MW00880307

ROGUE FOR PEACE

KELLI,

4/15/24

THANK YOU SO MUCH FOR YOUR ADVICE & ENTHUIASTIC SUPPORT! TO THE MOON WITH THE ARTS & OUR DREAMS!

– [signature]
BEN

Copyright © 2024 by Ben Johns

All rights reserved

For information about permissions to reproduce selections from this book, translation rights, or to order bulk purchases, write: benjohnsauthor108@gmail.com.

Cover design by Christian Storm

Johns, Ben
Rogue for Peace
9798879744415

1. Mystery, Thriller & Suspense / Thrillers & Suspense / Military.
2. Thrillers & Suspense / Psychological Thrillers.
3. Thrillers & Suspense / Suspense.

This is a work of fiction. Names, characters, places, and incidents either are the products of the author's imagination or are used fictitiously. Any resemblance to actual persons, living or dead, businesses, companies, or events is entirely coincidental.

facebook.com/RogueForPeace
instagram.com/rogueforpeace

ROGUE FOR PEACE

A THRILLER

BEN JOHNS

This book is dedicated to my mother.

Special acknowledgments to Joshua, Bob, and Kara
for your support.

ROGUE FOR PEACE

1

LIVESTREAM

Wilder straddled a telephone wire thirty feet off the ground as daylight struck just outside of Jerada, eastern Morocco. Shivering, he clung to a tree branch with one hand. His hair was messy and wet, but at least the rain had stopped. His knees stuck out from under a poncho shielding his laptop from the elements and flapping in the wind. He unjacked two micro alligator clips inside a metal box mounted to a utility pole.

Down below, Katya stood outside of their rental SUV and tugged her hoodie zipper up and down repeatedly. She looked up with severe but calm green eyes.

"Katya," Wilder exclaimed, "I got the livestream!"

"Tell me again," she said in a Russian accent. "What did you see?"

"At least a dozen people shot dead." His heart was pounding and he couldn't process the magnitude of the situation. He had done some shady things before, but nothing compared to this.

"Everyone is dead?"

"Except the military dudes," he said. "Crazy skills—perfect ambush. I saw the whole thing."

"Oh my God, I cannot believe this," said Katya. Her expression was stoic but inside she was scared.

Wilder asked, "What do we do now?"

"You say the soldiers ran away on foot?"

"Yeah—with the silver suitcase—except one guy. He drove off in the Humvee after they threw a couple bodies in it."

"What about the other bodies?"

"Inside the burning vehicles."

Katya got teary-eyed. "Something has gone terribly wrong."

"You think?" he asked sarcastically.

Katya was blunt. "I must go. I will come find you."

"What? No!"

She said, "Protect that intel with your life."

"Don't just leave me here!" yelled Wilder.

Stone-faced, she stared at him for a moment, then jumped in the car and sped away.

"I can't fucking believe this," Wilder cussed to himself. He gritted his teeth and mumbled, "Protect the intel. Don't get killed. Protect the intel. Don't get killed." The video rendered. He saved the file, shut his laptop and shoved it in his backpack.

Moments later the sound of a diesel engine roared as the Humvee rapidly approached. The brakes groaned and the vehicle idled beside the utility pole.

Navy SEAL Rex Hawthorne jumped out of the Humvee and aimed his Beretta M9 at Wilder. Hawthorne shouted in Arabic, "*Dae yadayk hayth yumkinuni ruyatuhum!*" He wiped blood spatter from his brow with his thick forearm.

Wilder didn't understand but his hands were up. He blurted, "Don't shoot! I'm American." It was all he could think of to say.

Hawthorne demanded, "The box! Give me the box!"

"I'm unarmed," said Wilder.

"Listen closely," Hawthorne said. "There are power shears taped to the back. Disconnect the box from the pole and throw it down."

"Throw it?" asked Wilder.

"You heard me. Do it or I kill you."

"OK, OK," said Wilder. He clipped the cable and unmounted the box from the pole.

With his finger on the trigger, Hawthorne flashed back two years earlier to rural Somalia. Wearing his desert fatigues, he lay face down in tall grass at the top of a bluff. A herd of goats ran past him, followed by an old-man shepherd wearing a kufi on his head and a sarong. Hawthorne assessed him as innocent but the shepherd posed a potential threat to the mission. Without hesitation, Hawthorne pulled his Beretta and shot him. Since then, every time he drew his pistol, he saw the dead old man.

Aiming the same pistol at Wilder, Hawthorne blinked his eyes and took a deep breath.

Wilder said, "OK, I'm ready to throw the box down."

Hawthorne shoved his Beretta in his belt. "OK, now drop it," he commanded.

Wilder let the box go. Hawthorne caught it, tucked the box under one arm and pulled his Beretta again.

Hawthorne had no time to deliberate. His cargo was top priority. The recent battle—explosions and machine-gun fire—had surely alerted the Moroccan military. Hawthorne kept his Beretta high and set the box inside the Humvee's cab. "Why are you here?" he asked.

Wilder said, "I cracked a code—it pointed me here."

"What code?"

"From a professor at UCLA."

"Is that true?" asked Hawthorne.

"Yes," said Wilder.

"Live or die," Hawthorne said plainly.

Wilder pleaded, "Please don't kill me."

Hawthorne perfected his aim and said coldly, "I do what I have to."

2

SURF SHOP AND BOUTIQUE

One week earlier, Wilder walked into a grungy surf shop in Redondo Beach. The young woman behind the counter said hi without looking up from her phone.

He said, "I heard the waves are frickin' huge today."

"The swell is twenty feet," she said. "Nobody's dumb enough to go out."

"Nobody except me," he said.

She looked up at him incredulously. He was skinny and not quite handsome, but there was a glow about him that attracted her. He took long, confident strides with his hands on his hips. "Where are your rental boards?"

She said, "I'm literally not renting you a board."

"Please?" he asked with a hopeful smile.

"You could die out there today."

Wilder casually leaned against the counter. "Life is boring without taking risks."

"You're an idiot." She acted annoyed, but he knew some women flirted that way and could tell she was interested.

"Actually I'm a computer programmer, so not an idiot."

"Then you're a nerd with a death wish."

"Come on," he nudged. "How much is the deposit?"

She looked him up and down. "You're not strong enough—and you obviously have no clue how dangerous those waves are."

"I'm plenty strong," said Wilder. "It's all muscle, from climbing."

"Like mountain climbing?"

"More like scaling buildings," he said. "Urban stuff."

She asked, "Do you even know how to surf?"

"Of course," he lied. "I surf big waves all the time. I just left my board at a buddy's house."

"Fine," she said. "You better sign the waiver then."

Wilder joked, "You should have to sign a waiver to work alone in a dump like this."

"Very funny. The rentals are under the sign that says RENTALS, if you can read."

Wilder picked a small board off the rack and filled out the waiver. He took off his T-shirt, vintage Nike high-tops and socks and shoved them into his backpack.

"You do have a nice ass," she said. "The water is really cold, you know."

"Hold my stuff behind the counter?"

"Sure," she said. "I'll be watching you on the surf cam. But if you start drowning, nobody's gonna rescue you."

"I got this." He walked out of the shop with the board under his arm.

A dude stood on a wall marveling at the surf. "Where should I paddle out?" Wilder asked.

"You crazy bro? You should NOT paddle out."

"I'm doing it."

The dude shook his head. "Then your best bet is over toward the pier."

"On it," said Wilder. Without hesitation, he trotted down the beach and into the turbulent water. He started paddling out and was plenty strong, but the waves were gigantic.

Wilder made it cleanly over two super-steep waves and the next one started to close out. He shoved the nose under and duck-dove, but the churning water pulled him back toward shore. He surfaced and ducked again as a massive ball of foam crashed over him. He spent almost all his energy fighting the current, but in a lull between sets he regained momentum and somehow cleared the break line.

He sat up on his board and caught his breath. Bobbing up and down over the huge rolling waves, Wilder felt a pang of fear. He gave himself a pep talk. "This is no time to chicken out. You got this."

He saw a gigantic crest approaching and knew it was his wave. Wilder turned the nose of the board toward shore and paddled with all his might. The surface of the humongous wave was moving fast, and Wilder accelerated into it. Toward the top, he stopped paddling and popped to his feet. For a split second, he stood up.

A gust of offshore wind flipped the board and tossed Wilder airborne like a rag doll. He hung upside down, arms and legs flailing. He inhaled deeply and plunged into the pit of the wave.

The thunderous slam of the wave instantly snapped the board in half. The crash dragged Wilder deep underwater. His body torqued and twisted. Losing oxygen, he lost his sense of up and down. Then his head cracked against the ocean floor. Hitting bottom gave him a glimmer of hope. His feet pushed off the sand and he swam upward. Finally, his head popped above the surface. He took another desperate inhale before the next wave smashed down on him. The rolling wave bounced him along the ocean floor and pulled him closer to shore.

Wilder jumped up to his feet in waist high water, raising both fists in the air triumphantly. Another wave swallowed him in a wall of froth, pulling him back out. Again, he fought for air, swimming for his life. This time, when his feet touched sand he lunged, clamored and crawled onto shore. He slumped on all fours and vomited water as stunned onlookers held up their phones.

Wilder shook it off and got up on his own, stumbling toward the surf shop. Inside, he told the woman, "The surfboard didn't make it. I guess you can keep the deposit."

"Holy shit." She was slack-jawed. "I have literally never seen anything like that. Are you OK?"

"I feel like a million bucks," he said, "but I do have dark blotches in my peripheral vision."

"Must be a concussion."

"Nothing a burrito and a Mountain Dew can't fix."

"You're lucky to be alive, man!" She put her arm and a towel around him.

He asked, "How come you let me go out there anyways?"

She rolled her eyes. "I told you not to."

"Can I have my backpack? I got a rolled joint in there."

She handed it over. "No weed inside."

"You smoke?" he asked.

"I'm more of a drinker."

"Gotcha," he said. "Let me guess. You hate your job, am I right?"

"Doesn't everyone hate their job?" she asked.

"Wait—I'm not done guessing," he said. "There's something you would way rather be doing. I bet you're a helluva chef."

She was genuinely surprised. "That's exactly right. How did you know that?"

"I'm good at reading people."

"It was a lucky guess," she said.

"Maybe," he said. "How's your charcuterie?"

She laughed. "I'm not that bougie."

"I don't even know what charcuterie means." He smiled. "Just heard it one time on a cooking show."

"Someday I want to have my own restaurant," she said. "Nothing fancy, just really good food."

Wilder said, "I hope you make it happen."

"Me too," she said. "Are you single?"

"What, tonight?" He rubbed his head. "Or like in general? Yeah, I'm single."

"Oh, I see," she said. "You're a slut."

"Why does everybody call me a slut?"

"Probably because you act like one," she said.

"It's not intentional," he insisted. "I get laid a lot, but really I'm looking for my soulmate."

"Well I'm not your soulmate," she said, and smiled.

"Gotcha." He smiled back. "My number is on the waiver." He ended the conversation on a high note by walking away.

*

Two miles away, Katya drove her moped down Roxbury Drive. A car sped by and cut her off. She fumed, raced after the car and pulled up alongside the driver at a red light. She popped the visor on her helmet and yelled in imperfect English, "Watch where you going!" The driver raised a middle finger through his sunroof. Katya gave the middle finger back, and the driver peeled out when the light turned green.

Katya Polenko was a Russian foreign exchange student at UCLA on a semester abroad. She got good grades and dreamed of living in California permanently. She wanted to start her own business.

She parked in front of an upscale boutique for women's accessories. She slung a big handbag over her shoulder and walked into the shop with her usual serious expression. After checking the place out for a few minutes, Katya was approached by a security guard.

"Excuse me," he said. "I'm going to need to see that handbag."

Katya clenched her fists and glared at him with her intense eyes. She protested, "I am so offended. I made this handbag myself out of quality Juchten leather."

The owner approached them. She was a middle-aged white woman with overdone cosmetic surgery. "It's OK, Carl. She's just looking around. Ma'am, I apologize. We have to be careful of shoplifters these days."

Katya frowned. "Is this how people do business in the US?"

The owner said, "Unfortunately, criminals love LA. You said you made that handbag yourself?"

"I did," said Katya. "I have started my business in Moscow."

"It's lovely. I know a few celebrities who would buy it."

Katya was unimpressed. "What if I told you I am a celebrity?"

"Are you?"

"Not yet," said Katya. "But you never know to who you are talking. You should treat your customers better."

The owner said, "It was an honest mistake. I'm sure he's sorry. Carl?"

Carl said, "No offense—just doing my job."

"You should find another job," huffed Katya.

"Charming," said Carl. "People in LA are gonna love you."

Katya stormed out of the boutique and back to her moped. Turning over the engine, she pulled out a tube of purple lipstick from inside her handbag. She peeled off the price tag and flicked it nonchalantly.

Katya smacked her lips and smiled in the handlebar mirror. *This color looks good on me*, she thought. She flipped her hair, put on her helmet and pulled back into traffic.

3

COFFEE AND FENTANYL

Wilder scaled a fifteen-foot brick wall and jumped down into a garden bed. He strolled across the backyard outside of the home of UCLA's Chancellor Sullivan. Wilder spotted the open back door of the mansion. He let himself in to an empty kitchen with a black-and-white checkered floor.

"Classy," Wilder muttered to himself. "Very French."

A pot of coffee beeped on the countertop. Wilder poured himself a cup. Moments later, the chancellor walked in.

"Wilder?"

"This coffee is horrible."

"What the hell are you doing in my house?" the chancellor asked.

"Special delivery," said Wilder, sliding a manila envelope across the counter. "That's two thousand dollars of high-grade fentanyl."

"You can't be here," the chancellor objected.

Wilder shrugged it off with a smile. "Cash only, just like always."

"We can only meet at our designated site, you know that."

"I got bored of waiting for you to call," said Wilder. "Plus, I always wanted to see the inside of this place. It's super nice."

"How did you get in?"

"I let myself in—and the back door was open."

"There are cameras all over this property."

"You're really pissed, aren't you?" Wilder asked. "Sorry

about that, but listen—I expected better coffee from a man of your stature."

"You're breaking and entering," the chancellor said nervously. "I have private security."

"Then give me my two thousand dollars and I'll leave," Wilder said casually.

"Fine," grumbled the chancellor. "You know what? Your parents didn't raise you right."

Wilder said, "My parents died a long time ago."

"Oh," said the chancellor, "that's unfortunate."

"Unfortunate, yeah." Wilder showed no emotion.

The chancellor dug into a kitchen drawer where he kept a pile of money. He paid Wilder and said, "This can never happen again. Not in my home—you understand me?"

"Loud and clear." Wilder shoved the cash into the front pocket of his jeans.

The chancellor's cell phone rang. "This is Ernie. Yeah I know. No, it's not a real break-in. It's one of my undergrads. I'm with him now. Yep. Just up to some mischief, you know how college students are . . . you called the police? That wasn't necessary . . . they're at the front gate? Yes, of course, let them in."

Wilder took one last sip and said, "I better run. I'm gonna be late to class."

"I gotta hide these drugs," said the chancellor.

Wilder said, "Later, Ernie. Step up your coffee game, would ya?" He sprinted across the lawn and over the brick wall before the police could see him.

4

THE LIMO

Two months earlier in Washington, DC, Arnold Renfree—the head of the Senate Intelligence Committee—walked down the stairs outside of the Capitol Building. He was an intransigent right-winger—extreme even for those who shared his radical views. Renfree hailed from Alabama and openly stated he wanted American history rewound to the days before the civil rights era.

A mob of press carrying cameras and microphones surrounded Renfree as he walked. "Senator Renfree," a female reporter said over the fray, "last week on the campaign trail, you said that blacks and Jews are untrustworthy bottom feeders. How can you explain that to the American people?"

"I like white people better," he answered. "So shoot me—but don't take my guns."

"Senator," said a man, "you continue to repost hate speech from the White Prophecy group on social media. Are you a white nationalist?"

"The WP is a great movement," Renfree said. "The silent white army needs a platform and they have the right to free speech."

"Mr. Renfree . . ." The press continued closing in. His limo driver waved them off and opened the side door.

No sooner had the door shut when the limo's phone rang from a number listed as No Caller ID. "This is Renfree."

"Tell me now is a good time to talk," said a digitally warbled voice on the other end.

"Hello, Karen," said Renfree. "I've been meaning to call."

"Let's be brief," said Karen. "Things are finalized here. Are your people ready?"

"Yes, they're ready." Renfree undid his tie and tossed it beside him. "I'm on my way to meet our two main contacts now."

"Be certain you can trust them," said Karen.

"I'm vetting them again myself," Renfree agreed. "They're fully committed to the White Power movement."

"Commitment is one thing," said Karen. "Finishing this job is another."

Renfree asked, "What would I do without you reminding me we can never be too careful?"

Karen continued, "Less than five people can know about an operation of this magnitude."

"We have found our most dedicated people," Renfree asserted, "willing to sacrifice everything."

"If you're wrong," Karen warned, "we have to kill them."

"That won't be necessary."

Karen said, "This is going to make 9/11 look like a trip to the candy store."

"Yes it is," Renfree concurred.

"Be certain. Do we understand each other?" asked Karen.

"Understood," said Renfree.

"We're very close to our goal."

"It's an incredible moment," said Renfree, and Karen hung up.

Renfree reached into the middle console for a box of cigars. He picked one and chewed on it a bit, then dialed a number. "Come on . . . pick up."

Sitting in his office in UCLA's South Wing computer science building, Professor Raj Singh stared at his cell phone too scared to take the call. He was a tall, good-looking man with a clean shave and a loose-fitting sweater.

The call went to voicemail and the professor took a deep breath before listening to it. "Raj, this is Arnold in DC. We're all looking forward to seeing your project out of beta. How's that going? We're paying you very well, so don't let us down by being late to deliver. You can piss me off all you want, but trust me when I say you don't want to piss off my partner. I'll assume we're all squared away unless I hear back. Oh, and our IT guys at the Pentagon are very impressed. Don't let them down either."

Professor Singh grasped the threat and nervously shook his head. He muttered to himself, "This is my legacy? How did I get here?"

Raj Singh was born and raised in the Punjab region of India, and he moved to the US to study computer engineering at Caltech, where he eventually got his PhD. He was recruited to teach at UCLA and soon afterward met his wife, an undergrad student from Tamil Nadu. Their love was deep, but he devoted more time to his work than to her. In the classroom, Professor Singh rejected heavy use of object-oriented programming and argued that shortcuts detracted from the fundamental art and science of coding. He warned against relinquishing control to AI without fail-safe measures. His core knowledge set him apart, and it led him to advanced tech discoveries.

He walked across his office and pulled a small satellite out of a box. He looked at it from a few angles and his hands trembled with a pang of fear. He heard a knock at the door, put the satellite back in the box and shut it. "Come in," he answered.

Katya stepped into the doorway, wearing a tennis outfit and a black leather backpack. "Professor Singh, I have a question . . ." She saw his face and her smile turned to a look of concern. "You look terrible. Is everything OK?"

He walked behind his desk and slouched into his chair with a heavy sigh. "As a matter of fact, nothing is OK. Are you a student of mine?"

"I'm Katya, from your bioinformatics class."

"You have a Russian accent, yes?" he asked.

"I am Chechen," she said, "but I grew up in Moscow."

His anxiety had been somewhat paralyzing and she was a welcome distraction. "Nice to meet you. Have a seat. How can I help?"

She stayed standing and prodded politely, "I'm curious, why are you so upset?"

"If you must know, it's my work," he said. "It's given me an existential crisis."

"But you are brilliant," she said. "Why a crisis?"

"I'm under contract," he explained. "I can't talk about it."

She smiled. "Well, if you change your mind, I'm a good listener."

His sullen look softened and he looked her in the eye. "You are very kind."

"I am kind to people I care about," she said.

The professor said, "Katya, is it?"

"Yes."

"Katya, may I give you some unsolicited advice?"

"You may."

"Be very careful if you ever sell your inventions," he said. "Be sure you know who your partners are."

"That is good advice," she said.

"Don't let prestige or money blind you. I've learned the hard way."

"I see." She stayed upbeat. "May I ask about the midterm project?"

"Of course."

She unzipped her purse. "I will show you where I'm stuck." Katya walked around the desk and set her laptop down in front of him. Her hand brushed against his, and he blushed. He could not hide his attraction.

Katya pointed at the photo on his desk. She asked plainly, "That is your wife?"

"It is."

"Do you have kids?"

"No."

"Neither do I," she said. "My only family is my uncle."

"Oh. Most of my family is in India." He turned his focus to the laptop screen. "There is your problem. This run command is incomplete."

"Really?" she asked. "Such a simple mistake. I don't know how I missed it."

5
THE LECTURE HALL

Wilder jogged to the computer sciences building and picked a wall near the front steps to practice his bouldering technique. He texted his best friend, Chuck, "I'm here, where u at?"

"Close," texted Chuck.

Wilder scanned around for cops. He lived for taking risks and usually had ice in his veins, but lately he worried about being arrested. Chuck had been warning him. One day he would wind up in prison or dead or dead in prison. Wilder's comeback to that was anything beats dying of boredom.

Chuck pulled up on his skateboard. He wasn't just Wilder's best friend, he was his *only* friend. Chuck's curly orange hair contrasted with his well-ironed shirt. He was a bit of an uptight, wimpy guy, but he was reliable and Wilder trusted him.

With a high five and their own handshake, they walked up the stairs to the front entrance. A woman in a sorority shirt passed them. Wilder said, "Hey, Jenny. How come you ghosted me?"

She glared at him, "Ugh. Don't even talk to me."

"Why not?" He shrugged and held up his hands.

She looked pissed. "We had so much fun. You took me to a Lakers game and I thought you were really hot."

"I think you're hot too," said Wilder.

"Then you called me fake rich." She pouted and crossed her arms.

Wilder explained, "You told me your mom was poor and remarried a rich guy."

"Fake rich, seriously?" she asked. "You don't say that!"

"It won't happen again."

"Damn right it won't." She gave him the middle finger and stormed off yelling, "Wilder Kole, you're just a slut!"

"Don't call me a slut!" he hollered, as she walked away.

Chuck elbowed Wilder and teased him. "Slut."

"Why does everyone call me that?" Wilder was always asking the same question.

"Fake rich?" Chuck shook his head. "She's right, dude. You don't say that."

"I wasn't wrong."

"That's not the point," scolded Chuck. "You gotta learn to hold your tongue. Boundaries, remember?"

"Whatever, I'm over her," Wilder said. "It's Katya I really like anyway." He ran his fingers through his hair and checked his T-shirt for dandruff.

Chuck asked, "Dude, are you wearing body spray?"

"Do you think she'll notice me?"

"*Everyone* is going to notice you. Why don't you just talk to her?"

"What do I say?"

"Just don't act desperate," said Chuck. "And don't be yourself."

"Very funny," said Wilder. "You look depressed. Everything OK?"

"I still can't believe Maria dumped me."

"You'll get over it. She's nice, but average."

"Average?"

"Pretty basic, yeah. So why can't I get a girl like Katya?"

Chuck said, "You sit in front of computers all day long."

"There's nothing wrong with that."

"You need to meet someone you're actually compatible with."

"Maybe you're right. All the women I like, I can't figure them out. I just need to crack their code."

Chuck rolled his eyes. "You can't hack a woman like she's a computer program."

"You can't?"

"Maybe you should just stick to computers," said Chuck. "Seriously, you're really gifted with tech but you're way too chill about it."

The only steady thing in Wilder's life was his love of computers. He spent half his childhood in the foster care system and it taught him to lie, cheat and trust no one. Unlike people, programming was reliable.

They walked into the lecture hall and down to the fifth row. Wilder took the aisle seat and mused, "Think Katya likes coding or is she just taking this class for credit?"

"Forget it," said Chuck. "She's probably into taller, better-looking dudes."

"Are you calling me short and ugly?" asked Wilder.

"You're just a scrawny little white boy."

"Says you, the Irishman," Wilder teased. "You're so white you're almost see-through. Plus I'm not scrawny, I'm slender."

"Yeah but I'm legit handsome," Chuck fired back. "Hey, listen—for real. You need to get your shit together with your classes."

"My shit's fine."

"You're probably the smartest guy in the room," said Chuck, "but if you fail your classes, there goes your scholarship."

"I know, I know. Brilliant how I set that up though, eh?"

Two years earlier as a senior in high school, Wilder hacked UCLA's servers and reversed his rejected application. He fixed his grades to 4.0, wrote his own letter of recommendation and granted himself a full ride. That hooked him on hacking and he started taking much bigger risks. His most recent scheme was nefariously breaking through firewalls and skimming off the tops of overseas bank accounts holding billions of dollars.

Wilder set up an elaborate network of dummy accounts through the dark web, eventually wiring the cash to himself. He never knew who he was stealing from, and they would never know who he was either.

"You *are* brilliant," Chuck said, smiling. "But you're too risky—and constantly breaking the law."

"Breaking the law is fun. And I haven't gotten caught, have I?"

"Push your luck and you will someday."

"Not me," said Wilder. "My code is too good."

"Whoever finds out about your offshore account stuff is not gonna forgive you for having shitty judgment."

"I'm undetectable," said Wilder. "My firewall alerts automatically shut everything down . . . Hey look, it's Katya."

Katya walked down the stairs of the lecture hall with her motorcycle helmet under one elbow. She headed directly to the front row. Examining her usual seat, she pulled out a Kleenex. She methodically wiped the seat from top to bottom, tucking the tissue in the outside pocket of her handbag.

"Same thing every time." Wilder said. "Do you think she has OCD?"

"Why don't you ask her?" snarked Chuck. "That's a perfect way to meet a girl—get her talking about her neurosis."

"I love how she dyed her hair black," said Wilder.

"You're so annoying," said Chuck.

"I love how she's Russian."

"She's totally out of your league."

"She's stylish and cool and . . . seems complicated."

"Meanwhile, you look like a grunge-era reject."

"C'mon man. The '90s are cool again."

"Not the way you're doing it."

"I rock my own look."

Professor Singh entered through a side door of the lecture hall and stepped up to the podium. He clipped a mic to his sweater and Katya approached him. She got close and quietly asked a question. Wilder walked up behind them to join in on their conversation.

"In Moscow," Katya said to the professor, "the coursework is not this difficult."

The professor said in a Punjabi accent, "Your question is a good one. It's top of the hour now and I need to start the lecture. Stop by my office and we can discuss it in detail."

Katya spoke with firmness. "I will. What time is best?"

"My office hours are nine to noon weekdays," said the professor.

"I will be there first thing tomorrow," she said in a husky voice.

The professor batted his eyes. "That will be just fine."

Wilder wedged himself into the conversation. "I'll stop by your office too."

Katya turned around and bumped right into him. "Watch where you stand," she snapped.

"Uh—hi, I'm Wilder."

"Good for you," Katya said, heading toward her seat.

Wilder walked beside her. "You're Russian, huh?"

"I'm from Chechnya."

"Isn't that Russia?"

"Technically," she said flatly.

"The Cold War is over, you know."

"I have heard that line before."

"You have?"

She added, "The Cold War never ended."

"We could end it together?" Wilder offered.

"I doubt that," she said with the slightest smile.

The lecture was basic, but Wilder liked the precision of the professor's code. After class, Katya left the lecture hall straightaway.

Chuck and Wilder sat outside on the lawn. Chuck said, "Dude, I gotta tell you something."

"What's up?"

“I took a paid internship at Channel 7 News.”

“Seriously? That’s huge.”

Chuck said, “It’s a B-roll editor on the graveyard shift, but that’s how you get your foot in the door.”

“Congratulations, boss.” Wilder gave him a bear hug.

“It’s a great opportunity. So I decided I’m dropping out.”

“Wait, what? You can’t drop out on me.”

“I need you to have my back on this,” Chuck said. “My dad is gonna be really pissed.” Most of Chuck’s anxiety came from his dad’s expectations. Chuck’s dad never went to college and worked double shifts as a warehouse manager so the family could have a better life.

“I would be pissed too if I was your dad,” said Wilder.

“You don’t even have a dad.”

The joke cut deep and Wilder’s face turned serious. “That’s cold blooded. My parents are dead.”

Chuck apologized, “That was way out of line. I’m really sorry.”

“Apology accepted,” said Wilder. “But don’t say that shit again. You and me gotta have each other’s backs.”

Even though Wilder hardly trusted anybody, loyalty was extremely important to him. He had plenty of issues, but one thing that rooted him in life was his mom and dad’s creed of always being faithful, woven into the story of how they fell in love. They were in the same Air Force unit and married between deployments to Iraq. Fighting alongside each other created an unbreakable bond. Their marriage vows “until death do us part” came true with a car accident that only Wilder survived.

“Don’t worry, I got your back,” said Chuck.

“You and me, we’re a crew of two,” Wilder said. “You’re all I got—until I find my soulmate.”

“You’re good at getting girls,” said Chuck, “but you gotta drop the soulmate thing.”

“People are naturally drawn to me,” said Wilder.

“Until they get to know you,” Chuck joked.

"But seriously, about the dropping-out thing," said Wilder. "You just can't."

"I already decided," Chuck said. "Real life experience is more important than a degree."

"Don't do it, dude. Stupid decision."

"That's real great coming from Mr. Stupid Decision himself."

"I prefer to be called Mr. Smartypants."

Chuck said, "You're a hacker and a drug dealer."

Wilder said, "Breaking laws is the fastest way to get ahead in life."

"You're basically a felon."

"Such strong words." Wilder grinned and then whispered, "You should see what I find online—like shit the CIA is doing. Technology is incredible these days."

"Your shenanigans are getting out of hand."

"It's a lot of money and it's fun."

"It won't be fun forever."

"Did you know they're controlling the flight of golf balls?"

"The CIA?" Chuck asked.

"Of course not, dumbass. Golfers."

"That's crazy. Anyways, I'm super happy about my new gig. Let's party later and celebrate."

Wilder said, "Now you're talking."

"Get us some whiskey and Coke."

"I'm on it," said Wilder. "Getting shit-faced is the best way to get over what's-her-name."

"You know her damn name."

"I'm just fucking with you. You're fun when you're drunk—it's the only time you really cut loose."

"Just because I'm not as reckless as you doesn't mean I'm uptight."

"You're a huge ball of stress, dude. You need to work on that."

"Don't be a dick," said Chuck. "OK, I gotta go."

"*Uvidimsya*," said Wilder.

"Huh?"

"That means 'see you later' in Russian."

6

A QUICK CALL

Katya drove her moped across campus, parked and tucked her helmet under her arm. She noticed a missed call from her uncle and FaceTimed him.

Uncle Timofey: Hi, Katya.

Katya: Hi, Uncle Timofey. Can we talk while I walk to my next class?

Uncle Timofey: OK. I have something important to tell you, but it can wait.

Katya: Hmm, alright . . . how are things in Moscow?

Uncle Timofey: Fine. Are you making friends in LA?

Katya: Not really. I'm lonely.

Uncle Timofey: Keep trying.

Katya: Today a security guard asked to look in my bag and I said fuck off.

Uncle Timofey: Careful with that temper, sweetheart.

Katya: I didn't punch him. That's progress right?

Uncle Timofey: Ha-ha, yes it is.

Katya: Are you still online dating?

Uncle Timofey: Yes, but women aren't interested.

Katya: You could fall in love with a goat.

Uncle Timofey: I need to try new things. Not as wild as you but something better.

Katya: Good. Don't come to LA, though. People here are shallow.

Uncle Timofey: Shallow is not the worst way to get by in this world.

Katya: The only person I find interesting is a professor.

Uncle Timofey: A man professor?

Katya: Ha-ha, yeah. He's not my type but I kind of like him.

Uncle Timofey: See? Your life has some things happening. How are your classes?

Katya: The education is good, not great.

Uncle Timofey: Great education isn't what you need anyway.

Katya: Right. I just need opportunity. LA has that.

Uncle Timofey: That's the spirit.

Katya: I could start my own line of purses here.

Uncle Timofey: You can do anything you want. In America or anywhere else.

Katya: I love how much you believe in me. It's so sweet.

Uncle Timofey: I mean it. You are sweet too.

Katya: Why don't more people see that?

Uncle Timofey: Because sometimes you're mean.

Katya: True. OK, I have to go. I love you.

Uncle Timofey: I love you too. Bye.

Katya tucked the phone in her handbag, wondering what could be so important that her uncle called to share.

7

MONTANA

A military jet touched down in Washington, DC. Each member of Navy SEAL Unit 20, aka KrayBULL, filed into two SUVs waiting on the tarmac. They drove to the Pentagon and the SEALs individually debriefed with intelligence officers about their mission in Guyana. It ended successfully—they freed both hostages—but a civilian was shot in the leg in the crossfire. It drew some diplomatic blowback but nothing people in DC couldn't handle.

Navy SEAL Rex Hawthorne was a white man from Montana, a tactical analyst, weapons expert and submarine pilot. He sat up tall with a husky build, answering each question directly.

A female intelligence officer asked, "Where were you positioned during the battle?"

Hawthorne answered, "Ma'am, I was on the roof across the street from the apartment where the hostages were being held."

"KrayBULL killed four targets. Who opened fire first?"

"I did," said Hawthorne. "My orders were to take the first clean shot at the targets I could get."

"How did it happen?" she asked.

"Two of them appeared in the window with the hostages out of view. I fired six rounds with my rifle. Both men fell out of view and I later learned they were kill shots."

"Was there any return fire in your direction?"

"Negative."

"The other two hostage takers fled the building interior.

You were not in the stairwell where the civilian was wounded, is that correct?"

"Correct, I stayed in my position on the roof."

"Ali and Perez from your team killed the other two targets in the lobby?"

"That's my understanding, ma'am."

"Those are all my questions," she said. "Can I get a nurse to rewrap that broken finger for you?"

Hawthorne held up his broken pinky, which he had wrapped to his ring finger with medical tape. "I'm good."

"Congratulations on meeting your mission objectives. Dismissed."

Before leaving, Hawthorne exchanged a few back-slap hugs goodbye with the KrayBULL men. He accepted a ride from an official to his hotel near the airport. A few blocks short, Hawthorne asked, "Drop me off at that church, would you?"

"Are you a praying man?" asked the driver.

"Always," said Hawthorne.

The next morning, he took a direct flight to Bozeman, a bus to Billings and an Uber downtown. Hawthorne ducked his head to step out of the car. He tossed his large duffel bag over his shoulder and climbed three flights of stairs to his small studio apartment. The door swung in and pushed his mail into a pile. His studio was otherwise empty except for a chair, a few suitcases and a mattress on the floor. He opened the window shade, let the sunlight in and sifted through the mail. He paused on a large envelope—from his wife—sighed sarcastically and said, "Fantastic."

His cell phone rang and it was his commander, Jansen. Hawthorne answered, "Hi, Commander . . . Tell me we don't have a new mission. I literally just got home."

"No choice as usual," said Jansen. "Our contact from Senate Intel called. They need us in DC in forty-eight hours."

"See you in forty-eight then," said Hawthorne. He hung up and looked in the empty fridge. He found some chili in the cupboard and stood in the kitchen eating out of the can.

Hawthorne texted.

Hawthorne: Eileen, I'm home for a few days. Do you want to talk?

Eileen: Hi. Did you get my letter?

Hawthorne: Yea but I didn't read it yet

Eileen: Why not?

Hawthorne: I just walked in the door. Divorce papers?

Eileen: Yeah, all the things we agreed on

Hawthorne: Did you already sell the truck?

Eileen: Yeah

Hawthorne: Ouch

Eileen: I'll be home late afternoon. Stop by if you want

Hawthorne: Is four OK?

Eileen: Fine

Hawthorne pulled up on a bicycle right at 4:00 p.m. He ditched it on the gravel driveway and walked around the side gate. He texted Eileen, "I'm here. Going to see Duchess."

"OK. Meet me on the porch," she replied.

Hawthorne's golden mare trotted up to him in the yard. He groomed her a bit and wrapped his big arms around her neck. He got teary-eyed and said, "We'll sell you to a friend and I'll buy you back, girl."

The screen door opened with a creak and slammed itself shut. Hawthorne's wife, Eileen, fixed her ball cap and motioned for him to join her. He walked across the lawn and up the porch stairs. She sat down in a wicker chair and said cautiously, "Thanks for coming over."

Hawthorne took in the view of their four-acre lot backing up to the Beartooth Mountains. He said, "I'm going to miss this place," and took a seat.

"What about me?"

"I'm going to miss you too."

She nodded with a lump in her throat. "Same here as a matter of fact."

Hawthorne noticed the divorce paperwork on the side table, ready with a pen. "Eileen, are you a hundred percent sure this is what you want?"

"I'm sure, Rex," she said.

"OK then."

"How long are you in town for?"

"I'm in DC day after tomorrow."

"Same old crap."

Hawthorne said, "Orders are orders."

"I will not miss this life."

"See?" He faked a smile. "We still have some things in common."

She said, "Pretty soon the military will be your only wife."

He said, "Low blow, babe."

"Please don't call me babe anymore."

"It's just habit."

"How's unit KrayBULL?"

"Strong as ever."

"It's a miracle more of you haven't died."

"You could say that."

"People called the landline while you were gone. I took messages."

"Names?"

"A Wendy and a Jacob. Who are they?"

"Nobody important," said Hawthorne.

"Tell me the truth," she said.

He got defensive. "I have always told you the truth."

"Except about your missions."

"You know I can't talk about them."

"Well?" she asked.

"Wendy and I went on a few dates awhile back."

"Christ on a crutch, Rex!" she exclaimed incredulously. "You gave her our home phone?"

He tried to explain. "We tried an open relationship before you asked me to move out, remember?"

"Seriously?" she scoffed. "When we fell in love, I thought we were gonna have a mostly traditional marriage. Now look at us."

Hawthorne gritted his teeth and tapped his foot.

She calmly reiterated her unhappiness, mostly to stay convinced of it herself. "I didn't know you wanted to be with other people."

"It was not ideal," he said, "but with me being gone so much, I thought it might actually save us."

"Isn't that just a load of crap, though?" she asked. "We should have known right then it was over."

"Maybe so," said Hawthorne. "Did you ever go on any dates?"

"Once," she said. "I met a man at the mall who was looking to buy property in Billings. I didn't much like him, though."

"Well I'm glad you tried."

"You know what?" Eileen shifted in her seat to look Hawthorne in the eye. "I'm not even sure if you would rather be with a man or a woman."

"Dammit, Eileen, I told you I was bi when we met," he said. "You're the one I fell in love with, period. That's what matters."

"Is it?" she asked.

"You're the love of my life," he said.

"You were never around, Rex."

"I meant to be."

She shook her head. "We can both do better than this."

"My heart is flat broken," he said.

They sat in a prolonged silence, which was for the best. He took a deep breath, signed the divorce papers one page at a time and put the packet back down on the table.

"Kind of a relief, isn't it?" She made an effort to be cordial. "I'm glad this is done."

"I'm not sure if things are ever really done," he reflected. "Only God knows that."

"You always were a philosophical man."

"My faith is the only thing that keeps me here," he said.

"Whatever God's plan is," she said, "I wish He would give us a memo sometime."

Hawthorne chuckled slightly. "That would be nice, yeah."

"Why don't you go say goodbye to your horse?" she offered.

"OK then." He stood up and said gently, "Don't be a stranger."

"I'm sure we will see each other from time to time," she said.

"At church maybe."

"Sounds good," she said.

They gave each other a cursory hug. Halfway down the stairs, he turned around and said awkwardly, "Take care, Eileen."

"Why don't you go around the side when you leave."

Hawthorne held his head high until she walked inside, and he frustratedly kicked up a cloud of dirt.

8

THE CAFÉ

After class, Wilder walked back to his dorm room and dumped his stuff on the floor. His flip phone, a burner line, buzzed from inside his backpack. It was Kim. She was the only one with his second phone number. Wilder never picked it up and it always meant the same thing: Meet me in an hour at the café. He finished a sandwich sitting out on his desk, smoked a joint and counted cash from his sock drawer.

Wilder walked past Kim's beat-up Honda parked in front of the café. She had a plastic lotus with a tassel hanging from the rearview mirror.

Kim sat in the back corner of the café in a white jacket with a fake-fur hoodie. She was Chinese American, born and raised in LA. She always talked trash and her laugh was contagious.

Kim greeted him with a smile. "You're late again, asshole."

"What year is that piece-of-shit Honda Prelude?" Wilder asked.

"It's a 1995 Si," Kim said. "The *Si* stands for Suck it."

The playful banter was always fun for both of them. Wilder asked, "Time for a new car, maybe?"

"She's got more miles in her. Besides, I was born in '95. Year of the Pig," Kim said.

"You're old as fuck. Hang on . . ." Wilder typed on his phone. "Google says the year I was born, 2001, is the year of the snake."

"That's fitting," she said.

"Why's that?"

"You're sly and impulsive, kind of like a snake. But you're not as cool as you think you are. You're just a typical LA dick."

"Well you're one tough bitch, aren't you?"

"There is no year of the *bitch* in my culture." Kim laughed and slapped the side of his head. "But I'll take that as a compliment."

"My mom and dad got married in '95," said Wilder. "That's for-fuckin-ever ago."

"But you were a foster kid, right?"

"Yeah, they died when I was really little. My grandma took me in but she died too—and I ended up with no place to go."

"You said your parents were alcoholics or something?"

"That's what they tell me," said Wilder.

She joked, "If you were my kid, I would be an alcoholic too."

"Too far," he warned.

"I'm sorry," she said.

He shook it off. "It's funny so you can get away with it. Know what? I'd like to know who's the real you when you're not hiding behind that sense of humor."

"I'm good," Kim declined. She zipped up her hoodie.

"Are you cold?"

"I'm always cold."

He looked at her feet. "Nice kicks. What are those, shell-tops?"

"Adidas forever." Kim pulled some pieces of paper out of her pocket and cut to the chase. "Here's the address for the rave on Saturday. And your VIP passes."

"Let me get two more," Wilder said.

She rolled her eyes and obliged.

"You're a gem," he said.

Kim said, "You're a stupid melon."

"What's that supposed to mean?"

"It's a Chinese insult. It means you're a bad egg."

"How do you say 'Go fuck yourself' in Chinese?" he asked.

"You're so high right now. Even if I told you, you'd forget."

"I brought your mail," Wilder said. They always had some kind of smooth exchange of cash for fentanyl patches. He dug in his backpack.

"Here's your chemistry book," said Kim.

The drugs were inside a cut-out section of the book, and he tucked it into his backpack. He handed her the envelope and they carried on casually.

"Don't deal to people you don't know," Kim said under her breath. "Cops are cracking down on the EDM scene."

"The kids can't get enough of this stuff," muttered Wilder.

"People who fly high need a smooth landing," said Kim.

He changed the subject. "When are you gonna take me to your cousin's food truck?"

"Who said I'm taking you?" She gave him the side eye.

"Are we not friends?" asked Wilder.

"Not really."

"Well I think we are."

"I don't run with scrubs. And I don't really do the friend thing. It's easier to just not trust anybody. That way you don't get hurt."

"I can relate to that. Come on, please?" asked Wilder.

She smiled. "OK, how about, let's just go now."

"Good action," said Wilder. "I have the munchies so bad I would eat anything."

"My cousin's truck is on the docks in Long Beach. It's not too far."

Kim pinned the gas pedal on the 405, zipping in and out of lanes. The engine grinded and the steering wheel shook.

"This car is sus!" Wilder yelled over the stereo. "Are we even gonna make it to Long Beach?"

"She's on her third engine!" Kim said, and laughed. "I got this!"

"That's my line!" said Wilder. "Hey, how did I get so lucky with you anyway?"

"What do you mean?" she asked.

"You're a hell of a provider," he said. "We're making bank together."

She smiled. "I saw that low-grade shit you were selling and I took pity on you."

"Whatever," said Wilder.

Kim hopped on the 110. They missed the worst of traffic and pulled up to the port in thirty minutes. A flock of seagulls stood around squawking on top of the food truck. Her cousin Kai had a huge belly and his face was sweaty. His voice boomed, "Here ya go, amigo, my specialty! Kalua pork sliders and fish tacos!"

"That looks delicious," said Wilder.

Kai smiled big and was instantly likable. "Stay away from my cousin or I'll hunt you down and kill you!"

Kim and Wilder ate lunch on the hood of her car, looking out at the water. She said, "You know how much cargo comes through this port? At least five billion dollars' worth every day. More than half of it is illegal."

"Is this where your fentanyl comes from?"

"I didn't say that," said Kim. "Eat your damn lunch."

"Seriously, this is the best fish taco I ever had," said Wilder.

"You're damn right it is."

A white man walked by them and said, "Fuck you, China girl."

Kim asked, "What did you just say?"

The man scowled, "You heard me. Go back where you came from, and take the kung-flu virus with you."

Kim walked slowly toward him, opening her jacket to show the man her Staccato CS in a shoulder holster. He ran away terrified.

Wilder said, "Woah. That was scary—and kind of beautiful. I had no idea you were packing."

"I'm so sick and tired of these racist motherfuckers. They're worse than ever. This happens to me like twice a week now."

"That really sucks," said Wilder.

"It's awful. Especially when they fetishize me."

"So you just show them your gun, huh?" Wilder asked with a tone of admiration.

Kim said, "I haven't ever done that before, but it felt pretty good."

Wilder smiled. "I always thought you were cool, but now I know you're a total badass."

"Time to go," she said. "That guy will call the cops for sure."

Kim drove Wilder back and dropped him off at the café.

Headed back toward campus, Wilder rounded a corner and walked past a row of boarded-up storefronts. A young man called out, "Help! Oh my God, help!"

Wilder couldn't tell where the voice was coming from until a young man jumped to his feet from inside a doorway. "He's dying," the young man said. He pointed to his friend slumped over on the ground.

Wilder hurried over. "What happened?"

"He's overdosing, man."

"On what?" asked Wilder.

"Heroin."

"I have Narcan," said Wilder, quickly unzipping his backpack.

"He's turning blue," said the young man. "Hurry!"

Wilder ripped the safety guard off the auto-injector. "Call a medic—he's gonna have withdrawals immediately." Wilder plunged the Narcan into the overdosing man's thigh. After a few long seconds, the man gasped, flailed his arms and vomited. Wilder tossed the injector back into his pack and stood up. "You're welcome," he said, and turned to leave.

"Wait," said the sick man's friend. "Stay with me."

"I can't," said Wilder. "I'm a dealer."

9

THE OFFICE

At 9:00 the next morning, Wilder walked to the professor's office. *It's way too early for this*, he thought. *She probably won't even be there.*

The office door was shut and he didn't bother knocking. He stepped in and there was Katya, whispering in Professor Singh's ear. He had his hands on her butt. Wilder blurted, "Am I interrupting something?" It startled them both.

"I should have locked the door," the professor said awkwardly.

Katya snapped, "Yes, you are interrupting."

The professor wiped Katya's lipstick off his mouth and stammered, "No, it's—um—these are my office hours. Come in."

Katya huffed. "He can wait. I was here first."

"I have a question about how to prep for the final," Wilder lied.

"I see," said the professor. "And you are?"

"Wilder Kole," he said confidently.

Katya frowned. "You need to come back when we are finished."

"No really, it's OK," said Professor Singh. "Wilder, why do I know that name?"

"Because I'm just about failing your class?"

"I remember now—you're my student who does the extra credit perfectly but never completes the assignments."

"Yours truly." Wilder flashed a satisfied grin.

"You're my first student to solve my Perl code problem."

"That was quite a piece of code," said Wilder.

"A classic coding conundrum," said the professor. "How did you solve it?"

"I guess I'm a nerd." He looked at Katya. "The cool kind, though."

"You are extremely rude," said Katya.

The professor said, "Ms. Katya and I were just discussing—"

"The homework," said Katya.

"Homework, right," teased Wilder.

"You're a total loser," said Katya. She clenched both fists by her sides.

The professor said, "He may be a loser but he is a very smart one."

"He doesn't look smart to me," said Katya.

Seemingly unprompted, the professor let his guard down and his mood shifted. "Hang on, let me have a moment of quiet." He looked blankly out the window. Katya and Wilder shrugged at each other. They could see something was truly troubling him. The professor got an idea and muttered to himself, "What do you have to lose that you haven't lost already?"

"What did you say?" Katya asked.

He turned to his desk and said in a subdued voice, "You know, it's a good thing that you're both here."

"You sure?" quipped Wilder, "Because I could come back later."

"I will hurt you," promised Katya, flaring her nostrils.

The professor fumbled in his desk drawer. "Listen, listen," he said with a quiver in his voice. "You're both such excellent students. There's something I want to share with you."

Wilder cocked his head. "This seems odd. Whatever it is, I'm in."

The professor unlocked a file cabinet and searched through it. Wilder snooped in a cardboard box in the corner of the office. "Is this a satellite? Wow, this is a satellite, am I right?" He picked it up in one hand. "This thing only weighs, what, five pounds?"

"Put that down right now," said the professor. "Yes, it's a satellite, and it's fragile. It's for a contract I'm working on."

"What is this thing attached to it, like a mini-transponder?"

"I said, put that down," insisted the professor. "Stop touching it."

Wilder put it back in the box. "Are you designing the software for that thing?"

"If you must know, yes, but it's top secret." The professor couldn't help but brag. "The transponder is short range, a few miles at best."

"What does it do?" Katya asked curiously.

The professor hedged. "Nothing particularly special."

"I'm very interested," prodded Katya.

The professor stared up at the ceiling. For a split moment he looked heartbroken. He had worked so many years on his proprietary technology and increasingly despaired how his contractor would use it. He took a deep breath and blurted, "I coded a universal disruption output signal. It overrides all existing transmissions while also going undetected."

Wilder said, "Sounds badass."

The professor said, "It has various functions. I'm being paid a lot of money for it."

"Who paid you, how much?" asked Katya.

Professor Singh said, "I am not at liberty to say."

Katya said, "Tell us more about this technology."

Professor Singh continued bragging. "We all know about the internet of things. The same is true in outer space. Everything is connected. Government satellites work around the clock to link to each other's frequencies and steal intelligence data."

Wilder said, "I heard they're all hacking each other all the time, and once a satellite gets breached, they have to power it down forever. There are thousands of them, basically a garbage dump in orbit."

"That's true," said the professor.

"What does your satellite do that is so special?" asked Katya.

The professor smiled and looked at Katya. He shrugged off his anxiety and said, "I might as well tell you. I created a covert temporary disable feature, which disrupts local device signals. It puts them to sleep or destroys them, depending on the program running."

"That sounds incredible," said Katya.

"I don't have a full enough picture to get why that's unique," said Wilder.

The professor's eyes lit up, and he turned to a whiteboard. He drew *X*'s and *O*'s with a dry marker and squiggly lines around each letter. "Let's say you've got a group of US satellites in an interlocked constellation with foreign satellites also. Countries like China and Russia . . . they're hacking the Americans and disrupting our operations, and the US is doing the same thing back."

"I'm following you," said Wilder.

"Well if you put out a signal pulse that fries nearby motherboards, depending on the situation, you would be knocking out your own satellites too." He scribbled lines all over the white board. "So I designed something better."

"You're working from the assumption that any foreign signal is bad?" asked Wilder.

Professor Singh said, "That is more elegant than reality, but yes, let's work from that assumption. Running my OS, a small satellite can freeze select signals and stitch other signals into them. While that program's running, anything else my satellite captures or installs goes completely undetected. It's the digital equivalent of a fake mirror. But not only that, my program can pick which satellites to skip over entirely. It creates another layer of imperceivability."

"You're a genius," said Katya.

"Not really," said the professor. "It was initially my idea, but making it happen required a team of computer scientists . . . friends at MIT, etcetera."

"Wow," said Wilder.

The professor said, “It’s cool technology and I should add, what works in space works on earth as well.”

“Sure, I get it,” said Wilder. “Dude, that’s fucking lit.”

“From there it gets more sophisticated,” said the professor, “because there are fine-tuned microgrid settings for infiltrating devices. A new version of steganography is the key to the whole thing.”

“I don’t know what that means,” said Katya.

Wilder said, “Random byte hiding. Are you using an LSB technique?”

Professor Singh nodded and said, “Katya, imagine having temperature control for different rooms, except now you control a city.”

Katya said, “A satellite can do that?”

Professor Singh said, “Much more. This kind of technology could change the flow of the digital universe.”

“And you can do that secretly, perhaps for military advantage?” asked Katya.

“Let’s just say this job is important and we’re staying one step ahead of the competition,” said Professor Singh.

Wilder pointed at the box. “Is that satellite operational?”

“Yes, but that is a model only. And we’re working on an underwater version, but that is an entirely different set of problems,” added Professor Singh. “Oh, never mind about all of this.” He popped the lid on the pen and waved his hand back and forth to dismiss the conversation.

“Fascinating,” said Wilder.

“Yes, is it not fascinating?” Professor Singh shuffled things around in his file drawer. “Ah, I found what I was looking for.” He tentatively pulled out a plastic sandwich bag holding two thumb drives.

Wilder said, “You’re a total stud for making that code. What’s in the bag?”

Professor Singh said, “Yes, yes. It’s one of my proud accomplishments.” His hand quivered as he reached in the baggie. He handed one thumb drive to Wilder and placed the second one gently in the palm of Katya's hand.

"What is this?" asked Katya.

The professor's voice wavered nervously. "Those are identical—it's my latest coding sequence," he said. He crossed his arms and took a deep breath.

"Why are you giving this to *us*?" asked Wilder.

"Well, you see . . ." the professor searched for words. "I can't share this with my colleagues, because I'm afraid they will steal it for their own." He hesitated another moment. "This code is special to me."

Katya held the thumb drive to her heart. "It's an honor that you give me this. What exactly would you like me to do with it?"

"Wilder, Katya—I'm giving you two a special project to work on together."

"I'm not working with him," she asserted.

"Sounds fun," said Wilder.

"Katya, I will give you an *A*, and Wilder, I will make sure you pass my class."

"I'm in."

Katya glared at Wilder, crossed her arms and said reluctantly, "I'm in."

"Good." The professor explained, "Each thumb drive has three folders holding a piece of programming code. Try to solve them and analyze them for errors."

"OK," said Katya. She put her hand on the professor's low back. "But I'm really doing this for you."

The professor said, "I believe you won't find errors, and I sincerely doubt you can crack all three."

"And the thumb drives are identical?" Wilder asked.

"Yes. Altogether I call the code sequence 'the eye.' "

"You named it?" asked Wilder. "Tight."

Katya stepped up close to the professor and in a quiet, sexy voice, she said, "I'll look at your work right away."

Wilder looked at the thumb drive incredulously. "Wait, you're trusting me with this? This seems like it's actually important."

"Yes, I am choosing to trust you," said the professor.

"That's not the wisest thing," said Wilder, "but I'm totally cool with this."

The professor nodded. "I'm a little stuck here. I could use your help."

Katya was effusive. "A man of your intelligence is asking *me* for help. I will not let you down."

The professor locked eyes with her. "That is certainly flattering," he said.

"Woah," said Wilder. "Get a room, you two."

"I doubt you can solve over half of the code. Work together on this, and don't share it with anyone else."

"Whatever you say," said Katya.

The professor broke from Katya's gaze. "I just remembered, I have an important phone call at ten o'clock. I have to ask you to leave."

"I'll come back tomorrow," said Katya.

"That would be nice." The professor smiled.

Wilder chuckled. "This is some serious hot-for-teacher action."

The professor blushed and tucked in his shirt. He said, "Stop by anytime during my office hours. That would be fine." He ushered them out the door and locked it behind them.

In the hallway, Wilder and Katya just stood there a moment looking at each other. Wilder asked, "What in the world was that about?"

She got in his face. "You're following me, asshole."

"No, I'm not," he lied but wasn't trying to sell it.

Katya grabbed him by the collar and shoved him backward. "Stay away from me. Otherwise, you will very much regret it."

"You would like me if you got to know me."

"I'm sure you're wrong about that," said Katya.

"OK, well, we gotta work together on this project," said Wilder.

"We do not." She turned and walked down the hall.

"Hey, wait," Wilder said, grasping at straws. "Have you ever been to an EDM rave?"

Katya stopped and did a slow pirouette. "Did you say rave? That is definitely one thing I want to do before I go home to Moscow."

He dug in his backpack and handed her a piece of paper. "Here's the address, it's this Saturday night," Wilder said. "And here's two VIP passes."

Katya snatched them from his hand. "Thank you. Now leave me alone. I mean it." She turned around and left.

Satisfied with himself, Wilder thought, *That actually went pretty well.* He held the thumb drive in his open palm. "Today is freaking interesting. Maybe I should wake up early more often."

Inside his office, the professor's cell phone rang and he sheepishly answered, "Hello, Arnold. Yes, we're out of beta. Send your guys to pick it up anytime."

10

THE MISSION

It was just before dawn in Al Hoceima, Morocco. A small Italian merchant vessel drifted toward a wharf under a thin layer of Mediterranean fog. All six members of Navy SEAL Team 20, aka KrayBULL, crouched low in the boat. Rex Hawthorne put the last of the crew's scuba gear into a disguised hull, covering the floorboards with netting. He was second officer in command.

Hawthorne pulled a coin out of his pocket and quietly prayed the same as he did with every mission. The other men joined him by bowing their heads. "God, may evil meet justice and our team survive. If luck comes my way I'll take it, and if there's no luck to find, I'll make it. Peace is your beating heart my Lord, amen."

Hawthorne flipped the coin into the water and watched it sink. He threw a rope around a dock post, then another. The men double-checked their gear, then heaved backpacks and duffel bags onto the dock. The driver, Officer in Command Barnaby Jansen, stood watch. The rest of the group filed off the runabout.

Commander Jansen was a tall white man with a New Jersey accent and special training in complex arena warfare. He tucked the keys under a mat and stepped off the boat last, giving Hawthorne the thumbs-up. The unit wore civilian clothing, each with a backstory about their business trip turned vacation.

Standing at ease, Ahmed Ali was an Iranian American, fluent in Farsi and Arabic, drone technology and an encryption expert. Next was Benito Perez, a Latino military brat, helicopter pilot and Air Force mechanic. Ray Jones was a black man from Chicago, technical adviser, handler of explosives and heavy weaponry. Then there was Leo Aganad, Filipino American, hand-to-hand combat marshal and naval engineer.

Hawthorne gave Jansen a one-armed hug and slap on the back. The team loved Jansen, particularly because of the way he saved their lives in Afghanistan. After the Battle of Takur Ghar, Jansen received the Medal of Honor for acts of valor. Later, Jansen became the Pentagon's main point of contact for SEAL Units 16 through 20. They gave him the code name *CR22A*, among other unknown monikers. Jansen led the way and the team walked up the dock.

At the foot of a tall barbed-wire fence, a man sitting on a low stool waved casually. Jansen held out a heavy handbag. The man looked at the cash inside and nodded. He handed Jansen a set of keys and buzzed them through the gate.

Without a word, the team from KrayBuLL loaded up a rusty truck with a hard topper. Jansen drove a mile, pulled down a gulley and parked in a grove of argan trees. They took a ten-minute break beside a shaded creek, then got back on the road. The team headed on the highway southwest.

Hawthorne and a few others napped, waking up when the truck bumped down a dirt road on the outskirts of Jerada. In recent years Jerada had grown into a big town but still had plenty of rural sprawl nearby. Jansen turned into a driveway, swerving to avoid a big pothole. He pulled to park next to a Humvee with a tarp draped over it. A vacant hut stood at the end of the driveway.

Team KrayBULL stepped out of the truck with their bags in tow. They looked around and saw a few distant houses but no people. Commander Jansen found the keys to the hut and Humvee under a pile of rocks. He walked to the hut, opened the door and motioned for his men to enter.

Jansen said, "Get some rest. I'm taking the back room for myself." He locked the door and lay face down on a cot. It was the only piece of furniture in the whole place. Fighting the urge to sleep, he sat up and grabbed a cell phone from his duffel bag.

In the front room, the other team members rested. Rex Hawthorne sat against a wall and cleaned his Beretta M9. He worked the tape around his two banged-up fingers. His pinky finger was rebroken and bent. *At least it's not my dominant hand*, he thought.

Hawthorne's face was calm and focused, but an unsettled fire burned behind his eyes. In idle moments, memories of combat cropped up involuntarily. His mind flashed with images of the caves of Tora Bora, and Fallujah was an unforgettable disaster that still gave him nightmares. In all of those battles, he fought alongside Commander Jansen, and they lost a lot of men. They both knew to never talk about it.

Hawthorne placed his hand palm up on his thigh. He grabbed the middle joint of his pinky finger with his free hand. With a slight grimace, he squeezed the finger straight and heard it pop.

Over the years he had broken twenty-seven bones, none of which had slowed him down much. Hawthorne always said he would've been dead or retired by now if it weren't for the love of Jesus and his faith in justice. He knew there wasn't always a crystal-clear right side in every battle, but he trusted he was among those going to heaven. Although sometimes it was at a heavy price, he knew in his heart the US ultimately defended freedom.

Hawthorne leaned over and unzipped a case with a VR headset, console and small jar inside. He tipped the jar and a black fly insect drone rolled into the palm of his hand. He pinched it in his fingertips and placed it on the ground. "Let's see whatcha got," Hawthorne said to himself. He powered on the VR headset and toggled the controls. The tiny drone lifted off and buzzed out the window. After a few attempts, Hawthorne landed the fly on a windowsill around the outside. *Holy cow*, he thought, *this little thing is powerful.* He checked his earpiece and hit the universal Transmit button.

The audio hissed, then came in clearly. He looked down with his headset and instructions appeared. "(1) Hold down universal Transmit and Start buttons, (2) toggle left to retrieve live signals." Hawthorne tapped an open audio line bouncing off a cell tower.

He heard Jansen speaking quietly. "Hello, Karen. We are in position. What's next?"

The other voice was digitally warbled. "You're gonna have to sell your boys on a change of plan."

Hawthorne wondered, *What change of plan? And who the hell is Karen?* He turned up the volume on the drone intercept mic control.

A different voice came through. "Y'all Navy SEALs make one hell of a team." Hawthorne placed the unmistakable Southern drawl and knew right away it was Arnold Renfree. Renfree was the head of the Senate Intelligence Committee and a far-right extremist. Hawthorne met him once and hated the guy's guts. Renfree had a politician's fake toothy grin and constantly made headlines with his blatant racism.

Renfree continued, "Back in my day, Navy SEALs were all white. Things have changed. But those darkies on KrayBULL sure do pull their weight."

Jansen sidestepped. "Very funny, sir. We've assembled a strong team."

Screw this racist son of a bitch, Hawthorne thought to himself. He had reasons to be concerned about Renfree. In 2016, Renfree got a team of Navy SEALs killed by pushing for an ill-advised mission off the island of Gabbi-Hu. Hawthorne mistrusted preemptive attacks, especially without the intel to justify them, and Renfree's fuckup was a case in point. He had goaded President Garner into flexing his power with a pointless strike. When the whole thing went south, DC swept it under the rug and the American public knew next to nothing about it.

Renfree said to Jansen, "Well, I hope you're ready for some real action. The WMD is en route, and our boys at CIA are ready to sell it. The team from Moscow is carrying their cargo with our Libyan friends in tow."

Hawthorne's eyes bulged in disbelief. He thought, *Did he just say WMD?*

"We are ready, sir," confirmed Commander Jansen. "I don't like lying to my team, but we do what we have to do."

Renfree smiled on the other end of the call. "Our friends at the Pentagon assured me it's an in-and-out job. Get to the site in Jerada. Provide perfect security for the sale and accompany them to escort the cargo. Make sure it's a clean exchange."

"OK," said Jansen. "When?"

Karen's warbled voice said, "You're going to have to lie low a few more days than expected. Four days tops. It's not easy making a nuke untraceable."

"We shouldn't even be talking about it," said Jansen. "No matter how secure the line."

"You're right as usual—and one hell of a leader," Renfree said condescendingly. "You make your country proud—and after this mission, you're going to be really, *really* rich. For the rest of your life, you can wipe your ass with hundred-dollar bills if you want to."

"What more do I need to know?" asked Jansen.

Karen chimed in, "It's simple by design. Everybody enters and exits on the one road to the site. Same as before, we jam all signals except ours. The exchange will also be invisible by satellite."

Jansen said, "Afterward, we leave with the tech box containing the video capture."

Renfree confirmed, "Yep, that's the same plan for y'all."

"What's it for—bounty?"

"Evidence, in case we need it."

"Understood."

Renfree detailed, "After the sale, you head south with our cut of the money. Provide cover for the WMD until it gets to the fork in the road. From there, our buyers peel off and where they go is not your business."

"Sir, why sell the nuke?" Jansen asked. "Aren't we handing it over to the enemy?"

Renfree snapped angrily, "Listen here, shitbag! It's *way* above your rank and pay grade to ask that question."

"Sir, you are right, sir," said Jansen.

Renfree said, "This plan is rock solid. Ensure the transfer of the weapon."

Karen said, "Be a pilot fish on the whale until you get to the fork in the road. That's it."

"Yes, sir," said Jansen. "Consider the job done."

Renfree lightheartedly asked a random question, "Do you like music, Jansen?"

"Sir?"

"What kind of music do you like?" asked Renfree.

"Um. Just about anything, I guess," said Jansen. "I really like Billy Joel."

"Ah, Billy. Classic. I like him too," said Renfree.

"Nice to have that in common, sir," said Jansen. "Thank you for trusting us with this mission. KrayBULL won't let you down."

"White Power," said Renfree.

"White Power," said Jansen. They hung up.

Sitting against a wall in the front room, Hawthorne heard every word. His jaw went slack and he started hyperventilating. Hawthorne rarely had panic attacks, but this one jumped him. His face turned peaked, and his muscles went weak. He was shocked by what he just heard. Commander Jansen was betraying the US in a literal nuclear situation. Hawthorne played back the conversation in his mind. How long had Jansen been a traitor? Why did he sign off with "White Power"?

Hawthorne steadied his nerves and slowed down his breathing. He fumbled again at the handset controls, and the drone fly buzzed back through the front window. Hawthorne landed it on the ground in front of him. He powered the drone down, pulled off his headset and sealed the fly in the jar. He put everything away just like he found it, sliding the case back in his duffel bag. Hawthorne put a damp towel over his face, still straining to catch his breath. After five long minutes, the panic attack fully subsided.

Ali threw a pebble at him. "Hey man, you alright?" he asked.

"Yeah, I'm fine . . . Must be something I ate," said Hawthorne.

"You can't bullshit a bullshitter," said Ali. "Talk to me."

Hawthorne said, "Join me outside. I gotta look at the Humvee engine anyway."

A wall of dry heat hit them as they exited the hut. Hawthorne popped the hood and they inspected the engine together.

"What's up?" asked Ali. "Something shook you—I can tell."

Hawthorne said soberly, "Besides God, you know nothing matters to me more than KrayBULL."

"Damn right," said Ali.

"After Fallujah, Tora Bora . . . We've been through hell and back."

"Literally."

"Swear to secrecy on this."

"Done."

Hawthorne said, "I just learned something that's gonna tear KrayBULL apart."

"Impossible."

Hawthorne whispered, "We got a loose nuke on our hands—and our real mission is selling it to the enemy!"

"What? That makes no sense."

"This is us committing terrorism," Hawthorne said. "And, get this, Jansen's in on it."

"Fuck that shit."

"I just overheard him confirm the plan."

"You gotta confront him," said Ali.

"I can't do that."

Ali said, "If you won't face him, I'll do it myself." He turned toward the hut. Hawthorne caught him by the shoulder. Ali spun around, cocked back his fist and held it in the air.

"I'm begging you to listen," Hawthorne said. "It's a fucking WMD."

Ali lowered his fist. "This really is some serious shit."

"Don't say anything," pleaded Hawthorne. "Just give me some time."

"Why should I trust you?" Ali argued. "If I stay quiet, that means I'm siding with you over Jansen's orders."

"This is duty over loyalty." Hawthorne said grimly. "If we tip off Jansen, we risk the nuke falling into the wrong hands."

"Duty over loyalty, huh?" Ali's stress was ratcheting up. "So what do we do?"

"We take out Jansen and I'm next in command."

"You're not serious," protested Ali.

"It goes against every fiber of my being," said Hawthorne, "but think about it—there's no better option."

Ali hung his head.

Hawthorne implored, "Please don't say anything. I'll draw up a plan and tell the others as soon as I can."

The front door of the hut swung open, and Jansen stood in the doorway. "What are you two doing out here?" he asked.

Hawthorne bluffed. "We were just checking the engine."

"We need to lie low," said Jansen. He took a long moment staring at his men. "Hawthorne. A word in private."

Ali nodded and went back inside.

"Get in the cab," said Jansen. He climbed in the driver's seat and Hawthorne on the passenger side.

"What's up?" asked Hawthorne.

"I got a bad feeling," said Jansen, "like we might not survive this one."

Hawthorne darted his eyes at his commander, then looked away. "I hate that feeling."

Jansen put his hand on Hawthorne's shoulder and made a request: "Say one of your prayers for us, would you?"

"Sure." They shut their eyes and Hawthorne slowly recited the Lord's Prayer. His mind ran through every mission their unit had been on, every battle and explosion—every time Jansen and he had saved each other's lives. ". . . and deliver us from evil, for thine is the kingdom, the power and the glory, forever. Amen."

"Amen," said Jansen. He looked out at the desert landscape and disdainfully said, "God I hate North Africa."

"We've seen a lot of action in these parts," reflected Hawthorne. "Somalia, Sudan, Eritrea, Libya . . ."

"It makes me sick, there are so many fucking Arabs this close to the Promised Land," Jansen snarled.

"Come on, man." Hawthorne tried to shrug it off like he always did when Jansen got racist.

Jansen carried on, "In the End Times, Jesus will kill every last one of them."

Hawthorne pushed back as diplomatically as he could. "Jesus is ready to forgive the sins of humanity. He holds a place for all of us in Heaven."

"Not my Jesus," said Jansen. He abruptly stepped out of the Humvee, slammed the door and walked back into the hut.

Hawthorne gritted his teeth and muttered to himself, "Not my Jesus. You motherfucker." He followed his commander inside.

11

TROUBLE ON CAMPUS

Wilder walked toward his dorm room thinking about Katya and what could possibly be on the thumb drive Professor Singh gave him. He felt a hand strongly grip his shoulder, turned around and saw a Latino man in a hoodie with a Smith and Wesson Equalizer TS at his hip. He shoved the pistol into Wilder's ribs. "Turn around and keep walking," he demanded.

"OK, OK," said Wilder fearfully. "Don't shoot."

"Get in the car," said the man. He pushed Wilder toward a sedan with tinted windows and jabbed the Smith and Wesson harder into his side.

"I'm cooperating," said Wilder.

The driver, a woman with a plaid shirt and ball cap, stepped out and opened the back door. The man shoved Wilder in the back seat with the pistol still drawn. The woman got back behind the wheel and they pulled away.

Wilder asked, "What is this? Who are you?"

The man said, "Shut up and listen, *güero*."

"Do what he says," said the woman. She brandished a pistol of her own.

The man said, "I'm Alejandro—call me Alex. You stole money from my boss and he's very upset."

"What money?" asked Wilder.

"Don't play stupid or I'll kill you."

"OK, OK."

Alex said, "Last night my boss looked up his bank account

and he noticed something strange. Ten thousand dollars of his money transferred directly to you. Come to find out you've been doing that every month. Did you really think you would get away with that?"

"I don't know what you're talking about," said Wilder. "I get trust money every month from my grandma's will, but I swear that's it."

"Well my boss isn't your fucking grandma," said the man. "We found you out, bro. We know you're pullin' that fancy computer dark web redirection bullshit. We got our own IT guys just like you."

Wilder knew he was caught. "Tell your boss I'm sorry and he can have his money back, with interest."

"Too late for that. He might kill you. But first he wants to know how the hell you did it."

Wilder said, "I'll tell you anything you want."

"That's right," said the woman. "You do that." She pulled a U-turn and headed back toward campus. The car pulled up to an empty spot outside Wilder's dorm room, which had its own basement stairwell and entrance.

The man said, "Now invite me inside like a good friend."

Wilder did what he said and the woman waited in the car. Once inside, Alex held the Smith and Wesson to his head and demanded information about how Wilder siphoned money from his boss. The offshore account was a fake bank in Panama. Wilder figured since the account had billions of dollars in it, nobody would notice if he skimmed off the top. He was wrong about that. Wilder opened his laptop, located the code, copied it to a thumb drive and handed it over.

Alex lowered his Smith and Wesson and took the thumb drive. "That's it?"

"That's it."

"You got any other thumb drives you want to give me?"

"What do you mean?" asked Wilder. A new layer of panic struck him.

Alex asked, “I don’t know—what *do* I mean?”

Wilder took a deep breath. “That’s everything, I swear.”

“This information better be real or I’ll come back and kill you.”

“It’s real,” said Wilder. “And it will never happen again.”

Alex smiled. “You are really scared shitless. Nobody ever point a gun at you before?”

“No,” said Wilder.

“Listen, gringo. We own you now, you get that?”

“Own me?”

“We might be back tomorrow, we might be back next week or maybe next year. But when we come knocking, you do whatever we tell you to do.”

“Who are you anyway?” asked Wilder.

“We’re the cartel de Casta, man.”

“Casta cartel? Oh shit, that’s bad.”

“You’re getting it now. We come knocking, you answer. Maybe we need a piece-of-shit hacker like you someday.”

“The other choice seems to be you kill me, so yeah—I’ll do anything.”

Alex said, “Exactly.” He pulled out his cell phone and dialed a number. “*Jefe, soy yo. Ya lo tengo todo. Sí—de ese mamón. Tiene un chingo de miedo, ja-ja.* OK, be right there, man.” He put the phone back in his hoodie pocket.

At this point, Wilder could see Alex had no intention of killing him, but he continued apologizing. “Tell your boss it will never happen again. You can watch while I destroy all the code on my end.”

“Fine, do it then,” said Alex.

Wilder pointed at his screen, dragged a folder into the trash and emptied it. “See? That’s it, for real. I’m not gonna fuck with this ever again, I swear.”

Alex said, “If it does happen again, you’ll never see us coming. You’ll just be dead.”

“Understood,” said Wilder.

Alex walked out of the dorm room and shut the door. Wilder looked in his hand at Alex's cell phone, which he stole from his hoodie pocket a minute earlier. The phone wasn't locked, and the most recent call was to Jefe, so he dialed him.

"*Bueno?*" said Jefe.

"Jefe? This is Wilder Kole."

"Wilder who?" asked Jefe.

"Yeah, I'm really sorry about stealing your money. It won't happen again—but you should send somebody more professional next time."

"The fuck you talking about?"

"Alex just stopped by and I stole his cell phone. But he got what he came for. I promise I won't mess with the bank account ever again."

"I should have him kill you right now," said Jefe.

"That would really lack style points."

"Style points? You got a huge set of *cojones*, don't you?"

"They're normal size, I would say," said Wilder.

Alex swung the door open and yelled, "Give me my damn phone, motherfucker."

Wilder tossed the phone to him. "Jefe's gonna be pissed you let that happen."

Alex was flustered. "You—fuck you, man. Next time I won't just scare you." He slammed the door behind him.

"Damn," Wilder said to himself, "that was a seriously fucked-up situation." It was true he had never been held at gunpoint like that, and he was rattled. Wilder sat down and cried for a moment. He opened his drawer and pulled out a joint. He smoked the whole thing and then he smoked another. It didn't make him feel better, but it took the edge off.

12

LEVEL UP

After the cartel incident, Wilder texted Chuck.

Wilder: You around?

Chuck: Yeah, what's up?

Wilder: Gotta tell you in person

Chuck: What are you into now?

Wilder: It's sort of serious

Chuck: Uh-oh . . . I'm at my dorm room

Wilder: I'm coming over

Wilder's mood slightly improved on the walk to Chuck's dorm. He stood outside with his hands on his hips, studying the building's facade to solve the problem of climbing it. He grabbed a jutting brick, got his footing and up he went.

After scaling three stories, Wilder looked down. He could see a small crowd of people watching him, and he waved with a smile. He hoisted himself up a challenging flat section, wedging his hands in a crack. His feet slipped and he dangled precariously, clinging with his fingertips. "Falling would be bad," he said to himself. He caught a toehold good enough to keep climbing. "That was a little too close."

At the fifth floor outside Chuck's room, Wilder's head popped up on the windowsill. He cracked open the window and climbed in.

"What the fuck?" asked Chuck.

Wilder acted casual. "Hey, bud."

"Why am I not surprised? And why don't you just use the buzzer like a normal person?"

"That would be boring," said Wilder. He strolled around the immaculately clean room, then tilted a picture frame on the wall by an inch.

Chuck fixed it to be level again. "What's this 'sort of serious' problem of yours?"

Wilder groaned and plopped down on Chuck's bed. "I'm sort of fucked," he said.

"You're way too cocky to ever say that. This must be bad."

"I just got held at gunpoint."

"Holy shit. Who? Why?"

"A dude from the Casta cartel," said Wilder. "It's the off-shore accounts."

"Oh my God," said Chuck in a panic. "I'm your best friend. They're coming for me next."

Wilder expected that reaction and felt genuinely awful. "Calm down, calm down." He slid off the bed and paced by the window.

Chuck compulsively flattened the blanket creases where Wilder was sitting. "I'm guilty by association. They're gonna shoot me in the kneecaps."

"I don't think so, dude."

"What makes you so certain?"

"Because I met their demands." Wilder was reassuring himself, not just Chuck. "They wanted my code to see how I hacked them. Plus—for a cartel it wasn't *that* much money."

"I told you something bad was gonna happen," Chuck said, worriedly. "We're up shit creek."

"I gave them my code." Wilder surmised, "Now they can fix their firewalls . . . and use my code to rob someone else."

"How can you be so calm?"

"I put up a good front," admitted Wilder, "but this one really scared me."

"Remember that time you accidentally hacked into the Pentagon mainframe?"

"*Shut up, dude!* We do *not* talk about that incident."

"Fine. I still can't believe they never caught you."

"Dark web security measures."

"Wilder, what are you gonna do if I show up dead?"

"Probably jump off a bridge."

The more Chuck thought about it, the angrier he got, "I should really kick your ass right now."

"I deserve it." They stewed in silence, then Wilder looked up hopefully. "I do have some good news, though."

"Don't try and downplay this."

"I'm not!" Wilder deflected. "But don't you want to hear the good news?"

"Tell me."

"I'm in with Katya."

"No way."

"Yep," he said. "I bumped into her at Professor Singh's office this morning."

"You were following her, weren't you?" asked Chuck.

"Kind of. I mean, she said she'd be there."

"Dude. Boundaries, remember?"

"I know, I know," Wilder said. "I got her attention, though."

"OK . . ." Chuck rolled his eyes. "Then what?"

"When I got there, she was making out with the professor!"

"Ha-ha, are you shitting me?"

"For real." Wilder laughed. "And then, out of the blue the professor gave us some important code—like an assignment to work on together."

"That's crazy. Are you gonna do it?"

"She said no to that," said Wilder. "I'll just work on it myself. But hey, Katya knows who I am now."

"You're brave, I will give you that."

"Plus I gave her VIP passes to Saturday's rave."

"I don't know how you do it."

"Maybe it's because I have no boundaries."

"Zero boundaries," said Chuck.

"Why would I need boundaries when I got swagger?"

"You do get laid a lot—but you always fuck it up."

"I don't *try* to fuck it up. Women love me—then they hate me."

"The shit you say cuts deep."

"I see things in people," said Wilder. "*Somebody's* gotta tell them."

"It doesn't work like that," scolded Chuck.

"Like you know anything about women."

Chuck said, "You're just a slut."

"I'm not a slut," protested Wilder.

"You are too."

"Then I'm an *accidental* slut."

"Yeah right," said Chuck.

"I wanna fall in love," insisted Wilder. "I'm just—"

"Looking for my soulmate," they said in unison.

Chuck laughed. "I know you believe that soulmate crap, but you push girls away to not get attached."

Wilder nodded. "You're probably right . . . so will you go to the rave with me?"

"Not this weekend."

"Come on, boss."

"No."

Wilder twisted his arm. "I got another VIP pass with your name on it."

"Fine."

"Righteous!" Wilder fist-bumped Chuck.

"No more offshore account bullshit."

"I promise."

Chuck nagged him, "Why don't you just stop doing illegal shit? Like when are you going to grow up and stop dealing drugs?"

"As soon as I save up enough money."

"What's enough?"
"I got this," said Wilder.
"You do *not* 'got this.' "
"I *got* this."
"Do not," said Chuck. "Also—you're a slut."
"Don't call me a slut!" Wilder said, laughing.

13

EDM

Chuck parked his car on a dimly lit street in the warehouse district south of downtown. He turned to Wilder in the passenger seat and asked, "Exactly how much are you making off dealing fentanyl?"

"So far, about enough to pay for your education three times over," Wilder bragged. "A lot of that went into my computer hardware, but I have a big stash tucked away."

"Don't you feel guilty pushing drugs?"

"Nope."

"You know damn well some of these kids are gonna end up shooting heroin. And overdosing and stuff."

"Not my problem," said Wilder. "These kids are gonna get their fix from somebody. It might as well be me."

They stepped out of the car and walked toward the rave. There was a line of people a block long. Chuck asked, "Isn't fentanyl for major surgeries or something?"

"Yep, originally," Wilder said. "And if you're high on coke and molly, a half patch of my shit will bring you down easy. A whole patch is a magic carpet ride." They walked to the front of the line and Wilder flashed a VIP card. The bouncer nodded and motioned for them to pass.

Inside the warehouse, electronic dance music was pumping. Lights bounced off misty clouds of sweat above the crowd. Wilder scanned the scene and said, "I gotta go. My best clients are in the VIP room."

"Alright, catch ya later," said Chuck. "Hey, kick me a few joints before you go."

Wilder climbed a flight of stairs to the loft space. He held up his pass and they waived him through.

Inside the room about a hundred people made a small rave of their own, lit by globe lamps and kaleidoscope patterns on the walls. Psychedelic down-tempo pumped from the speakers. A half dozen naked women painted head to toe in gold wandered slowly through the crowd, selling cigarettes and cocaine. On a row of vinyl couches, clusters of people were making out, having sex in couples and trios. A pile of people writhed around on the floor. With enough people high on molly, there was usually an orgy going. Wilder knew they would be buying from him once they started to come down.

Wilder's main buyer was a black kid from Lincoln Heights no older than sixteen. He bought half Wilder's supply right off the bat. "Good action," Wilder said. In the far corner Wilder caught a glimpse of a dark-haired woman straddling a man in a chair. His hands explored her body. She pulled off her shirt, showing a lace bra.

Wilder walked closer and said, "Katya! I thought I recognized you!" She whipped her head around, and Professor Singh tilted at an angle to see. Wilder said, "You two! Oh my God, fancy seeing you here!"

Furious and wild-eyed, Katya stood up, took two steps toward Wilder and punched him squarely in the eye with a straight right hand. He fell on his back and Katya pounced. She mounted Wilder and unloaded a flurry of punches to his head. "You! Motherfucker!" He couldn't defend himself and she knocked him unconscious.

Moments later, Wilder came to, seeing stars. Katya's angry face and bloody knuckles came into focus. In his periphery, he saw people gathering around. The professor pleaded with her, "Katya, what in the world! So much violence is unnecessary."

She had already tipped into a state of rage and was squeezing Wilder by the throat. Wilder reached up and grabbed a handful of her hair. He pulled hard and to his surprise he was holding a black wig. His vision was still bleary but he could see Katya's bald head. Wilder was shocked and she was absolutely mortified.

Katya furiously gritted her teeth, cocking her arm back to punch Wilder again. Instead, she snatched the wig from his hands and put it back on her head. Onlookers were too stunned to move, including Professor Singh. Katya stood up and put on her shirt. Livid and humiliated, she grabbed the professor by the arm. "We are leaving immediately." She spit on Wilder. "I already warned you. Leave me the fuck alone. Next time I will really hurt you."

Wilder sat up and used his sweatshirt to stop the bleeding under his eye. One of the gold-painted women crouched down next to him. "Want a line of coke? It's on me."

14

THE SITUATION

At a quarter past midnight in Jerada, SEAL Team Kray-BULL minus Commander Jansen sat in a tight circle in the hut. Hawthorne double-checked to make sure Jansen was sleeping in the back room.

"What the hell is this about?" Jones asked. "If this is an emergency meeting, why don't you wake up Jansen?"

"Keep your voice down—and hear me out," said Hawthorne, looking each man in the eye. He had been praying and his mind was clear. "We're in some really deep shit."

"That's obvious," said Aganad. "What's the situation?"

Hawthorne said with tears in his eyes, "This is unimaginably bad. Jansen is compromised."

"Compromised?" asked Aganad.

Hawthorne handed him a note. "Everybody read this and give it back."

"Holy fuck," said Aganad. "Is this real?"

"It's real," confirmed Hawthorne. "The choice is yours what you do with this intel, but I'm asking you—please—follow me."

Perez read the note. "Is this some kind of joke?" Hawthorne's face was dead serious.

Ali acted like he didn't know. "Shut the hell up." He passed the note to Jones who was the last one to read it.

"Mother of God," Jones whispered. "We're dealing with a nuke?"

Hawthorne grabbed the note back and earnestly said, "Yes, and not only does Jansen know about it, he has no plans to tell us."

"Are you sure the intel is good?" asked Perez. "And Jansen is in on it?"

"Positive," Hawthorne said. "I tapped a secure line with Jansen taking orders from Arnold Renfree with Senate Intel—and another player named Karen. I heard everything I needed to. Our stated mission is not why we are here."

"Then why are we here?" asked Aganad.

Hawthorne said, "If we go through with this, we will be covert security escorts supporting a clandestine cell inside the US government. We're selling a nuke to a group of Russians working with Al Qaeda sympathizers."

Jones almost threw up in his mouth. "Russia and Al Qaeda? That's beyond treason."

"I'm begging you," said Hawthorne. "I know this is uncharted territory, but we can't let this happen. Will you join me?"

"What about orders?" Aganad asked. "What about loyalty?"

"This is duty over loyalty." Hawthorne could tell his words hit home so he repeated himself. "Duty over loyalty."

"This is seriously heavy," Ali said.

Hawthorne pleaded, "Look deep in your hearts. With a nuke on the loose hundreds of thousands of lives are at stake."

Jones shook his head in dismay. "OK, I'm in. There's no possible justification for selling a nuke like that."

"How did they get to Jansen?" asked Ali.

"No idea," said Hawthorne.

Perez asked, "You want us to disobey command, just like that?"

Hawthorne said, "I know how serious that decision is, but Jansen's actions are incomprehensible. Please."

"Why should we trust you over Jansen?" Perez asked.

"Because there's too much at stake," said Hawthorne. "Watch—his behavior will be different. His eye twitches when he lies."

"OK then, what do you propose we do?" asked Jones.

Hawthorne said, "We take Jansen out."

"No fucking way," Aganad protested.

"He's betraying us all," Hawthorne said forcefully. "It's the only way."

Perez knew he was right. "Want me to kill him right now?"

"No," said Hawthorne. "We need Jansen to carry out the orders."

"Makes sense," said Perez. "Then what?"

Hawthorne said, "On my command, we kill Jansen and blow up the whole scenario. We seize the nuke and the evidence, then do our best to disappear."

"That's a hell of a plan," said Ali. "When?"

Hawthorne said, "Looks like we're lying low for another few days. The situation is fluid."

"I need more," said Aganad. "Why would *any* Americans *ever* sell nukes to the enemy?"

Hawthorne said, "I've been asking that same question all day. My best guess is there's a group of double agents in the Pentagon. Maybe they're running a bait and switch, or maybe they just hate America."

"Either way, we can't let it happen," said Aganad.

Hawthorne grabbed his lighter and burned the note. "We need to be all in on this. Anybody not all in, speak your mind right now."

Each of them nodded silently.

Hawthorne said, "It's done then. Same time tomorrow, we meet again. I'm drawing up a battle plan. Nobody says a word to Jansen."

In a long silence, their sullen faces spoke volumes about the gravity of the situation.

Hawthorne said, "I'll secure the tech evidence, and the rest of you get the nuke. Anything goes wrong, I take the fall on this."

15

NEWS FROM MOSCOW

On Sunday evening, Katya was in her dorm room alone. She called her uncle Timofey in Moscow.

Timofey answered, "Good timing. I was just finishing breakfast."

"Hi, Uncle Timofey. Sorry it took me a few days to get back to you."

"It's not a problem. What are you up to?"

"Just sitting in my dorm room. You said you had something important to tell me."

"That's right. Is now a good moment?"

"Yes. What is it?"

"I have news about your father."

The mere mention of her father landed like a punch to Katya's gut. She flashed back to her nine-year-old self on the day of her mother's funeral. Her father dropped her off, saying he would be right there. She watched him drive away, and a stranger walked up to her. "My name is Timofey. I'm your uncle. Come with me, I will take care of you." She asked the strange man where her dad went, and Timofey said, "He had to go away." Katya's dad never came back.

She held the phone away from her ear. Disassociating, her eyes glazed over and the blood flushed out of her face. "Katya?" asked Timofey.

More memories flooded in. She was in the classroom sitting at her desk, pulling out clumps of hair and feeling horrified. The other kids stared and pointed. On the playground, a fat boy bullied her with taunts. She socked him in the eye and threw him off the top of the slide. He broke his arm and the other kids looked on fearfully. Later, at the doctor's office with her uncle, the doctor explained, "Katya, losing your mom and dad is a really scary thing. It's unusual but sometimes scary and traumatic events can make your hair fall out. I know you're very sad, but I have some nice wigs—which color do you like? Black? OK, let's see how it fits . . ."

"Katya, you still there?"

"Yes, Uncle Timofey," she replied quietly. "It has been many years since we talked about my father."

"I know," he said compassionately.

"Well then, what is it?"

"He has died."

Katya's jaw dropped. She sat motionless.

Timofey asked, "Katya, did you hear me?"

"Yes."

"I'm very sorry. I know your relationship with him was complicated."

"You're calling it a relationship?" she asked angrily.

"He gave me a letter many years ago. He told me to only share it with you after he died."

"I don't know what to say," said Katya.

Timofey continued, "I'm so sorry for your loss, my dear."

"You held this letter in secret all these years?"

"I am sorry for that too. He made me promise. Now open your email. I just sent you an encrypted file. It's a scan of a handwritten letter to you. The password to open the letter is your mother's maiden name."

"I'll read it now."

"Close the file after you read it. It will become corrupt and not open again."

"OK."

Katya hung up and opened the email attachment on her laptop. She read the letter and buried her face in her hands.

16

THE POOL

Professor Singh's wife, Lakshmi, stepped out of the taxi. She rolled her luggage up the driveway and into her house. All the lights were on, which was odd because she thought he would be asleep by now. She called his name, "Raj?" He didn't answer. "Honey, I'm home." She checked the bedroom and then the kitchen. The sliding glass door was open and she went out to the patio.

"Raj? What are you doing out here in the middle of the night?" Under the glowing light of the swimming pool, he appeared to be on a raft. She approached and saw Professor Singh's body floating face down and motionless. Blood covered the concrete and dispersed into the water.

"RAJ!" Lakshmi screamed. She fell to her knees next to a kitchen knife. "No, no. Noooo!" Trembling in horror, she buried her face in her hands. She saw the professor's laptops and computer hardware at the bottom of the pool. "Why?" she cried. After a few minutes of stunned silence, Lakshmi pulled her cell phone out of her purse.

"9-1-1, what's your emergency?"

"My husband . . . he's dead. At our home, in the swimming pool." She gave them her name and address. "There's a knife, and so much blood."

Two police cars parked in the driveway, and the officers made their way around the side of the house. A few cops put a blanket over Lakshmi's shoulders and asked her questions. The other officers surveyed the scene.

"Don't step in the blood," one said.
"No perp on the property as far as I can tell."
"Looks like a suicide."
"Is that computer equipment?"
"I saw that too. Odd, isn't it? Yeah, probably suicide."
"People do strange things before they kill themselves."
"Maybe he was into child pornography or something."
"Have some respect, would ya?"

*

On Monday morning, Wilder sat ten rows back in the lecture hall, wearing a ball cap to shield his black eye and stitches. Katya sat in her usual seat. Chuck said, "Your face looks worse today. She landed those punches perfectly, didn't she?"

"Shut up," said Wilder.

"Do you still think she likes you?" Chuck prodded.

"Fuck you."

At the top of the hour, a white policeman and a black federal agent walked to the front of the class with adjunct professor Ms. Cruz handing them a mic. The policeman said, "Good morning. My name is Lieutenant Alan Oxford with the LAPD, and this is special agent Marvin Petersen with the FBI. We're very sorry to have to announce that Professor Raj Singh died over the weekend at his home." There was a collective gasp in the auditorium. The lieutenant continued, "We offer our sincere condolences to his family and community, including his colleagues and students affected by this sad news."

Agent Petersen said, "The police and FBI have no further information to share at this time, but I can tell you that circumstances around Mr. Singh's death warrant a special investigation. If you have any information as to his death, or if you observed anything unusual about Professor Singh's behavior in recent weeks, I'm asking you to contact the authorities directly. You can call the police and they'll put you in touch with the people in charge of this investigation. Thank you."

Ms. Cruz took the mic from Agent Petersen and said with a heavy heart, "The UCLA faculty and leadership are terribly saddened by this news. We're here to support you as students, including any counseling and academic support you may need."

Katya turned around in her chair and spotted Wilder. She furrowed her brow and faced the front again.

Ms. Cruz continued, "Class will resume next week, and everyone will receive a passing grade this quarter as long as you complete the remaining coursework." Her lip quivered. "We offer our respects to Raj Singh and his family. Our staff will do everything we can to make this time as smooth as possible for you. Class is dismissed."

Wilder waited for Katya to look back at him again, but she didn't. She packed her things and left the lecture hall straightaway.

17

CREATING A BOND

On the lawn outside of the lecture hall, Wilder turned to Chuck and said, "I'm shook. I can't believe Professor Singh is dead."

"I know dude," said Chuck. "I wonder what happened."

"He died," Wilder said sarcastically.

"Duh," said Chuck. "You know what I mean."

"I'm curious too," said Wilder.

"Poor guy," said Chuck. "Anyways, I gotta go to my next class."

"I thought you said you were dropping out," Wilder prodded him.

"I'm trying to do it all right now," said Chuck, "but the graveyard shift plus school is killing me."

"Awesome that you're making it happen," said Wilder. "Alright, catch ya later."

Wilder headed back toward his dorm room and felt a tap on his shoulder. It was Katya. She kept her composure but was clearly upset.

"Professor Singh . . . I can't believe it," she said.

"Crazy, right?"

"It is so sad."

"I don't know what to make of it," said Wilder. "But yeah, it's sad for sure."

"I am sorry for beating you up." She sounded sincere.

"It's OK."

"Can we talk?"

"Alright," Wilder said. "Wanna walk to north campus with me?"

"OK. Let me get my Vespa and I can walk with it."

"Sounds good."

Katya got her moped and pushed it over to Wilder. "Ready."

Wilder said, "About the other night—sorry I tore your wig off."

"I do NOT want to talk about that."

"Let me guess, your hair won't grow."

"I SAID, I do NOT want to talk about that," she repeated angrily.

"Alright, alright—I get it." Wilder nodded.

Katya whispered, "Professor Singh is dead . . . this does not seem real."

"I know, right? One day you're alive, the next day you're a goner. I have to admit I'm morbidly fascinated."

"Do you think we are suspected in his death?" she asked.

Wilder made a confused expression. "No . . . why would you say that?"

"I don't know," she said.

"Wait, Katya—could you be the last person who saw him?"

"Before he was killed?" she asked.

"Who said he was killed?" asked Wilder.

"I mean died," Katya corrected herself. "Perhaps he was killed."

"Maybe it was suicide."

"We can't know."

"Not without looking at the police report," said Wilder.

Her face was striking and serious. "Can we do that?"

"Maybe. Why do you think the FBI came to class today?"

"We should not talk like this," she said. "Is there somewhere we can be alone?"

"How about my dorm room?" he asked, feeling mischievous.

"Yes, let's go," she said.

"I have to warn you, my place is a total mess," said Wilder.

"I hate that," she said, "but right now I don't care. We need to talk."

"OK, fine. But don't judge me. I wasn't expecting a guest—least of all you." He started to smile but winced in pain instead.

"I really hurt you, didn't I?"

"It's OK," said Wilder. His mouth and temple were still throbbing nonstop, but he really wasn't mad about it, especially now that they were connecting.

Outside his dorm, Wilder led her down a half flight of stairs into his basement entrance.

"Welcome to my humble abode." Wilder bowed with his arm outstretched.

Katya gingerly stepped inside and gasped. "Oh my God. It's disgusting."

Wilder stepped over a spilled can of beer, mopping it up with a hoodie. "I'm really sorry about that." He tossed his dirty clothes under the bed and picked up a box of leftover pizza.

She put her hands to her mouth and stammered, "This is so horrible, but I—I can get over it."

Wilder shut the door behind her. She turned to him and shoved him against the wall.

He flinched. "Don't hit me."

She pushed him again and took a step back. "Don't be a loser. Can you not see something very serious is happening?"

"Ow," said Wilder, rubbing the back of his head. "Yeah, you're right. This situation is super screwed up."

She pointed to a rack of computer towers and a pile of tech gear in the corner. "What is all of that?"

He said, "That's my server farm and firewall setup—and some experimental stuff."

"Did you build it all?"

"Most of it, yeah," said Wilder proudly.

"That is very cool." She seemed impressed.

"I think so."

"Wilder, I have to tell you something."

"Yeah?"

"It's a secret."

"My lips are sealed," said Wilder.

"You won't believe me."

"Relax. What is it?"

Katya said, "After I enrolled into UCLA, the CIA approached me in Moscow and offered me a job as an informant."

"Woah, woah," said Wilder. "Holy shit."

"I have no idea what I am doing," she said. "I am scared. Nobody was supposed to get hurt."

"Much less turn up dead." Wilder shook his head in disbelief. "Why did they recruit you?"

"They told me to get close to the professor," she explained. "He had information they wanted."

Wilder smirked. "Well you definitely got close to him. You were damn good at that."

"It was easy to do."

"What happened after you two left the party? If things were anywhere near as good as the VIP room, maybe he died happy."

"I had fun with him," said Katya.

"Did you get the intel?"

"I think it's the code on the thumb drives."

Wilder nodded. "That adds up. So you're like . . . literally a spy?"

"I guess so."

"This is so classic. The smokin-hot Russian girl is a spy."

She said, "Well you have a thumb drive also. Now you are a spy with me."

He found that entertaining. "I guess you're right. But I only work for myself."

"What does that mean?"

"Nothing, I'm kidding."

"I don't get it," said Katya.

"Never mind," he said. "Look, I know this is a serious

situation. The thing is, I never take anything seriously at all. It's how I get by."

Katya frowned with disappointment. "I thought you could help me."

"Of course I can help you," said Wilder. "No problem."

She looked hopeful. "You can?"

"Sure. So—did you give the CIA your thumb drive?"

"My LA contact asked if I had information and I said no. I decided not to tell them about the code."

He asked, "So you're a good liar, eh?"

Katya replied defensively, "I lied because I'm scared for my life."

"I don't care if you lie," said Wilder. "Actually, I respect you more if you do."

"Oh," said Katya.

"But you're really working for the Russians, right?"

"No," she said earnestly. "No way. First of all, I am Chechen. But I do love Russia. And I'm only loyal to myself."

"Why's that?"

"My government destroys the lives of normal people," she said.

"The US does that too," replied Wilder.

"I guess there is bad and good everywhere," she said.

"True, but . . . you're acting strange. There's something you're not telling me."

She balked. "I don't know what you want me to say."

"Forget it," he said. "So you said bad and good—do you believe in pure evil?"

"Yes, I do."

"Same."

Katya said, "I believe that when a person sees something evil, they must fight it."

"Nice," Wilder agreed.

She reflected, "Otherwise, how can we know we are not evil ourselves?"

"That's really deep."

"Is it?"

"Yeah. So what made you decide to come to LA in the first place?"

"I want to start my own business," she said.

"Doing what?"

"Selling high-end women's accessories."

"I could picture you doing that."

"Thank you." She changed the subject. "So . . . Wilder . . . did you see what was on your thumb drive?"

He said, "Yeah, I spent a bunch of time with it, but I'm still working on the code. How about you?"

"No," she said. "I was too afraid, so I hid it instead."

"In a way that's smart," Wilder said. "Also, Katya, I really like you. You're a little mean but I think you're amazing."

"You don't even know me," she said.

"Facts," he said.

Katya said, "I'm not so mean. People always think I'm awful but I'm really very kind and loyal."

"I could see that," said Wilder. "But you do have a pretty bad temper."

"That is true." She nodded. "I'm violent when I am angry."

"I can vouch for that," he joked.

"I'm not going to keep apologizing."

"I don't care about that," he said.

"Good."

"So," he said, "Can I take you out to dinner sometime?"

"Sure."

Wilder glowed.

"How about now?" Katya suggested. "I am hungry."

"Totally, yeah."

"I feel like having a hamburger," she said.

Wilder bragged, "I know a place that has the best burgers in LA."

Katya smiled. "Let's go on my Vespa."

"You know it's stupid to have a moped in LA, right?"

"Shut up."

"Actually, that's perfect," he said, "because I don't have wheels."

"You disrespect my ride," she teased, "but you don't have one?"

"Ha-ha, you got me on that one."

"Can we come back here after?" Katya suggested. "I want to talk about the code."

"Good vibes," said Wilder.

*

It took Katya a few tries to start her moped. "You have to ride with no helmet."

"What's the max speed on this thing, like thirty miles an hour?"

"Shut up and get on."

Katya took Sunset Boulevard to Barrington Avenue. The night sky was purple. They got to the restaurant in good time and both ordered cheeseburgers. Wilder also got fries and a shake.

He found a table outside.

"So, Miss Katya," he said, "if you say you're kind and loyal, then why are you so mean sometimes?"

She explained, "I had a bad childhood and I'm not like other people."

"Same here," said Wilder. "But I guess I channel my anger differently than you."

After an awkward silence, Katya blurted, "My father abandoned me."

Wilder tilted his head. "He abandoned you? That's awful."

"When I was nine years old, he drove me to my mother's funeral. My father left me there with a stranger. He was the man who raised me. I grew up calling him uncle."

"Wait—first your mom died, and then your dad left you . . . at her funeral?"

"There's more story—but yes."

"Intense."

Katya said, "I have one strong memory of my father, from when I was very little. On the coffee table in the living room, he had a ceramic brick with the coat of arms from Chechnya. I dropped it on the floor and it broke. He was very angry and yelling."

"If it meant so much to him, he shouldn't have left it on the coffee table."

"So much yelling," she said.

Wilder shared some of his story. "My parents died when I was three. My childhood sucked, but I always knew they loved me."

"Both of your parents died?"

"Yeah, we were in a car accident. They died at the scene. And I survived."

"What happened after they died?" she asked.

Wilder said, "My grandma raised me for a few years but she died too. After that I was a foster kid."

"You were an orphan. That sounds like a hard childhood."

"Yep, it was. So are you and your uncle close?"

"Yes, we are." Katya fought back tears. "There's more."

"What is it?" he asked.

"Uncle Timofey called me yesterday and . . . my father recently died himself."

"I'm so sorry," said Wilder.

She lowered her head. "We are talking about death too much."

"It's real, though," he said.

Her lip quivered. "I don't know why this makes me cry. I never knew him and I did not love him."

He said, "Losing a parent is sad under any circumstances."

"My uncle surprised me with this news," she said. "I don't know what to feel." Katya dabbed under her eyes with a napkin and faked a smile.

Wilder said, "Don't judge yourself for crying about it."

"Some first date," she said.

"One to remember for sure," Wilder said, and smiled.

Her expression turned serious and she lowered her voice. "This was too much for me already. And now I find out the professor is dead too—and I know nothing. What do I do?"

"I don't know, Katya. But I got your back."

"Thank you."

"Whatever you want to talk about—or don't want to talk about—is fine."

"The code," she said quietly, "but not here. Let's go back to campus."

They hopped on the moped and took the same route back. Katya parked by Wilder's dorm room.

Inside, Katya said, "I can't stop thinking about it. What do you think happened to the professor?"

"No idea, but what about the code?" asked Wilder.

She asked, "What about it?"

"It's not a coincidence."

"It can't be," she agreed.

"Out of the blue he gives us the code, and the next thing you know he's dead."

"What does the code mean?" asked Katya.

He said, "They're programs of some sort but I don't know what they do. Do you have any idea?"

"I'm asking you," she said bluntly.

"Well, at least it brought us together," said Wilder with a glimmer of hope.

She rolled her eyes. "You're not my type."

"What's your type?"

"You are smart and you are cute. Too smart maybe," she said. She pointed a finger into his chest and he stumbled backward. "You are not strong and you are not dangerous."

"I can be strong," Wilder insisted, "and I'm plenty dangerous."

"You are just a nice guy who will not leave me alone."

"I'm not that nice."

"Too nice for me," she said.

"I can be whatever you want me to be."

"You can't be taller."

"You're right—that I can't do."

"Or better looking." Katya smirked.

Wilder said, "Yeah but the code connects us. It's like a puzzle we can work on together."

"I'm very scared about it," she admitted.

"Some spy you make," he joked. "I'm scared too, but this is also very cool in a way. I like solving problems."

Katya asked, "Can you solve the code? I want to know what it says."

He said, "I think I can crack it, but even then I have to figure out what it means."

"We do it together." She smiled.

Wilder got stars in his eyes. "Finally, something cool happens in my life."

"Yes!" Katya agreed. "America is very boring."

"You and me, we'll be like Bonnie and Clyde," he said.

"Who are they?"

"Like a perfect team." He smiled. "Totally OG."

"I'm excited about the code," she said.

"Me too," said Wilder, "and Katya . . . I really want to hook up with you."

She paused and stared at him. "Make a move then."

Wilder kissed her on the lips. "Damn," he said.

"Does it hurt?"

"Yeah, but I could care less."

She said, "We don't have to kiss."

"Plenty of other things we can do," he said.

Katya grabbed his inner thigh and moved her hand up. Wilder put his arms around her and pulled closer.

She looked down and exclaimed, "Oh no!"

"What?"

"You're bleeding on my favorite blouse."

"Aw fuck."

Katya frowned. "I need to get water on this."

"Total buzzkill," he said.

"Where's the bathroom?" she asked.

"Down the hall," he said, motioning. "Here—take one of my shirts."

Katya came back wearing Wilder's T-shirt and holding her wet blouse.

"You look super-hot," he said.

"It's way too big on me."

He drew himself toward her. "Where were we . . . ?"

She turned away. "Some other time. Now I'm just bummed."

"But you got it on with the professor." Wilder knew he had stuck his foot in his mouth.

She clapped back, "That is not a nice thing to say at all."

"Crap, I'm sorry."

"Rude! You're such an idiot," Katya said. "That was totally different."

"I apologize, really. My bad."

"It's not like I actually liked him or anything."

Wilder perked up. "But you like me though?"

"I didn't say that," she said.

"Maybe a little?"

"OK, a little."

"That's an amazing thing to hear," he said, holding a Kleenex to his lip.

"Whatever," she said. "We really should be talking about the code."

"Agreed."

"But let's do it tomorrow," Katya said. "I am tired and want to go back to my dorm."

Wilder tried to hide his disappointment. "You sure you won't stay?"

"I'm sure," she said.

"OK, then. See you tomorrow."

"What time?"

"Let me check my calendar," said Wilder sarcastically. "For you, I'm pretty sure I can free up some time."

"Noon?" Katya offered.

"I'm glad you didn't say earlier," said Wilder. "I like to sleep in."

"I will text you." She kissed him on the cheek and left.

18

READY

The night Hawthorne called the emergency meeting, KrayBULL's men slept poorly. The sun rose and it was hot by 9:00 a.m. Jones and Perez did push-ups, and the others sat around resting. Commander Jansen called the group to the back room. They watched him closely as he rolled out a map on the floor.

Jansen said, "I just got word from the Pentagon. Our mission has changed." His eye twitched—it was the tell he was lying. In that moment, the KrayBULL men knew in their guts that Jansen was a traitor. Any lingering doubts about following Hawthorne vanished. Jansen pointed at the map. "We've been ordered to the location of this mine to provide security for our top-brass CIA in North Africa. We get there first, and we leave last."

"What's CIA's objective?" asked Hawthorne.

"We're swapping intel." Jansen lied. "We make sure our guys don't get killed in the exchange. Orders came from high up and that's all the detail I was given. Our mission stays in Jerada and we make a clean exit. KrayBULL is big enough to handle the operation alone."

Hawthorne nodded. "OK. We wait until go-time and follow your lead."

Jansen said, "Our IT guys have arranged a tech blackout, with the exception of what we capture on video. That makes our evidence of the exchange highly valuable."

“For future blackmail?” asked Perez.

“Not ours to know,” said Jansen. “Just make sure nobody dies on our watch.”

Ali said, “Never be in a hurry to meet the grim reaper.”

“Damn right,” said Jansen. “We’re security and partial escort. Those are the orders. That’s all for now.”

“That’s it then,” said Hawthorne. “Let’s do it.”

Jansen said, “This operation has no name and never happened. We keep the mission quiet in every way.”

*

Later that day, Commander Jansen reconvened the team. “OK, let’s go over it once more, then we go silent.”

Hawthorne said, “Summarizing. You give the word, and we move at dawn. We’re security escorts for CIA intel transfer and safe exit. IT placed a tech box to fry and dry a patch line, and the second tech box is autorun video capture. The exchange of intel and securing all tech is mission critical.”

“Right,” said Jansen. “We rendezvous here and leave the country.”

The soldiers all put their hands in.

“Kray,” said Jansen.

“BULL,” said his men.

Hawthorne rubbed a silver dollar in his palm and said a silent prayer.

19

THE CODE

Wilder stayed up all night working on the code. He woke up at ten, shaved and showered. He made his bed and picked up laundry, then smoked a joint and spent some more time with the professor's code. He used an old, reconfigured laptop without internet connectivity.

Noon rolled around and Katya didn't text. It took every ounce of self-control for him to not text before she did. Finally, at one o'clock Katya texted she was on her way. She showed up at two.

"Right on time," joked Wilder.

She looked around the room, then pointed at the top of his mini fridge. "Is that the same pizza as yesterday?"

Wilder said, "Yep. It's always better when it's a day or two old."

She grimaced and shook her head with a smile. "That's horrible and disgusting. How do you live this way?"

"I know—I'm a lazy bastard. But at least I cleaned up, can you tell?"

She furrowed her brow. "This is not clean. I take medicine so I don't freak out when I see things like this."

"That's OK," he said. "I used to take antidepressants but now I just smoke weed."

"Does it work?"

"Most of the time. Again, sorry I'm such a slob."

Katya said, "I will survive." She hung her head and let out a sigh.

Wilder leaned over to make eye contact. "You seem different today."

"I'm very sad. About my father."

"Want to talk about it?"

"No," she said firmly.

"OK, that's fine too."

She bit her lip and then her expression softened. "Actually, yes—maybe talking could be helpful."

"OK. What's up?"

"The other day, when my uncle called, he also sent me a letter. My father wrote it many years ago, and he wanted me to read it after he died."

"Intense. What did the letter say?"

Katya said, "Remember when I told you I am not really a spy?"

"Of course I remember."

"My father was a real spy. I knew nothing about this until two days ago."

"Woah," said Wilder. "What else did the letter say?"

"He explained why he left me."

"That's huge. Why?"

Katya said, "When I was nine years old, my mother died. My uncle always said it was cancer, but the letter said she was poisoned."

"Poisoned? By who?"

"The Russian Federal Security Service. They tried to kill my father, but they killed my mother instead."

"Oh my God. That's awful."

"My father abandoned me because he thought they would kill me too."

"Why did they want him dead?"

"He was a Chechen rebel from Argun. The Russians did not trust him. My uncle told me my father was from Chechnya, but he lied about everything else."

"Maybe he had to lie."

"My father's letter explains. He surrendered in the Battle of Grozny, and the Russian Federation forced him to join them. After that, he moved to Moscow and met my mother."

Wilder said, "Your father never should have left you."

Katya locked eyes with Wilder. "I agree completely. He betrayed me. He was a coward and I do not forgive him."

Wilder said, "Nobody should bail on their kid no matter what. Blood is thicker than mud."

"What does that mean?"

"Family comes before anything else."

"I feel sick in my stomach," Katya said. "Can we be done talking about this?"

"Of course," Wilder said.

"I need to sit down." She resisted the impulse to wipe down the chair before she sat in it.

"You have OCD, am I right?"

"Yes, but it's not as bad as it looks." She asked, "What about the professor's code?"

Wilder pulled up a chair and turned his laptop to face them. "You still haven't looked at it?"

"No. I'm not very good at computer programming."

"You're not? Professor Singh said you were like a top student."

"I have paid someone."

"Gotcha."

She lit a cigarette from her purse.

"You can't smoke a cigarette in here," he said.

"Don't be boring."

"Of course not," Wilder said. He stood on a chair and removed the battery from the smoke detector.

She smiled. "I am not actually bored. Not when I'm around you."

He said, "You're too sexy to be boring."

"Don't be cute, I hate that."

"Not cute. Not nice," said Wilder. "Got it."

"Nice is OK sometimes," she said.

"Nice and dangerous."

"Yes."

"Definitely not boring," said Wilder, taking a drag off Katya's cigarette.

"Boring never," she said.

"So you're a freaking spy, huh?"

"Do you really think I am a spy?" she asked.

"You're working with the CIA, aren't you?"

"OK fine. I'm a spy. But nobody in Russia knows."

Wilder chuckled. "And I'm supposed to believe that."

"I would make a bad spy," she said. "Plus, my nose is too big. I could not disguise it."

"You don't have a big nose," he said. "Look at mine."

"You would make a bad spy too," she said, and smiled.

Wilder said, "Honestly, your nose isn't big. It's a little long I guess, but it fits your face perfectly."

"Is that supposed to be flattering?"

He said, "I tell you what: I'll work on my flattery and you get better at lying . . . spy."

"I'm not a real spy," she insisted.

"Not until you got into UCLA—right, right."

"It's true. Let me tell you. It was the day after I got my acceptance letter to UCLA. A man called me from Moscow State University. He said it was for foreign exchange class registration. He told me to come to their office, and when I got there, the man tells me he was CIA. He said he has a job for me. If I stay quiet about it, he will pay me $100,000 up front, and $100,000 more when I'm done."

"Two hundred grand?" asked Wilder. "What exactly was the job?"

"He told me to get close to Professor Singh and put a device in his office—to help them find some special intelligence."

"Wow," said Wilder. "They gave you all that money up front?"

She nodded. "In cash."

"Then what?" asked Wilder.

"Then nothing. The man said they would contact me when they need me."

"And now, here we are."

"Yes, here we are," said Katya. "Now show me the code please."

"You know they're probably listening, right?" asked Wilder.

"Maybe," she said.

Wilder asked, "For real though, how do I know if I'm helping the CIA or the Russians?"

"You're helping me. And I already told you—"

"I'm just kidding," he said. "I believe you. And even if you're lying, you know what, fuck it."

"No, don't fuck it, Wilder," said Katya.

He said, "I mean fuck it, like, *fuck it*, we might as well do this."

"Oh, that is a relief. I don't want to do this alone."

"Don't act helpless," said Wilder. "I'm not that naive."

"I don't know that word."

"I'm not an idiot," he said.

"Of course you are not an idiot," she said. "You understand the code."

"I've been called a genius. I do this stuff for fun, and yeah—I spent all night on it."

She mocked him. "You don't look like a genius."

"Don't underestimate me," he said.

"I don't."

"OK, look at this—it's three pieces of code organized into three folders. I solved the first two problems, but I still have no idea what they mean."

"You did that?" It excited Katya.

"Yeah. Honestly, they were simple programs—not that hard to solve."

"I could not have done it. What does the code say?"

"I pulled out a few messages. Here, I'll show you." Wilder turned his laptop so she could see better.

"I'm impressed." She leaned over and ran her hand down his abs.

Wilder raised his eyebrows and pointed toward the bed. "This code can wait, you know?"

"Later," she said.

"You sure you're not just teasing me?"

"Don't be cute. It's annoying."

"You know what I really think?" asked Wilder.

"What?"

"I think you don't like letting people get too close. This mean and serious thing you have going—that's your armor. Beneath all that, there's just a little girl with a huge heart."

Katya paused in a moment of surprise. "Maybe you are a little bit right."

"You know what else I think?" He was pushing it too far, but he couldn't help himself.

"What?"

"First off, I think you're a double agent, and second, you switch sides because you don't really love yourself."

"You asshole." That truly angered Katya. "I am not a double agent."

"Too far?" asked Wilder. "Damn, I'm sorry—I have horrible boundaries."

"Yes you do!" She glowered.

"But really, it's OK to let your guard down," he said. "Relax."

"Did you just tell me to relax?" she asked. "Fuck you."

"Alright, alright. Fuck me, fine."

"Show me," said Katya.

"The code. Got it."

Wilder tapped a sequence on his keyboard.

"Is this Linux?" asked Katya.

"Yeah. I have a ghosted dual boot."

"I'm embarrassed to say I don't know what that means."

"I hide the important stuff I'm working on with a unique login system I designed myself," Wilder bragged. "Unless you enter my exact sequence—including cadence of keystrokes—the machine boots like a regular PC and the laptop looks clean. It's more sophisticated than just a password."

"What does that mean?"

"You can still type in my password but never get to Linux. It's a rhythm-based log in."

"That is hot," said Katya.

"I think so too." Wilder grinned.

"Where can I put out my cigarette?"

"That empty beer can is fine."

"Ugh—that is so gross," she said.

"Smoking is gross," said Wilder.

"Good point." She dropped the butt in the beer can. "Where's your garbage?"

"There," he pointed.

She walked over to it and gasped at the mold inside the garbage can. "Oh my God. I thought you said you cleaned. How can you live like this?"

Wilder got a little defensive. "Trash is supposed to be nasty. I'm sorry—I'm trying, and I can tell it really bothers you."

"For the moment, you're excused," said Katya. "I'm here for the code."

"OK well, first of all, it's three programs and the third one is impossible. It's in some kind of hybrid AI language. I've never seen anything like it."

"What about the first two programs?" she asked, massaging his shoulders.

"I solved the first bit of code right away. The professor embedded extra letters and numbers, and all I had to do was extract them to make the program run. Like I said, pretty easy."

"What happened when you ran the program?"

Wilder said, "It generated two names and this ominous number sequence: 911 2.0."

Katya said, "911 2.0 . . . what does it mean?"

"Like a second 9/11, I guess. Maybe it's a terrorism warning."

"What are the names?" asked Katya.

"The first one is Arnold Renfree."

"Who is he?"

"A senator from Alabama, a total right-winger. I researched him outside of my firewall on a double-locked VPN. Renfree is so far right even the worst media outlets don't report half the shit he says."

"This man is a United States senator and the code has his name?"

"Yeah."

"Great job, Wilder!" Katya was enjoying the suspense and laid it on thick with a sexy voice. "I'm even more impressed than before." She pulled up her chair and sat closer.

"There's more. This guy Renfree is also a big dog. He's the head of the Senate Intelligence Committee."

"What's that?" asked Katya.

"A very powerful position. Dude gets briefings from top Pentagon officials—important shit. He knows things they might not even tell the president."

"Why did you not tell me this before?" she asked.

"I didn't have a reason to. Besides, it's just a name. I have no idea what it means."

"It certainly must mean something," said Katya. She grabbed his forearm and looked at him earnestly.

"Yeah, I'm getting that now," said Wilder. "There's more about him too. This guy is a real son of a bitch."

"How is he a son of a bitch?" asked Katya.

"He's a full-on white supremacist. The worst kind—like real evil. A lot of people hate this guy, especially the far-left progressives. They want him ousted from the Senate."

"Ousted?"

"Removed. They're really pushing for it. A couple Liberals made a website and posted every offensive thing he ever said."

"Like what did he say?" asked Katya.

"He actually said, 'Slavery was economically necessary and the US should bring it back.' "

Katya said, "That is very bad."

"Right? Total douchebag. And look at this," Wilder pointed at his screen. "And I quote, 'The answer to America's problems is an unstoppable wave of White Power, rising violently by necessity.' "

"That's terrible. How can he say such things publicly?" she asked.

"That one got leaked. He was in the Senate chamber talking to another right-wing radical from Kentucky. Someone caught the audio on their cell phone."

"People like him must be why they say Americans are so racist," said Katya.

"Racists are everywhere," said Wilder. "And nothing's gonna change unless we do something to stop it."

"You sound like a—how do you call this—snowflake?"

"Call me what you want, but I'm actually a Libertarian."

She said, "I think everyone just wants power and money."

"Yeah, that about sums it up," he said. "But this guy Renfree is on a totally different level of white supremacist. It's beyond me how someone this demented gets to be head of Senate Intelligence."

"Maybe he is really good at giving blow jobs," joked Katya.

"You might be right," agreed Wilder.

"OK," said Katya. "So . . . why did the professor put this man's name in the code?"

"Professor Singh had to have known something." Then something occurred to Wilder. "Katya, do you think he knew he was going to die?"

"Yes. I do think that," said Katya. "He must have learned something very serious."

"Yeah. Or he was in on something bad the whole time."

Katya asked, "Wilder, what's the second name in the code?"

"Karen."

"Just Karen?"

Wilder nodded.

"Is that a woman's name?"

"Yeah, but it's also an insult," explained Wilder. "Don't be a *Karen*."

"What's a Karen?"

"It's like the uptight white lady at a restaurant who demands to speak to the manager. It's a funny reference."

"I don't get it," she said.

"Sometimes people put jokes in code. I think the professor was dissing Renfree by calling him a Karen."

"So maybe Karen is not a person?"

"Maybe, maybe not."

She said, "If the first piece of code is Renfree's name and this 'Karen' . . . what about the second piece of code?"

"It took me longer, but I cracked the second code too. I don't entirely know what it means either, but this one seems like a big deal."

"Show me."

"OK look. I fucked around with the code for a long time—it's really well written. It's got basic logic but the program launches its own algorithm—not self-evident. I kept hitting walls and then I remembered a program I once sequenced myself—braiding monoalphabetic substitution ciphers."

"Huh?" Katya was befuddled.

Wilder said, "It's hard to explain, but that's how I cracked the code."

"I am dying to know what it says."

He grabbed a notepad and scribbled on it. "By reversing the algorithm, I created a file with a string of partially legible data. The first part is N 34° 18'36", W 2° 9'36". Latitude and longitude coordinates."

"I don't understand."

"These numbers are geographic locators. In Morocco—some town called Jerada."

"Morocco?" asked Katya.

"Yeah, North Africa. Weird, right?"

"What about the rest?" she asked, pointing at the screen.

"There's two IP addresses."

"What for?"

"No idea—they don't exist," said Wilder. "Nobody ever registered them. There's no website or anything else."

She asked, "There are two of them?"

"Yeah, two."

"What else?" Katya asked.

"Well, then there's a day and time."

"What day?"

"Four days from now."

"Wilder, this could be something really big."

"I think you're right," he agreed. "OK, so there's the algorithm itself—it's not just for solving this program, it has to be designed for something else. Then there's one last part. It's an encrypted image—a satellite photo with an overlay of Jerada's electric grid. Look how simple it is."

"Electric grid?"

"Yeah, the main power line to the whole town runs right here. See that? It's on the southern road to Jerada. The grid goes up to this mine site and then stops."

"Mine site?"

"Yeah, like a coal mine. Jerada's whole economy is basically underground metals and minerals. And a shit ton of coal."

She asked, "What are these two numbers 1 and 2 printed on the satellite photo?"

"No idea. Unless . . ."

"Unless what, Wilder?" She squeezed his upper thigh.

"See the number 2? That's right on the power line. And look, there's number 1 at the mine site. Maybe someone is transmitting a signal on the local grid."

"Huh?"

"Like passing top secret information or something," said Wilder.

"Could it be?" asked Katya.

"Yeah, I think someone is using that power line as a transmit signal."

"Wilder, you are literally a genius," Katya said.

"It's just a theory. But why would they do it that way?" he wondered aloud.

"To send a signal?" she asked. "Professor Singh must have known."

Wilder snapped his fingers. "Remember what he said about his satellite technology? It can knock out all the RF waves. Cell towers, everything. It's like an internet kill switch. If that program runs, everything goes dark, no signal in or out. Until the RF comes back online, you could transmit whatever you want over that power line and no one would know."

"That makes sense completely, Wilder."

"You could fry a signal—embed, stitch or something—for however long you program it for."

"I'm not following that."

"If they set it up right, whoever is doing this could even knock out the rest of the electric grid, and still transmit a signal over the line . . . I don't know how, but it's possible."

"Wow," said Katya. "It seems like you do know how."

"But why?" Wilder wondered. "Who's behind it and what are they doing?"

"I think we should find out." She looked at Wilder and smiled. Her eyes were fiery and alive. "This is too exciting."

"Totally."

"How are the two pieces of code connected?" she asked.

"Million-dollar question."

"We need to find out."

Wilder's mind drifted a moment and he said, "I just thought of something crazy."

"What crazy thing?" she asked.

"When I researched this Renfree douchebag on the dark web, I found out he's gonna be a guest speaker at a white supremacist convention. Well it's not a convention, it's a black-tie event at a country club. In Burbank—tonight."

"Tonight?" Katya was intrigued.

"Yeah," said Wilder. "It's invite only. An elite gathering of grade-A assholes. Renfree's cover is calling it a campaign fundraiser. It's pretty damn secretive but they're covering all their bases. I was able to figure it out and even see the guest list."

"Let's go," she said wide-eyed.

Wilder grinned. "Exactly what I was thinking. Let's get close to this motherfucker and size him up."

"Really?" Katya bounced with exhilaration. "How do we get in?"

"Leave that to me."

"Yeah, but how?"

Wilder said nonchalantly, "We add ourselves to the guest list. Piece of cake."

"Are we going to disguise ourselves as white supremacists?"

"Let's do it," said Wilder.

"Oh my God, this is so amazing," said Katya. "Back in Moscow, the CIA told me almost nothing, but they did teach me about disguises." She pulled him out of his chair and gave him a huge hug.

Wilder held her tightly.

"Tonight is going to be so exciting," she said. "I know exactly what to wear."

20

THE COUNTRY CLUB

That night, Wilder and Katya went to LAX and rented a car. Wilder took the wheel and they reviewed their backstories on the drive to Burbank. Wilder followed the map on his cell to a private golf club.

A couple blocks away, Wilder pulled over and Katya carefully reapplied makeup to his face. She did a good job of covering up the bruises, making sure no glue was visible on the fake beard. Lastly, she gave him a pair of yellow-shaded sunglasses.

"Very stylish," Wilder said.

"You look great," Katya assured him. "How about me?"

"Absolutely stunning," he said.

"Every woman should have at least one good black dress," she said.

Wilder said, "With those legs, you're going to turn heads, for sure."

At the gate, Wilder rolled down his window, and a security guard scanned the digital tickets. They got in without a hitch, gave the keys to the valet and headed to the ballroom.

Katya grabbed him by the hand and took them straight to the bar. Wilder ordered a scotch on the rocks. He motioned to Katya. "What will you have, my love?"

"Pinot gris if you have it." She spoke in a German accent, which was smart because her American English was not good.

A few minutes later, an emcee walked onstage and tapped a microphone. "Ladies and gentlemen, please be seated. Senator Renfree will be joining us shortly."

Katya and Wilder took a seat along with the hundred or so others. Flanked by his security, Renfree entered a side door, waving and smiling. The group clapped politely.

"Is that all the applause I get?" Renfree joked into the mic. "Come on people, you can do better than that!"

The audience clapped harder and a few men whooped from the back.

"White Power!" yelled Renfree, pointing to the crowd.

"White Power!" the audience hollered back.

He smiled with all his teeth and then settled into a solemn voice. "We all know why we are here. It's urgent. We have to stop the rising tide of the blacks and all the other colored people. We must stop the Jews. Jews are the reason there are so many colored people in the first place."

Huh? Wilder thought to himself.

"That's right!" An elderly lady stood and pumped her fist.

"Nice to see you, Angie." Renfree waved at her. "When I look at a lovely woman like you, and all of the amazing people here today, I think about my favorite fourteen words."

"Fourteen words," people replied back, and everyone nodded.

"We must secure the existence of our people and future for our white children."

"Damn right!" hollered Angie.

"I love your spirit. You know . . . those words are so sacred," said Renfree. "I don't know why they aren't in the Bible."

"Amen," said people in the crowd.

"In fact, I bet those words *were* in the Bible and somehow the Jews took them out."

Heads nodded and people clapped.

"Now we all know what God wants, right? He wants white people to take action. The white race must eliminate or be eliminated. And you, the very people gathering here today, you are the chosen ones."

Applause erupted.

"You are the spark that will ignite the fire of the Global White Alliance. And once that fire starts burning, it won't stop. We will torch the world as we know it down to the studs, and all that will be left is white people."

"Burn it down!" Katya yelled. Wilder smiled approvingly and put his arm around her.

Renfree took a long look at Katya and pointed. "Yes! That's what I'm talking about."

Katya sipped her drink and kissed Wilder's cheek.

Renfree was rolling now. "There is a great poison, not just in this nation, but all over the world. Dark people are multiplying everywhere—taking over like a cancer. Well I've had enough of this so-called melting pot, this multiculturalism crap."

The audience booed.

"I've had enough with the weakening of our white brothers and sisters. We need only one race on this planet, and now is the time for the uprising of the superior race, an all-white humanity."

The audience gave Renfree a standing ovation.

"The Aryan race must have purification. Now is the time for the Global White Alliance to rise!"

The crowd chanted, "G-W-A! G-W-A!"

"The white revolution starts here!" yelled Renfree. "Look around the room. We are the spark to light the fire. Are you with me?"

"G-W-A! G-W-A!"

Renfree motioned for people to sit back down. "OK now . . . you all know about the White Prophecy. The WP is all over social media and getting more and more news coverage. Great job, by the way, helping spread the good word. I love info wars. But a lot of people think The WP is just a bunch of rumors."

"The rumors are real!" a man shouted from the back.

"That's right," said Renfree. "But let people believe it's a conspiracy theory if they want, so long as word keeps getting out."

"The WP!" another man screamed.

"There are also a lot of people who know it's real. Keep spreading the word. The first sign of the Apocalypse is coming, and it's gonna be a big sign too. And once that happens, the GWA will rise."

"G-W-A!" yelled the crowd in unison.

Wilder shifted in his seat and Katya grabbed his thigh. They both knew about the White Prophecy. Everyone did. *It's real*, Wilder thought to himself.

Renfree had a gleam in his eye. "After the spark, we will call every white person into our global army—God willing, stocked up on serious firepower. We all must join the battle. GWA will be silent no more."

"Bring it on!" a woman yelled. "I got my weapon stockpile!"

Renfree said, "The world will soon see how unstoppable the Global White Alliance has become. Now is our time to ignite the silent white majority, to kill or enslave every black and brown person in the nation and on the planet. And every last Jew must die."

"G-W-A!"

"And listen closely, my friends," said Renfree. "To cleanse the world of this evil, this global parasite of non-white people, we have to do it right. We can take no chances, and we must make it clear that the enemy is to blame. They are attacking our existence. We are simply defending ourselves."

"He's a great speaker," whispered Wilder to Katya.

Renfree said, "We pin this war on them, the darkies and the Jews are the aggressors. They are to blame—they are the ones triggering the Apocalypse. And if we don't fight back, the end of times will be coming for all eternity. G-W-A!"

"G-W-A!" yelled the crowd.

"The Global White Alliance will rise!" cried Renfree, turning red in the face and raising his arm like Hitler.

"G-W-A!" The crowd returned the Nazi salute.

*

Renfree's speech went from fiery to calm and back again. "So here's what we're gonna do. We start with China. After China, we spread our army's righteous annihilation to every nation of color. And while we're at it, we take this country back by force."

"Take this country back!" hollered a few men.

"Thanks to the WP we have already infiltrated the military!" yelled Renfree.

"Damn right we have," said a woman.

"The battle is near," said Renfree, now in a subdued voice. "And y'all know . . . you know how much I hate black people."

"Mm-hmm," said an old man. "Me too!"

"But every once in a while they have good ideas. Take Malcolm X for example. When he said, 'by any means necessary'—that's the spirit we need. We attack with all the power we have. God is calling on us to defend ourselves."

"It's God's will!" Wilder called out.

Renfree said, "Now is the time. We can wait no longer."

"No more waiting," Katya said.

Renfree pointed at her and smiled. "That's right. Look for the signs of the Apocalypse, my friends. Stoke the white fire of righteousness in every corner of God's earth. G-W-A!"

The crowd kept chanting, "G-W-A! G-W-A!"

Renfree carried on for a few more minutes and then thanked everyone for coming. "Enough out of me, my friends. Enjoy yourselves tonight. There's champagne coming around. Let's all toast to the Global White Alliance."

The crowd gave thunderous applause and a standing ovation. Wilder leaned over and said in Katya's ear, "Really inspiring, isn't he?"

"Very much so," she said. "Get me a drink at the bar, would you?" She kept an eye on Renfree moving through the crowd.

"Another glass of white wine?" asked Wilder.

"See if they have a rosé," she said.

"You got it, my love."

Katya flipped her hair and made her way toward Renfree.

"That was a powerful speech, Senator," Katya said.

Renfree locked eyes with her. "Thank you. I don't believe we've met."

"I am a guest of Archibald Winthrop." She pointed toward the bar.

"How do I know that name?" asked Renfree.

"Archibald is an American arms dealer based in Poland."

"Ah, yes, of course." Renfree smiled. "And you are . . . ?"

"I am Lina."

"Are you Polish?"

"I'm from East Germany," she said.

Wilder tapped Katya on the shoulder and handed her a glass of rosé. He knocked back his scotch rocks, set it down on a table and shook Renfree's hand vigorously. "Arnold, those were exactly the words I needed to hear today."

"Just trying to keep our base inspired," said Renfree. "Your date tells me you're an arms dealer."

"Yep," said Wilder. "Based out of Warsaw."

"How's business there?" asked Renfree.

"Never better, especially with the war in Ukraine," said Wilder. "But once the GWA uprising starts, I'm sure sales will go through the roof!" He laughed and patted Renfree on the shoulder.

Renfree grinned, "You're my kind of guy. What's your favorite firearm?"

"No disrespect to our American manufacturers," said Wilder, "but I have a real soft spot for the Russian-made Kalashnikov AK-15."

"I can appreciate that," said Renfree. He looked again at Katya, this time from her body up. "You two have a nice evening."

"White Power," said Katya.

"White Power," said Renfree.

Wilder winked at Katya with a satisfied smile. They stayed

another ten minutes and made their way to the exit. The valet brought their car around.

Wilder headed toward LAX to return the rental car. "Wow," he said. "What a complete son of a bitch."

"He's a monster," Katya agreed. "The Global White Alliance must be stopped."

"I totally agree," he said. "They are fucking scary."

"This man Renfree is a very bad man. I think he is actual evil."

"Yeah, he's a fucking maniac."

They returned the rental car and then took an Uber back to UCLA. "Want to come back to my place?" asked Wilder.

"Yes, I do," she said.

"Good," he said, "because I have something to tell you."

"What is it?"

"Hold your horses," he said.

"You won't tell me now?" asked Katya. "It must be something good."

"It's definitely something good."

Katya said, "Now you are the one teasing me."

Inside Wilder's dorm room, Katya took off her high heels and smacked Wilder's butt. "I can't believe we just did that!"

"That was a total rush," said Wilder.

She said, "I absolutely hate that man, Renfree."

"Such a douchebag, right?"

Her tone got serious. "GWA is a terror cell."

"Full-on domestic terrorists," Wilder agreed.

Katya asked, "What is it you have to tell me?"

"I planted a mic on him."

"A microphone?" She gasped.

"Yes."

"On Renfree?"

"Yep. A string mic."

"What's that?"

"It's like a tiny piece of sticky thread with its own hotspot and audio system. I read about it online, so I made my own."

"Really?" she asked incredulously.

"Yep. I planted it on his shoulder when I shook his hand."

"I am beyond impressed," said Katya. "You just became very much sexier."

"Before you get too excited, let's see if it works first." He pulled a dongle out of his desk drawer and plugged it into his laptop.

"I can't believe you did this," she said.

"I'm full of surprises," said Wilder. He opened the app and turned up the volume. "That should do it."

Sure enough, Renfree's voice came through clearly. Katya and Wilder hugged each other.

"Driver," Renfree said. "Take the long way to my hotel. Go down Melrose, would you? I like to see the nightlife."

"Yes, sir," said the driver.

"Hand me the phone in the middle console."

"No problem, sir."

Wilder and Katya listened in amazement as Renfree punched numbers into the phone.

"Hello, Karen," said Renfree. "Yeah, it went great. Nice crowd. Hang on a sec, would ya? It's stuffy in here."

The mic popped and then muffled to mute.

"Shit," said Wilder. "He must have taken his jacket off."

"I can't hear anything," said Katya.

Wilder hung his head, "Unless he puts his jacket back on, or moves it or something, we're shit out of luck."

"Wait," she said. "Don't give up yet."

Wilder sighed, "This tech's battery life is an hour tops."

Minutes later, the mic signal went dead and they hadn't heard any more of Renfree's conversation. Wilder shut his laptop with a frown.

Katya said, "Well at least now we know Karen is a real person."

He gave a satisfied shrug. "Yeah, he did say Karen. That was awesome, eh?"

"Amazing," she said.

"We still have no idea who Karen is though. Probably a code name."

"Yes, but what you did was brilliant—and very brave."

"Life is short," he said. "Take chances."

"Wilder," she said.

"Yeah?"

"Help me get out of this dress."

"For real?" he asked.

Katya nodded and turned her back to him. "Unzip it," she said.

Her dress fell to the floor and underneath she was wearing only a thong. She turned back around and he stared at her body.

She said, "Don't just stand there, take your clothes off."

Wilder pulled his shirt over his head and just about fell over pulling his pants down.

"Wait," said Wilder. "I have condoms."

"I don't use condoms," she said.

"Are you on birth control?" he asked.

"No," said Katya.

"You like living on the edge."

"Yes, I do," she said.

"Me too."

"Don't you dare touch my hair." Katya pressed her body against his, leaning into the desk. She wrapped a leg around him and they fucked standing up. She flung Wilder onto the bed and got on top of him, digging her fingernails into Wilder's chest.

"Katya—"

"Don't talk."

It was better for Wilder than Katya. Sweaty and catching their breath, they lay side by side staring at the ceiling.

Wilder said, "I did not see that coming."

"Neither did I," said Katya.

"That was incredible," he said.

"Now maybe I am the one who will not leave you alone," she said, and laughed.

"Really?" asked Wilder.

"No . . . well, maybe," she said, slapping him softly. "You are a lot more fun than I thought you would be."

"See? I'm not just a nice guy," he said.

"You have a lot to learn," said Katya, putting on her thong.

He gazed at her and put on his boxers. "I'm a fast learner."

"Tonight was great," she said.

"Want to stay the night?" asked Wilder.

"Sure," she said.

21

THE ITINERARY

They slept until late morning. Katya rolled out of bed and found one of Wilder's joints in a drawer. She sat at his desk wearing one of his T-shirts and kicked up her feet. The smell of weed woke him. He stood up, outstretched his arms and took a few drags of the roach.

"You want a coffee?" Wilder offered. "I have a Keurig that makes a good cup."

"No thanks—I don't do caffeine."

"Weed and espresso is like the perfect combination."

She was eager to talk more about the professor's work. "Because of this code," she said, "we know something is happening in Morocco."

"Something big," said Wilder.

"Huge."

"Should we tell the CIA?" he asked.

He saw the sparkle in her eye. "No."

Wilder nodded in agreement. "This is exciting. *You* are exciting."

"You are too." She smiled.

"I bet that motherfucker Renfree is right in the middle of this."

"He is an evil man," she said.

"Global White Alliance, my ass," said Wilder. "And that White Prophecy conspiracy theory he was going on about—that's all over social media. There's talk about signs of the

Apocalypse, all kinds of crazy stuff. It's scary to think about an uprising of a silent white army."

"It's hard to believe so many people will follow."

"It's simple. People like simple. What's unbelievable is that it's real."

She sighed and said, "So many people have lost their minds."

"Way too many," he said. "And they've got Renfree, a psychotic madman driving them all off a cliff."

"And Karen, whoever she is," said Katya.

Wilder said, "Right. Hey—this weed is giving me the munchies. Wanna order delivery?"

"We could be here all day," said Katya suggestively.

"I'm not going anywhere," said Wilder, rubbing her thigh.

"Do you have more pot?" she asked. "I am pretty high and it feels good."

"I never run out of weed." He grabbed an ounce of kine bud from a box in his dresser.

"Let's go to Morocco," Katya suggested impulsively.

"Go to Morocco?"

"Why not? The code points us there."

"That's crazy," he said.

"I think it's crazy *not* to go."

Wilder joked, "Because life is otherwise nightmarishly boring?"

"Life can be so boring"—she giggled—"especially in America."

"You seriously want to go to Morocco?"

"Why not, Wilder? If we don't do something, I think nobody will."

"Gotta live dangerously," Wilder muttered. "OK, when?"

"The day after tomorrow?" she suggested.

"That would put us there right on time," he said. "Let's do it."

Katya's face glowed. "Oh, this is so exciting! Wilder, I'm starting to really like you."

"Well I hope I don't fuck it up," said Wilder.

Katya said, "This is so romantic."

"Isn't it, though?" He was on cloud nine.

"Oh, sweetie, your lip is bleeding again." She dabbed it with a Kleenex and mocked him. "I should not have beat you so badly."

"For real, though. You took me out with the first punch."

"You deserved it for following me," she said.

"I wasn't *that* bad, was I?"

"I have seen much worse," she said.

"With a woman like you, I wanted to show some guts and get your attention."

"I hated you until two days ago, but you did have my attention."

Wilder laughed. "Alright, partner in crime, what's our plan?"

"We need plane tickets," she said.

"Two tickets coming right up," he said. "My treat."

"Are you rich?"

"Not officially. But I hack offshore bank accounts."

"Offshore?"

"I wire myself money from time to time"—Wilder winked—"to support my education."

"You steal this money," said Katya.

"As a matter of fact, I do."

"Wilder, how do you say . . .? I underestimated you."

"I have stories," said Wilder.

"I like stories," said Katya.

"OK, plane tickets . . . we should fly into Rabat." He hit some keys on his laptop and a few moments later gave Katya the thumbs-up.

"Done?"

"Yep."

"Wonderful," she said. "Wilder, that was a risky thing you did with Arnold Renfree."

"Wasn't that awesome?"

"Do you really like danger this much?"

"I live for it to be honest."

"I do too," she said.

"I can see that more and more," said Wilder.

*

There was a knock at the door and it startled them both. Wilder opened the door slowly and laughed. "It's the pizza guy. I totally forgot we ordered delivery."

"It's smells like some seriously dank weed in here," said the delivery guy.

Katya stood there in a T-shirt and underwear and gave a little wave with her fingers. Wilder was still only wearing boxers. He tipped the pizza guy extra with a small bag of kine bud.

"Wow man, this like totally makes my day, dude."

"You're welcome, get out of here," said Wilder.

"This is all so absurd." Katya laughed. "Are we really going to Morocco?"

"Damn right we are."

"OK, so we fly into Rabat—then what?"

"I don't know," he said. "Should we rent a car?"

"Yes," she said, "and in a country like this, we can find a guide."

"What for?"

"They speak many languages. Outside of big cities we can use an interpreter."

"Good idea," said Wilder. "Like if someone asks what we're doing in Jerada."

"What *are* we doing in Jerada?" Katya asked.

"Like what's the plan, or what's the lie?"

"Let's start with the lie," she said, smiling.

"How about trekking?" he suggested. "Let's say we love nature."

"That's a good idea."

"I looked it up and Jerada is surrounded by mountains."

"Show me a map."

Wilder pulled one up on his monitor. "OK, there's Rabat and there's Jerada."

Katya pointed. "Why don't we go to El Aioun? We can find a guide there."

"How easy is it to find a guide?"

"Very easy," she said. "They know that foreigners always have money."

"I can bring plenty of cash," said Wilder.

"Good."

Wilder's gears were turning. "OK, so what happens when we get to Jerada?"

She said, "Show me the satellite image of the town again—the one with the electric grid overlayed."

Wilder looked closely. "This is the part that is so interesting. See how 1 and 2 are on either side of town? Those numbers must be the key."

"You say this number 1 is where there is a mine?" asked Katya.

"Coal mine, yeah. And 2 is right on the power line outside of town."

"What is this white square next to the mine?" she asked.

"At first I thought it was the roof of a building, but the shadows are odd. I think it's a giant canopy."

"What's that?"

"Like a tent," said Wilder.

Her heart raced. "Something is happening at that mine. We need to get as close to it as we can."

"This whole thing is super sketchy," said Wilder.

"I like it," she said.

"They've got to be transmitting a signal."

"What makes you think that?"

"I've just been piecing it together," he said. "OK, hang on . . . let's say shit's going down at the mine. What if somebody sends a transmission, like streaming a video or something? It makes sense."

"What makes sense?"

"Whatever is happening is top secret, next-level stuff. Whoever is behind it can't risk anybody finding out. So they take down literally every possible signal transmission except for their own."

"That's your theory," said Katya. "Tell me more."

"Imagine you could somehow take control of the local internet. If they knock out cell towers and they stay out of satellite view, whatever happens in Jerada slips under the radar."

"How do you know all of this?" asked Katya.

"I understand computers and I think like a criminal."

"You're good at solving problems."

"Breaking the law is fun."

"You don't look like someone who deals drugs and steals money online."

"Thanks—I guess?"

She said, "And you could use a little help with your wardrobe."

"How very fashionable of you." He smiled.

"But you do look good naked," said Katya.

"You're not so bad yourself."

"Not so bad?"

"You're incredible."

"That's better."

"I just thought of something," he said. "I should hide my burner phone before our trip."

"What's a *burner* phone?"

He dug his flip phone out from under his bed. "I use it for dealing." He removed the SIM card, put the phone parts in a Ziplock baggie and then inside another baggie.

"You must deal a lot of drugs," she said.

"Yep." He put on pants and a shirt, then shoved a roll of duct tape down his collar. Katya watched him with curious amusement. He lit a joint and it dangled from his mouth. "Gimme five minutes."

"Where are you going?"

"Up."

Barefoot in his open doorway, he leaned over to grab a drain spout and quickly ascended. Katya stepped outside and watched him casually speed up the side of the building. He tossed the joint and disappeared over the third-story rooftop.

Wilder looked around and saw no one. He busted out the duct tape and wrapped the double-bagged cell phone. He mounted the package under the lip of the roof. "That should do it," he said to himself, and climbed back down.

Katya greeted him in his doorway. "You're a climber."

"In my free time."

"Get in here," she said assertively, and closed the door behind them.

They had sex another time and fell back asleep.

*

Late afternoon, Wilder once again woke up after Katya, and she was sitting at his desk like before. She asked in a quiet voice, "What do you think the professor knew?"

"Who knows? He wrote the code, so he must have had intel."

"Yes, but *what* intel?"

"Maybe we will find out in Jerada."

"Wilder, what is our plan?"

"I know." He snapped his fingers.

"You do?"

"We get there at night . . ."

"And?"

He logged into his laptop. "We somehow make a digital intercept at the number 2 site on this map. If a signal comes through, we capture it. If I set it up right, nobody will know we were there."

"Intercept?"

"Yeah, I can rewire it, stitch us in . . . and use a laptop like a receiver basically. I haven't done it before, but theoretically it's pretty straightforward."

"Astounding," she said. "You are very good at this. You're like a real spy."

Wilder was feeling confident. "Thanks, you are too. But that's because you're literally a spy, right?" He was joking but suspected it was true.

"I am not a real spy," Katya insisted. "I am an informant just like I told you."

"But your father was a spy . . . what about your uncle?"

"My uncle is not a spy either. However, he did teach me how to fight. Moscow can be a difficult place for women."

"Sounds like he took good care of you."

Katya said, "He is protective."

Wilder asked an ill-advised question. "So . . . how come you're bald?" He immediately knew he was out of bounds.

"You will never see me without my hair again," she said sternly.

"Oh damn. I'm really high or I would not have asked that."

Katya's lip quivered. Her eyes pooled with tears. She said, "I have a medical condition called alopecia totalis. After my mother died and my father left me, my hair fell out in a matter of weeks. It was very traumatic. I can never grow my hair again."

"Katya, I'm really sorry. I should not have pushed you to talk about it."

"No, you should not have," she agreed.

Wilder took a deep breath. "A condition like that is a private thing. I promise not to bring it up again."

"Good," she said. "I would rather you asked me about my father."

He said, "I guess neither of us really had parents, since mine died when I was three."

"I remember," she said. "That is very sad."

"They were good people but they struggled with addiction,"

he explained. "My dad's blood alcohol level was over the limit in the car accident that killed them."

"What was it like after they died?" asked Katya. "You lived with your grandmother?"

"My grandma was very loving, but she was old and pretty much drank herself to death."

"Addiction must run in your family."

"It does," said Wilder.

"And now you deal drugs," she said plainly.

"Go ahead and judge me, I've heard it all before."

"What happened after that?"

"I ended up in group homes . . . You know what? I really don't wanna talk about this anymore."

"I can understand."

He said, "Let's just say you and I both had fucked-up childhoods."

"In this way we understand each other," she said.

"True."

Katya said, "I would be happier if my father had died sooner. Is that bad to say?"

"Not really. Death is gonna happen when it happens," said Wilder. "You know what? This conversation has gotten way too heavy."

"You're right." She suggested, "Let's talk more about Morocco."

"OK."

"Can you believe our first vacation together is this?"

"First vacation . . . I like the sound of that," said Wilder.

"This is a real-life spy mission," said Katya. "If we do this, you and I are connected forever."

"This is all so awesome," he said. "Maybe we should download some nature photos for our trekking backstory. I can give them a future time stamp."

"Smart," she said.

"I got another idea. If we're going to capture a video signal of something, we can embed it in a hidden channel of some other video."

"We can do that?"

"Yeah, it's easy," said Wilder. "Alright, lemme set up this machine with the right code. This capture device is gonna be totally badass."

"*You* are the badass one," she said. "Wilder, I am scared but I'm also having a lot of fun."

"Me too," he said.

Katya ran her hands through Wilder's hair. "Thank you."

"What are you thanking me for?"

"You are a real man. You're taking a big chance with me."

"You're more woman than I deserve," Wilder said with raw vulnerability. "You're everything."

"Everything is a lot."

"Well, I never met a woman like you."

He worked on his laptop late into the evening. Katya fell asleep on the bed. He put a blanket over her and texted Chuck.

Wilder: Dude are you awake?

Chuck: Yeah I'm at work, what's up?

Wilder: You will not believe who's asleep in my bed right now

Chuck: Who?

Wilder: Katya!

Chuck: Wow, dude. How did you pull that off?

Wilder: Never stop believin'

Chuck: It's a miracle, ha-ha

Wilder: Yeah, it is. I need you to do me a favor . . .

Chuck: Uh-oh, now what . . . ?

Wilder: In a few days I need you to stop by my dorm room and run a script. Me and Katya are going on vacation

Chuck: Vacation?

Wilder: Yeah, we're really hitting it off. She has a wild side too

Chuck: Are you for real?

Wilder: Yeah, boss, the romance is thick. We will be back next week

Chuck: Where you going?

Wilder: Not telling

Chuck: Not telling? What are you into now?

Wilder: Nothing bad, I promise

Chuck: Why can't you run the script from wherever you're at?

Wilder: It needs to run through the server behind my firewall. It's just a monthly deposit

Chuck: I'm not getting mixed up in your accounts again

Wilder: It's just a script. All you gotta do is double-click on it

Chuck: Alright fine. When?

Wilder: Three days from now

Chuck: OK. I can't believe you're hooking up with Katya!

Wilder: Me neither. I'm gonna be incommunicado for a bit

Chuck: That's OK. I'm busy AF at work

Wilder: Thanks man. Peace

22

MAKING THE TRIP

Wilder and Katya flew to New York City, and from there it was a direct flight to Rabat. They deboarded and stood on the tarmac in the dry heat. Katya leaned over to say something to Wilder, and just then a plane took off noisily. They both laughed and he put his arm around her.

After the baggage claim, they each went through customs. "What's the purpose of your trip?" the agent asked Wilder.

"Vacation," he said.

"Is it your first time to Morocco, Mr. Kole?"

"First time. I can't wait."

"You flew from the US. You're not staying very long."

"Yeah, four days is super quick, I know."

The man stamped Wilder's passport. "Enjoy your trip."

Wilder walked through the gate and waited for Katya. She was answering a lot of questions, seeming to know when to be friendly and when to be serious. Wilder wondered if Russians have a harder time, or maybe the customs guy just wanted to flirt with a pretty woman. She winked at Wilder and twiddled her fingers at him. He felt a pang of irrational jealousy fueled by willingness to do anything to keep their good thing going. Sex and espionage—a week ago he could never have imagined any of this.

At the rental car booth, Wilder put the car in his name. "Do you have anything bigger, like an SUV?"

The woman at the counter adjusted her glasses. "Americans always want a big car. How about this one?" She pointed to a picture.

"That'll work," said Wilder.

Outside the terminal they walked toward the rental car and two Moroccan men descended on them. The men insisted they knew Rabat's finest places including a tea house with excellent hashish. One of the men made the mistake of touching Katya's hair. She slapped him across the face.

"Don't fucking touch my hair," said Katya.

The men were speechless. Wilder said, "She means business. Leave us alone." Wilder loaded their bags and climbed into the driver side of the SUV.

"You OK?" he asked her.

"I'm fine," she fumed.

"You good if I drive the first stretch?"

She nodded and he drove onto the main highway heading east. He could see Katya was still upset, and he said, "I know they really invaded your personal space, but we're foreigners. We have targets on our backs."

She said, "Maybe next time he will think twice before touching a woman."

They hit a wall of traffic, and Wilder regretted not buying a connecting flight east. After several hours of stressful driving, they arrived at the town of El Aioun. "This trip is almost more transportation than vacation," Wilder said. "But it's still romantic, right?"

"Yes," she assured him, "it's romantic and very exciting." Katya leaned her head out the window to see better. "There," she said. "See the red tower of the mosque? I read about it. That is Mosquée Mohammed VI."

"Did you practice pronouncing that?" Wilder asked. "It sounded great, ha-ha."

She said, "It's a tourist attraction. We can find a guide there."

They stood outside the car, looking across the empty plaza. A man in flip-flops trotted toward them. "Cheerio, friends.

They call me Samuel." He spoke in a British accent and fiddled with his curled-up mustache. "Perchance, are you looking for a guide? I can recommend a top-notch hotel and a restaurant you couldn't possibly forget."

Wilder quipped, "This guy speaks better English than I do."

Katya told him, "We need someone to accompany us to Jerada—tonight. We have a full day planned for tomorrow and want to see the desert."

"The desert is nice," Samuel said, "but I think you will much prefer the beach at Cap de l'eau."

"Jerada," Katya asserted plainly. "That is where we are going."

Samuel nodded, acting particularly gracious because he was eager for the job. He offered to take them for Moroccan cuisine nearby.

"Not interested," snapped Katya. "No more delay. Are you coming with us or not?"

"Straightaway, yes, of course." Samuel climbed in the back seat and began to describe the sites around them.

Katya said, "Stop talking."

"Very well," Samuel said. "You must be tired from your trip."

The sun set as they drove into Jerada. Wilder parked in front of Hotel Paraiso. Samuel carried their bags and helped check them into their room. His translation came in handy because the clerk spoke a local dialect and hardly a lick of English. Samuel opened their hotel room door, handed over the key and waited expectantly. Wilder dug in his pocket and handed him a twenty-dollar bill.

"Much obliged," Samuel said. "Very well, I'll wait in the car until you need me next."

"Tonight we are taking the car," directed Katya. "Alone."

Samuel said, "There's not much by way of nightlife in this town."

Wilder said, "We're going stargazing. I'm from LA, and I can't remember the last time I saw a dark night sky."

Katya told Samuel, "You stay here in our room and watch

our things." She motioned to Wilder and he gave Samuel another twenty.

"Cheers. Just say the word. I'll wait for you in the lobby."

Wilder stuffed his backpack with cables and gear. "I'm good to go." He patted his fanny pack. "And quite fashionable, if I do say so myself."

"You look like a tourist," said Katya. She was dressed in all black and motioned to the door. They hurried to the car but kept a low profile as they pulled away.

"I need a cup of coffee or something," said Wilder. Katya handed him an energy drink she bought at a pit stop in Fez. Night fell and the road got bumpier away from the center of town. Katya held up her cell phone's flashlight to their printed map. "Look ahead, do you see where the road turns left? Just before the corner is our spot."

Wilder pulled over at the power line. He parked between a couple of large bushes beside a ledge overlooking the valley. Distant lights shone from buildings and the moon was rising. Katya looked all around, paranoid they might be followed. Wilder pointed up at a canopy through the windshield. "Well, this is lucky. Looks like I can climb this tree." He leaned over for a kiss and she pecked him on the cheek. "That's it?" he asked.

"For now," she said softly. "Once we do this job, we can celebrate and make it a real vacation. We can have sex all day if we want to."

"That is pretty damn good incentive," he said with a smile.

"Don't be a loser."

"Let's go to Casablanca."

"Just like the movie," she said.

"Yeah."

"Anything you want, Wilder. Right now I need you to focus."

"You can count on me," he said. "Look up on that pole, I was right! There's some serious hardware hooked up."

"You're so good at this," she said. She dug into her purse and handed Wilder a prescription bottle. "Here, take these."

"What is it?" he asked.

"It's modafinil," she said. "Don't take more than two."

"Is this speed?"

"It's a very strong amphetamine."

"Where did you get this?"

"A doctor in Moscow."

Wilder rubbed his palms together and popped two modafinil. "Let's do this," he said, smiling. "Looks like that box is all hooked up, whatever it is . . . transmission, intercept, some kind of encryption device, who knows?"

"Maybe all of that?" Katya wondered. "I'll keep watch. Are you ready?"

"Ready as I'm gonna be." He grabbed his backpack and put on his headlamp. "It sucks that it rained last night. It makes those power lines more dangerous."

"You are so brave. Your country would be proud."

"Yeah, but no one can ever know we were here," said Wilder.

"Right," said Katya. "No one can ever know."

Wilder nodded. "It's a good plan. If we get intel, we pass it along anonymously back in the States."

"Don't use your headlamp unless you have to," she said worriedly.

They climbed out of the car and stood cliffside by the tree. Wilder knew better, but he looked down at the drop-off. A fall would kill him for sure, he thought. The trunk was slippery. Katya webbed her hands, hoisted him by his feet and raised her arms overhead. Wilder strained to reach the lowest limb. He pushed off with a leap and caught a handhold. Wilder clambered up, and from there the tree was easy to climb.

High off the ground, Wilder straddled a branch and shimmied toward the power line. He made it to the tech box with the branch dipping precariously under his weight. Luckily, it was simple for Wilder to pick the lock. He opened the panel and was blown away by what he saw. He resisted the urge to take a picture. Instead he analyzed each connection, a slick setup with four microcomputers and some kind of military-grade transmitter. He followed the smallest wires with his fingers, figuring out how they fed into the transponder junction.

He turned on his headlamp and moved quickly. As if on cue to make things more difficult, the wind picked up. The branch bounced and swayed, and Wilder held the power line for balance. He grabbed a utility knife from his fanny pack, stripped a piece of rubber and exposed two tiny brass wires between the transmitter and the microcomputers. One of the wires was shiny and encased in a thin layer of plastic, and Wilder could tell that was the wire piping in the remote signal from whatever nearby device was patched in. Picking the correct wire lowered his chances of shutting off power to the town.

Wilder muttered to himself, "Don't fuck this up." He waited for a lull in the wind and carefully stripped a half inch of the signal wire. Holding the knife in his teeth, he grabbed some wires from his backpack, putting two alligator clips on either side and USB connectors in the middle. Wilder engineered the setup himself and it looked like tiny jumper cables. With the USB ports connected and the wires dangling, he booted his laptop and logged into his ghosted Linux OS. Wilder's fingers trembled but he was totally in the zone. The modafinil was doing its job.

Wherever the signal was coming from, Wilder could see it was strong enough to fry his motherboard. He ran a signal booster, thinking it might actually suppress the signal and act like a surge protector. He attached the alligator clips and held tiny scissors in his fingers. Wilder took a deep breath. "Here comes the moment of truth."

Wilder snipped the wire between the clips and stared intently at his monitor. The signal dipped for a split second and was back to full strength. Triumphantly, he raised both fists in the air. Wilder's laptop wobbled. He caught it with one hand, and he damn near fell off the branch—his cockiness had for a moment gotten the better of him. His heart pounded and he turned off his headlamp. Looking down at the dark cliffside road, he spotted Katya's figure and gave a vigorous thumbs-up. She waved both hands excitedly and got back into the car.

Now we wait, Wilder thought. He shut the panel with the wires connected and he felt a righteous, calming surge of adrenaline. A strong wind picked up and it started to drizzle. "Perfect." He shrugged. He put on a sweatshirt and draped a poncho over himself and the box. The setup would work fine as long as it didn't rain sideways.

23

THE BATTLEGROUND

At 4:00 a.m., Wilder sat shivering on the tree branch with his laptop linked to the power line and feeding into the box. Every few minutes, he checked the screen. Finally, a surge of packets came through as a video signal. Wilder was riveted that he guessed right. He was also grateful the modafinil was tamping down his anxiety. He launched his application and executed the stitch-capture campaign. Wilder's steganography code embedded the video feed into an invisible channel on an already downloaded four-hour deejay set from his favorite EDM artist. Wilder hit Record, and the incoming video packets came through under his digital cover file. He double-checked the feed and pounded his chest with a fist.

Wilder watched the livestream video encoding on his screen. Dimly lit objects took shape. He identified the cave-like entrance to the mine and the flat desert floor. The camera appeared to be mounted on the far side of a pavilion without walls. Otherwise, the scene was empty. Wilder tossed some twigs at the SUV's windshield.

Katya stepped out of the car. "Is it working?" she asked.

"I told you it would be a video signal!" he said. "I have eyes on the mine entrance."

"Really? That's amazing."

"Something is about to go down, I can feel it," said Wilder.

"Keep going. I'll keep hiding in the car."

He intently monitored the incoming packets of video.

Nothing yet. At just before dawn, Wilder heard engines approaching. As the sound got louder, he clung to the branch and prayed to a god he didn't believe in.

"Please, God, don't let them see us," Wilder whispered to himself. "I don't want to die."

Katya lay on the back-seat floor of the SUV. A military Humvee whizzed by, heading toward Jerada. A minute later, a ten-wheeler and a van approached. The vehicles rumbled past. Last came a limo followed by a box truck. They sped past, and the sound of their engines faded. Wilder let out a sigh of relief. He looked again at his laptop and returned to watching the video.

Minutes later, the Humvee pulled into the camera foreground. Six men got out, each of them carrying M249 SAWs. It was Team KrayBULL. They spread out with precision. Ali paced a hundred feet left, and Perez and Aganad walked the same distance right. Jones hauled a long black bag to the mouth of the cave, positioning himself behind a boulder. Center frame in the foreground of Wilder's video, Hawthorne and Jansen stood behind the parked Humvee.

Wilder watched the ten-wheeler and van roll into frame, parking past the mine entrance. Last came the limo and the truck, grinding to a halt in front of the mine. The driver of the limo got out with a visible limp. He was a tall white guy with a long gray beard and desert army fatigues. Wilder didn't know, but it was Sergei Podkopaev, a veteran Russian war hero well known in Moscow. Muscovites knew the lore of his days with Naval Spetsnaz Spec Ops, but he was considered washed up. He had a string of mental health crises in public, during which he carried on with vitriol about Muslims and was involuntarily hospitalized. Sergei motioned and a half dozen men stepped out of a truck, flanking their leader with Kalashnikov AK-12s.

From the ten-wheeler and van, several guards stepped out with AK-47s pointed toward the dirt. The last man climbed out of the ten-wheeler, a white guy in a pink blazer and fedora.

It was Liam Aldridge, director of CIA in North Africa. Liam raised his hand, waving slowly to the man with the beard. Sergei pulled a flask out of his shirt pocket, raised it in Liam's direction and took a long swig. It was a signal, and also a telltale sign of a real alcoholic.

The back door of the limo opened. An unarmed black man with a tight Afro and sunglasses stepped out. His name was Izhad Esfahani, an Iranian nuclear scientist. Esfahani's bodyguard was right behind him carrying a Glock. His bodyguard had a turban, light skin and a clean shave. After a still moment, Liam tipped his fedora and walked toward Sergei and his Russian guards. Liam and Sergei stood close to each other and talked.

Two miles away at the power line, Wilder watched the scene on his laptop video, wondering who these men were. He looked at Sergei and thought, *That guy looks like Fidel Castro if he was a basketball player.*

Sergei opened the back doors of the box truck, lugging several duffel bags to the ground and unzipping them. Liam looked inside and gave the thumbs-up. They zipped the bags back up and one of Liam's guards stacked them on a cart. All of the guards shifted to keep position, holding their rifles at the ready. Sergei motioned to his men to stand at ease.

Liam walked to the back of the ten-wheeler and pulled out a large steel suitcase. He motioned, and Esfahani approached, kneeling beside the open suitcase and closely inspecting the contents. Esfahani nodded and closed the suitcase, then stood up and shook Liam's hand.

From his position at KrayBULL's Humvee, Hawthorne shouted, "Chesapeake!" He drew his Beretta and fired point-blank into the back of Commander Jansen's head. Blood burst from Jansen's face. Hawthorne was in command now.

An instant later, Jones popped up into view at the mouth of the cave with a grenade launcher over his shoulder. He fired a grenade and the box truck exploded, engulfing guards in flames. The ambush was on and KrayBULL had the upper hand. Sergei, Liam and the others stumbled to find cover but they had nowhere to run. They fired their weapons in chaotic desperation.

KrayBULL's right and left flanks unleashed M249 fire. Hawthorne switched his Beretta for his SAW, opening fire over the Humvee hood. The truck exploded a second time. One by one, bodies dropped just like Hawthorne planned it.

Esfahani dove onto the suitcase. Sergei put Liam in a headlock, shielding his body and firing his Makarov pistol. KrayBULL's crossfire pumped Sergei and Liam full of bullets. Both men fell in a cloud of dust. Another burst of shooting and the ambushed men were all down. Pools of blood stained the sand. KrayBULL held their fire. The man in the turban rolled over and fired more shots. Another blast of machine-gun fire shot him dead. Smoke billowed from the exploded truck and filled the pavilion.

Esfahani was the only man KrayBULL didn't shoot because he was on top of the WMD. "Get the nuke!" shouted Hawthorne. He sprinted toward Esfahani who lay face down on the suitcase with his hands over his head. Hawthorne kicked him onto his back, pulled a hunting knife from his belt and slit Esfahani's throat.

He grabbed the suitcase and yelled, "Blackwell!" which meant the job was done. Team KrayBULL got out of their positions but kept their rifles held high as they surveyed the scene. They stepped around the bodies one by one, making sure that everyone was dead. The only KrayBULL casualty was Commander Jansen, which meant everything went to plan. Hawthorne stood over Jansen and said, "You left me no choice."

Hawthorne handed the suitcase over to Ali. "Get the package home," Hawthorne said.

"Let's go," said Ali.

Hawthorne lifted Jansen's body over his shoulder and ran over to the Humvee. He threw the body into the back.

"Get the rest!" shouted Hawthorne. Perez, Jones and Aganad each grabbed the high-asset bodies—Sergei, Liam and Esfahani—hauling them over to the Humvee and piling them inside.

Back at the power line, high up in the tree, Wilder's adrenaline surged. He exclaimed, "Holy shit! I saw the whole thing!"

Katya paced back and forth outside of the SUV. "Oh my God, Wilder, what happened?" She was nearly in hysterics. Even from their distance, the battle was thunderously loud.

Wilder said, "A lot of guys are dead. At least a dozen. I'm still recording."

"Keep going, Wilder," said Katya.

Back at the mine, Ali strapped the suitcase to Perez's backpack. Jones and Aganad aimed their weapons on the roads and surrounding area. They saw no one. Unit KrayBULL quickly loaded the remaining corpses of the bodyguards into the back of the ten-wheeler. Next, they threw in the bags of cash to get rid of as much evidence as possible. "Back up," said Jones, standing thirty feet away and hoisting the grenade launcher once more.

Ali, Perez and Aganad moved away from Jones and ran around the side of the mine.

"Fifteen seconds," yelled Hawthorne from outside the Humvee.

"Fire in the hole and roll out!" said Jones.

"Go!" yelled Hawthorne.

Unrecognizably burned bodies would buy time for a cover-up. Jones launched another grenade into the ten-wheeler and ducked. The back of the cab erupted in a giant fireball, and the pavilion ceiling caught fire. Jones sprinted to join the other three SEALs.

Hawthorne fled in the Humvee with the bodies. The rest of his team escaped on foot and headed down into a valley. They couldn't be sure their contacts at SEAL Unit 16 were executing Hawthorne's command, but they expected an Italian helicopter to pick them up at a mountaintop a mile away. It was a messy plan altogether, with attention-drawing warfare and too much time on the ground. But improvising in the arena lends itself to imperfection. They had twenty minutes to get there and the terrain was rough.

Across town, Hawthorne sped through the streets in the Humvee. He passed a group of mortified police officers standing outside their cars. They were frozen and didn't pursue because the explosions and machine-gun fire had put the fear of death in them. The police captain was already on his cell phone with regional military command. He yelled and pointed in confusion.

Hawthorne pinned the gas pedal, knowing he had a small window to flee with the bodies and retrieve the tech. If KrayBULL could pull this off, the Pentagon and Italian Ministry of Defense could spin the incident as an extraction of their own forces. However unlikely, they could avoid an international outcry and pin it on a local cell of terrorists. None of that came into play for the moment. It was kill or be killed, escape or surrender.

*

Back at the transmit box, Wilder was still up in the tree with his laptop. Overcome with paranoia, he stayed glued to the video.

"What did you see?" asked Katya.

"It was a deal gone bad. A lot of heavy bags, I'm guessing it was cash . . . there was a large silver suitcase."

"Suitcase? What did the men look like?" Katya asked.

"Hard to tell much," said Wilder. "Everybody's dead except the group of military dudes that ambushed them. They all left on foot, except one guy in a Humvee. Katya, we gotta get out of here."

She said sternly, "Wilder, what exactly did you see?"

"I-I don't know. First there was a tall guy with a long gray beard. He had a lot of bodyguards. They all did. And there was some dude with a hat and a jacket, a black guy in sunglasses and another guy wearing a turban."

"You said a tall guy with a gray beard? Was he limping?" asked Katya.

"Yeah. How did you know? He was drinking from a flask."

"He was drinking from a flask?"

"Yeah," said Wilder, "but not anymore he's not."

Katya hung her head. She recognized Wilder's description of the man. He was a friend of her uncle and well known in Moscow—a high-profile military veteran who had succumbed to PTSD.

Wilder watched the video rendering on his laptop. "Katya!" he exclaimed. "I got the livestream!"

"Tell me again," she said. "What did you see?"

"At least a dozen people shot dead."

"Everyone is dead?"

"Except the military dudes," he said. "Crazy skills—perfect ambush. I saw the whole thing."

"Oh my God, I cannot believe this," said Katya. She looked up at him with an empty sadness. "Something has gone terribly wrong."

"You think?" Wilder said sarcastically.

Katya said, "I must go. I will come find you."

Wilder yelled, "What? No!"

Stone-faced, Katya said, "Protect that intel with your life."

Wilder's heart dropped. "Don't just leave me here."

Katya stepped into the car and started the engine. She pulled away, speeding in the direction of El Aioun.

"I can't fucking believe this." Stunned and stuck in the tree alone, Wilder repeated, "Protect the intel. Don't get killed. Protect the intel. Don't get killed."

Birds chirped in the morning sun, an oddly beautiful moment in a nightmare situation. Wilder looked back at his laptop. The video finished rendering and the livestream was feeding on the split screen. Dark smoke billowed out of the bombed trucks beside the empty limo and van. The only other things left behind were blood and shell casings.

Wilder said to himself, "Somebody's gonna find me. I'm a dead man." He was so scared he crapped his pants. He checked the livestream recording file to make sure it wasn't corrupt. "If I'm gonna die, at least I can save this video." He had captured the whole massacre on his laptop. Whatever it meant, the video was important.

Practically paralyzed with fear, he prepped himself to climb out of the tree. Wilder heard the distant sound of the Humvee's diesel engine, and he regretted his decision to stay put. How could he possibly escape? He visualized diving off the branch and down the cliff, but that would probably kill him.

Hawthorne's Humvee roared as it approached. Wilder was petrified and he perched still on the branch. The Humvee's brakes groaned, and Hawthorne parked beneath Wilder with the engine still running.

Hawthorne opened the driver's side door and aimed his Beretta at Wilder before his feet hit the gravel. He wiped the blood spatter off his brow. He pointed his pistol and shouted in Arabic, "*Dae yadayk hayth yumkinuni ruyatuhum!*"

Wilder didn't understand but his hands were up. He blurted, "I'm American." It was all he could think to say.

There was a long silence.

Hawthorne demanded, "The box! Give me the box!"

"Don't shoot!" cried Wilder.

"Listen closely," Hawthorne said. "There are power shears taped to the back of the box. Disconnect it from the pole and throw it down."

"Throw it?" asked Wilder.

"You heard me. Do it or I kill you."

"OK, OK," said Wilder. He clipped the cable and unmounted the box from the pole. "I'm ready to throw it down."

Hawthorne shoved his Beretta in his belt. "OK, now drop it," he commanded.

Wilder let the box go. Hawthorne caught it, tucked the box under one arm and pulled his pistol again.

Hawthorne had no time and his cargo was top priority. The battle had surely alerted Moroccan military. He kept his finger on the trigger and set the box inside the Humvee's cab.

"Why are you here?" he asked.

Wilder replied, "I cracked a code—it pointed me here."

"What code?"

"From a professor at UCLA."

"Is that true?" asked Hawthorne.

"Yes," said Wilder.

"Live or die," Hawthorne said plainly.

Wilder pleaded, "Please don't kill me."

"I do what I have to." Hawthorne stepped up to the side of the cab and lowered his pistol. "Consider yourself lucky, kid."

"Oh, thank God." Wilder smiled with a mix of fear, relief and unearned confidence in the face of death. Wilder asked, "Who are you?"

"Nobody."

"I'm nobody too," Wilder said.

"Nice to meet you," Hawthorne said.

"Why don't you kill me?"

"What has to be done is done." Hawthorne ducked into the Humvee. Gravel spun under the wheels, and he drove away in a cloud of dust.

24

THE SECOND AMBUSH

Down in the valley, Ali led KrayBULL's charge through thick brush. Perez had the suitcase on his back, and Aganad followed closely behind with Jones at the rear. They crossed a stream and headed up the other side. They were making good time, but the ascent had multiple cliffs. Ali had picked their route carefully using a satellite image, but they could not avoid being exposed.

Perez stopped to tighten his straps. The suitcase weighed seventy pounds and he was drenched in sweat. "Keep going," he said.

Ali said, "Quick—through the gap."

At the base of the cliffs, Jones and Aganad flanked Ali and Perez to provide cover. No one seemed to be following them.

"Clear," said Jones. They entered a small ravine that narrowed at the top. Back in single file, they found handholds and scrambled over the rocks. The higher they went, the steeper it got.

Perez lost his balance and precariously tipped backward. Aganad spotted him and shoved Perez back to his center of gravity. "Keep going," said Aganad.

Approaching the top of the largest cliff, Ali ran right and Jones went left. Aganad and Perez inched upward at the center of the incline.

Perez froze in his tracks and raised his fist. Aganad stopped too. Perez signaled to Aganad he saw unknown soldiers just above them.

Perez drew a pistol that he had pried out of a Russian bodyguard's hand back at the battleground. He turned on Aganad and shot him in the neck at close range. He pulled out a second pistol, his own, and fired into the air.

"Ambush!" yelled Perez.

Ali sprinted in Perez's direction to protect the nuke. Each KrayBULL soldier drew their SAWs. Perez caught sight of Ali and pointed to a boulder above them. Ali turned to look, and Perez blindsided him with a barrage of machine-gun fire, killing him instantly.

Jones charged toward the gunfire and over the ridgeline. He looked left, right and center, not knowing where the attack was coming from. Jones ducked for cover gripping his rifle at his chest. He caught sight of Perez crawling toward him with the nuke still on his back.

Jones and Perez were the only two left alive now. They crouched down, covering each other. Silence. After a long pause, Perez tipped the barrel of his rifle at Jones's head and pulled the trigger.

Perez waited for the sound of the helicopter and then ran into the clear. With the other KrayBULL men down, Perez was the only one to arrive at the scene. He waved both hands and ducked low as the chopper swooped in and landed.

The pilot was alone in the chopper and expecting four SEALs. Perez boarded and yelled, "Ambush! Two attackers and three SEALs down! I'm all that's left!"

"Three SEALs down?" screamed the pilot.

"Dead!"

"Are you sure?"

"Yes!"

"No man left behind!" said the pilot.

"Dead! Call it in—ambush!"

The pilot yelled into the headset mic, "*Imboscata! Imboscata!*"

With one bullet left in his Russian firearm, Perez fired a shot through the pilot's temple and his body went limp. Perez ripped off the headset and said, "Four men down! Ambush! I need a flight corridor to Tangier."

"Ambush?" said the soldier on the end of the line.

"Navy SEAL Team KrayBULL needs full diplomatic cover from the Pentagon. Don't start a war. No escort and no backup. I repeat: No backup." He smashed the headset, unbuckled the pilot and tossed his body out of the helicopter.

Perez lifted off in the chopper and headed north, flying low to try and evade radar detection. He angled toward Algerian air space without crossing into it, figuring his flight path would cause alarm between the bordering nations—and buy him time. He then curved the chopper solidly back over the Moroccan mainland, taking a direct path toward Tangier.

Perez mentally assessed the improvised mission. He let Jansen die back there, and he could have tipped him off. Together, they could have killed the rest of KrayBULL—but then the sale of the nuke might never have happened. Perez had the nuke, and that's all that mattered. He told himself it had to be this way. It was what Jansen would have wanted.

Back in the valley, behind a cliffside boulder, Aganad wasn't dead yet. The gunshot from Perez had collapsed his carotid artery, and he pressed his hand firmly in the side of his neck. Blood gushed between his fingers. Aganad gasped and pulled out his cell phone. He made a voice text for Hawthorne. "Perez has the bomb. It was no ambush. The rest of us are down." Aganad hit Send and died.

25

JUST A TOURIST

Wilder sat up in the tree feeling utterly terrified and elated at the same time. He was so close to death—and yet so alive. A half dozen police cars sped by beneath him. He muttered to himself, "Protect the intel. Don't get killed." He made sure his laptop was secure in his backpack and scrambled down the tree.

Once on the ground, he chuckled deliriously. "I shit my pants too. What a fucking mess." He kicked off his high-tops, pants and underwear. He tossed the underwear cliffside and wiped the crap out of his pants with a handful of leaves. He put his pants and shoes back on, slung his backpack over his shoulder and waddled back toward town.

Another fleet of police cars approached with their sirens blaring. Wilder dove into the bushes and they sped past. When the coast was clear, he got back up to his feet. "Protect the intel, don't get killed," he repeated to himself. "You're just a tourist."

Besides his fear of being killed, Wilder was petrified by the thought of Moroccan prison. He walked back through town, looking perfectly pathetic and drawing a couple of stares from the locals. He walked to the hotel and headed straight to his room.

"My heavens!" said Samuel. "You look terrible. Woah—and you smell worse. Did you shit yourself, lad?"

"Yeah, I had a bad acid trip," said Wilder. He shlepped himself into the bathroom and locked the door.

Samuel said through the door, "I don't think it's safe here.

There were explosions and gunfire, did you hear them? It must be something to do with the military."

"Yeah, I heard it," said Wilder. "Give me a few minutes." He got in the shower and ran the water hot. He hung his head low and breathed deeply. Something had changed inside him.

Words kept running through his mind on repeat. "Protect the intel. Just a tourist."

He dried off, put on clean clothes and sulked on the side of the bed.

Samuel stood by the window drinking a cup of tea. He felt a mix of compassion and amusement. "Where's your lady friend?" he asked.

"No questions." Wilder packed his bags sadly.

Samuel smirked. "You crapped yourself on acid and you lost the girl, eh? I hate it when that happens."

"Fuck off," said Wilder. He was exhausted and stared blankly ahead.

"Fair enough," said Samuel. "Not at all the vacation you were hoping for, is it? Maybe things will somehow get better."

Wilder spun a lie. "Katya ran off with some other guy. She took the car and everything."

"She took the car? That's a crying shame, lad. I tell you what—why don't we have a continental breakfast while we wait for her to come back?"

"She's not coming back," said Wilder bluntly.

"No?"

"No." Wilder picked up her things one by one and threw them in the trash. Wilder said, "We need to hitch a ride back to El Adi-*idiot*, or whatever you call your damn town."

"That shouldn't be too difficult," Samuel said. "Cheer up if you can, lad. There are plenty of beautiful women in the world. She looked like a good one, but if she's run off with some other man, you don't want anything more to do with a woman like that. Trust me."

"Just stop talking," said Wilder. "I feel bad enough already."

An hour later Wilder sat under the hotel awning while Samuel found them a ride. A family of eight was crammed into a sedan and they liked Samuel's price. They would make room, no problem. The driver shoved two kids in Wilder's lap, and Samuel was smooshed between two sweaty old ladies, one with her butt in his face. Samuel looked at Wilder and shrugged.

Wilder watched the landscape go by. The images of the massacre played over in his head. He remembered one of the last things Katya said. "Something has gone terribly wrong." Who was she? Why did she betray him? Was she telling the truth about working with CIA? Whatever the case, she double-crossed him and pulled the wool over his eyes all too easily. Wilder felt like the stupidest man on earth.

His thoughts snapped back to the killings and he winced. He remembered the moment when Hawthorne pointed the Beretta and spared his life. Wilder figured somebody would kill him soon enough. Maybe today, maybe tomorrow. He wasn't dead yet, but he didn't feel relieved anymore—only defeated. *Protect the intel.*

The car approached a police barricade and a cop ordered everyone out. He singled out Wilder and said in Darija, "Who is this man?"

"*Sayih*," said Samuel. "American tourist. I am his guide."

Two officers inspected Wilder's backpack. They pulled out his passport, laptop, and digital camera.

"Those are for my vacation photographs," said Wilder innocently.

"Should we take them?" asked an officer.

"No need," his supervisor said. "He's just a tourist."

Wilder's face betrayed nothing.

The supervisor waved his hand and said, "Let him through."

The car pulled through the barricade. Samuel said to Wilder, "This is too much trouble in one day for my liking."

A while later, they arrived to El Aioun and pulled up to the mosque with the red tower. Everybody piled out and Samuel handed Wilder his bag. "Well, my friend. I guess that's all you will need from me—unless you might like to try the beach?"

"That's all." Wilder could see Samuel was waiting for a tip. He dug in his pocket and handed him a hundred-dollar bill. "That was in my pants—you might want to wash it."

"I should say so," Samuel said with a laugh.

Something caught Wilder's eye. "Samuel, look!" The rental car was parked across the plaza. Wilder ran over to it with Samuel jogging behind him. He peered in the window. The car was empty and the keys were still in the ignition. Wilder looked all around for Katya, but somehow he knew she was long gone.

Wilder said, "That's the second-luckiest thing to happen to me today."

"What's the first luckiest?" asked Samuel.

Wilder thought to himself, *Not getting shot*. Instead, he said, "Having an extra pair of pants."

He said goodbye to Samuel and pulled up Rabat on Google Maps.

26

ROAD TO ROME

Hawthorne sped in the Humvee back to the hut just outside of Jerada. He parked next to the old truck, jumped out and surveyed the scene.

He popped the rear window of the truck and lowered the hatch. He walked back to the Humvee, opened the side door and looked over the bloody mess of the four dead bodies. He choked up seeing Jansen at the bottom of the pile. First he hoisted Izhad Esfahani, somehow still wearing sunglasses despite his head dangling from a half-severed neck. He tossed the body into the back of the truck. Hawthorne looked over the corpse of CIA's Liam Aldridge. He knew the man, not on a first-name basis, but enough to know he could never trust him—a fact now verified. Hawthorne tossed Aldridge beside Esfahani, shoving them in a row to lie in the truck as flat as possible.

The heaviest body was the Russian, Sergei Podkopaev, who had two gunshots to the forehead. "We finally got you, motherfucker." Hawthorne loaded his body into the back of the truck. He returned to the Humvee and stared at Jansen's dead face. "Traitor," Hawthorne muttered under his breath, hoisting him over a shoulder. He wedged Jansen's body next to the others and threw a tarp over them. Inside the cab, Hawthorne crawled around on top of the bodies, making sure the tarp fully covered them.

He ran into the hut and made a few trips back and forth. Hawthorne piled his unit's packs and duffel bags on top of the dead bodies. He brought the tech bag with him in the front passenger seat, with a separate bag for the transfer box holding the video evidence of the massacre. Behind the wheel of the truck with the engine idling, Hawthorne applied makeup, a black wig and mustache.

He planned to leave on the same route KrayBULL had entered Jerada. He knew he might have company, so he kept his Beretta by his side and the SAW below the tech bag in the passenger seat. After a mile, he came to a police barricade across the road.

Hawthorne opened the glove compartment and pulled out a magnetic police siren. He turned on the light and mounted it to the roof. He approached the barricade and held a badge out of the window. An officer signaled for him to stop and stared at Hawthorne for a long, tense moment. The officer then nodded and let him through. Hawthorne was ready to kill them all and felt relieved he didn't have to.

He took the police siren down and drove the speed limit. For the next ten miles, military vehicles raced in both directions on the highway. He drove without incident all the way to the Port of Al Hoceima.

Hawthorne headed toward the rendezvous point at the pier. As far as he knew, the plan was still in place for the rest of the crew to meet at the boat. Hawthorne assumed KrayBULL had succeeded in securing the nuke, and the next step was to flee the country with it. His plan was to secretly deliver the bomb to the US Navy installation at NATO Base Sigonella in Sicily. En route, Team KrayBULL could sink the bodies in the Mediterranean and hopefully make them disappear. Back on US soil, Hawthorne had a trusted contact in DC who could get word of the nuke recovery mission to the Secretary of Defense.

Hawthorne's head ran through a hundred scenarios of what would happen if the bodies were discovered, much less what would happen if the wrong people found out about the nuke. God willing, the Pentagon and Kremlin would never know about the meeting with CIA, Russian Spec Ops and the Iranian nuclear scientist. That plus the involvement of the Al Qaeda type operatives was enough to start World War III.

Hawthorne pulled the truck up to the pier. He grabbed the tech bag, transfer box and his own gear. He unlocked the fence, stepped onto the dock and looked around. The rest of Team KrayBULL wasn't there. No vehicles, just one random fisherman packing his things. His crew was supposed to be waiting for him with the nuclear cargo. Where the hell were they? He got a very bad feeling about it.

Hawthorne pulled out his cell phone and powered it on. He saw the voice text and played it back. Aganad's voice came through. "Perez has the bomb. It was no ambush. The rest of us are down."

Oh my God, thought Hawthorne. *Perez turned on us! He was in on Jansen's plan!* Even if Aganad was still alive, there was nothing that could be done for him now. Extraction was impossible, and his message meant the rest of his unit was dead. If Perez got away with the bomb, he would be long gone.

Agonizing over the magnitude of the failure, Hawthorne thought, *If Perez has the nuke, what in God's name will he do with it?* It dawned on Hawthorne he needed to flee immediately, not just from Moroccan forces but from a possible dragnet from the US government too. Perez would either go totally dark or relay false intel to frame Hawthorne. Either way, they were the only two KrayBULL men left alive. If push came to shove, it was one man's word against the other.

There was no time to haul the bodies onto the boat. Hawthorne blocked the consequences out of his mind. He packed everything but the bodies onto the small vessel. Alone and afraid, Hawthorne escaped the scene and pointed toward Italy.

Hawthorne contemplated the tech box holding the video of the massacre. Someone went way out of their way to make this video evidence. But they didn't anticipate KrayBULL blowing up the scenario. Hawthorne mulled it over a few minutes more and dropped the box into the Mediterranean. "I hope that was the right decision," he muttered.

Hours later, Hawthorne arrived in Naples, moored the boat illegally and walked away. His disguise was meticulous, and he had condensed the gear into one pack. He headed straight for the bus station and bought a ticket to Rome.

27

THREE FLIGHTS OFF GRID

After faking the ambush, killing three KrayBULL men and the pilot, Perez flew the helicopter toward Tangier. The battle in Jerada drew plenty of attention. The Moroccan military followed Perez's flight from afar with orders not to engage with the helicopter. Tensions spiked between the Moroccan government, Algeria and US. Saber rattling gave Perez the advantage of time for subterfuge. Militaries stood down to prevent escalation by unknown causes and fear of being baited. The Americans had the most credible explanation because it was closest to the full truth. The Pentagon owned up to a covert operation by Navy SEALs having gone wrong in Jerada, declaring Spec Ops survivors needed a window to exit Morocco.

In the air above Tangier, Perez hovered over a downtown building and landed on the roof. He killed the engine and shoved the suitcase with the warhead into an oversized duffel bag. He ran for the rooftop door and shot the deadbolt. Ripping open the door, he fled down several flights of stairs and into a parking garage. He located his escape vehicle, stitching together his improvised plan with the former one. Perez and Jansen were always meant to deliver the nuke—but not like this.

He put the bag in the trunk and quickly disguised himself in a business suit. He drove to the exit, went two blocks and entered another parking lot beneath another large office building. He parked, popped the trunk and converted the suitcase carrying the warhead into a carry-on piece of luggage with wheels.

He took the elevator to the main lobby, walked out the front entrance and hailed a cab. Perez handed the driver a piece of paper and said, "Take me to this address." The driver recognized the name of the private airport. Assuming his passenger was very wealthy, he acted professionally and skipped small talk. He hoped for a big tip. At the airport entry, Perez indeed tipped the man handsomely.

Perez boarded a private jet. The captain opened the cockpit door and greeted him. Perez handed him a card and an envelope with cash, keeping a firm grip on the suitcase. "I'm the only passenger today."

"I was expecting two of you," said the pilot.

"Change of plan," said Perez. He sat down and reclined on a wide leather seat. He handcuffed the suitcase to his wrist, and the jet flew straight to Dubai.

Perez crossed the tarmac and got on another private jet. Again, he was the only passenger. He never let the suitcase leave his side. He ate a good meal, night fell and exhaustion set in. With an abundance of caution, Perez locked himself in the bathroom and slept a few hours. The plane touched down the next morning in Shanghai. A car was waiting for him.

Navy Commander Chen, wearing a tan business suit and orange tie, waved so Perez would know he was his man. He was a Chinese American and spoke with a Boston accent. "Mr. Perez?"

"You must be Mr. Chen." Perez shook his hand.

"Welcome to Chinah."

"Shanghai is a nice city," said Perez. "Too bad I won't be staying long."

"The smawg here is awful," said Chen.

"There's a lot of pollution for sure," said Perez.

"Can I take your luggage?"

"No thanks, I'll just carry it with me."

They climbed into the car, and Chen gave the driver instructions in Chinese.

Chen asked, "Where's yah colleague?"

"He couldn't join us today."

"Why not?"

"He died," said Perez.

Chen's face changed. "I'm sorry for your loss, sir."

"It's OK," said Perez plainly. There was an awkward silence so Perez made up a lie. "After our business trip in Europe, we went climbing in the Alps—north face trilogy. We had a bad accident on Mount Eiger, and two guys died."

"Gawd, that's awful."

"Mountaineers know the risks."

"Were you able to recover the bodies?"

"Just get me to the port. I don't want to talk about it."

Chen said, "Whatever you say, sir. Everything is set on our end."

They hit traffic in midtown and the street was like a parking lot. "God I hate China," said Perez.

"Traffic is bad today," said Chen.

Perez said, "It's not just that, there are so many Chinese people."

"Are you kidding?" asked Chen.

"No, I really hate Chinese people," said Perez.

"Excuse me?" He was offended but mostly confused. "You know I'm Chinese, right?"

Perez said, "You're not getting my humor."

"That's because it's not funny," said Chen.

A little girl ran out in front of their car and circled around it. Her older brother chased her down, tagged her in the back and ran away. It reminded Perez of his own kids.

Perez said, "They're so cute when they're little."

Chen glared at him. "Are you for real right now?"

Perez backtracked. "That's not what I meant. I have kids about that age. They grow up too fast."

The car arrived at the Port of Shanghai. Perez casually held the suitcase by his side, but he was prepared to kill if someone tried to take it. They walked to the end of the pier and joined two white men in the US military wearing civilian clothing.

They made a friendly greeting, with one of them reaching out his hand. Perez gripped it strongly and looked the man in the eye.

"You the engineer?" asked Perez.

"Yours truly. Bailey, sir."

Stein was the lowest in command. He said, "Pleasure to meet you, sir."

"Pleasure," said Perez.

Bailey said, "We're all set to transport the cargo, sir."

Chen led them up a walkway onto a huge vessel with the word *Garganta* painted on the side of the ship. The four men stepped onto the main platform and walked through stacked rows of shipping containers. Chen said, "One thing I don't get . . . why this ship? Why don't you set sail from one of our own locations—or take a faster boat?"

"That is not your business, Commander," said Perez. "Your job is sworn silence."

"Sir, yes sir," said Chen. "The money will help my family a great deal, sir. It's a hell of a contract. Tell the guys in DC thank you."

"Will do," said Perez.

Chen led them to a 10-by-20-foot shipping container marked with a stripe of bright orange paint. He unlocked the deadbolt and swung the door open. The container was retrofitted for personnel transport, with fifty gallons of water, a large box of food and a neatly folded pile of blankets and clothing. In the back, there was a makeshift portable toilet and a large metal trunk.

Perez said, "Looks like this is home sweet home for the next few weeks." He stepped inside the container and motioned to Bailey and Stein.

"Let's make the most of it, sir," said Bailey.

Chen stood outside the container. He said to Perez quietly,

"I still don't understand all this effort. Why not take an unmarked Navy ship? What kind of cargo is this?"

Perez glared at him. "I dare you to ask me one more question."

Chen said, "Yes, of course. Sincere apologies."

Perez pounded his chest and said, "White Power."

"Huh?" asked Chen.

"I said White Power," said Perez.

"You're not even white."

"Of course I'm white," insisted Perez.

"You don't *look* white," said Bailey.

"Isn't your last name *Perez*?" asked Chen.

"My biological father is from Mexico," said Perez. "But I'm a güero."

"What's a güero?" Chen asked.

"A white man," said Perez.

"Whatever you say." Chen shrugged. He had grown accustomed to racism among the ranks.

Perez repeated a little louder, "White Power."

"With all due respect, Perez, go fuck yourself," said Chen. "Remind me to kick your ass next time I see you off duty."

Chen swung the door of the shipping container in order to shut it.

"Wait," said Perez, catching the door with his hand. "Hey, man, I'm sorry. I come from a really racist family."

"Apology accepted," said Chen. "The money's incredible so let's just drop it."

Perez continued, "I'm still working on understanding my white privilege."

"Now you're just making it worse," said Chen.

"I'm honestly sorry."

"Drop it," said Chen.

Perez dug in his pocket. "Hey—can you do me a big favor?" he asked.

"What kind of favor?"

He handed Chen an envelope. "Can you mail this letter to my wife?"

"Why don't you give it to her yourself when you get back to the States?" asked Chen.

Perez paused. "Just . . . put it in the mail for me, would ya?"

Chen said, "Sir, you outrank me. Of course I will. But you should really pull your head out of your ass with that White Power shit."

"Sometimes I snap," said Perez. "I think it's PTSD."

Chen said, "You seem pretty lost. Get some rest back home."

"You're right," said Perez. "I need some rest."

Chen shut the door of the shipping container. Inside, Bailey lit a flashlight and asked, "Is this enough food and water?"

Perez said, "Turn that thing off and sit down. Nobody talks until we're out on the open sea."

After what felt like an eternity, the *Garganta* pulled away from the port. An hour later, Perez checked his watch and turned on a lamp. "OK, we're in the clear now," he said.

"Two weeks and the mission's over," said Bailey.

Perez leaned toward the line officer. "You didn't tell me your name, soldier."

"It's Stein, sir."

"Is that a Jewish last name?"

"It's German and Jewish."

"You're not Christian?"

"My family converted to Christianity a long time ago."

"That's good," said Perez. "How do I know you're not secretly a Jew?"

"Sir," said Stein, "in 1935 my great-grandparents were recruited to work for the Gestapo. They served Nazi Germany. It's complicated, but that's the truth of it."

"And your great-grandparents, they were Jewish?" asked Perez.

"Originally, yes."

"Well that's some family history right there," said Perez.

"Not exactly something you bring up at a Thanksgiving dinner party."

"No, sir," said Stein.

Perez said, "Thanks for sharing that, son. So how do I know I can trust both of you?"

Stein said, "You can trust us both completely, sir."

"That's right," said Bailey.

Perez asked, "Which one of you can I trust more?"

"Equally," said Bailey. "One hundred percent."

"Good. Bailey, you're the engineer and you outrank the Jew."

"Sir, I'm not a Jew," said Stein.

"You know what?" said Perez. "You talk too much."

"He's usually super quiet," said Bailey.

"There's one way to make him more quiet," said Perez. He pulled a Beretta out of his inside jacket pocket with the silencer already mounted.

"What? Please, no," begged Stein.

Perez shot the man dead. He looked at Bailey and shrugged. "I wasn't planning on doing that, but I didn't like him."

Bailey put his hands up. "Don't shoot."

Perez smiled and said, "I can't kill *you*—you're the engineer."

"Thank you, sir."

"No problem."

There was a long, awkward silence.

"What the hell are we going to do now?" asked Bailey.

"What do you mean?" asked Perez

"After a couple of days his body is going to start to decompose," said Bailey. "We're stuck in this shipping container for two weeks."

"I didn't think about that," said Perez.

Bailey said, "I thought Navy SEALs were supposed to think of everything."

"Nobody's perfect," said Perez.

"That's a hell of a thing to say after killing someone."

"He looked like he could jeopardize the mission."

Bailey shook his head. "Look—I know none of us have met—and that's by design. But we were all vetted very carefully."

"I know."

"You didn't have to kill him."

"You're right," said Perez. "His body is gonna stink to high hell."

28

WHEN THEY FLIPPED

Two months earlier, Perez and Commander Jansen stood on the sidewalk outside of a diner. Jansen checked his watch. Perez asked, "Are you going to tell me what we're doing here?"

"Waiting," said Jansen sarcastically. He had a good sense of humor, but his mood was generally serious. Perez was uncomfortable around Jansen because he had a unique talent for exploiting people's weaknesses. His deep-set eyes could stare any man down. He once brought Perez to tears about his Mexican ancestry, accusing him of being disloyal to GWA.

"Exactly what is it we're waiting for?" Perez was eager to know.

"Our ride." Jansen pointed. A limousine rounded the corner and pulled up to the curb. The driver jumped out and opened the passenger door.

Perez and Jansen sat across from Senator Renfree, who lit a cigar. He half smiled and said with a Southern drawl, "You must be Perez. Nice to meet another member of Team KrayBULL. Do you know who I am?"

Perez said, "No, sir. I recognize your face but I can't place it."

"I'm Arnold Renfree, from Alabama and head of the Senate Intelligence Committee."

Perez said, "It's an honor, Senator."

Jansen told Perez, "He's a friend."

"White Power," said Renfree.

Jansen echoed, "White Power."

Perez looked around the limo in a questioning way. Renfree said, "Relax, son. This ride has been thoroughly checked for bugs. It's just us talking here."

Perez asked, "How do you know *I'm* not bugged?"

Jansen confirmed, "You're wearing military-issued clothing head to toe, and you're carrying the cell phone I provided you, correct?"

"Correct," said Perez.

"Then you're not bugged," said Jansen.

Perez said, "You can never be too careful, Senator."

"Call me Arnold."

"Yes, sir," said Perez. "I mean, Arnold."

"Tell me something . . ." said Renfree with twisted amusement. "What drives the son of a Mexican to join the White Power movement?"

"My biological father means nothing to me," said Perez. "I'm disgusted by his heritage."

"But he's still your dad," Renfree prodded.

Perez said, "My mom raised me all by herself, mostly on NAS Jax Base. I'm a purebred military brat—as American as they come."

"But you're not white," said Renfree.

"Yes, I am white, Arnold. I am white." It struck a nerve with Perez but he had learned to keep his cool about it.

Renfree pressed him. "Then why don't you change your last name?"

"I thought about that," said Perez, "but when I joined the Global White Alliance, I figured my last name could be an asset. It provides cover."

"A man like you doesn't need cover," Renfree scoffed.

"I always wanted the last name Himmler," said Perez.

"Interesting," smiled Renfree. "Well then, you're Himmler to me."

"Thank you, Arnold."

Renfree said, "Jansen here tells me you're extremely loyal to the white supremacy movement."

"Absolutely," said Perez firmly.

"OK, then," said Renfree. "Let's get down to brass tacks. GWA is rising. New White America's time has come."

"Damn right," Jansen chimed in.

Renfree continued, "GWA's gonna show the full strength of our military. We'll start by wiping China off the map."

Perez said, "That's a good place to start."

"If that doesn't work, we'll take America back by force and fix things on home soil first."

Jansen said, "We need to take this country back."

Renfree asked, "Perez, are there any limits to your loyalty?"

"No limits whatsoever, Arnold. The rise of the master race is inevitable."

"Isn't Hitler's vision grand?"

"It's a prophecy," said Perez.

"That's right," said Renfree. "Once we ignite the spark, the silent white army will rise up with hellfire. And the word is out. All through the military and every white American with any sense at all. We're winning the info wars. Good people know what's coming and they are ready."

"I've seen it in the ranks myself," said Perez. "White people are ready for the uprising."

"We believe the same thing—that's good. Now is the moment for the pure Aryan race."

Perez said with disdain, "Every black and brown person will be killed or enslaved. And Jews wiped off the map."

"It's genocide time," said Jansen with an approving pat on Perez's shoulder.

"OK then," Renfree said plainly. "Let's talk about how we're going to bomb LA."

"We're bombing Los Angeles?" asked Perez.

"I'll fill you in later," said Jansen.

"It's a necessary step," said Renfree, putting out his cigar.

"Who knows about this?" asked Perez.

"Very, very few people," Renfree said sternly.

Perez said, "Not the president, I hope."

Jansen retorted, "Of course not—he's black."

Perez shook his head. "I still don't understand how we ended up with a *second* black president."

Renfree agreed, "He's an ignorant bastard who doesn't understand the threats our nation faces. But you understand, Perez, don't you?"

Perez nodded. "You can trust me with this operation, sir. It's an honor to be selected as Aryan warrior for the first wave of the White Uprising."

Renfree said, "This is going to be a beautiful war." He smiled and looked out the window distractedly. "Do you like music, Perez?" It was an odd moment for a question like that.

Perez answered, "Yes, I do, Senator."

"Arnold. Call me Arnold. What kind of music?"

"Mostly hip-hop," said Perez.

"So you like music by the blacks," said Renfree. "Me too. It's a shame when we kill them all they won't be around to entertain us. You know who I really like? Michael Jackson. *Thriller* is the best damn album ever produced."

Renfree rolled down the inside window between them and the driver. "Driver, play the album *Thriller* for us." He rolled the window back up. "So Perez, you ready to handle the job of being Jansen's right-hand man?"

Perez said, "I have never been more ready, Arnold."

Jansen reassured Renfree. "I groomed Perez and he has what it takes. I saw him kill ten Taliban children in front of their parents. He enjoyed it. A lot of soldiers think they have ice in their veins until they confront a situation like that."

Renfree laughed. "I would like to see that. Do you have any video footage I could watch?"

Jansen said, "I don't think so, Arnold."

"That's too bad," Renfree said. "I like watching people die."

"Well, I like killing people," Perez said. "So we should get along just fine."

"That's the spirit!" Renfree chuckled. "Next time you kill somebody, get it on video for me, would you please?"

"My pleasure," Perez said.

Renfree said, "Jansen is right. You're just the man for the job."

Jansen told Perez, "We have a rock-solid team for this mission. Most of us have never met—and odds are we never will."

Renfree leaned forward and said, "Jansen will fill you in. KrayBULL is going to aid the sale of a nuclear warhead—you two will transport it to Shanghai and then on to LA. Behind Jansen, you're second-in-command."

Jansen said, "The enemy is getting stronger and the time is now to destroy them."

"The sooner we attack, the better," added Perez.

"That's right," agreed Renfree. "In a few years, China will have a strong enough military and technology to overtake us. Starting the war now is our best chance for victory."

"Wait . . . are we the bombers?"

"Exactly right," Renfree said, "You're a team of four. Boarding a Chinese vessel with a direct route to LA. Two weeks later, at the Port of Long Beach, you'll detonate the WMD and LA will be a nuclear wasteland."

"A WMD? Oh man, this is a lot bigger than I imagined."

"You will be a supreme martyr of the Global White Alliance," said Renfree. "Do you have any reservations?"

"No, Arnold. You picked the right man. I can't think of a higher honor," said Perez.

Renfree said, "Good, because otherwise I have to kill you."

"It makes sense," said Perez. "We ignite the Great Race War. LA is just the beginning."

Renfree said, "You got it, boy. This is how we win World War III. By starting it."

Jansen said, "We frame China by launching the nuke from a commercial cargo boat sailing out of Shanghai."

"Brilliant design," said Perez. "But that's a long route to carry the bomb. Boat delivery all the way from China has liabilities."

Renfree explained, "This scenario is so off the radar it will escape suspicion. Just imagine it. This will be our new Pearl Harbor, a thousand times worse than anything our nation has ever seen."

Commander Jansen agreed, "With a first strike coming from China, our military will retaliate with full force."

Renfree said, "That's the plan. Just a second . . ." Renfree again talked in a lighthearted way that clashed with the conversation. "Driver, put on the song 'Pretty Young Thing.' "

Perez assessed Renfree as a psychopath but he went with it. "Great song. Probably my favorite song by Michael Jackson besides 'Smooth Criminal.' "

"I knew I would like you." Renfree smiled. "My friend, this plan is foolproof. We nuke LA and it triggers all-out war. Blaming China for the nuke will force the US to strike back with WMDs of our own. We have plenty more nukes closer to their mainland. One way or the other, we will wipe them out. It's beautiful in its simplicity."

Jansen said, "A lot of nukes could drop."

Renfree was unfazed. "GWA will rise like a phoenix from the ashes."

Perez said, "It's God's will."

"The day of reckoning is here," said Jansen.

Renfree said, "When it dawns on China how many of our nuclear subs are launching in the South China Sea, their military will scatter like cockroaches. We will put an atomic cloud over their whole damn country."

Jansen said, "Great plan."

Renfree said, "Here's to GWA and New White America."

"I wish I could be there to see it," said Perez.

"You can watch from heaven." Renfree's eyes gleamed. "You make God proud."

Perez surmised, "If nukes drop, Americans will follow any declaration of war to preserve what's left."

"Right," said Renfree. "They don't need to believe it's the rise of Aryan rule, they just need us to help crush China, and then we move on to the next enemy, and so on."

"Who's next?" asked Perez.

Renfree said, "The Muslims."

"There are a lot of Muslims," said Perez. "Gotta deal with them."

"Yes, we do," agreed Renfree. "But for now, we need all our friends in the Middle East. Not just the Israeli Jews. The Arabs too, especially the terror cells. They operate in a part of the world where we can't navigate without them as partners."

Perez asked, "What's our plan B? What if the bomb somehow doesn't blow?"

"Have faith," said Renfree. "For one thing, our info wars have radicalized people. We have infiltrated social media and all corners of the internet with the vision of GWA. It has captured the minds of a significant portion of the US military—maybe even the majority. And soldiers aren't just paying attention to GWA. In their hearts, they have already joined us."

Perez asked, "How do you know they'll join the cause if they don't know it's real?"

"If you tell the same lie enough times, it becomes real," said Renfree. "And if you tell the lie well enough, they make the movement happen themselves."

"GWA's gone viral," said Perez.

Renfree continued, "Our most viewed video is the secret oath to the global militia."

"I like that," said Perez.

"That damn oath video has planted the seeds of a white uprising in America, Europe, Russia . . . all over the world."

"I have read the stories," said Perez. "Nice to know our guys behind the info wars are so effective. It feels good to know I'm not alone."

Renfree said, "You're never alone when you're doing God's will."

The limo pulled into a tunnel, which took them to a garage below the Pentagon. Jansen said, "OK, Perez, there's someone else we need you to meet. Are you ready?"

"Always," said Perez.

Jansen said, "We've got a briefing with Uri Nowak, the Assistant Secretary of Defense for SO/LIC. Don't even mention the White Alliance."

Renfree smiled. "Nowak has a lot of sway at the White House."

"Is he with us?" asked Perez.

Jansen said, "Just don't mention the White Alliance. That's an order."

"Yes, sir."

Renfree said, "He's a quiet little guy, but when he speaks you listen."

Jansen said, "Our visit with Nowak today is to advise about CIA operatives in Pakistan. We stick to that."

Renfree said, "Keep a low profile, and if you ever talk about GWA inside of the walls of the Pentagon, I will kill you myself."

"Understood," said Perez. "Do you have a moniker, Arnold?"

"Son," said Renfree, "You shouldn't ask that."

"Sorry."

Renfree said, "They call me Thenos, the first head of the snake. If I die, the second head rises from a deep sleep. That's Karen."

"Karen?"

Jansen told Perez, "Stop asking questions."

"No, it's fine," said Renfree. "Karen is a known but ambiguous threat, which frankly scares the piss out of the Pentagon."

Perez said, "It's not a good name like Thenos."

Renfree said, "Well, Karen is a very dangerous person who basically runs the silent white army."

Jansen said, "You should forget all this immediately."

"Understood," said Perez.

Jansen and Perez stepped outside the limo. They were

saluted by Jennifer Landry, aide to Uri Nowak, Assistant Secretary of Defense for Special Operations and Low Intensity Conflict. They saluted back. The limo drove off with Renfree inside. Landry said with a Connecticut accent, "Jansen. Perez. I'm Landry. Assistant Secretary Nowak looks forward to meeting with you. It's a real honor to meet Navy SEALs from the KrayBULL unit. Especially you, Commander Jansen. I have read all about your acts of valor in Takur Ghar, sir."

Jansen said, "Thank you, Landry, but I prefer not talking about it."

Perez emphasized the point. "We don't like talking about it." It was a true statement, not a deflection. When Perez flashed back to Fallujah, those memories haunted him most. He could still smell the white phosphorus and burned flesh. Weekly and sometimes daily, his mind replayed the day his best friend's head was blown off. He was less than a foot away. Those images had infiltrated Perez's consciousness. Walking beside Landry, Perez thought about that moment and quivered involuntarily.

Landry noticed Perez was disturbed and said little else. "Right this way." They took an elevator and she walked them to Nowak's office.

Jansen, Perez and Nowak saluted one another. Nowak had a crew cut and was at least six inches shorter. Looking up at them, he said, "Gentlemen, come on in."

Inside the office, Nowak asked tactical questions about the war and Afghanistan's central northwest border with Pakistan. Jansen detailed the role CIA played when the war started, passing intel to Spec Ops after Al Qaeda and Taliban insurgents were entrenched. Nowak acknowledged the difficulty of subterranean warfare and complemented Jansen on his valor. He hardly acknowledged Perez's presence, but he was sizing him up, nonetheless.

After the meeting, Nowak said, "Commander Jansen. Pleasure to see you. You've got a strong team in KrayBULL. Keep up the good work." He turned and said, "Perez, nice to meet you."

"Secretary Nowak, it's an honor," said Perez.
"Thank you, Secretary," said Jansen.
Nowak walked them to the door.

29

SOME TRIP

Back at the mosque Mohammed VI, Wilder sat inside the rental car running the AC. Across the plaza, Samuel sat under a cluster of palm trees. Wilder jumped the curb and drove across the plaza's ceramic tiles. Rolling down his window, he asked, "You still up for taking me to the beach, Samuel? It couldn't make my vacation any worse." He figured if he was going to die he might as well see the Mediterranean first.

Samuel admonished him. "You can't drive on this plaza. Get back on the street." Unconcerned, Wilder pulled forward slowly with Samuel walking alongside the car. "OK, Wilder. Let's go to Cap de l'eau. It's the perfect beach town and I know a very nice restaurant—"

"Ease up on the tour-guide thing, will ya?" said Wilder.

"Very well."

"Can you drive? I'm so tired I can't see straight."

"Not a problem. May I recommend the hotel Brise de l'ocean?"

"I can't wait," said Wilder sarcastically.

Once inside the hotel room, Wilder face-planted on one of the twin beds. Samuel asked, "What more can I do for you?"

"Just leave me alone for a while," said Wilder.

"Of course. I'll wait in the car and be ready at a moment's notice."

After a few hours of sleep, Wilder called his airline but couldn't change his flight. He thought to himself he could wait two more days to fly home. What difference would it make? If a spy or government official came for him, they would never find the hidden stream on his laptop.

Wilder pulled up the video from Jerada. He watched the whole thing again, replaying the ambush scene with Team KrayBULL opening fire and all the people dying. Wilder assumed correctly that KrayBULL were American Spec Ops. Their movements were precise, and they were perfectly positioned for a surprise attack. Wilder wondered what went down before the gunfire. What was in that suitcase? He rewatched Perez strapping the suitcase to his pack and the other men loading dead bodies in the Humvee. At the end of the clip, Wilder froze the frame on Hawthorne's face. He was definitely the man Wilder encountered at the power line.

Wilder shivered at the thought of Hawthorne shooting him up in that tree. He shut his laptop and cradled it while drifting off. Startling awake, he called room service and ordered a twenty-dollar cheeseburger with two sides of bacon and a slice of chocolate cake. He scarfed it all down, so hungry he even ate the parsley sprig. Stepping out onto his patio, he stared out at the sea. Something had shifted in Wilder's spirit—maybe because his days seemed numbered, maybe because he was holding highly sensitive intel.

He carefully calculated his next moves. He figured now was the time to take his biggest risks, because he now had both the professor's code and the video. Whether or not someone came to kill him—today, tomorrow or any other day—he had come too far to not protect the intel.

With the sun setting, Wilder strolled out to the rental car. He told Samuel he didn't need his services anymore and gave him a generous tip. Samuel said he would catch a bus home, and once again they parted ways.

With an air of determination, Wilder walked to a grocery store big enough to have electronic supplies. He grabbed a travel sewing kit and two thumb drives, purchased one with a credit card and the other with cash. Back at the hotel lobby, he asked the clerk for a paper clip and returned to his room.

It dawned on him there could be cameras in his room, and he chided himself for not thinking of it earlier. With his laptop in hand, he sat on his bed with his back against the wall and blanket over himself. He launched Linux, his ghosted dual-boot OS. The moment had come to take a few of the biggest risks of his life. Wilder inhaled and exhaled deeply and muttered, "Fuck it, let's do this."

He saved the video's decryption key file on a thumb drive, copying the three parts of the professor's code as well. He methodically dismantled the thumb drive with the paper clip and carefully analyzed the parts. The SD card was intact—it was about half the size of his pinky nail. With the needle from the sewing kit, he poked tiny holes in the upper inside eyelet of his left high-top. He pried apart the eyelet and gently inserted the SD card into it.

Left shoe, top lace, Wilder thought to himself. *Now I gotta keep my eye on my shoes—not just my laptop.* He put some random vacation photos on the second thumb drive to serve as a decoy. He flushed the broken thumb drive parts down the toilet.

Now came the bigger risks. He dove back under the blanket on the bed. *Time to hide this shit in plain sight,* thought Wilder. He uploaded the encrypted video to YouTube. Unless someone had the key, they could never see the hidden channel with the massacre video. It was now backed up in the cloud—on YouTube, no less. One copy of the key was on his laptop, and the other copy was on the SD card in his shoe's eyelet. It was logical, and given the circumstances, it met Wilder's standards for security. He needed one backup for each critical component of intel.

"Here comes the hardest part." His heart pounded. "Save the best for last." A year back, by sheer luck he came across a back door to a Pentagon mainframe. It scared him shitless at the time—in fact, it still did, and he had never used it again. In a seemingly random folder in the Pentagon's maximum-security cloud, he found an AI-generated decoding algorithm. It was an unrecognizable piece of code in a language he had never seen before. Wilder needed the algorithm now.

He located his hidden bookmark link on the dark web where he had discovered the Pentagon's AI decoder. He pulled up the third folder with the program from Professor Singh. The piece of code was also in a programming language he couldn't recognize—almost like multiple kinds of code were mashed together into randomized sequences. He figured only military AI could have made it, so only military AI could hack it. *Here goes nothing*, he thought.

He opened the Pentagon app, fed it the professor's impossible problem number 3. He hit Run and waited anxiously. Wilder raised his eyebrows and muttered, "Holy shit, I think it worked."

Within seconds, the AI decoder spit out words in English: "Long Beach Bay. October 26, 7:00 a.m." Wilder had no idea what it meant but he memorized it. He could see the program was hung up trying to decode a small percentage of information. Suddenly, the program crashed.

Wilder knew that was his one chance, and he didn't dare try running it again. You don't just infiltrate Pentagon files like this without raising internal alarms and having firewalls slam shut. If he tried to access the program again, they would find him for sure. His dark web presence was stealthy but not undetectable.

Wilder shut his laptop and spent a few minutes praying his cloaking software was foolproof. He half expected people to storm his hotel room and kill him. Instead, nothing happened except the sea breeze blowing the curtain through the open patio door. He walked to the bathroom mirror and stared at himself.

"What have I become?" he said to himself. "Protect the intel. Don't get killed. You're just a tourist."

On the beach out front of his hotel, Wilder hung his backpack over one shoulder with his laptop and high-tops inside. He bought a bottle of beer and walked up to his knees in the sea. If this was his last sunset, it was a good one.

He sat on a beach chair and drank another beer. He ruminated about Katya—he simply couldn't get his mind off her. Wilder drank another beer, switched to Margaritas and barely made it back to his hotel room on his own two feet.

He sent five texts in a row to Katya.

Wilder: So I guess this is it then . . .

Wilder: Can we talk? I love you

Wilder: Are we over? Well it was fun

Wilder: You know I would die for you, right?

Wilder: I'm sorry drunk texting I do love you, tho

He got ahold of himself and stopped texting.

The texts went from delivered to read, so he knew Katya saw them. What Wilder didn't know was she was boarding a plane at the airport across town. An hour later her flight touched down in Rome. She headed straight to her hotel room and called her uncle Timofey.

"Hi uncle Timofey, you'll never guess where I am."

"Where?"

She said, "If I told you I was in Rome, would you believe me?"

Timofey said, "Anything is possible with you. What are you doing there?"

She explained, "I took an impulsive trip to Morocco. I was with a friend but we went our separate ways. And I always wanted to go to Rome, so here I am."

He asked, "Was it a man friend?"

"Yes," she said. "We had a romantic moment but it didn't work out. So I'm making the most of it."

He asked, "How long will you be in Rome?"

"A few days only."

"*Bozhe moi*, Katya. What surprise will you come up with next?"

She laughed. "I don't know, but don't make an elephant out of a fly."

"OK," he said. "Have fun."

She said, "Thanks, Uncle. They give tours of Rome by moped. I'm going to see as many famous places as I can."

"That sounds just like you."

"Ha-ha! Yeah, I guess it does," she said.

He said, "Get back to LA safely."

"Yes, of course," said Katya.

30

THE PRESIDENT'S DAILY BRIEF

Jenna Scofield, President Garner's chief of staff, walked into the Oval Office with a serious but calm demeanor. She delivered the president's daily brief with intel from ODNI, CIA and an unknown source within the IC. Per usual, the president invited Scofield to have a seat and he silently read the whole thing.

Prior to becoming a politician, Garner had an extensive career in the military and rose through the ranks. In 1981, he joined elite company as the fourth black man in US Army history to be appointed to three-star lieutenant general. He conducted successful operations in Lebanon, Grenada and Panama, and his stories of heroism helped him get elected. His wartime experiences had left a scar on his soul, but nothing changes a man like being commander in chief.

Garner ran his hands over his gray hair in his habitual, neurotic way. "Well if this isn't a shit show, I don't know what is." He shoved the papers aside.

The massacre in Jerada made Morocco a global hot spot overnight. The brief acknowledged several unknowns and scant details about KrayBULL's failed mission. No one knew where to find Navy SEALs Perez or Hawthorne, why they fled or what went wrong.

President Garner was in disbelief. "Have you read this, Jenna?"

"I have," Scofield confirmed.

"Fucking hell. There are disastrous implications to an unexplained battle with CIA, Russian and Al Qaeda operatives."

"That intel is highly classified," she said. "The amount of confusion is to our benefit."

He said, "Remind me to thank the Moroccan prime minister for letting us move in so quickly."

"Noted," said Scofield. "It was another team of SEALs that seized the dead bodies. SEALs don't leak intel."

"Who moved the bodies away from the battle zone?" asked the president.

"Navy SEAL Rex Hawthorne," she said.

"Why?"

"Probably covering his tracks," she said, "but he ran out of time."

"What do we do now?" he asked.

"We call it a top-secret military operation that went sideways and ultimately ended well."

"But it didn't end well," Garner retorted.

"A good lie will buy us some time," Scofield said.

"A good lie, OK, fine," said the president. "What about the rest of the brief? What's this about increased chatter with the Global White Alliance?"

"GWA is a threat we should take seriously."

He asked, "Do people seriously believe the White Prophecy crap on social media?"

She said, "People will believe almost anything these days."

"How many people are we talking about?"

"Hundreds of thousands of followers in America alone."

Garner downplayed it. "Our nation has bigger problems. The idea of a white supremacist military uprising is ludicrous."

"It's not just talk and social media," Scofield warned. "GWA is infiltrating the military. The extremists claim to be speaking for the silent masses."

"Haven't they always? What's new here?"

She said, "They could set doomsday scenarios in motion."

"What—like mass riots in our major cities?" he asked. "Power grid attack? What are we talking about here?"

"We don't know, Mr. President."

"Compared to that battle in Morocco," he said, "I'm not too worried about the Global White Alliance. I know evil incarnate is out there—but these extremists are mostly isolated."

"It's in the PDB for a reason," said Scofield. "All it takes is a few brilliant and maniacal leaders to lead this herd off a cliff."

"I appreciate you being direct—and I get it," said Garner. "GWA is truly a threat. But I won't be speaking on the matter publicly."

"Sounds good, Mr. President."

"Keep me posted up to the minute about Morocco," he said. "I want to know everything."

31

THE SWITCH

Just south of the Vatican, Hawthorne entered an apartment complex. The receptionist didn't recognize him. Hawthorne gave the password: "*Buongiorno, mio cugino mi ha lasciato una chiave.*"

The receptionist's eyes widened in surprise, and he nodded. "You must be the cousin of Signora Bucelli."

"Yes."

The receptionist handed Hawthorne a key, then called upstairs to see if the resident was home. Hawthorne's undercover doppelgänger answered the landline on the wall. He was an Italian businessman who went about his normal life and was rarely called upon. "*Molto bene.*" The Italian left his cell phone behind, exited the flat and went quietly down the back stairwell. He opened the basement door with an extra key, passed the boiler room and opened another door. He walked silently down a hall and faded into the dark.

Moments later, Hawthorne walked up the main set of stairs, entered the flat and spotted the cell phone waiting on the kitchen counter. He picked it up and texted. "Hello my sweet. I have the rest of the day off and would love to see you. I'm home. Come visit?"

After a few seconds, a response came: "Ciao, amor. I'll tell my boss I'm leaving early and be right there."

Foreign service officer Alexander Brenton walked out of the US consulate headquarters. It would have been faster by taxi but he stayed on foot. He walked into the front lobby of the apartment and the receptionist said, "*Buongiorno*, Alexander. Head on up."

Brenton knocked and let himself in. Hawthorne stood in front of the bathroom mirror sorting through a travel hygiene kit.

"*Come stai?*" Brenton stepped in the bathroom doorway. "*E'bello vederti.*"

Hawthorne looked up. "English is fine."

"You look awful." Brenton kissed Hawthorne on the lips and put his hand on his chest.

Hawthorne caught him by the wrist and said, "I'm not in the mood for that."

Brenton asked, "What is it?"

Hawthorne said, "I've had a very bad business trip." He was speaking in code.

Brenton looked concerned. "Did you lose any clients?"

"All but one."

Brenton took a step back in shock, holding himself up in the doorway.

Hawthorne nodded grimly and whispered, "All of us are dead except Perez."

"They're gone?"

"That's just the tip of the iceberg." Hawthorne's expression showed how critical the mission was, but he couldn't tell Brenton anything.

Brenton went back to speaking in code—it was futile to try to be of any comfort. "Well, you can always find another job. I'm sorry, love. How long are you in town?"

Hawthorne gritted his teeth in consternation. He had come to terms with how poorly things had gone but he refused to accept ultimate failure.

"Come sit with me in the kitchen," offered Brenton.

Pacing slowly around the flat, Hawthorne rolled a coin across his knuckles. He slapped it on the kitchen table.

"Honey?" Brenton tried to get through to him. "I asked you a question. How long are you in town?"

Hawthorne looked up and said, "Just one night. Let's spend it together, just the two of us."

"Nice try at making me feel special. Why don't you stay longer?"

"I can't," said Hawthorne. "I was hoping to stay in. Can you get us some fast food?"

"Sure, dear," said Brenton. "What are you hungry for?"

"Honestly, nothing. But I know I should eat."

"Fine, I'll pick something good. You know what, though?"

"What's on your mind?" asked Hawthorne.

"I'm tired of us being a secret."

"You know we can't tell people about us."

"Because you're bi?"

"Nobody gives a damn about that," said Hawthorne. "This is deep cover."

"How's your wife?" Brenton asked with a critical tone.

Hawthorne replied, "We signed the divorce paperwork last week."

"Are you still in love with her?" Brenton pushed the issue. "I mean, is she more attractive to you than I am?"

"Not anymore."

"Tell the truth. You at least owe me that."

"I always tell the truth," said Hawthorne. "The love I have for Eileen will never go away—but it's you I want to be with."

"I'm not just some man to you?"

"That is an idiotic question."

"Then tell me why I feel so irrelevant," Brenton complained.

Hawthorne said, "I'm here, aren't I?"

"You'll be gone tomorrow. What happened to you relocating here?"

"I still want to."

"Do you, though?"

"Stop," Hawthorne said. "I'm in the middle of a job gone wrong."

"I know." Brenton teared up. "I just want to be the only one you love."

"You know that's not how I want to live. I don't wanna argue about it."

"I'm just saying—"

Hawthorne slammed his fist on the kitchen table. "Are you not getting how serious this situation is?"

Brenton had never seen Hawthorne so emotional about an operation. He said, "You're really losing everything, aren't you?"

"Just go get us some food."

Brenton said, "You know what? Sometimes I don't know whether to tell you I love you or to go fuck yourself."

Hawthorne said, "You just said both."

Brenton lost his cool and swiped the keys off the table. "Anything else?"

"Get me a small bottle of contact lens solution that I can take on the airplane."

"Fine!" Brenton slammed the door on his way out.

32

FCO—ROME

The next morning, Hawthorne stood at the bathroom mirror and carefully fixed his eyes. He applied a transparent gel to his medial canthus and tear ducts, swelling his skin to alter the lining around his eyeballs. He put in contact lenses with microlaser-printed corneas matching his doppelgänger's color patterns. The lenses changed how fractals of light struck his eyes and would obscure his true identity from airport cameras.

Hawthorne knew his Italian counterpart would be off grid for as long as needed, reappearing only after learning his return flight schedule. Hawthorne zipped his leather carry-on suitcase, tucking his passport and cell phone into the inside pocket of his jacket. Brenton sat at the kitchen table holding back tears.

Hawthorne casually said, "*Ciao, mi amor*. See you in a few days."

Without looking up, Brenton said, "See you soon." But he knew they might never see each other again.

"I don't want to miss my flight," said Hawthorne, preventing a drawn-out goodbye.

At the FCO airport, Hawthorne cleared security and strolled into the gift shop near his gate. He was very confident in his disguise, but nonetheless he steeled himself to be approached by agents—Italian, American or otherwise. By now CIA had definitely put out a flyer to bring him to DC for questioning.

Hawthorne looked up from a magazine. He caught Katya's green eyes and her pupils dilated wide. The mutual attraction was instant. Hawthorne kept his unassuming expression, and Katya was stoic as always. Electricity passed between them, and they calmly looked each other up and down.

They both were thinking the same thing. Somehow they both knew each other were deep cover. Hawthorne noticed the slightest tremble in Katya's hands and they betrayed her. Also, her hair was too perfect. Then again, so was his—she also knew the subtle details to look for. Each wondered what the other knew.

Katya and Hawthorne cunningly admired each other's calculated outfits. Her red and white Vespa T-shirt was well on brand for a tourist. Hawthorne's Italian designer clothes were expensive yet plain. She looked away first. Minutes later, they stood at the same gate, boarding the nonstop flight to LA, both flying first class. Katya took her seat and ordered a glass of white wine. Hawthorne walked nonchalantly past her, confirming his first impression. *She's beautiful.*

She glanced up at him and had a similar thought. *He's handsome and tall enough.*

He sat a few rows behind her. After takeoff, the plane leveled out. Hawthorne walked to the bathroom up front and stood in line. Katya unbuckled her seat belt and joined him.

"What's in LA for you?" she asked with the slightest smile.

"A business trip," he said perfectly.

"You're Italian, yes?"

"I am from Rome. You have a Russian accent, am I right?"

"Yes. Have you ever been to California?"

"I go one or two times a year. The food is awful."

"I agree."

Hawthorne pulled a money clip out of his blazer pocket. "Too bad. I forgot to exchange my euros for dollars."

She mocked him. "Does anyone still use cash?"

"I like to sometimes," he said. "They call me Marcus. And you are . . . ?"

"Katya."

Knowing that they were both deep cover made the sexual tension even hotter.

"What brought you to Rome?" he asked.

"Traveling for pleasure. How do you say—it was on my bucket list."

"You're traveling alone?"

"Not originally," explained Katya. "My boyfriend and I broke up in Morocco."

Hawthorne's ears pricked up but he didn't flinch.

She continued, "My vacation was going badly. Then I thought, I'm already so close to Rome. So I went."

Hawthorne poured on a little Italian charm. "Let me guess, you broke up with him."

"Yes," she said. "What makes you ask?"

"You seem like a very nice woman." It was a simple enough compliment but his delivery hit home.

"Thank you," said Katya sincerely. "Most people think I am not nice. The truth is I'm very kind and loyal to my friends."

He asked, "What's in LA for *you*?"

"I'm an exchange student at UCLA."

Hawthorne raised an eyebrow. "I hear it's a nice campus."

Katya said, "Very nice. But as you say, the food is terrible."

He bragged, "I make a dish of carbonara better than anywhere you will find in LA."

"I do like Italian food," she said.

He added, "And my *cacio e pepe* is to die for." Hawthorne pulled a business card from his money clip. "I'll be in LA for a few days. Call me and I'll make you dinner."

"I might do that," said Katya. She tucked the card into the inside pocket of her clutch. She noticed a photo of a man on Hawthorne's money clip.

"Who is that?" she pointed.

"One of my lovers," he said.

She asked, "You are bisexual?"

Hawthorne winked. "I don't care who you tell." They exchanged closed-mouth smiles. A passenger exited the bathroom and he entered. Katya was next. She sat on the toilet and pulled out the business card. Knowing not to keep a gift from a stranger, she memorized the phone number, tore up the card and flushed it. However, a speck of paper with GPS tracking capability had sloughed off inside her clutch.

Hours later, the flight landed in LA. They separately passed through customs. She walked toward the exit, and Hawthorne caught up with her. "Katya? Are you planning to call me?"

"I haven't decided, Marcus." She smiled. "Maybe if I'm bored."

"Then I hope you get bored." He noticed multiple Homeland Security officers were watching them and he tipped her off. "There are a lot of people looking at you."

"It happens most places I go," she said plainly.

Just then, he recognized a CIA colleague he worked with closely. Hawthorne caught Katya by the arm, pulled her close and kissed her on the lips.

The kiss took her breath away and she asked, "What was that about?"

He said with quiet urgency, "I saw someone I didn't want to see. I have to go."

He walked briskly toward a janitor's closet and picked the lock with his money clip. Hawthorne knew the underbelly of the airport and had a clean escape route in mind. He slipped inside and started to run.

Katya hurried to the door and caught it with her hand. "Wait!" She chased after him.

"Why are you following me?" Hawthorne called back.

Katya yelled, "I need you to kiss me without some stupid excuse."

He stopped in his tracks and she walked right up to him. They kissed passionately and their hands explored each other's bodies. Hawthorne dropped the Italian accent and said in a deep voice, "Katya, this is serious. I gotta go."

He took off running again, and she yelled, "What's your real name?" But he was already gone.

She walked back out of the janitor's entrance. Four confused CIA contacts shrugged their shoulders to ask what was up. She shrugged back with a look of mischievous innocence. They let her leave the airport, but now the pressure was ratcheted up even higher. Katya never broke her persona and got to her dorm room an hour later.

33

IATA—RABAT

The day of his flight, Wilder drove from Cap de l'eau to the Rabat-Salé Airport. He carefully checked the eyelet on his left high-top and made it through screening without incident. He boarded the plane and took his seat. Wilder glanced at the old lady next to him. For a moment he let himself wish she were Katya. He was still heartbroken but mostly feeling extremely anxious. He kept as calm a demeanor as he could muster.

After liftoff, Wilder felt a wave of relief. He tucked his laptop under his thigh, zipped his hoodie and took a nap.

The plane touched down in New York City, and Wilder passed through customs. Two white men in sunglasses were waiting for him. "Wilder Kole? Come with us." They led him through an unmarked door into a room with a table and two chairs. "Have a seat." Wilder gulped and asked what this was all about. The two men stood in the corner and said nothing.

A black woman entered the room from another door. Her silver stilettos clacked as she walked. Her name was CIA Special Agent Carmen Jefferson. She had hoop earrings and straight hair to her shoulders. She slapped a file folder on the table and pulled up a chair across from Wilder.

"Lovely office you have here," said Wilder, "but it could use a few windows."

"Skip the humor," said Carmen.

Wilder was failing to deflect his nerves. "Nothing wrong with a little humor," he muttered.

"Cut the crap. Wilder Kole, born August 20, 2001, correct?"

"Correct. And you are . . . ?"

She flashed an unamused, closemouthed smile, staring at Wilder intently. "You've had quite a life. My notes say you were three years old when your parents died. You were in a car accident in the Grand Canyon."

"Yeah, the accident." Wilder remembered it in flashes. A fireman cradling him outside of a wrecked vehicle, his three-year-old self looking back at his dead parents inside. He stared Carmen in the eye and said, "It's a bad memory."

"Marla Johnson—your grandma—adopted you, but she died of a heart attack when you were six."

"People have a way of dying on me," quipped Wilder. This memory was more vivid. Grandma Marla was drunk as usual. She was in the kitchen yelling at Wilder about tripping over his skateboard. She clutched her chest and collapsed to the floor, twitching. Her mouth gaped wide open and her inhales got weaker and weaker until she stopped moving.

Carmen continued, "After that you were put in foster care—ended up in group homes. As a teenager, you ran away ten times."

"At least. What's this about?" asked Wilder.

"I like to understand what motivates a person to a life of crime."

"Me?"

"Yes. Let me give you just one example. It says here you've always gotten mediocre grades, and yet miraculously UCLA accepted you. My team found glaring discrepancies between your high school transcript and the one UCLA has on file. I'm guessing you hacked their servers."

"No idea what you're talking about," Wilder lied.

"But that's just the beginning." She skewered him with calm, angry criticism. "You're not too clever, but you're extremely smart. You have coding skills at the level of an MIT student. So tell me, why don't you build a real résumé for yourself instead of dealing drugs?"

"You're talking to the wrong guy," he said.

Carmen pointed at him with a long fingernail. "Here's where the shit gets deep for you," she continued. "Six weeks ago, Karen Masterson from Beverly Hills attended a rave. She overdosed on fentanyl and just about went into a coma. You sold her that fentanyl."

Wilder faked a muted outrage. "This is ridiculous." He was ready with a defense but knew he was caught. "You can't prove that."

"You're lucky she woke up. Only problem is, now she can implicate you," Carmen said. "You're facing multiple felony convictions." She paused and let that sink in. "But that's not why you're here, and you know it. So why are you here, Wilder?"

He deflected. "Well if this is speed dating, you're really hot, but I have a girlfriend already."

"Not funny in any way. Talk."

He said, "There must be some mistake."

"No mistake." Her face was stone-cold serious.

"You're with the CIA, am I right?" Wilder asked.

"Correct. I am CIA."

"You're the CIA?"

"CIA," snapped Carmen. "There's no *the*."

"I'm confused," Wilder said.

"It's not *the* CIA, it's just CIA. That's how you say it."

"OK, CIA." He smiled. "You're really sensitive about the word *the*, aren't you?"

"You don't say *the* God, do you? It's just God."

"Beautiful, sensitive *and* CIA," Wilder wouldn't quit with the jokes. "I can see why we make a good match."

"Don't be cute and don't think you can confuse me. I deal with assholes like you all the time." Carmen motioned to the two men. "Go through all of his belongings," she said. "Tell Shareem to do a full scan of his laptop. Now, Wilder, is there anything you want to tell us before we find it?"

"Nothing to declare," said Wilder. "But can I get a glass of water? Plane rides always dehydrate me."

"No," said Carmen. The men left the room with his things.

Wilder wondered if they would crack his code and find the video of the battle in Jerada. He was confident in the cloaked OS he programmed, but he was worried, nonetheless. He thought, *If they find the video, I'm screwed.*

"Now," said Carmen, "I'm going to ask you some very important questions."

Wilder leaned over and farted loudly. "Oh man, I'm sorry. This happens when I fly."

Carmen shook her head, mildly disgusted and unamused. "Let's move on." Carmen slid an 8 x 10 photograph across the table. "What's your relationship with Katya Polenko?"

"Katya? She's a Russian foreign exchange student in my bioinformatics class. But I'm sure you know that."

"Go on."

"Katya is my girlfriend—sort of—at least she was until a few days ago. She looks great in this picture—can I keep this?"

Carmen raised her voice. "Stop. Fucking. Around. If you're going to avoid life in prison, I might be the only person who can help you."

"Life? Oh Jesus." Wilder's stomach gurgled.

"You two flew to Morocco four days ago, and now you're flying back alone. Why is that?"

"You'd have to ask Katya."

"Not good enough, Mr. Kole."

He flashed again to the images of the battle and aftermath, with the Navy SEALs dragging bodies around and loading them into the Humvee. Again he returned to worrying. Could the men who took his laptop possibly find the video? "It was an impulse vacation," Wilder answered. "I was trying to prove I could be exciting and romantic." Half-truths made the best lies. He showed some real emotion by channeling his feelings of rejection.

"Morocco is a long way to travel. Aside from being lovers, what's your relationship?"

"That's all, I swear. She wanted to go see the mountain desert and we picked Jerada. I was down for whatever she said. After we got there, this dude sold us acid. He was pretty good looking, I guess, and Katya ran off with him while we were tripping."

"Stop lying. If you don't give me something, I can't help you."

"OK, OK. Here's something," said Wilder. "Katya said she was working with the CIA—without the *the*."

"She told you that?" asked Carmen. "When?"

"Is it true she's with you guys?" Wilder asked.

"I'm asking the questions."

"She told me that after Professor Singh died."

"What else did she tell you?"

"She said she sucked at programming. Katya needed my help decoding a message Professor Singh gave her." Carmen leaned forward and Wilder spun a lie. "She said the professor was CIA too. He asked her to deliver the message to his contact at the University of Rabat. She had the idea to use a Morocco vacation as a cover story."

"What coded message? What contact?"

"I don't know, and I don't know." It was true that he didn't know because those were lies he made up on the spot.

"Is that when you and Katya became romantically involved?"

"Yes."

"What happened after you arrived in Rabat?"

"We skipped going to the university. She said someone approached her in the New York airport while I was in the restroom. They said to avoid the Moroccan connection and not to hand off any code. So when we flew into Rabat, Katya got the idea to go to Jerada."

Carmen stared at him. "Why Jerada?"

"There's a lot of nature. Going to the desert was supposed to be our cover. We were planning camel rides and stuff."

"Your credit card record shows you stayed one night in a hotel," said Carmen. "What exactly happened in Jerada, Wilder?"

Wilder closed his eyes and he thought about the battle video. He said, "Well, we got to the hotel lobby and Katya started talking to this guy, almost like she knew him. He was good looking, like I said."

"What did he look like?"

"He had on a pink blazer. Suntan."

"And I'm supposed to believe this man sold you acid?"

"I was lying about the acid part."

"Why did you lie?"

"Because I'm scared. I was trying not to tell you about the Katya CIA thing."

"She really threw you for a loop, didn't she. What else are you lying about?"

"Nothing else, I swear. We got to our room and Katya started acting funny. All of a sudden she was in a hurry. It was like midnight and she said wanted to get something to eat. She said she was going to the lobby and she would be right back . . . Well, she never came back."

"Stop lying, Wilder."

"I'm not lying. She ditched me in Jerada."

"Who else was with you?"

"Our guide. His name was Samuel."

"Did he seem like a real guide to you?" asked Carmen.

"Yes," said Wilder.

"You're saying the last time you saw Miss Polenko was in Jerada on the night you paid for the hotel room?"

"Yes." He was starting to sell his lies.

"Then what?"

"Then nothing. I waited and waited. Katya wouldn't answer her texts and I tried a bunch of times. The next day I realized she wasn't coming back. I was really heartbroken, honestly. So I figured fuck this—and I told my guide to take me to the beach."

"What did your guide look like?"

"He looked Moroccan."

"What does that mean?"

"He had dark skin."

"How dark?"

"Not as dark as yours. Am I being racist?" Wilder asked.

"Not at the moment. Do you have a picture of this man, Samuel?"

"No. But he had a British accent and spoke Arabic too. He had one of those turned-up mustaches and beat-up sandals. I remember the sandals because they looked like they were about to fall off his feet."

Carmen was reading every small expression on Wilder's face. He was nervous but committed to his lies. She said, "Keep talking."

"What else do you want me to say? Can I use your restroom now?" He was uncomfortably bloated but glad to have it shift his focus. "I'm thinking maybe I can just fart it out, you know?"

Carmen said, "You can use the restroom when I'm done asking questions. Then we're gonna take a break and I'm gonna ask you *more* questions. And we're not done until I say so, got it?"

"Got it," said Wilder, trying to buy time to spin more lies. "You know it's kind of hot when you boss me around, right?"

"Stop acting like a fool," said Carmen. His antics were beginning to piss her off. She said, "I can single-handedly make your life a living hell."

"At this point, I'm counting on it," said Wilder.

Carmen pulled another photograph from her file. "Do you recognize this man?" He didn't. She showed him another. "What about this man?"

He looked down at the photo and got a lump in his throat. It was Sergei Podkopaev who he saw get killed on video.

Carmen said, "That's a yes. Talk."

"Yes, yeah." Wilder thought fast. "He was in the lobby too, at the hotel in Jerada."

"What was he doing?"

"He was standing around and looking out the window, drinking tea or something. That's all I remember, I swear." It was a good enough lie.

Carmen paused and took a deep breath. Silence hung in the room. She slapped her palms on the table, shoved her chair back and paced around the room. For the first time, she looked annoyed. She tugged at the lapels on her jacket, pointed at the photo and sternly asked, "Do you have any idea who this man is, Wilder? This is Sergei Podkopaev with the Russian Federal Security Service."

"A Russian fed? Holy crap!" said Wilder.

"He's former KGB."

"You're shitting me."

"I am not *shitting* you, Wilder. This is an extremely serious matter."

"Is Katya KGB?"

"There is no KGB anymore."

"Oh."

"We know Katya works for the Russian secret service, but we don't know in what capacity."

"Damn. I'm so stupid. Is she connected to Sergei?"

"Not that we know of. Sergei served in Russia's war with Afghanistan. He's a Spetsnaz veteran, which is equivalent to our Navy SEALs."

"Sweet Jesus," said Wilder. "Did Katya lie about working with the CIA?"

Carmen didn't answer that. She said, "We think Sergei is part of a splinter group of Russian spies in North Africa. He's been working with Libyan militiamen linked to Al Qaeda."

Wilder broke into a cold sweat. "Well, I didn't know that. I didn't know any of this."

"For the first time today, I actually believe you," said Carmen.

"Why are you telling me this?" asked Wilder. "I'm just a guy who fell head over heels for a beautiful woman. I mean, look at me . . . look at Katya. Don't you get it?"

Carmen slowly strolled behind Wilder. "You're beginning to see now how serious this situation really is. Come on Wilder—this is your chance to do something good for your country. If you give me more, I can arrange for a reduced sentence. If you help us catch the bad guys, you'll get more than clemency. I guarantee it."

Carmen gave Wilder a toilet break with guards watching his every move. She brought him a sandwich with a cup of water and interrogated him for another two hours. She pressed him particularly hard about Professor Singh, issuing threats of life in prison along with the clemency carrot.

Finally, Wilder relented and gave up more of the truth. He confessed that the professor gave him a thumb drive with code on it. He said Katya got the code too. Then Wilder carried right on with his lying and claimed he never cracked the code. He said the professor's death made him so paranoid that he destroyed the thumb drive. Carmen asked where the drive was, and Wilder told her truthfully that he dropped it in a bottle of beer.

Carmen asked, "Why did it take you so long to tell me? Did you honestly think I didn't know?"

Wilder said, "I figure I'm in so much trouble—and I know so little—that truth and lies aren't much of a consequence."

Carmen scoffed. "You don't even want to help me, do you? You're just thinking about yourself."

"Help you with what?"

She said, "You're not striking me as a man who loves his country."

"I love America," he assured her. "I have trouble with authority of all kinds, but I love the hell out of my country."

Carmen told him that agents searched his dorm room top to bottom and they found the destroyed thumb drive. CIA took all of his technology into custody and so far had found nothing connecting him to the professor. Wilder continued doubling down on his bluffing. He said, after the professor died, he destroyed his thumb drive, and that's when Katya approached him. He lied, claiming he didn't save a copy, and told the truth that he didn't know where Katya put hers. At one point, he asked for a lawyer, and Carmen assured him a lawyer would only make things worse.

Wilder sensed that Carmen didn't know the details of the massacre in Jerada. The two men came back into the room with his laptop. The computer looked clean, they said. Wilder suppressed a proud smile and gave a fake one with a shrug. His cloaked OS had gone undetected, and the battle scene video was sitting right on his hidden desktop.

Wilder thought to himself, *Sometimes the simplest piece of coding is the most elegant.* He was so tired he was starting to see things, and he played that up a little.

Carmen mumbled something inaudible to the men and dismissed them. She said, "Today you're catching a break because we need your help catching the bad guys."

"Who exactly *are* the bad guys?" he asked.

"Most of them are Russians," said Carmen.

"And the Arabs too?" said Wilder.

She said, "We don't know their level of involvement."

Wilder said, "But they must be terrorists."

"You know not all Arabs are terrorists, right?"

"Of course I know that," he said, feeling stupid.

"In this case, they are in fact terrorists, so you had it right," said Carmen. "But it's the Russians we're after. And until you prove otherwise, Wilder, you're one of the bad guys too."

"I swear, I'm innocent," Wilder said.

"You're not innocent by any stretch of the imagination," she said. "We will find out the worst thing you're guilty of and make you pay accordingly."

A man walked back into the room with the rest of Wilder's belongings. He whispered something in Carmen's ear and left. Carmen glared at Wilder.

"Listen," said Carmen. She crossed her arms impatiently. "We're offering you one shot at a deal."

"You're not taking me to prison?"

"Not yet, we're not," she said.

"What kind of deal?"

"For now, we let you go. You go back to your everyday life, like everything's normal, you got me?"

"I got you," he said.

"My team is watching your every move. We need to know who you're in contact with and track whoever comes to find you."

"What about my provider, Kim?" Wilder asked. He had already spilled the beans about his drug connection.

"She's small potatoes," said Carmen. "We'll tell the DEA about her some other time."

"I'll do anything you want," said Wilder.

"Are you sure?" Carmen teased him. "Because if you want I can put you in jail right now." She showed a glimpse of humor, but it was also a promise.

"Are you giving me back my laptop?" asked Wilder, unzipping his backpack.

"No," she said. "Apparently you're not dumb enough to leave anything on your computer that implicates you of any crimes on your little trip to Morocco. However, we are keeping your laptop. That should come as no surprise."

"I told you already—"

"And your phone has been replaced with this one. Here you go. Goodbye for now, Wilder."

"Hey wait," said Wilder. "I've been acting like an asshole today. I'm honestly really scared and nervous. I apologize."

"Accepted," said Carmen.

"You're a consummate professional," Wilder said. "Can I shake your hand?"

Carmen shook Wilder's hand for the briefest of moments. Her stilettos click-clacked as she crossed the room. She kicked a doorstop with her heel to prop the door open. "You're free to go, Mr. Kole." With that, she walked away.

Wilder stood alone in the room, adding life in prison to his list of things to worry about. These past few days he had experienced the worst anxiety he had ever felt, ups and downs mixed with heartache. He looked in his backpack and saw CIA was kind enough to leave him his Xanax. He took three.

A man walked in and escorted Wilder to his connecting flight to Los Angeles. Aboard the plane and more relaxed, he pulled out Carmen's security clearance badge, which he removed from her lapel when they shook hands. He chuckled to himself and stuffed it in his seat pocket.

Wilder smugly looked down at his shoes. They never found the video, and he was wearing a copy of it in his damn shoe—not to mention the professor's code. He felt pretty glorious because it was definitely some next-level spy shit. He leaned back and thought about his laptop, quietly celebrating that agents hadn't solved his configuration. On the flight home, he replayed the battle scene in his mind, wondering what the hell would happen next.

34

BUMPY LANDING

They put Wilder on a red-eye flight to LA. He deboarded and took an Uber to his dorm. He recognized a car in the parking lot. Alex from the Casta cartel stepped out. "We need to talk," he said.

Wilder warned him, "You might want to leave me alone. I'm being followed by the CIA."

"Don't bullshit me, man," said Alex.

"Look," said Wilder. He pointed across the street at a man in sunglasses conspicuously standing around. "And look." Wilder pointed again, this time at a woman looking through binoculars on a balcony.

"Oh damn, you ain't lying," said Alex. He got in the car and sped off.

Wilder stepped inside his dorm room and set his bags down with a sigh. His bed was unmade, with Katya's underwear and an empty pizza box on the floor. The place looked just like he left it except his server farm and tech gear were gone—and there was a new laptop sitting on his desk. He knew the room was bugged to the nines. Wilder took a hot shower and collapsed on his bed, but he couldn't sleep.

He remembered Carmen's orders to return to his normal life as if nothing were different. So he decided to retrieve his flip phone from the roof. He opened his outside door, grabbed the drainpipe and started climbing.

The agent on the sidewalk tapped his earpiece and asked, "What's he doing?"

"No idea," replied the woman on the balcony.

Wilder touched his feet down on the roof and slipped out of their sight. He located the flip phone beneath a low overhang and unwrapped the duct-taped baggies. No sooner had he put back the SIM card when his flip phone rang. It couldn't be coincidental. It must have been Kim—she was the only one with the number. What did she know? Their rule was to never talk on the line—a phone call was just a cue to meet.

Wilder climbed down and tossed the phone on his bed. A few bong hits later, he slung his backpack over his shoulder and headed for the café. Kim was late and he sat in the corner tapping his foot nervously. He wondered again if Kim knew something.

One table over, a man in a baseball cap slowly turned around in his chair. "Hello, kid." The man was well disguised, but Wilder knew Hawthorne's voice right away.

"Oh crap, it's you." Wilder's anxiety shot through the roof.

Hawthorne pulled up a chair at Wilder's table. "How was the rest of your trip?"

"You just ruined my high."

"Calm down."

"How did you know to call my flip phone?" Wilder asked.

"You're conspicuous." Hawthorne had tired eyes and a sun-weathered face. "We don't have much time."

"Who are you?" asked Wilder.

He muttered, "If I told you I was Spec Ops, would you believe me?"

Wilder said, "I don't know what to believe anymore."

Hawthorne shook his head. "You have no idea how deep this shit is, do you?"

Wilder agreed, "No idea." He looked defeated, and the stress had frayed his last nerve. "You know, the CIA is watching my every move."

"Looks like they put some rookies on you." Hawthorne tilted his head in the direction of two agents lingering in the front entrance.

Wilder gulped. "Total buzzkill."

Hawthorne said, "You took a trip to Morocco with a Russian spy. She got what she needed from you and disappeared. Right?"

Wilder insisted, "She said she was an informant."

"Katya is a good kisser too," Hawthorne said with a coy smile.

"What?" Wilder was incredulous. "You kissed her?"

Hawthorne nodded. "There's some real heat between us."

"No fucking way," said Wilder.

"It wasn't a planned thing," said Hawthorne.

"I don't believe you."

Hawthorne vise-gripped Wilder's arm. "I think you know what went down in Jerada."

Wilder grimaced, "I don't—"

"It's written all over your face," said Hawthorne.

Wilder gave up pretending and whispered, "You were there. What was in the suitcase?"

"You don't want to know," replied Hawthorne. "Listen. Tomorrow somebody's going to try to kill you. What time? I don't know."

"I *knew* somebody was trying to kill me," whispered Wilder. "Now I *know* I'm not paranoid."

"No—you're paranoid too," Hawthorne said bluntly.

"The CIA will protect me."

"They're not going to lift a finger to stop you from getting killed."

"Why not?"

"Because you're disposable."

Wilder's heart sank. Suddenly the threat of prison was sounding pretty good. "They said they needed me."

"Don't take it personal, kid," said Hawthorne. "I'm disposable too."

"Why would anyone want to kill me?"

"You were pretty fucking obvious on your so-called vacation. Everyone—including the bad guys—knows about the disaster in Morocco. They pinned it on you."

"But I don't have anything to do with it," pleaded Wilder.

"I know that—but they don't."

Wilder asked, "What about Katya?"

Hawthorne said, "I'm way ahead of you on that."

"Did you really kiss her?"

"I wouldn't lie about a kiss," said Hawthorne.

"Damn you." Wilder was jealous. "So what you're saying is I'm a dead man."

Hawthorne said, "Here's the thing, kid. Never rush to your death."

"I don't want to die," said Wilder nervously.

"There's a chance for you," said Hawthorne. He dug a piece of paper out of his jeans pocket and handed it to Wilder. "If you want to live, go to this address right now."

"Why?" asked Wilder.

"There's a teacher friend of mine who owns a dojo. Her name is Maria but you can call her Sensei. She was my hand-to-hand combat trainer but she's on the nonviolent path now. She swore off military involvement."

Wilder was tracking him. "OK . . ."

"But she owes me one last favor and I've decided to spend it on you."

"Are you for real?"

Hawthorne nodded. "Maria's not too happy about it, but she's honoring my request."

"What's the request?"

"To give you a fighting chance to live when your assassin pays you a visit," said Hawthorne.

"Sweet Jesus," said Wilder. "Why?"

"I think you're on the right side. And like I said, she owes me a favor." He stood up and headed for the door. "Oh—and one more thing."

"What?" asked Wilder.

Hawthorne lowered his voice. "On the way out of Jerada, I picked up some hitchhikers."

By hitchhikers, he meant dead bodies and Wilder knew it. "I dropped them off at a pier in Al Hoceima."

Wilder asked, "Why are you telling me this?"

"I'm not telling you—I'm telling the guys who are listening through your phone."

"Oh shit," said Wilder. "I get it now."

"You seem like a good kid, and this situation has gone nuclear."

"You look scared," said Wilder. "I thought SEALs weren't supposed to get scared."

Hawthorne said, "Good luck not dying tomorrow. And get your ass over to that dojo." On his way out the door, he tipped his cap to the CIA agents who had followed Wilder into the café. They were too amateurish to ID Hawthorne until he was gone.

35
THE DOJO

An hour later, Wilder stood in front of the dojo. The sign said CLOSED, and Wilder was about to knock when Sensei Maria opened the door.

Sensei was short and stocky with shaved blond hair. She had clear eyes and a long scar across her jaw. "You must be Wilder. Come in. Take off your shoes."

"Thanks for having me."

"No small talk," she said. "I'm doing this because I owe Hawthorne a favor. Honor is honor."

Wilder said, "He said you swore off violence."

"That's correct," she said. "But in your case, this is self-defense, so it's not as bad."

Sensei stepped onto the mat, motioning to Wilder to join her. "Make a fist," she said, so he did. "If you punch somebody like that, you're going to break your thumb." Wilder blushed. He didn't know the first thing about fighting.

Sensei spent fifteen minutes teaching Wilder the proper stance, firmly grounded yet flexible, ready to defend and attack. "Your form is not great, but it will have to do. Wait here a minute." Sensei went into her back office and came back with a thick roll of masking tape, two hunting knives and a photo printout. She methodically taped a large box around Wilder. She walked over to one corner.

"This is your outside entrance." She walked to another corner. "And this is the door to the hallway."

"Is this my dorm room?" asked Wilder.

"Yes," Sensei said. She taped an X toward the middle. "Stand right here and get in your stance. Turn and face the outside entrance."

"OK."

"Here's a photo of your attacker," Sensei said. He was an ugly white man with neck tattoos.

"Sweet Jesus," said Wilder. "He looks like a mean dude. How do you know he's the one coming to kill me?"

"CIA spotted him at LAX this morning. His name is Dimitri Andropov. He's here for a hit job, not tourism."

Wilder was petrified. "Why can't somebody stop him?"

"That's not how it works."

"Well, why not?"

"Pay attention, Wilder."

"OK. Go on."

"He's going to enter the room, and once he sees you have no gun, he's going to come at you with his switchblade."

"Why can't I have a gun?"

"He would shoot you first, without a doubt."

"Oh," said Wilder.

"He's gonna prefer you die painfully—to get revenge."

"Revenge?"

"Yes," said Sensei. "Hawthorne told me about your appearance in Morocco. A group of Russian spies had no problem tracking you down. Dimitri is with them."

"I'm just a victim of circumstance," Wilder said.

"You really kicked the hornet's nest."

"But I didn't actually do anything."

"Doesn't matter." Sensei handed Wilder a knife and raised her own. She walked to the corner and turned to face Wilder again. "Dimitri will size you up. Remember, he wants you to have a terrifying, painful and slow death."

"Fucking hell," said Wilder. "What if I scream and run?"

Sensei said, "He won't care if you scream—a guy like him has fled a murder scene a thousand times."

Wilder dropped his head in defeat. "What is even the point of this?"

"Focus," she continued. "You're in your stance. He's getting ready to attack."

"OK." Wilder practiced his stance.

"Look only at the left side of his neck. Dimitri has a tattoo of playing cards with the Ace of Spades showing. When his neck turns, the ace goes out of view and the attack has begun. His first move is with his head, understand?"

Wilder nodded.

"You right-handed?" Sensei asked.

"Yes."

"Good. Hold your knife in your right hand. He's going to love that you're trying to defend yourself. What's the fun of killing an unarmed man, right?"

"Like this?" Wilder held the knife up.

Sensei showed Wilder the correct grip and said, "This blade has never seen a battle it didn't win."

She went over and over the moves of Dimitri's predictable attack. She explained each footstep and showed Wilder his defense. Sensei taught Wilder to move left while rolling outside to the right, which would make the attacker miss. She insisted Wilder move in one fluid motion. "Shift and roll, now knife in both hands, turn and thrust into the back of his heart."

Sensei taught him the same sequence a hundred times. After two hours of training, she said, "That's it."

"That's it?" asked Wilder.

"You're as good as you're going to get," she said. "If you don't kill him with that move, you're going to have to improvise, and your chances of survival will be almost zero. Dimitri Andropov does not miss twice."

Just like that, Sensei walked to the front door and opened it. "Now, I kindly ask you to leave."

Wilder put the knife in his backpack and laced up his high-tops.

Sensei said, "If through some small miracle you survive this attack, don't set foot in my dojo again."

"Yes, Sensei," said Wilder. "Thank you." He wasn't sure if he was supposed to, but he bowed.

She gave the slightest bow back. "Finish this—and I hope you find peace." She ushered Wilder out the door and shut it behind him.

36

THE ATTACK

Exhausted, Wilder shuffled into his dorm room. He ate most of a pizza and smoked a joint but didn't feel high. That night he barely slept a wink.

The next morning, Wilder sat up in bed and ate his leftover slices. He remembered he had one more modafinil, dug it out of his backpack and swallowed it. He moved his desk chair a couple feet behind the imaginary *X* marking his attack stance. And he waited all day.

At dusk, the outside doorknob jiggled. Someone was picking the lock. Wilder pushed back his chair and took his stance. He put his left foot forward and right foot back, holding the knife chest high.

The door opened a crack, and Dimitri Andropov poked his head in. He looked at Wilder, scanned the room and calmly stepped inside. Dimitri shut the door softly and tucked his pistol behind his back belt line. He was uglier in person than in the photo at the dojo. Pulling a Karatel tactical combat knife from his thigh pocket, he rubbed his hands over greasy hair and tightened his ponytail. He smiled a toothy grin, showing a gold canine. "*Privet*," said Dimitri. "That means 'hello' in Russian."

"I know what it means." Wilder inhaled deeply, gripping the knife handle tightly.

Dimitri assured him, "When you killed my comrade Sergei, you said hello to death."

Wilder stood motionless and stared at the Ace of Spades on Dimitri's neck tattoo. Wilder heard Sensei's voice in his head: *When the card turns, the attack has begun.*

Dimitri's head shifted, the card turned and he lunged forward. Wilder swiftly slid his front foot sideways and twisted his torso like a bullfighter. He fluidly whipped his whole body around as Dimitri thrust the knife blade, grazing millimeters past Wilder's throat. Wilder buried his hunting knife into Dimitri's back. It pierced through the rib cage behind his heart, and Dimitri face-planted on the floor.

Blood spurted around the knife protruding from Dimitri's back. Wilder stood there panting incredulously. Dimitri quietly laughed, his hand reaching around and pulling out the knife. He rolled over to his knees and stood up slowly. "Not bad." He waved Wilder's knife at him. "Now you die by your own blade."

Dimitri charged again. Wilder snatched his laptop and swatted the knife across the room. The men collided and Wilder fell to his back. They grappled and Wilder tried to get a headlock, but he was overpowered. With a cruel laugh, Dimitri pinned Wilder and rained down punches. Wilder grabbed a fistful of hair and ripped out a chunk with bloody skull tissue attached. Dimitri dropped an elbow on Wilder's forehead. Blood and hair covered Wilder's face. Dimitri slammed the back of Wilder's head into the linoleum, knocking him out.

Dimitri waited for Wilder to return to consciousness. Terror in his eyes, Wilder bucked and flipped over to his stomach. Dimitri punched the sides of Wilder's head. Wilder flailed his arm behind him, grabbing in desperation for whatever his hand could find. He jammed his fingers under Dimitri's chin. Wilder pushed so hard he dislocated his own shoulder, with his fingers crawling up Dimitri's face to the eye. Instinctively, Wilder plunged his thumb into the orbital. A sack of fluid ruptured inside Dimitri's eye socket. Thick bloody slime burst down Dimitri's face. Wilder wriggled his thumb all the way to the last knuckle, two inches into the man's head. Hot blood flooded down Wilder's arm. Dimitri squealed, "*Moy glaz! Moy glaz!*"

Wilder hooked his thumb and Dimitri's eyeball popped out. Wilder felt the squishy ball in the palm of his hand and squeezed hard. Dimitri instinctively yanked his head back. Sinew and tendons stretched and snapped. The eyeball detached in Wilder's fist and Dimitri screamed, "*Oh Bozhe!* My eye!"

Wilder tossed the eyeball into the pool of blood and hair. Struggling to stay conscious, he rolled over to his hands and knees. Dimitri kept wailing, and he stood up staggering backward with his hands by his face. Blood spewed like a fountain out of his eye socket, pulsing with the beat of his heart. Wilder got to his feet, slipping in the pool of blood and still seeing white spots in his periphery. He dove at Dimitri and both men fell. Blood squirted in every direction. Wilder wrapped both hands around his throat and squeezed Dimitri's windpipe. Dimitri gurgled and choked with his hands spastically swatting around his neck. Wilder scooped the bloody laptop off the floor and raised it into the air. He thrust the thin side of the laptop into Dimitri's jugular with a loud crunch. Dimitri's trachea and vertebrae broke and his head flopped to the side. His one good eye rolled back and his body went limp.

It was over.

Wilder's neighbor Luis pounded on the hallway door. "Hey! Are you alright in there?"

Dizzy and covered in blood and hair, Wilder shouted, "I'm OK! Just watching a horror movie!"

"Horror movie?" the voice said. "You fucking kidding, man?"

"Yeah! Horror movie! Fuck off!" said Wilder.

"Turn that shit down!" yelled Luis through the door. "I was about to call 9-1-1!"

"Leave me alone!"

"Fine! And fuck you too!" yelled Luis, storming down the hallway back to his room.

Wilder sat curled in a ball, rocking back and forth. The room came into focus. There was so much blood. Wilder threw a couple of towels down and they were instantly soaked. He picked up the eyeball and it looked back at him. He threw it against the wall with a splat.

There were only a few feet of floor space not covered in blood. Wilder stripped his bloody clothes and scrubbed down his body. He stood naked and panting in the full-length mirror. He poured a liter of water over his head, gingerly patting it dry. He wrapped a bandanna around his forehead to cover the gash. Wilder palpated the bloodied back of his head, putting a baseball cap over the bandanna. He found a button-down shirt and pants in the closet, away from the blood spatter radius. Once fully dressed, he tiptoed around Dimitri's body. Wilder grabbed the blanket off his bed and cleaned his bloody shoes. He wiped off his laptop and muttered to himself, "Is there anything in this room *not* covered in blood?" He tossed the laptop on the mattress and walked out the door.

Wilder headed to a dive bar called Murphy's Pub, a block off campus. He winced in pain but tried to walk casually. He sidled up to the bar, showed his ID and ordered a whiskey double with a beer chaser. Wilder found a dimly lit booth in the back. Three or four rounds later, he was sufficiently drunk, and before he knew it the bar was closing.

He stumbled back toward his dorm room. Where else was he going to go? Wilder was dismayed but had also drunk enough to block out the harshness of reality. In his stupor, he decided he would deal with it all tomorrow.

Fumbling for his dorm room key, Wilder braced himself for the body and blood. Inside the door, he found the room pristinely clean. He wobbled and slurred, "Well, I'll be goddamned! What the fuckin' FUCK in fuckin' hell!" Wilder fell on his bed and passed out. For the first time in three days, he slept until sunrise.

37

FAILED TRANSFER

Late that same night, at her secret apartment in Burbank, Katya sat at the kitchen table, and a text came through on her phone: "Hi, Katya, next semester's early registration is happening now. Please come into the foreign exchange student office ASAP."

Katya replied, "OK."

"Please bring all of your personal information."

It was time for Katya to hand over her copy of Professor Singh's code to her contact. She had hidden the thumb drive in a less obvious place than her apartment unit—the electric room by the garbage dumpsters on the ground level of the complex.

Katya grabbed a bag of trash, stepped out of her unit and headed downstairs. She tossed the bag in the dumpster and picked the lock of the electric room. Hawthorne popped out of the shadows holding his Beretta. He put Katya in a rear naked choke.

Katya punched over her shoulder, striking Hawthorne's face. She collapsed to her knees in a failed effort to flip him. They both fell to the ground. Hawthorne kept her in a choke hold and shoved his pistol into her temple. Katya gave up fighting back. All he had to do was pull the trigger.

"Give me the code," said Hawthorne.

"Who are you?" she asked.

"The man you kissed in the airport."

"How did you find me?"

"The business card."

"I threw it away," she said.

"That wasn't good enough. Where's the code?"

"In the main breaker panel," Katya said, pointing to the wall.

"Get up." Hawthorne forced her to stand.

"There's a key in my pocket," she said.

"Open it." Hawthorne held his Beretta against her head while she opened the lock. The thumb drive was mounted with electric tape above the flip switches. Hawthorne ripped off the tape and grabbed the drive, zipping it in his jacket pocket.

He asked, "Has anyone else seen this?"

"No."

"Did you make any copies?"

"No."

It was true. Katya couldn't confirm what was on the thumb drive, and she had chosen not to try and find out. She didn't want to blow her cover by accidentally launching an autorun program.

"Anything to say before you die?" Hawthorne asked.

She said, "I'm sorry I didn't call you."

Hawthorne recalculated. "Killing you draws more heat. Tell whoever you work for—no more mercy."

He tucked his Beretta inside his jacket and Katya lunged. With quick reflexes, Hawthorne deflected her attack, striking her in the back of the head with the pistol's magazine. The blow knocked Katya out cold, and Hawthorne caught her as she fell. He lowered her to the ground and slipped out the side door. He jumped in his car and sped away with the thumb drive.

38

SOME GOOD, SOME BAD

Renfree was an early bird on a private golf course just outside of DC. His cell phone rang.

Renfree: Talk to me Karen.

Karen: I've got some good news and some bad news.

Renfree: Good news first.

Karen: The shipment is on its way.

Renfree: Wonderful. Amazing.

Karen: Bad news is KrayBULL's down seventy-five percent of its men. Hawthorne is AWOL and we think he killed his unit.

Renfree: What?

Karen: Perez is the only one left.

Renfree: Where's Hawthorne now?

Karen: He popped up in LA. He led CIA to Jansen's body in the back of a truck in Morocco. His corpse was in the company of some very shady international characters. Also dead.

Renfree: Jesus Christ. Is that intel under wraps?

Karen: For now, but it's impossible for the Pentagon to spin it. If word gets out this will be very bad.

Renfree: This all falls on Hawthorne. Pin it on Hawthorne. And find him.

Karen: That's not as easy as you think, Arnold.

Renfree: You said he showed up in LA.

Karen: He's a master of deception.

Renfree: I don't care. Find him.

Karen: There's more bad news.

Renfree: More? What is it?

Karen: Hawthorne contacted some kid who got the tech evidence.

Renfree: A kid?

Karen: A young man at UCLA by the name of Wilder Kole. An amateur spy but apparently some kind of computer genius.

Renfree: Kill the kid.

Karen: We tried.

Renfree: Don't try—do it.

Karen: We think Hawthorne and Kole are working together to disrupt the shipment.

Renfree: Capture and kill them both.

Karen: That's our plan—I just wanted you to know what's happening.

Renfree: Clean up this mess, goddamn it!

Karen: Wait—there's more.

Renfree: There's still more? For Christ's sake!

Karen: Hawthorne and the kid got their hands on some secret code.

Renfree: Does that threaten the mission?

Karen: We don't know.

Renfree: Dammit. Please tell me that's all the bad news.

Karen: That's all of it.

Renfree: Fix this!

Renfree hung up and pocketed his cell phone.

His caddy said, "That sounded like a stressful call."

Renfree took a deep breath and suppressed his anger. "That could have waited till I got back to the office. Can't a man golf in peace anymore?"

The caddy asked, "Who's Karen? I don't think I ever heard you talk to her before."

Renfree was seething. "Shut the fuck up and give me my nine iron."

*

Meanwhile, aboard the *Garganta* in the middle of the Pacific Ocean, Perez and Bailey contended with the horrific scene of Stein's decomposing body inside the shipping container. They had wrapped it in garbage bags, but the fully bloated corpse smelled intensely like rotten meat, fruit, eggs and cabbage. Black liquid seeped across the floor, and they ran out of extra blankets and clothing to soak it up.

"The stench is unbearable," said Bailey.

"Truly," said Perez.

"The intestinal bacteria are gonna keep multiplying."

"Not exactly a first-class ticket we got here."

Bailey asked, "Think we could at least crack the door?"

"No way," said Perez.

"I know," agreed Bailey, "but it's making me crazy."

Perez gritted his teeth. "Just one more week, man. Just one more week."

39

CRUCIAL ENCOUNTER

The next morning, Wilder's flip phone rang and then stopped. He sat up in bed and rubbed the crusted wound on the back of his head. A minute later, a second call—just one ring. Then a third call—it rang over and over, which was Kim and Wilder's code to pick up.

"Hello?" said Wilder.

"Congratulations, kid." It was Hawthorne on the line. "You survived."

"Barely," said Wilder.

"Meet me at the cafeteria right now."

Wilder put on a new ball cap and headed out the door. He spotted three pairs of people following him. Inside the south campus cafeteria Wilder didn't see Hawthorne, so he grabbed a dining tray and served himself waffles with a cup of coffee. Wilder found a table to himself and a guy sat down next to him. He had long scruffy blond hair and a neon shirt.

"Hey, kid," said Hawthorne.

"Wow," Wilder said. "I didn't recognize you at all."

Hawthorne said quickly, "Our friends took my tip and found the bodies in Al Hoceima."

A day earlier, another team of Navy SEALs recovered the corpses of KrayBULL Commander Jansen with Aldridge from CIA alongside the Russian and Al Qaeda affiliates.

"Bad situation," said Hawthorne.

"You think?" asked Wilder sarcastically.

"But I shoved a note in the Russian's mouth."

"What did the note say?"

" 'GWA has the nuke.' "

"There was a *nuke* in the suitcase?"

Hawthorne nodded. "Now in the hands of the enemy."

"Why didn't you tell me before?" asked Wilder.

"I thought you were a dead man."

"GWA's behind this?"

Hawthorne leaned in. "Where's Professor Singh's code?"

"My shoe." Wilder pointed to his left high-top.

"Your shoe?"

"In the eyelet."

"Hand it over," demanded Hawthorne.

Wilder pried open the eyelet with his thumb and forefinger and pulled out the SIM card. Hawthorne snatched it out of his hand.

"I cracked everything but one piece of code," said Wilder. "It needs a Pentagon-caliber AI decoder."

Hawthorne pressed him, "What does the code say?"

"Arnold Renfree."

Hawthorne concluded. "He must have helped sell the nuke."

"Why?"

"Doesn't matter," said Hawthorne. "What else?"

Wilder said, "Another date, time and place."

"It's the bomb," said Hawthorne. "What day and time?"

"Seven a.m. on the twenty-sixth."

"A week from today. Where?"

"Long Beach Bay."

"That's all in this SIM card?"

"Yes."

Wilder felt the barrel of a pistol in the back of his head, and another pistol pointed at Hawthorne. Two feds in plainclothes had them cornered. Hawthorne, pinching the SIM card between his thumb and forefinger, slowly raised his hands in the air. Wilder followed suit.

"Shoot to kill," said the man targeting Wilder.

Two shots rang out. Hawthorne and Wilder grimaced and the federal assailants crumpled to the ground. Students in the cafeteria yelled in panic. Some hid for cover and others ran for the exits.

Wilder turned around to see where the shots came from. To his disbelief, Kim stood behind him holding a smoking Staccato CS.

Hawthorne dove on top of one of the assailants and shot him three times in the head. He fired finishing shots into the other fed too. Screams in the cafeteria grew louder, and students crushed each other in a mob toward the exits.

"Kim?" cried Wilder. "Where did you come from?"

"No time to talk!" she said.

"You saved my life," said Wilder.

"Get out of here!" Kim yelled.

Hawthorne said to Kim, "I owe you one," and bolted—with his Beretta in one hand and the SIM card in the other. He sprinted toward the kitchen, hurdled the counter and disappeared through a back exit.

"Wilder! GO!" shouted Kim, but he was frozen with fear.

In an instant, six more feds surrounded Kim and Wilder. One of them barked, "Drop your weapon!"

Kim dropped her pistol. "I'm FBI!" she exclaimed.

"Hands behind your head! Down on the ground!" They yanked Wilder and Kim and pinned them face down on the floor. Agents cuffed them both. Police car sirens blared outside the cafeteria.

With knees on their backs, Wilder's and Kim's faces mashed into the ground. They looked at each other. Wilder asked, "You're FBI?"

Kim's expression was so different that he hardly recognized her. "Don't tell them anything." Wilder quickly surmised Kim's partnership with him as his drug provider was deep cover. FBI had good reason for those measures. After they discovered

Wilder was skimming money from offshore bank accounts, the agency became alarmed—not by the scale of his theft but rather the perfection of his computer programming. Kim had been monitoring him for months, gathering intel as to whether there were any bigger fish to go after. She discovered not a fish but a whale.

Feds pulled Kim and Wilder to their feet and forced them to walk. A swarm of agents escorted them out of the building. Officers shoved them into separate vehicles.

*

Inside the Pentagon, Lieutenant Esther Hadwick got the news and headed straightaway to the office of Defense Secretary Tilford. She apprised him, "There's been a shooting involving feds in LA. Two of our men are dead at the hands of an FBI agent named Kim Lee."

Tilford asked, "Why would an FBI agent kill our own men?"

"She was protecting a Navy SEAL—Navy SEAL Rex Hawthorne—the only confirmed survivor from unit KrayBULL."

"Not KrayBULL again."

Hadwick said, "We have audio of Hawthorne linking himself to the dead bodies from the pier in Morocco."

Tilford asked, "Is Hawthorne in custody?"

"No sir—he got away."

"Get Hawthorne at all costs."

"Yes, sir," said Hadwick.

Tilford said, "Get the president on the phone."

President Garner sat anxiously at his desk in the Oval Office with the landline to his ear. He dabbed the sweat off his brow with a handkerchief and listened intently as Tilford described the shooting at UCLA. The president said, "I have no idea what to make of this. You tell me. All I know is we have to keep the massacre in Morocco as quiet as possible."

"We will do our best, Mr. President," said Tilford.

Chief of Staff Jenna Scofield walked into the Oval Office. The president hung up the phone and looked at her with a befuddled expression. "Jenna," he asked, "what do you know about the shooting in LA?"

Mrs. Scofield shook her head. "Nothing. I just got the news while you were on the line. Rex Hawthorne's a war hero—but now he's linked to murdering our own guys. Before long, the American public will know everything."

Garner said, "Get ahead of it. Tell the press we're working round the clock to bring Hawthorne in. Play up the hero with PTSD thing. Make him sound crazy, but not a victim. And for God's sake, project confidence like we have a clue what the hell is happening."

*

Back in LA, news cameras outside the police station surrounded the car transporting Wilder. Officers rushed him inside and put Wilder alone in a concrete cell. For over an hour, he sat handcuffed on a cold metal bench.

Finally, someone opened the cell door. With a click-clack of her stilettos, Ms. Carmen Jefferson stepped through the doorway. She glared at Wilder with her arms crossed.

Wilder quipped, "I see you went with the white pantsuit today. It goes really well with your skin."

Carmen calmly nodded to the officer who trailed in behind her. The officer led Wilder down a hall into an interrogation room with a giant mirror. Carmen followed them in and said, "You can uncuff him now. And leave us be." The door shut and Carmen stood with her back to Wilder. After a prolonged silence, she turned and said, "You're lucky to be alive."

"You can say that again," said Wilder.

She began the questioning. "What do you know about Kim Lee?"

"She's my provider. I deal what she sells me. Until today that was it."

Carmen asked, "Ever have any idea she was working with FBI?"

"No."

"Wilder, this is a matter of national security. Tell me everything Professor Singh gave you before he died."

"I already told you—the professor gave Katya and me thumb drives. As far as I know, it was three pieces of identical code."

"Where is the code now?" asked Carmen.

"Gone."

"You gave Hawthorne a copy that was inside your shoe eyelet."

"You got me there."

"You destroyed your backup files?"

"Yes," he lied. "I had it on my hard drive but I wiped it clean." Truthfully, the backup files were on his laptop that Carmen seized in the airport. But Wilder trusted no one.

"Why did you destroy the evidence?"

"I was terrified," said Wilder.

"Where is Katya?"

"No idea."

"Where is her thumb drive?"

"Again, no clue," said Wilder.

Carmen pivoted on her heels. "What's your connection to Rex Hawthorne?"

"You already know everything," he said. "You have been following me every moment since I arrived in New York."

"You don't have anything else?"

"Nothing . . . Did Hawthorne get away?"

"For now."

"How the hell does he do that?" Wilder marveled.

"He's highly trained."

"With the amount of people following me, you should have caught him."

"Well, it's not that easy."

"He's that much of a badass, huh?"

"Enough. What's this about a WMD?"

"Hawthorne said the threat was real."

"I heard the audio from the cafeteria," Carmen said firmly. "Do you believe him?"

"Yes, I do. Absolutely."

"Why is that?"

"Gut feeling. Look, I know what the code says," said Wilder. "Someone's planning an attack on US soil."

"Lies." Carmen dismissed him. "Do you have any idea how many unsubstantiated threats our country receives on a daily basis? Why is this time any different?"

"I don't know," said Wilder.

"You gave Hawthorne Professor Singh's code—plus a time, place and location."

Wilder said, "San Pedro Bay, off Long Beach."

"Do you really think terrorists are trying to bomb LA?"

"I do. This could be a nuclear meltdown."

She scoffed, "Give me a damn break, will you?"

Carmen repeated all the same questions from the first interrogation. Wilder answered consistently. Late afternoon, a man walked into the room and gave Wilder a meal. Wilder ate ravenously. The man whispered some things to Carmen and she nodded.

Carmen said, "My superiors are taking you into CIA protective custody for further questioning. And you and I . . . we aren't done yet." The man pulled out a pair of handcuffs.

Wilder groaned, "Those things are really painful."

"Wait," said Carmen. "Give us another minute."

"Of course, Miss Jefferson."

"I'm against this," Carmen said, "but it came from higher up. You get one phone call." She reached into her inside breast pocket and pulled out a cell phone. She dialed a number and handed him the phone.

"Hello?" It was Wilder's best friend, Chuck.

"Hey, boss."

Chuck was in distress. "Wilder is that you? Are you alright?"

"I'm fine."

"Holy crap, dude, you're all over the news. Where are you?"

"In CIA custody at the police station," said Wilder.

"The news says somebody tried to kill you?"

"A couple times, yeah," said Wilder.

"What the hell have you gotten yourself into man? Wait—don't tell me, I don't want to know."

"Chuck, listen," Wilder said. "No matter what happens, I want you to know—you're the best friend I ever had."

"You too." He choked up. "You're my best friend too."

"In case I never see you again . . ." said Wilder.

"Don't talk like that," said Chuck. "This whole thing is out of control, but whatever it is, I know you're on the right side."

"The feds don't see it that way."

Chuck said, "Dude, the internet is blowing up. Everyone has a different story about you. Nobody knows what's real."

"What are they saying?" asked Wilder.

"The media is calling you an innocent civilian, just a student who happened to be on campus when the feds got shot," said Chuck. "Some guy named Rex Hawthorne is on the run. He's a fucking Navy SEAL. Do you know that guy?"

"I met him before," said Wilder dryly.

"Wilder . . ." said Chuck. "Who *are* you?"

"I'm just me, boss."

"Well, you're in some serious shit, man."

"I figured that out already," said Wilder sarcastically.

Chuck said, "This woman with the FBI, her name is Kim Lee . . . they're calling her a hero."

"She's definitely a hero," said Wilder. "She saved my life."

"They say she was fighting an LA faction of the Global White Alliance. I thought GWA was a conspiracy," said Chuck. "Dude, you gotta tell them everything. Whatever happens, happens."

"I told them everything already," Wilder lied.

"Good," said Chuck. "They questioned me too, you know."

"Who did?"

"CIA."

"You talked, right?"

"Yeah," said Chuck in a dejected voice. "I'm an accomplice to your crimes."

"They can't pin anything on you," Wilder protested.

"They already have."

"I'm so sorry. I never meant for any of this to happen."

"I'm free for now," said Chuck. "You know what's really crazy? I already got guys from three different TV networks asking me for interviews. You're like instantly famous, dude."

Wilder asked, "You're not gonna interview, are you?"

Chuck answered, "My lawyer says that's a bad idea. He's some court-appointed asshole, but he's right on this one."

"No interviews," said Wilder. "Chuck, I'm guilty of some shit, but you're fucking innocent."

"They're gonna press charges on me."

"They can try," said Wilder. "But you're innocent."

"My lawyer says if I plead guilty and testify, I might avoid a sentence."

Carmen interrupted, "Time's up, Wilder."

Wilder clenched the phone with both hands. "Chuck, I gotta go. Try not to worry about me, OK?"

"Yeah, right," Chuck scoffed. "OK, man. I love you."

"I love you too," said Wilder. He hung up and an agent cuffed him. Wilder's eyes drooped sadly. He asked Carmen, "Where are you taking me?"

"CIA is taking you to a safe house. We need to ask you more questions," she said, "and we need you alive for that. Goodbye for now."

Agents led Wilder down a flight of stairs and into a parking garage. They loaded him into a van with tinted windows on all sides. The back of the van was set up like a paddy wagon with two benches on either side. Everyone climbed in.

The van drove a few blocks away from the station. One of the agents got Wilder into a headlock. Another man shoved a sock into Wilder's mouth and duct taped it shut. Wilder struggled to breathe through his nose. He screamed a muffled sound and his eyes bulged in panic. Someone pulled a black pillowcase over Wilder's head. They yanked him to the floor and zip-tied his ankles. He desperately struggled to get enough oxygen. Something struck the side of Wilder's head. He heard his skull crack and lost consciousness.

"Safe house, my ass," said one of the men.

40

THE BLACK SITE

Wilder lay on the floor of the van, tied and bound with a hood over his head. The tires squeaked and echoed as they drove through a parking garage. The van went down several floors. His captors climbed out, tugging Wilder by the handcuffs and pushing him to walk. The men ushered him through several metal doors that loudly slammed behind them. Someone shoved Wilder to his knees and pulled the hood off his head.

Two white men stood over Wilder—one was short and the other man was fat. The short one ripped off the duct tape and pulled the sock out of Wilder's mouth. He said, "Don't bother yelling. No one will hear you."

The fat man said, "Uncuff him. Let's put him in the cage." They shoved Wilder in a cramped wire crate. He tried to sit up but his head hit the ceiling.

"Welcome to your luxury suite!" the short man said with a chuckle.

The fat man put his face up close to the cage. He had welts of acne on his peaked face. He smiled with charred, chipped front teeth—the mouth of a crack addict. "Hellooo there, I'm Simon. This is my associate Bobby. We're gonna get to know each other real close like."

"Let me out of here," said Wilder.

"I'm afraid I can't do that," said Simon. "Why dontcha settle into your new home? We'll pay ya a visit later on." They fist-bumped each other and left the room.

Wilder slumped forward, shivering and hugging his knees. It was cold and damp. His eyes scanned the room—all concrete, about fifty by one hundred feet. The overhead fluorescent lights flickered. There were empty cages next to Wilder's. Shower heads and a fire hose hung on the far wall, next to plastic industrial-sized laundry bins. There were gurneys in the corner, a stack of folded chairs and a garbage can.

Wilder heard the door unlock, and the torturer Simon walked back in with a plate of spaghetti and meatballs. He pulled up a chair in front of Wilder's cage. "Hungry?" Simon asked.

"Yes," said Wilder.

"That's too bad," said Simon. He twisted his fork in the spaghetti and took a big bite. "*Mmmm-mmm*," he mocked. "This is delicious, but I just ate." Simon tossed the plate into the garbage can and left the room.

Each passing minute was like an eternity. Wilder sobbed, fearing this was the end.

Hours later, Simon and Bobby led another hooded captive into the room. Wilder saw the shell-top Adidas and woman's frame, and he immediately knew who it was. The men pulled off her hood.

"Oh Jesus, Kim!" Wilder cried. "They got you too?" Her face was cut and bruised, and her eyes looked empty. They ripped the duct tape off her mouth and locked her inside the cage next to Wilder.

Wilder clung his fingers against the cage and asked, "Are you OK?"

"Stupid question," she said with a hollow shred of humor. "Of course I'm not OK."

"What are they going to do to us?" asked Wilder.

Kim said, "I don't know . . . Try to break us I guess."

"Like torture?"

"Yeah," she said. "If you have to shit, go in your shoes."

"In my shoes?"

"Yeah, otherwise you're gonna end up lying in it."

"I am not shitting in my shoes," said Wilder.

Kim said, "Maybe they'll give us receptacles, but I wouldn't count on it." She leaned against the side of the cage and hung her head. She knew all too well about the torture playbook they could be facing.

"So you're FBI, huh?" Wilder asked her.

"Yeah," she said. "Your computer programming was too good—it raised alarms across teams at the agency. Our engineers traced your robbery scheme with offshore bank accounts, and they worried what else you were capable of."

"I'm capable of way more than that," he said.

"That's evident," Kim said. "I signed up to get close to you, and being your provider was an easy fit—all of which brings us here. A black site. To be tortured."

"I'm sorry."

"You're only sorry you got caught," she said. "Didn't it ever cross your mind that I gave you the flip phone as a monitoring device?"

Wilder felt stupid. "Somehow it never occurred to me."

She shook her head. "I always knew you were too cocky. Sooner or later it was gonna get you killed."

Wilder remembered the video of the Morocco massacre and the code. "I'm gonna die knowing the evidence," Wilder lamented. "It was all for nothing."

"Try to conserve your energy," advised Kim.

"Are they just gonna leave us here in these cages?" asked Wilder. "Like animals?"

"Probably."

"Where are we?"

"Somewhere no one can find us," said Kim.

"Oh God." Wilder started to hyperventilate. "Kim, I can't take this."

"Shut it," she said. "I've been beaten. Not exactly in the mood to process your feelings."

"I am so sorry," said Wilder, overcome with guilt. They sat and stared blankly into space.

Simon walked in and Bobby followed him carrying a rope. They pulled up three chairs. Bobby unlocked Wilder's cage. "Come on out, don't be shy." Wilder slowly crawled out of his cage and stood up.

Simon yelled, "Why do you hate your country so much?" He punched Wilder in the stomach and kneed him in the head. Wilder fell over and Bobby dragged him onto a chair, strapping him tightly to it with the rope.

Simon teased, "You're not even going to fight back?"

Bobby giggled. "Prolly not a good idea to fight back."

Wilder groaned in pain.

Simon again yelled, "Why do you hate your country so much? When did you join the enemy?"

Wilder stuttered, "I-I'm not the enemy."

Simon punched Wilder in the nose and blood poured down the front of his shirt. Simon said, "Why do you hate America, huh?"

"I don't hate America," said Wilder.

Bobby kicked the chair over and Wilder bounced on the concrete. Bobby kicked his ribs and head a few times, untied him and dragged him back into his cage.

Kim had the same round of questions and beating. They shoved her back into her cage. Simon dug in his pocket and pulled out two rolled-up garbage bags, shoving one through the wires of each cage.

"What's this for?" asked Wilder.

Simon smiled. "Well, don't try to kill yourself with it. We won't let you do that."

Bobby was gleeful. "That's your widdle night-night blankie."

Simon ordered Bobby, "Alright, feed them!"

Bobby went and fetched some Tupperware containers. He scooped brown glop with his hand and shoved the food through small doors in their cages. "Dinner is served," he said, and laughed.

For days on end, Kim and Wilder were stuck in their cages. They were dehydrated, starving and terrified. The room was so cold they spent most of the time in their plastic bags. To count the days, Kim reached through the bars and scraped marks on the wall. She counted a week but time stopped making sense.

The anxiety gave Wilder migraines. "Why don't they just kill us?"

Kim said, "They will eventually, but there's worse torture coming."

Bobby set up a strobe light in front of them and turned off the overhead fluorescents. They blasted heavy metal on a repeating loop from ceiling speakers. Wilder and Kim went three days without sleeping and they both cracked. Wilder hallucinated that he was a newborn baby being cryogenically frozen as part of an experiment. Kim still knew where she was but feared she had gone irretrievably insane.

Finally the music stopped and the overhead lights came back on. Simon and Bobby walked in. Simon ordered, "If the prisoners are still alive, feed them." Wilder and Kim each got a slice of bread with a bottle of water. With a shred of human dignity designed only to prolong the torture, Simon promised he would let them sleep.

Hours later, Kim and Wilder awoke to the door opening and slamming shut. A white man in a suit walked to the far corner of the room. He set up an old-school handheld video camera on a tripod. Another figure appeared in the doorway. Wilder squinted to see and gasped. It was Katya. Stone-faced, she paced across the room.

Wilder cried, "Katya? No, no, you can't be part of this."

"Long time no see," she said with indifference. "The circumstances certainly have changed, haven't they?" She pulled some lipstick from her purse, applied it and popped her lips.

"Katya, help us!" Wilder pleaded and banged on his cage.

"There is no help for you," she said, pulling up a chair and fixing her bangs in her makeup mirror.

"Why are you doing this?" asked Wilder.

Katya answered, "You have no idea who I am."

"I thought I knew you," said Wilder.

"My name really is Katya—that much is true."

"You're a double agent," said Wilder.

Katya said, "It's more complicated than that, Wilder."

"Tell me then," said Wilder. "You owe me that."

Katya spat on the floor. "I owe you nothing. But since you asked, I once was a covert operative helping the Russian Naval Spetsnaz. And now I serve the Global White Alliance."

"You're with Russian Spec Ops?"

"Yes. But I don't work for Russia anymore," Katya said.

"I bet you know Sergei Podkopaev," said Wilder. "Hawthorne killed him."

"I know the intel," Katya said plainly. "Hopefully I can thank Hawthorne personally someday. I always hated Sergei and only wish I had killed him myself."

The man in the suit finished setting up the camera and stood beside Katya. "Wilder Kole . . . you are quite the mischievous son of a bitch, aren't you?"

"Why do I recognize you?" asked Wilder.

"That's Arnold Renfree," said Kim.

Wilder remembered. "Renfree?"

"Yours truly," he said. "Nice to meet you again. Sorry it's not as comfortable here as the country club."

"You white nationalist motherfucker," Kim said. "You're running a domestic terror cell."

Renfree said, "*Shh.* Don't give it away—that would spoil the fun." He motioned to Katya. "Get me a latte, would you?"

"Get your own fucking latte," snapped Katya. Renfree raised his finger as a warning. Katya scoffed and dialed her cell phone. She put it on speaker and said, "Simon, get the boss a latte."

"That's better," said Renfree smugly.

"What kind of latte?" said Simon through the phone.

Renfree said, "Sixteen-ounce nonfat with extra vanilla and no foam."

"Did you hear that?" Katya asked.

Simon said, "Right away, sir. Ma'am. Whatever."

"Get me a cranberry muffin," Katya said. "And come back with our other friend." She hung up and gave Renfree the middle finger without looking at him.

41
UNDERWATER

Renfree mounted a handheld video camera on a tripod. He hit Record, walked up to Kim's cage and kicked it. "Kim Lee. Our little hero with the FBI. I'm going to enjoy killing you."

"Rot in hell," said Kim.

Renfree looked at Katya and asked, "Should we try and get them to talk?"

"Your call," said Katya.

"There's nothing to say," said Kim.

"There isn't?" Renfree chuckled.

Wilder declared, "It was *you* who sold the nuke to the enemy. Just so you could turn around and bomb the US. You're pulling the strings on this whole damn thing, aren't you?"

Renfree puffed his chest proudly. "Why yes, yes I am."

"Why? Why are you doing it?" asked Wilder.

Renfree asked, "Do you simply hate America, Wilder?"

"No. Why do you guys keep asking that?"

"Well I do. I *hate* the America we see today. Our country has forgotten who we really are. We have grown weak."

"You fucking scumbag," said Kim.

Renfree said, "We're going to take this country back."

"What's your lunatic plan?" asked Wilder.

Renfree said, "I'll tell you—because it will make your death all the more agonizing."

Wilder said, "Killing us won't change anything, you bastard. Your plan will fail."

"You sure have a mouth on you, son," said Renfree. "You should show more respect."

"Would it make any difference?" Wilder asked.

"No," said Renfree, and he smiled. "No, it wouldn't. But I do like talking about the nuke, so I'm glad you asked. We sold it for a *lot* of money. The sale didn't go too well because Hawthorne and his SEALs blew up our plan, along with a ten-wheeler carrying fifteen billion dollars. We got the bomb, though. That's what really matters."

"*Who* got the bomb?" asked Wilder.

"We did," said Katya. She was listening while looking at her phone.

"Who's we?" asked Kim.

Renfree said, "The New Americans of the GWA. Our Russian and Al Qaeda friends were part of it, but we were going to kill most of them anyway. Hawthorne's team beat us to it, so at least he made that part easier for us."

"Did you say *New Americans*?" asked Wilder.

Renfree growled, "It's a new era for this country. The true rise of White Power is here, and we're going to bomb LA to take our country back."

"Go ahead and try," Kim said, and spat at him.

Katya retorted, "You stinking, low-life Chinese. You're not a real American. How did you even get in the FBI?"

Kim said, "I was born in LA and this is my fucking country."

"Damn right," said Wilder. "Fuck you, Katya."

"Your plan is gonna fail," said Kim. "Your whole sick vision is gonna crumble."

Renfree said, "You're wrong about that. Our guys are going undetected on a ship heading right to the Port of Long Beach. We've got just two days before . . . *Boom!*"

Wilder said, "It's just like Professor Singh's code said."

Katya smiled and did her lashes. "He led me to everything. I had no idea it would be so easy."

"You goddamn psychopaths," said Kim. "New Americans? Bombing ourselves?"

Renfree snarled, "A truly white America is coming. The time is finally here. If LA is what it costs to have that, who gives a fuck? As it stands, this shithole city represents everything wrong with America as we know it. So many Latinos, blacks, Asians, queers—it's disgusting is what it is."

"We're what makes this city great," said Kim.

Renfree scoffed. "Know what else? All this socialist BS talk about racial equality and justice—it makes me want to puke. When we watch LA burn to the ground in a nuclear hellfire, all that commie Hollywood crap is gonna burn with it."

Wilder said, "Your plan is white supremacy and fascism? That's your New America?"

"Exactly," said Renfree. "We drop the bomb and blame it on China. Of course the US has to strike back, right? We're gonna win World War III. We need this war to start now, and we need America behind us—even if the people don't get the White Power thing yet."

"You're completely insane!" yelled Wilder.

"Sociopathic, yes. Insane, not so much," said Renfree.

Kim protested, "It won't work. Whether you bomb LA or not, the truth will come out. Americans will find out the GWA is the real enemy."

Renfree said, "In that case, we will have a civil war on our hands, and GWA will win that too. Same outcome eventually, so who really cares?"

"Who cares?" asked Wilder incredulously. "I fucking care."

Renfree looked at Katya and asked, "Where's my latte?"

"Don't look at me," said Katya. "I told Simon."

"It better not be cold when it gets here," Renfree said.

On cue, Simon walked in and delivered the latte and muffin. Then he yelled through the open door, "Bobby, bring in the next captive!"

Bobby dragged a man across the floor. His face was so badly beaten that Wilder could barely recognize his own best friend.

"Chuck!" cried Wilder. "Oh God no!"

Chuck looked helplessly at Wilder.

Wilder said, "I'm so, so sorry. I'm the one who got you into this."

Chuck muttered, "It's OK. You didn't know."

Renfree said, "Alright, enough with the reunion. Put them on the boards."

At Renfree's command, Bobby put Chuck in a headlock and pulled him toward one of the gurneys. The other captor, Simon, forced Chuck onto his back and strapped him onto the board. Buckles clanked and they bound him face up in the fetal position.

"Fill the tubs!" Simon barked at Bobby.

Bobby pushed three plastic laundry bins against the wall underneath the showerheads. He turned the knobs and began filling each tub with water. Simon yanked Kim out of her cage. They constrained her on a gurney board next to Chuck, and Wilder came next, strapped so tightly he couldn't budge an inch.

Wilder looked at Kim. "What are they doing?"

"Waterboarding us," she said.

Renfree looked at the video cassette to make sure it was still recording. "Simon, is this a fresh tape?"

"Yessir," said Simon. "It's got two hours on it."

Renfree said, "That's more time than we need for these three." He sipped the last of his latte and threw the cup on the floor. "Somebody pick that up."

Katya rolled her eyes angrily. "Pick it up yourself, asshole."

Renfree said, "You are such a bitch. I admire that about you."

Katya paced anxiously back and forth. She did not like torture. It gave her bad memories.

Eyes gleaming, Renfree said, "God, I love waterboarding. You'll be on the brink of death, over and over. You're drowning like rats in my laboratory."

"Go fuck yourself," said Kim.

Renfree pulled the tripod and camera over to the waterboard station. "Simon, how long is it going to take to fill these bins with water?"

"Just a minute."

Katya wiped a tear from her eye. She sat facing away, crossed her legs and distracted herself on her cell phone.

Kim asked her, "You've been tortured before, haven't you?" Katya said nothing, but her face betrayed her feelings. She was once a prisoner of war.

Wilder pleaded, "Katya, you know this is wrong. It's not too late! Help us!"

She answered flatly, "Long live the Global White Alliance."

Renfree said, "You're damn right."

Katya's hands trembled. She dug in her purse for a piece of gum.

"Hang 'em up!" Renfree laughed. Simon and Bobby pushed the gurneys over to the tubs. Renfree insisted, "Put Wilder in the middle so he has the best view. Torture his friends first." They hoisted the boards onto hooks above the tubs. Wilder, Kim and Chuck hung suspended, looking down at the water in terror.

"Chuck is innocent!" screamed Wilder. "Torture me and let him go!"

Renfree said, "It is far, far too late for that, Wilder."

"I'll tell you everything," said Wilder.

"There's nothing to tell anymore," said Renfree. "All I want is for you to suffer unimaginable pain. And then, after a while, I'll let you die."

"You sick motherfucker," Kim said. "You can kill us, but your plan to bomb LA will fail."

Renfree ran a finger down Kim's cheek. "Imagine the mushroom cloud. People's skin melting from the bone, hundreds of thousands dead in an instant. Farther from the blast, millions more suffering radiation poisoning . . . It's really too bad you won't be around to see it."

"You will never take down our country!" Kim said.

"And this is only phase one," Renfree said, smiling. "Things will get worse after that."

Kim closed her eyes in dread, and prayed, "In the name of God, help me, Jesus."

"Oh, so you call yourself a Christian?" asked Renfree.

"A real Christian," said Kim.

Renfree's face turned purple, a vein bulging on his forehead. "Jesus Christ is MY savior, not yours!" he yelled. "It's God's will that the Aryan race reign supreme, in America and worldwide!"

Katya moved her chair by the door and turned away from them. Renfree walked over and put his hand on her shoulder. He asked, "What's the matter, Katya? Aren't you going to watch?"

"I don't need to," Katya said. "I know what happens next."

Renfree walked back toward his victims. "Are the tubs full?"

Bobby said, "Full enough, sir."

Simon turned off the water and said, "I love this part."

"Who's first?" Bobby asked.

Renfree said, "Put the Chinese girl under, and Wilder's best friend, too."

Bobby said, "It might be hard to pull 'em both up in time."

"So what?" Renfree sneered. "Try not to let them die right away, but whatever happens, happens."

Simon and Bobby unhooked the board holding Kim. "You won't get away with this," she said, and they submerged her in the water. They hustled over to Chuck and unhooked his board.

"No! No!" yelled Chuck. They dropped him in the water and Wilder looked away in agony.

Simon and Bobby hoisted Kim out of the water. She coughed and gasped, and they put the board back on the hook.

Wilder exclaimed, "Chuck is drowning! Get him out!"

Renfree laughed. "You heard the man. Get him out."

They pulled up Chuck and hung his board on the hook. His head was limp. His body twitched and his eyes sprung open. Chuck vomited water, choking for air.

Renfree said, "That was really, really close to dead. Good job, fellas."

Katya turned around in her chair, forcing a grin. "Who's next?" she asked.

Renfree said, "Wilder, of course."

"We can't let him miss out on the fun," Katya said without emotion. She was disassociating because of her PTSD. She pushed through the dizziness and slowly applauded.

Renfree asked, "Any last words, Wilder?"

"For the love of God, don't do this," begged Wilder.

"Well if the love of God won't save you," said Renfree, "then it's God's will that you die."

"You're the devil," said Kim.

Suddenly, machine-gun fire erupted from another room. Renfree and his henchmen looked utterly confused.

Katya grabbed her Glock 19. "Renfree, get behind me."

He cowered behind Katya, and Simon and Bobby drew pistols from their belts.

The door flew open and Hawthorne rushed in with an M249 SAW. Simon and Bobby fired. Bullets hit the wall around Hawthorne. He sprayed them with machine-gun fire and the two men fell dead.

"What took you so long?" Katya asked Hawthorne. She spun around and pointed her Glock at Renfree.

"Don't shoot. I-I'm defenseless," he said.

"You die," said Katya, unloading two shots in his chest. Renfree's knees buckled and he collapsed in a heap. Blood poured out of his mouth and he writhed in pain.

Renfree whispered with a gurgle, "White Power." Katya emptied her clip and his head exploded like a pumpkin.

Katya said, "That's the first person I ever enjoyed killing."

"Help!" cried Wilder.

Hawthorne said, "Let's get them down."

Hawthorne and Katya hoisted down all three of them, unstrapping them from the boards. As Wilder and Chuck staggered to their feet, Kim scampered to Simon's body, grabbing his pistol. She pointed it toward the exit and moved swiftly.

"Get the camera," said Hawthorne. Katya yanked it off the tripod and they fled. Kim and Katya took the lead, Wilder and Chuck followed and Hawthorne was the last man out.

They ran past the bodies of people Hawthorne killed storming the black site. They got into the garage and the group stood there alone.

Adrenaline surging and shivering with fear, Wilder and Chuck hugged. Hawthorne handed them each a pistol. "We're gonna have company. Shoot to kill."

Katya reloaded her clip and said, "Wilder, I'm sorry. I was deep cover. This is war."

Wilder asked, "Why do I hate you so much and still love you?"

"Talk later," said Hawthorne.

"Where's your ride?" Kim asked.

Hawthorne pointed. "My motorcycle will fit three of us, max."

Katya pointed at a convertible. "I'll take that car. Wilder, come with me."

"Do it," said Hawthorne.

Katya and Wilder climbed into the car. She said, "Alarm's off—that's lucky." She ripped apart the ignition lock assembly, touched two wires together and hotwired the engine. Katya squeezed Wilder's thigh. "Cool, right?"

"Totally," Wilder said. "You're back to being hot as hell again. Get us out of here."

Hawthorne saddled onto the motorcycle, with Chuck in the middle and Kim on back. He yelled, "Katya! Follow me!"

42
RUN

Hawthorne throttled the gas on the motorcycle, speeding up to ground level with Chuck and Kim holding on tight. Katya followed them in the stolen convertible with Wilder by her side. He stared at the pistol in his hand. "I don't know how to use this."

Katya turned off the safety and handed it back. "Point and shoot."

As Hawthorne approached the street, two SUVs pulled up and blocked the exit lanes. It was feds working for the GWA. Hawthorne stopped the bike and swiftly assessed. "Chuck, fire left, Kim, fire right! And hold on!"

Hawthorne hit the throttle and the motorcycle peeled full speed ahead. Federal agents leaned out of the SUVs' windows and fired gunshots. A bullet whizzed past Hawthorne's head and another two ripped into his bulletproof vest. Kim fired multiple shots into one of the SUV's windshields. Return fire ripped into Chuck's thigh. He screamed in pain and dropped his pistol.

In a split second, Hawthorne weaved and straightened the motorcycle. With only inches of clearance, Hawthorne ripped the bike between the SUVs. The motorcycle caught air and landed in the street. Hawthorne made an out-of-control wide turn, careening onto the sidewalk and narrowly missing a telephone pole. He stopped to look back and the motorcycle's engine died.

"The bike is stalling!" said Hawthorne.

"My leg! I'm hit!" cried Chuck.

"Get us out of here!" said Kim.

"Hold on!" said Hawthorne, but he couldn't restart the engine.

The SUVs lurched into reverse, swinging around in the street to face them. Kim fired several more rounds and emptied the pistol's chamber.

Katya's convertible came flying out of the garage, T-boning the SUVs and smashing them together with a loud metallic crunch. The front end of the convertible crumpled severely, shattering the windshield into pieces. Katya pulled away. "Shoot, Wilder, shoot!"

Wilder fired shots at the SUVs and the feds fired back. Bullets ripped into the convertible's hood and interior, narrowly missing them both. Katya floored it and turned down a narrow side street.

Finally, Hawthorne got the motorcycle started again. "Yes!" He followed Katya and the SUVs were right on their tail. Hawthorne handed Kim a grenade. "Throw it!" he yelled.

Kim pulled the pin and hurled the grenade behind her. It bounced on the concrete. The SUV in closest pursuit drove over it and the grenade blew. The explosion lifted the vehicle off the ground and the engine erupted. Flames engulfed the SUV and it rolled into a parked car. The vehicle behind it was blocked by the flaming wreck.

A man on fire ran out of the SUV. He dropped to his knees and fell over dead. Another explosion erupted from inside the vehicle. The second SUV did a U-turn to route around the crash.

Moments later, Katya hit the brakes and Hawthorne's motorcycle pull up next to them.

"Katya, the bike's dying!" said Hawthorne. "Make room!" Hawthorne climbed into the convertible and stood on the middle console. He reloaded the magazine in his SAW. Chuck leaned on Kim and limped toward the car in agony. Kim hopped onto the trunk and hoisted Chuck into the tiny back seat. He wailed in pain.

"Chuck, are you shot?" asked Wilder.

"My leg!" yelled Chuck. "It hurts so bad."

"Go!" yelled Kim.

Katya punched the gas.

"Wait—is today Saturday?" asked Wilder.

"Who fucking cares?" Kim asked.

"Yeah, it's Saturday," Katya said. "Why?"

"We're in the warehouse district. Keep going straight."

"I know what you're thinking," said Kim.

"There's a rave tonight for sure," said Wilder.

"And?" asked Katya.

"There's safety in numbers. Take us to the rave," said Wilder.

"He's right," said Hawthorne. "The feds will be swarming us."

"Bad idea," Katya said. "But I don't have a better one."

"Wilder, which way?" asked Hawthorne.

"Take a left!" said Wilder. As they turned the corner, the second SUV caught sight of them. Katya sped past a long line of people standing on the sidewalk. She pulled up to the rave entrance and slammed on the brakes.

"How do we get in?" asked Wilder.

"Ask nicely," said Kim.

"We have guns," said Hawthorne.

They all jumped out of the convertible. Chuck was limping badly. Kim threw his arm around her shoulders. Someone yelled, "That dude is bleeding." A dozen people took video on their cell phones as the chaos unfolded.

Hawthorne waved his rifle and the bouncers ducked. "Don't shoot!" Everyone followed Hawthorne in and they ran through the dancing crowd. The music's bass boomed and laser lights flashed. A bouncer watched them disappear into the sea of people. He dialed 9-1-1 and said, "This party just became a battle zone."

The shot-up SUV pulled up, followed by several more cars. Federal agents held up badges, yelling, "FBI! Out of the way!" A SWAT team filed out of an armored vehicle.

Hawthorne and the gang shoved their way through a pit of dancing ravers. Kim yelled ahead, "Chuck is losing too much blood! I have to fix this gunshot wound." She carried Chuck into the women's bathroom and laid him on the ground.

A group of young women screamed, and all but one teenager ran out. She asked, "Did someone shoot that guy?"

"Yes," said Kim.

"Oh my God," she said. "You have a gun."

"Give me your jacket," Kim said.

"Why?"

"He's gonna bleed to death. I have to tie his leg off."

Struck with fear, the young woman sheepishly shook her head.

Kim said, "I'm FBI. Help me save this man's life."

The young woman gave Kim her jacket. Kim told her, "Somebody out there will give you another jacket. Give me your phone and purse too."

"OK. Just don't shoot."

"Password?" Kim asked.

"Two thousand five," said the woman.

"Is that the year you were born?" asked Kim. "Jeez, you're a baby."

"You didn't have to rob me," she said.

"You'll get your stuff back. Chuck, this is gonna hurt."

"Don't let me die," said Chuck.

"Not on my watch," said Kim. She ripped a sleeve off the jacket and tied a knot above the bullet wound. Chuck screamed.

Kim said, "Give me your ball cap too."

The woman had enough and stomped her foot, throwing the Dodgers hat on the ground. She stormed out of the women's restroom. Kim put the hat on and told Chuck, "For the record, I'm a Giants fan."

Kim dialed a number.

"Hello?" her cousin Kai answered.

"Kai, I'm in deep shit. Come get me."

"Kim?" he asked. "Where are you?"

"I'm texting you my address. Hurry up." Kim pulled up Google Maps and found a nearby rendezvous. "We're at a rave next to a furniture warehouse called Andy's. Meet me on the corner of Third and Jackson."

"OK, I'm on my way," said Kai. "My food truck isn't that fast, though."

"Just get there," said Kim. "Watch out, the feds are all over us."

He pulled up the address on his phone and said, "You're lucky I'm close by. Gimme ten minutes."

Kim hoisted Chuck and he clung to her shoulders as they headed out of the bathroom. With him grimacing in agony, she hurried them along the periphery of dancers. The crowd got thicker. "Coming through," said Kim, bumping into people.

"What are we doing?" asked Chuck.

"I know this building. There's a men's lounge with a basement exit," said Kim.

On the other side of the crowd, Wilder was thinking the same thing. He showed Hawthorne and Katya the way. Their path converged with Kim and Chuck, and the gang was reunited. Everyone hugged for a moment, then kept moving toward the back exit.

Behind them, the SWAT team closed in, but they kept losing their sight lines. Feds were shutting down the party, but music kept blasting anyway.

The gang got to the middle of the main stage and Hawthorne hoisted everyone up. Two bouncers closed in, and Hawthorne knocked one of them out with one punch. The other bouncer backed off. Hawthorne and the crew ran across the stage and it bought them time.

"This way!" yelled Wilder.

Everyone's adrenaline was surging and Chuck looked bad.

Kim bumped into a dealer friend of hers wearing a glow-stick necklace, and she asked him, "What do you have?"

"What the hell happened to you?"

"Don't ask," said Kim.

"I have some awesome molly. Pure MDMA."

Kim fished two hundred dollars out of the stolen purse. She said, "Fine. Got anything faster to go with it?"

"I got Oxy," said the dealer. "You could crush it up."

"Gimme the Oxy too." Kim paid and gave the pills to Chuck. "Take these. Chew them well before you swallow."

The crew made it to the men's lounge, and once again Hawthorne pointed his rifle. The bouncer put his hands up and jumped out of the way. Hawthorne demanded, "Show me the exit," and the bouncer pointed sheepishly to the back. The crew climbed a half flight of stairs and busted through a doorway.

They stood in a dark alley.

Kim said, "My cousin's on his way to get us."

Hawthorne said, "That alone won't work. We have to split up again."

"OK," said Katya.

Chuck moaned in pain.

Hawthorne asked, "Kim, do you still have the camera?"

"Yes, it's in this purse."

Hawthorne said, "Great, find a way to make sure that video goes public. Stay with Chuck if you can. Where's your cousin's ride?"

Kim pointed to the left. Hawthorne nodded and started heading in the other direction. He motioned for Katya and Wilder to come with him. Hawthorne paused and said, "Hey, Kim. You're one hell of a soldier."

Kim said, "I saved your life, and you saved mine."

"I guess we're even," said Hawthorne.

"This shit ain't over," said Kim.

Hawthorne said, "Go!"

They hurried in opposite directions. Kim and Chuck somehow made it to the corner outside of the furniture store without being noticed by anyone.

Kim found a dumpster. "Get in," she said. They climbed inside. She shut the lid, peering out of a crack to keep a lookout for the food truck.

Chuck said, "I feel warm all over. The Oxy is working."

At a different intersection, Hawthorne, Katya and Wilder ran into the street. A black SUV pulled to a stop in front of them. "Feds," said Hawthorne. He pointed his rifle at the driver and Katya took aim on the passenger side. The two men inside were caught off guard, and they got out slowly with their hands up.

Hawthorne commanded, "Firearms and cell phones, now!" The agents handed them over.

Katya and Wilder climbed into the SUV and Hawthorne took the wheel. They sped away, and the agents stood in the street cussing.

They maneuvered through traffic and pulled away from the wild scene unfolding in the warehouse streets. Hawthorne pitched the cell phones out the window.

Wilder said, "I can't believe this is happening."

Katya asked, "What now?"

Hawthorne said, "We switch vehicles. I know a place in Santa Monica." He got on the interstate and drove in and out of traffic at a hundred miles an hour. The SUV screeched down an exit, smashing against a guardrail.

Hawthorne said, "This engine has power but the handling sucks."

Katya said, "You drive like a man who's done this before."

Wilder held on for dear life. "Don't die, don't die," he said to himself.

Hawthorne pulled up in front of an auto body shop. He shattered the office door window with his elbow, kicked out the broken glass and climbed through. The alarm sounded. Hawthorne typed numbers on the alarm pad and the ringing stopped.

Katya and Wilder stood there a moment looking impressed, then followed him through the door. Hawthorne grabbed a set of keys off a hook in the garage, pushed a button on the key fob and a silver Maserati started its engine. "That will do just fine," said Hawthorne.

He filled a shop sink with water and threw in the computer tower connected to the surveillance system. He opened the garage door. "Y'all lie down in the back seat."

Wilder climbed in first and Katya lay down on top of him. Hawthorne drove to Highway 10 and headed east.

"Holy Moses," said Wilder. "We're getting away."

43

THE NEWS AND MANHUNT

Kim peeked out of the dumpster as her cousin Kai pulled up in his food truck. Droves of ravers filled the streets walking back to their cars. Federal agents searched the warehouse and checked people at the exits. There were too many people for the feds to manage an organized dragnet.

Kim threw open the lid of the dumpster. "My cousin's here! Chuck, get ready."

"Ready," he said.

They tumbled out of the dumpster. Kai's belly jiggled as he ran around the back of the food truck to open the doors. He saw Chuck's leg and said, "That's a lot of blood. How much trouble are you in?"

"A shitload," said Kim. "Get us out of here."

Kai drove away, and a police car pulled him over. "Oh no!" he said. Kai stepped out and lied that he was selling food outside of the rave and had been instructed to leave. The police officer told him it was a crime scene and to get out of the neighborhood.

Back on the road, Kai said, "That was too close! Kim, we gotta get him to a hospital."

"No hospital!" said Kim.

Chuck begged, "Just take me to the ER and drop me off."

Kim said, "No. There's something we have to do. You work at Channel 7—on La Cienega and South Fairfax, right?" Chuck nodded. Kim shouted, "Kai, take the 405 to the 90 and get us to La Cienega."

"I'm on it!" said Kai.

"How do you know where I work?" asked Chuck.

"I'm FBI," said Kim. "I know a lot more about you than that."

It dawned on Chuck. "Are you thinking to play that videotape live on air?"

Kim nodded. "Can you do that for me?"

Chuck said, "Technically, yes. But even if we get to the live edit room, they'll never let us air it."

"Leave that to me," said Kim.

Chuck laughed, then winced in pain. "What's another crime on top of all the other crimes we already committed? Maybe if I bleed to death, I won't end up in jail anyway."

Kim clapped back, "None of this matters if LA gets nuked!"

Chuck said, "How do you know the nuclear threat is real?"

Kim had lost patience with people not getting it. "It's fucking real, Chuck! This is really happening."

"Then we're all going to hell," Chuck said.

Kim said, "Focus. I promise I'll get you out alive. You'll be a hero."

"What if I don't want to be a hero?"

"Would you rather be a coward in the very moment your country needed you?"

"OK, you're right," Chuck said. "I'm all the way in. I'm just in a lot of pain and really scared."

"Is the Oxy helping any?"

"A bit. Have any more?"

Kim gave him what she had left. Chuck chewed and swallowed it down.

"Take some deep breaths," said Kim. "Try to calm yourself."

The food truck bumped along and Kai switched freeways. From the 90 he took the exit at La Cienega. Chuck felt a pleasant wave in his body. "I think the Oxy and Molly just hit me at the same time."

"Good," said Kim. "It will help you have less fear."

"What's the plan?" asked Chuck.

"Whatever it takes, I get us to the newsroom and you put that tape on air."

Kai pulled into the parking lot. "We're here!"

Kim grabbed the camera and hoisted Chuck out of the truck. He pointed to a side entrance. At the door, Kim knocked and a security guard opened it. "Hi, Leroy," said Chuck. "Let us in."

"Chuck? What the hell happened to you?" Leroy asked.

Kim held the pistol under Leroy's chin. "You heard the man. Let us in."

Leroy burst into tears and wet himself. Chuck pulled the keys off his belt and pointed to the stairs. "Up," he said. Chuck leaned heavily on Kim and bounced on one leg up the stairs. Leroy ran out of the building and called the cops.

Kim waved her pistol at three more people on the way to the newsroom with the live edit console. The man at the switch hopped out of his chair and fled. Kim locked the door behind him. Chuck patched the camera with an HDMI cable and hit *Play*.

The torture cages and waterboard scene went live on the LA airwaves. It was a brutal scene and nobody watching it could look away. Renfree was fully in frame, spouting his vitriol. His tirade was mercilessly incriminating: "The true rise of White Power is here . . . and we're gonna watch this city burn to the ground in nuclear hellfire."

The news crew in the other room gasped. The footage rolled of Hawthorne bursting in and killing Renfree. Katya was in frame helping Hawthorne. The number of viewers skyrocketed to tens of thousands. Chuck let the whole video play back on live broadcast, including showing Hawthorne and Katya rescuing the waterboard victims.

"Are you sure that played live on air?" asked Kim.

"Positive," said Chuck. His eyes were glazed over and he smiled with pride.

Moments later, police officers kicked in the door to the

newsroom. "Drop your weapon!" yelled an officer. Kim dropped her pistol. "Hands where I can see them!"

The officers handcuffed Kim and Chuck. One of them looked at Chuck and said, "This man needs immediate medical attention."

"Take them to the prison hospital in Orange County," said the ranking officer. Moments later, Seahawk helicopters landed on the roof and Marines Special Forces swarmed the news station. Spec Ops outranked the police and seized Chuck and Kim. They restrained them and hauled them to the choppers, lifting off and flying toward Marine Corps Air Station Camp Pendleton.

The news broadcast of torture footage went viral internationally, and so did videos of the rave scene. By sunrise, US citizens and particularly people in LA were in total panic about the nuclear threat.

The White House press secretary issued a statement from the Pentagon, declaring the video was a deepfake with bold-faced lies designed to terrorize the American public. He assured everyone it was a false threat of a nuclear attack. He claimed Arnold Renfree was alive and well, on a hunting trip in the backwoods of Alaska. The press secretary repeated multiple times that there was no imminent nuclear or other danger to US citizens.

For the moment, the majority of Americans believed the official lie from the White House and Pentagon. But in LA, the highways were clogged with people fleeing the area. The nuclear threat, however implausible, completely terrorized everyone.

*

In the West Sitting Hall of the White House, with security flanking him, President Garner and the First Lady watched the video of Renfree torturing civilians, then Hawthorne breaking in and the murders. Garner was stunned.

"Renfree? How can it be? And this Hawthorne character... That's the same Navy SEAL at the center of the crisis in Morocco and on the run after the UCLA murders."

"I know, love," said his wife, Judy.

"Judy, I-I don't know what to do."

"Our people will know what to do, Henry," she said.

Garner said, "My intel says the kid Wilder Kole is just an amateur spy, can you believe that?"

"He doesn't look like an amateur," said Judy. "Sometimes even the best intel isn't right."

Garner continued, "The Russian woman, what is she—a triple agent? It's bad enough that we got Wilder Kole running with FBI, CIA and a Navy SEAL! And now this horrible murder scene—and a nuclear threat. And we can't interrogate Renfree about it because he's fucking dead!"

An hour later, Secretary of Defense Michael Tilford headed over from the Pentagon. He joined President Garner, now stationed at his desk in the Oval Office. Tilford was a lanky man with a buzz cut and a hard, clenched jaw. He had stellar credibility in the defense department.

Although the explosive video had caught Tilford off guard, there had been signs of an imminent threat in recent weeks. Tilford had made it his top priority to pass daily briefings to President Garner about the rising white supremacy movement—including the Global White Alliance. Until this week, he considered every hypothetical wartime scenario with the GWA to be extremely low probability.

"Mr. President, I know what you're asking yourself," said Tilford. "I can tell you definitively, the video of Arnold Renfree is real and he's dead."

"This is an absolute shit show," said Garner. "Very, very bad—and not just for my presidency. This endangers our country as we know it."

"That seems accurate," Tilford said. "My team has thought through different scenarios. We need to keep selling the video to the public as a deepfake. I advise you to do that, Mr. President."

"OK . . . then what?" asked Garner.

Tilford said, "Our best people are already working on a deepfake video of our own. We're creating a crash scene of a private seaplane in the Alaska backcountry. Renfree liked to hunt elk. The story is believable, and we have a library of never-seen footage mixed with AI content to work from."

Garner said, "This is what I call a 'good lie.' One worth making."

"I agree wholeheartedly," said Tilford. "If our country keeps inching toward the possibility of a civil war, one day an uprising could actually happen. We have to pour water on the idea."

Garner slammed his fist on his desk. "It's that damn White Prophecy movement. I knew I should have taken a firmer position on that. Well, tell me, what else do we have? The American public is in full panic mode. We need more."

"That's our assessment as well, Mr. President. We believe it's best to frame Navy SEAL Rex Hawthorne for this whole thing."

"Hawthorne?" asked Garner. "Is there any truth to it?"

"Not much, sir."

Garner said, "Well it does make sense. That's a good lie also. A Navy SEAL going psycho homicidal is very compelling."

"Agreed, Mr. President. We declare him a domestic terrorist."

Garner said, "You don't have to keep calling me Mr. President. It's annoying."

"OK, sir," Tilford said.

"Sir is fine," said Garner. "And this plan sounds good. Truthfully I fucking hate it, but it's the best we got, right?"

"It is. With Hawthorne, we've got a threat that matches people's fears. We blame the worst on Hawthorne and stick to that story."

"It fits," said Garner. "Please tell me there are still no leaks about the disaster in Morocco."

"No leaks whatsoever, sir," Tilford assured him. "It's a good thing our top soldiers were first to the crime scene."

"That cannot leak."

"All our men swore secrecy."

"Good," said Garner. "Imagine the hell that would break loose if that news got out. I mean, American soldiers lying dead next to Russian and Al Qaeda operatives? That's simply too much for anyone to handle."

"Agreed, sir."

"Christ, that intel is honestly terrifying—and I have seen some shit."

"That's understandable," said Tilford.

"I thought I was going to have a heart attack," said Garner. "My doc says I might have had a mild stroke."

"I hope not, sir."

"That stays in this room."

"Of course. And sir, I just want to validate—what happened in Morocco is scary stuff. We still don't have a theory we're satisfied with."

"What an absolute disaster," said Garner. "OK. Blame Hawthorne. My team will tell me what to say—and what not to say."

Tilford said, "I think it would be wise to let me be your primary spokesperson on this."

Garner nodded. "I'm gonna need a great speech on this one. Could take some time."

A half hour later, Tilford stood behind a curtain preparing to speak to the press corps. He gritted his teeth and nervously choked on a sip of water.

The White House press secretary exited the podium, and Tilford stepped up to the mic. He corroborated the lie that the torture video with Arnold Renfree was a deepfake. Tilford made Hawthorne the central character in a sensational story. Creating a diversion was the best move, and everybody loves a manhunt.

Tilford declared, "The Pentagon is on high alert—not because of this false nuclear threat—but because Navy SEAL Rex Hawthorne is an extremely dangerous domestic terrorist—wanted dead or alive." Tilford dramatized the lies and made accusations referencing nonexistent evidence.

Tilford recounted Hawthorne recently murdered his entire team of Navy SEALs overseas. He fled home to the US—paranoid and delusional, with extreme PTSD and heavily armed. Tilford said, "Hawthorne is a violent, psychotic and highly trained killer, last seen in the LA city limits. We don't know how many lives are at stake with a psychotic Navy SEAL on the run. It's an urgent matter of national security—we are hunting him down."

To further spin the lie that the video was a deepfake, Tilford declared Wilder and Katya to be Hawthorne's accomplices—also armed and dangerous. Tilford framed Katya as a Russian spy out to kill Americans. He claimed Wilder was a brainwashed computer genius helping Hawthorne. As part of the manhunt, Tilford announced the immediate deployment of the National Guard to capture or kill all three of them.

He dodged further questions from the press, citing the urgency of the military operation and the need to conserve every tactical advantage. Tilford called upon American citizens to assist in the national manhunt. "Help us catch the bad guys. This is a manhunt of unprecedented magnitude. If you can't join the manhunt, then do your best to go about your daily lives. I promise you this: We will find him."

44

SNAKE IN THE GRASS

Meanwhile, in a hospital room at Camp Pendleton, medics removed the bullet from Chuck's leg, saving it from amputation. As soon as Chuck sat up on the surgery table, feds began interrogating him about the live broadcast video. High but lucid, Chuck told the feds everything he knew. In another room and recovering from her own injuries, Kim was tended to by a physician and questioned. She corroborated Chuck's story and also told them everything she knew. Their stories held together, but the feds dismissed the plot to bomb LA as inconceivable.

Back at the White House, President Garner was now fully briefed and increasingly believed the nuclear threat. He secretly ordered every available team of elite Special Forces to LA, using National Guard deployment as cover for the operation.

That same evening, the president prepared to speak live from the Oval Office. "How do I look? Is there anything in my teeth?" He deliberated about what to say right up to the moment of going on air.

President Garner addressed the public with a sober, earnest tone. "An hour ago, I issued the order to launch the biggest manhunt on American soil in our nation's history."

Garner said Hawthorne's mind had snapped, creating an immediate danger to civilians, police and military. He discerned correctly that the public would not be able to handle any more truth about the WMD.

The president hurried to the Situation Room after he debriefed his speech with his chief of staff. Already inside with his elite team, Secretary of Defense Tilford rubbed the sides of his jaw and forehead. He was angry and tense. Two Secret Service officers flanked Garner along with his personal physician, who worried the president would have a stroke or heart attack. The commander in chief had been covering up some major health problems. He asked for Tilford's assessment and let him air his grievances.

Tilford said, "Here's what we know. Arnold Renfree is dead, and he played a key role in the American faction of the Global White Alliance. We've got a deepfake video of his death ready for release—and we must cover up the truth of how bad this situation is."

"Are we a hundred percent that the torture-murder video wasn't a deepfake itself?" asked the president.

Tilford fumed. "Things are rarely a hundred percent, but we're pretty damn close to it on this one." The president had no reply and simply blushed with a dazed look on his face.

Uri Nowak, Assistant Secretary of Defense for SO/LIC, walked into the Situation Room, tucking his clearance badge into his inside breast pocket. Nowak sat silently and shook his head with a frown. He used a handkerchief to polish the medals and decorations on the chest of his uniform.

What no one knew was that Nowak was the second head of the snake of the Global White Alliance. Now that Renfree was dead, he was the only head of the snake. Nowak was the one with the mysterious moniker *Karen*. He had waited a long time for the most damaging moment to reveal himself and strike. *Stay patient*, he thought to himself. *It's almost time*.

Tilford continued, "Mr. President, the Pentagon needs you to issue another executive order."

"What order?" asked Garner.

"Declare Hawthorne a nuclear threat and take us to DEFCON 1."

"That seems extreme," said Garner.

A vein bulged in Tilford's forehead. "Son of a bitch, Mr. President! What about this situation doesn't seem extreme to you?"

"I know you're right. But I just don't know . . ."

Tilford slammed his palm on the table. He was not done cussing at Garner. "Issue the goddamn executive order and stay out of the Pentagon's way! Then go home to the First Lady and that fucking shit dog of yours."

"Get ahold of yourself, Tilford." Nowak hadn't said a word up to this point and the room fell quiet. He said plainly, "The deepfake cover story will only hold up for a few hours—definitely not twenty-four. Airing the new video with Renfree going down in a plane crash is crucial. We frame killing Renfree in Alaska as part of Hawthorne's plot to bomb LA. The American public needs to know two things. One, LA could end up in a nuclear meltdown, and two, Hawthorne is behind it all."

Garner said, "Everybody shut up. I need to think." He paused for a full minute, turned to his executive secretary and said, "OK—Tilford and Nowak are right. Tomorrow morning, I'll go live on air from the Oval Office again. This threat—this nuclear threat—I don't believe it, but I believe it. This situation is spiraling out of control, and the American people need to know I can handle it."

The president left the room abruptly. Tilford instructed his team to dispatch thousands of spies in California, the Southwest and major US airports. "Turn over every stone and find Hawthorne," he said. His face turned beet red and he demanded, "No leaks about this mission! No leaks! And find the goddamn terrorists, whoever they are!"

"Our best troops are already on it," affirmed Nowak.

Tilford added, "And nobody even think about telling me you understand what we're really dealing with. I've seen the intel. We don't know shit—except we got a possible WMD somewhere off Long Beach. Stop that bomb!"

Tilford's anxiety was far worse than normal. He carried on with his tirade. "This shit-eating situation is way too goddamn fluid! For fuck's sake, somebody get me a full assessment of the nuclear scenarios."

With the manhunt declared, top generals issued orders for all soldiers on base to report to duty at Camp Pendleton. Tanks rumbled, and a huge fleet of Humvees and buses rolled out of an airplane hangar. Loading up their military gear and preparing for the days ahead, soldiers were fully armed and ready. Sergeants debriefed their units, ordering them to leave their cell phones behind and stay off the civilian grid as much as possible. Forces were ready at a moment's notice.

The manhunt for Hawthorne, Wilder and Katya was fully operational. Thousands of soldiers in tanks, Humvees and buses drove out of Camp Pendleton. The northbound highway to Los Angeles shut down for all vehicles except the military.

45

DESERT WINGS

Fleeing LA that same night, Hawthorne drove east on the 10 with Wilder and Katya ducking low in the back seat. They were running out of gas, and Hawthorne pulled into a truck stop in Fontana. He wore a ball cap and hung his head at the pump to keep a low profile.

Hawthorne overheard two truck drivers having a friendly argument outside of their rigs. One said, "That shit on the news was a hundred percent deepfake. No way Arnold Renfree tortured those people and said all that."

"Yeah but the White Prophecy is real," said the other man. "Some dude like him must have been running WP the whole frickin' time."

"Maybe, OK. But he died some other way. The gawd dayum media just tryin' to brainwash us."

"Listen here. It's all bullshit if you ask me."

"Where you from?"

"Alaska. You?"

"Lotsa places. Mostly Mississippi."

"Where you headed?"

"Florida."

"Well you best be gettin' the move on then. That's a long haul."

"Good chattin' wicha."

Hawthorne finished pumping gas and got back in the car. He drove two hours inland and the sunrise painted the sky. He switched freeways twice and ended up on a road with no traffic. Finally, Hawthorne pulled over and said, "This is the closest spot to where we're headed. Let's go."

Katya sat up rubbing her sore neck. Wilder startled awake from a vivid dream. "You would not believe the nightmare I just had," he said. "Where are we?"

"Mojave Desert," said Hawthorne. Sand stretched in every direction around the two-lane highway, with no one else in sight. Shrubs and Joshua trees dotted the landscape. Distant mountains glowed orange in the morning sun.

"It's absolutely beautiful," said Katya.

Hawthorne popped the trunk and tossed each of them a water bottle. He left the keys in the ignition and walked across the highway. "We go north—just under a mile," he said.

"Where to?" asked Wilder.

"You'll see," said Hawthorne.

"What about the car?" asked Katya.

Hawthorne said, "It exposes us, but we don't have time."

Their shoes dug into the sand, and Hawthorne scanned the horizon. He corrected their direction a few times, and Katya jogged to catch up with him. She held his hand, and Hawthorne smiled at her.

Wilder protested. "Holding his hand, really? Katya, haven't you put me through enough?"

"Relax," said Katya. "Isn't that the advice you gave me once?"

"It's OK, Wilder," said Hawthorne. "Fighting side by side has a way of bringing people close."

"That's right," agreed Katya. "Besides, you and I had immediate chemistry. Didn't we?"

"Absolutely," Hawthorne said.

Wilder asked, "Isn't it bad enough you already dumped me once—and now LA is about to become a nuclear wasteland?"

Katya dismissed Wilder with a wave of her hand. She kept flirting and squeezed Hawthorne's bicep. "You are very strong."

"Strength is a matter of soul," said Hawthorne. He chuckled. "But yeah, I'm pretty ripped. Somebody call a veterinarian, these pythons are sick."

"I don't get this joke," said Katya.

Wilder rolled his eyes. "Fawwwk. Why don't you just rip my heart out of my chest?"

Katya asked, "Could you see yourself with a woman like me?"

Hawthorne said, "Sure could."

She said, "On the airplane you showed me a photo of one of your lovers."

Hawthorne said, "That's my boyfriend—he's stationed in Rome."

"And you're married to a woman. I stalked you online, so I know."

"Eileen and I are filing for divorce."

"Honestly," said Katya, "I don't understand how you could be bisexual."

Hawthorne said, "You should work on that then." It was a naive thing for her to say, but he also liked her.

Katya corrected herself. "You know what—I'm being closed-minded. Who you are is not hard to understand."

"You love who you love," said Hawthorne.

He was far more preoccupied with the mission at hand and what it all meant. Since the massacre at Jerada, and now faced with nuclear annihilation, he had fallen into a spiritual reckoning. All these years, he followed orders and fought wars without asking to what end. In reflection, he landed on his deepest truth. If he truly served God and stood for peace, then the war had to stop for him. The nuke added certainty that this would be his last mission—one way or the other. "Let's pick up the pace," he said. "We're halfway there."

Wilder said, "Hang on, hang on—Katya, who the fuck are you really?"

"Good question," said Hawthorne.

"What do you mean?" Katya asked.

Wilder asked, "First off, are you serving Russia or America?"

"I was trained as Russian special military intelligence," she said. "But now I work for both countries, depending on the circumstances."

Wilder interjected, "Why should I believe anything you say?"

She continued, "When I learned about GWA, I knew I had found my one true reason to fight. I will do everything in my power to stop them."

"That I believe," said Hawthorne. "You've been through hell and back to get that close to the enemy."

"So you trust me?" she asked Hawthorne.

"Hell, no," said Wilder.

"I'm asking him," she said, "slut."

"Why does everyone call me a slut?" asked Wilder.

She said plainly, "Because you're a slut."

"Katya, to answer your question," said Hawthorne, "yes I do trust you."

"Good," she said, and nodded with a smile. "Because you should."

"I'm wondering . . ." Hawthorne said. "You know what you're fighting against—but do you know what you're fighting for?"

Katya reflected, "I think we are fighting for the same thing."

"War on war is different than making peace," said Hawthorne.

"Words of a warrior," she said.

"Wait a minute," Wilder said. "Katya, when did you infiltrate the GWA?"

"Two years ago," said Katya. "The CIA recruited me much earlier than I told you."

"What did they recruit you for?"

"To fight Moscow's faction of the Global White Alliance."

Wilder added it up. "At the country club when we met Arnold Renfree, did you already know each other?"

"Of course we did," she said.

Wilder pressed, "What was your relationship?"

"I was his Russian counterpart."

"What the hell does that mean?"

"What does it matter now?" she asked.

Wilder yelled, "Were you just going to sit there and watch me get waterboarded to death?"

Katya clapped back sternly, "I called Hawthorne and he saved us all. That is not hypothetical."

"Enough already," Hawthorne said. "You two can sort that crap out later. We have to stop the nuke. Besides, we're here."

"Where?" asked Wilder.

"All I see is desert," said Katya.

"Wait till you get a load of my hideout," said Hawthorne.

Hawthorne walked up to a tall cactus and roundhouse kicked it. He split the cactus open with a few more front-kicks. He plunged his arm into the trunk and pulled out a shovel.

Wilder exclaimed, "Did you just pull a shovel out of a cactus?"

"Looks exactly like the real thing, doesn't it?" remarked Hawthorne. He yanked off a piece of flesh from the base of the cactus trunk. He opened a small panel, pressed a few buttons, and an antenna emerged from the top of the cactus. Hawthorne walked over to a clearing between some bushes and started digging.

"What are you digging for?" asked Katya.

"I built a bunker right beneath us," said Hawthorne. "Only a few people know about it." He shoveled furiously, clearing sand off a metal hatch in the ground. He yanked off a piece of plastic, flipped a switch and stepped back. A thick metal lid automatically slid open. Sand poured down a ladder leading into the hideout.

Hawthorne motioned for them to enter. "Welcome to my underground lair."

"Oh my God, this is so dope," said Wilder, climbing down the ladder and triggering several motion-detector lights. "Holy shit, this place is huge."

Standing in the sand, Katya hugged Hawthorne tightly. "I have never met a man like you," she said, "and I would follow you to the end of the earth."

"Let's just hope earth as we know it doesn't end," said Hawthorne.

"Could you really see yourself with me?" asked Katya.

"Maybe." He pointed to the open lid of the bunker. "Get in."

"That's what she said." Katya smiled and climbed down.

Inside the hideout, Hawthorne cleared cobwebs hanging from the ceiling. He pulled bedsheets off racks of gear throughout the space. "Sorry about all the dust."

"It smells awful"—Katya coughed—"but this is an unbelievable setup."

Hawthorne flipped a breaker and powered on a computer system mounted on the wall. He popped open a few laptops linked to cables running across the floor.

Wilder marveled at the gear. He sat himself down in a flight chair and put on a VR helmet. He pulled a glass visor over his eyes and it powered on. "Is this a 4D AI display?" he asked. "This is the real fucking deal right here."

Hawthorne told Wilder, "I'm gonna need you to operate that console you're playing with."

Katya walked past a row of assault rifles, examining a rocket launcher and some weapons she could not identify. "Where did you get all of this hardware?" asked Katya.

Hawthorne explained, "There's a naval weapons base not too far from here. Years ago, I trained on the base and in the mountains surrounding the area. We played war games, a lot of top-secret stuff. Over time, I stole decommissioned machines from the storage bay at the base, and during our games I tucked them away."

Katya asked, "How did you get them to this hideout without being noticed?"

Hawthorne said, "I'm not gonna tell you all of my tricks." He walked into a second room with a thick glass window separating it from the rest of the bunker. Katya and Wilder followed him. In the center of the room there was a vehicle with a cloth draped over it.

"What's that?" asked Katya, pointing at the covered vehicle. Hawthorne tugged on the cloth and revealed a large translucent drone.

Wilder's jaw dropped. He walked around the drone and said, "I can see right through the exterior. Look at that electrical system inside! What the hell am I looking at?"

Hawthorne said, "That's an early prototype of a cloaking aircraft. Completely invisible in flight."

"Does it work?" Wilder asked.

Hawthorne said, "Eighty percent of these explode on takeoff, but I'm sure they have fixed that bug by now."

"What will we do with it?" asked Katya.

Hawthorne said, "More on that later. Wilder, we need to talk about Professor Singh's code."

Wilder said, "I told you everything I know. Wait a minute, did you crack the rest of the code?"

"Yeah, I cracked it."

"The copy I gave you?" asked Wilder.

"No, but that was pretty cool how you stored it in the shoe."

"My device didn't work?"

"The SIM card got destroyed underwater. I had to flee in the sewers."

"Of course you did, you're a Navy SEAL," said Wilder. "Then how did you get the code?"

"Katya gave me her thumb drive," said Hawthorne.

"I did not *give* it to you," she said.

"So wait—I went through all that trouble for nothing?" asked Wilder.

Katya explained, "After I flew back to LA, I set a meeting to hand off the thumb drive to my one good contact, but Hawthorne intercepted it."

Wilder asked Hawthorne, "Did you solve the third problem—all of it?"

He answered, "Yeah, I ran it through an AI Spec Ops decoder." He held up the thumb drive and plugged it into a laptop. He handed Wilder the computer and sat him down in the flight chair. Hawthorne and Katya huddled around Wilder and they looked at the screen together.

Wilder pulled up the code. Like the Morocco problem, it was latitude and longitude coordinates with a day and time. "See? That's what I was trying to tell you back in the cafeteria on campus. Those coordinates are the Port of Long Beach."

Hawthorne pointed to the screen. "The shit is going down tomorrow morning."

"Tomorrow's the day? Jesus," said Wilder.

Hawthorne said, "Here's the part of the code the AI cracked . . . it says *Garganta*."

"*Garganta* . . ." Katya said, scratching her head.

Hawthorne said, "I looked it up. The *Garganta* is a vessel owned by a Chinese global shipping company."

It dawned on Katya. "Is the nuclear bomb on that boat?"

"Exactly," said Hawthorne. "I ran the shipping routes to see which vessels will be in the Long Beach port tomorrow. The *Garganta* is scheduled to dock this afternoon, arriving from Saigon. If we don't act now, that WMD is going to level LA."

Wilder asked, "What do we do?"

Hawthorne said, "I have a plan but it involves a significant amount of improvisation. We have a couple hours to talk it through, but first I have to make a phone call."

46

FULL FORCE

In the morning, President Garner made the grave announcement to the public: "However unlikely, Navy SEAL Rex Hawthorne is possibly in possession of a dirty bomb. The threat of a WMD on US soil is real."

The Pentagon fully deployed the US military in Southern California. Citizens of greater Los Angeles watched in horror as the region went into lockdown.

The internet exploded with conspiracies and loud chatter about the WP. White supremacists took to social media, claiming now was the time for GWA to rise in full force. Within the ranks, soldiers argued bitterly about the extent to which the Global White Alliance had infiltrated the military. For the moment, all US troops were following orders, but top generals worried the military could unravel.

A huge fleet of Army helicopters lifted off from Camp Pendleton and dispatched to the LA skies. They fanned out over all major highways and roads, patrolling neighborhoods nonstop. The LAPD and police forces within a two-hundred-mile radius created freeway checkpoints, paralyzing traffic.

People stormed grocery stores, stocking up on emergency rations. Shelves emptied and fights broke out in parking lots. Thieves took to the streets, smashing windows and looting. Anarchy gripped Los Angeles and buildings burned. The outbreak of violence was multiple times worse than the Watts and Rodney King riots combined.

A swift uprising of white supremacists spilled into the streets. All across greater Los Angeles, mobs of white vigilantes roamed neighborhoods and highways packing automatic weapons. Fueling bedlam, the white mobs began shooting people of color at random, chanting, "W-P!" and "G-W-A!" Race warfare swept LA.

Massive numbers of previously silent white citizens sided with the Global White Alliance. A massive surge of white people organized into militia units. Guerrilla combat erupted, led by white gangs: Peckerwood, the Aryan Brotherhood, Proud Boys, QAnon extremists, the Abergils and LA crime family.

Gangs of people of color fought side by side. The Casta cartel joined with the Mexican mafia. Pacts formed to join forces with Triad, the Bloods, the Crips, Yakuza, Bahal Na and many more. Everyday citizens joined their side too. At first, people of color fought back with equal force, but a new surge of white nationalists popped up from every corner. The show of white force was overwhelming, and nobody was safe.

The Pentagon had no choice but to declare martial law in the state of California. The news rocked the nation. Violence broke out in other major cities, but nowhere near the LA chaos. The US military was still holding together, but rumors were flying about the White Prophecy and signs of a GWA uprising.

CIA needed every last shred of intel to stop the bomb and the uprising. Back at Camp Pendleton, special investigator Carmen Jefferson arrived to interrogate Chuck and Kim. They were held in two separate prison cells under close watch.

Carmen interrogated Kim first. Abusing FBI privileges, Kim had committed egregious federal crimes and was probably in prison for life. However, Carmen acknowledged the complexity of the situation. Kim was now a nationally famous figure and "potentially one of the good guys." Carmen said she would personally look out for Kim and Chuck's safety, a promise that rang hollow. She learned nothing new from either of them.

When Carmen interrogated Chuck, it was abundantly clear he was in way over his head. Chuck was collateral damage and had no place in the world of espionage. Ms. Jefferson told him, "You're in deep trouble. The stunt you pulled is starting a damn war. But if the whole torture video turns out to be real—and a terror plot gets disrupted—you could still be the man of the hour."

*

Meanwhile, at his office in the Pentagon, Tilford sat reading a print copy of the letter Perez had sent to his wife. Lieutenant Esther Hadwick stood beside his desk with her hat tucked under her arm.

Tilford asked, "Is this a goddamn suicide note? We've got fucking martial law in California, and now another SEAL who's lost his mind? Would somebody please tell me what is going on?"

"I would explain it if I could, sir," she said.

"At ease, Esther. How long have we been working together, and you still act like a soldier every time you walk in."

"Just trying to show respect," said Esther.

"Get a load of this letter . . ."

> Dear Linda,
>
> I always wanted to die in your arms. At least we will still die together even though we're still apart . . . Death is coming so I wanted to at least say goodbye.
>
> Love always,
> Benny

Tilford scowled. "First of all, that is completely pathetic. Second of all, doggone it, what does this letter mean?"

Esther gave her assessment. "Sir, it is definitely cryptic and reads like a suicide note. Benito Perez has never gone off the radar like this. If you add that to Rex Hawthorne's erratic behavior, this situation looks even more serious. One suicidal, homicidal Navy SEAL poses a threat of its own. Now it looks like we might have two of them."

Tilford said, "You're right. Navy SEALs don't just go AWOL for two damn weeks. What in God's name has Perez gotten into, mailing a suicide note from China? I'm still trying to wrap my head around that fucking viral video of Rex Hawthorne killing Arnold Renfree!"

"That's understandable," Esther said.

"We sold the deepfake lie, but the truth will come out. The American public is dumb but not *that* dumb."

"You're right," said Esther. "Even if they don't want the truth, people will know it before long."

"And by the way, Renfree had it coming!" said Tilford. "He went completely off the fucking deep end! Torturing our own citizens? In the name of the motherfucking Global White Alliance? I never even believed that group was truly dangerous! Now, look at what's happening in LA. Who's to say that won't happen nationwide? This whole situation is completely insane."

Tilford opened a desk drawer and pulled out a bottle. He poured himself a full glass of bourbon. He took a large gulp, frowned and said, "The worst part of all this is Arnold Renfree made the nuclear threat. If he wasn't dead, I would torture him myself."

"Permission to speak freely, sir," said Esther.

"You don't need my goddamn permission. What's on your damn mind, Esther?"

Esther said, "I always thought Senator Renfree was a cocksucker, sir. He was a white supremacist Nazi sympathizer and a two-faced asshole."

"Well OK, Esther, but tell me what you really think," said Tilford. "That's true, he was a doggone bastard. What do you make of this White Power international movement crap? You think these extremist sons a' bitches are stupid enough to start a war they can't win?"

"No idea," said Esther. "But I do know Renfree deserved to die."

"Yeah, that scumbag must have gone straight to hell." Tilford rubbed his jaw with his fingers. "Crap, I'm getting a migraine. I'm gonna need to take another painkiller."

Tilford's executive assistant Jonathan said over the intercom, "Urgent call for you, sir." Tilford waved Esther out of the office.

"Who's on the line, Jonathan?" Tilford said through the speakerphone.

"Rex Hawthorne."

"Did you say Hawthorne? Put him through—and find out where the damn call is coming from."

Tilford knocked back his glass of bourbon and poured another. "Hawthorne? What in God's name are you doing?"

Holding a burner cell phone to his ear, Hawthorne leaned against his weapons wall in his bunker. He wasn't worried about the call being traced because the transmitter routed through a Spec Ops satellite. He said, "I'm gonna give it to you straight, because unlike most top brass in the military, you don't have your head all the way up your ass."

"Dammit Hawthorne, tell me what the hell is happening."

"The uprising you're seeing in LA is just the tip of the iceberg."

"What else you got?"

"Tomorrow. Seven a.m. Long Beach Port," Hawthorne warned.

"What about it?" Tilford fumed.

"If you don't take action, a nuclear bomb is gonna wipe out LA," said Hawthorne.

"Hawthorne, you're out of your mind!"

"You're right," said Hawthorne. "I *am* out of my mind. You should be too because this is war."

"What war exactly? You mean the rioting in LA?"

"This is far, far bigger. We are truly at war."

"Who's we?" Tilford took another large gulp of bourbon.

"All of us," said Hawthorne. "You. Me. Everybody."

"I think you're full of shit, how about that?" said Tilford.

"We're at war with ourselves," said Hawthorne. "The enemy is within."

"Give me a damn break." Tilford had lost all patience. "Tell me something, Hawthorne. Why am I looking at a goddamn suicide note from your pal Perez, the only other survivor from KrayBULL who—by the way—has been AWOL two weeks?"

"Perez is the suicide bomber," Hawthorne said. "He's gonna detonate that nuke in Long Beach. Tell the president."

Tilford gritted his teeth. "You're just making this stuff up. For crying out loud, you're America's most wanted man."

"You're gonna have to believe me. Or else."

"Or else what?"

"Would you rather be wrong and have LA blown off the face of the earth?"

Spitting angry, Tilford yelled, "I would rather be right and at home having sex with my wife!"

"There's still time to stop it," said Hawthorne. "This is an extreme threat."

Tilford said, "We are way ahead of you, asshole. We already deployed a hundred teams of Special Forces to Southern California. Not to mention ten thousand Marines on the ground in LA, plus the National Guard. The manhunt for you made a pretty fucking good cover, but now we have martial law!"

"Did the president authorize that?" asked Hawthorne.

"I talked him into it," said Tilford. "If you think *I'm* confused, President Garner is ten times as bad."

Hawthorne asked, "The Global White Alliance is rising up, am I right? There's a full-on race war starting in LA."

"The GWA has gotten to a lot of people, it's true. But LA has a big riot every twenty-five or thirty years. They'll kill each other for a while and things will settle down eventually."

"Wow, that's morbid."

"It's true though, isn't it?"

"Shut up and listen," said Hawthorne calmly. "There comes a time when you have to decide. Are you on the side of war, or are you on the side of peace? Are you an angel, or are you a demon?"

"You're talking about demons right now?" Tilford yelled into the intercom. "Go fuck yourself, Hawthorne! When I find you I am gonna hang you by your balls!"

"The only balls we should be talking about is you growing a pair."

"Hawthorne, you're really taking the piss out of me, you know that?"

"Listen. Two weeks ago, I was as close to dead as I have ever been. On the run, all alone. I knew I had to solve the nuclear threat on my own. I ran a piece of critical code through an AI program that I stole from Ridgecrest awhile back . . ."

"Another felony to add to your life sentence if you live through this."

"And now that I'm sharing the intel, you won't even listen, you schmuck."

"Oh, I'm listening. To a bunch of horse crap."

"I've had a lot of time to reflect back on my life," said Hawthorne. "I have been fighting too many years and done a lot of terrible things, on the battlefield, off the battlefield, all over the world. I always thought that I was on the right side. I was fighting for all the right reasons, serving and protecting America. It turns out all too many of those battles were based on lies."

"For God's sake, Hawthorne!" said Tilford angrily. "Are you getting moralistic on me? Why don't you shove a stick of incense up your ass and we can sing some John Lennon songs together?"

"I'm not getting *moralistic* at all," said Hawthorne. "I'm declaring war on the United States."

"*What?*" asked Tilford.

"That's right," said Hawthorne. "You didn't believe me when

I told you I'm fighting for peace, so you leave me with no choice but to declare war."

"You're declaring war?"

"You heard me."

"We're already at war with you! You're wanted dead or alive."

"I mean *war*. I lied about Perez. It's me. I am the terrorist who's gonna bomb LA."

"What?"

"Tomorrow morning in Long Beach. Be a hero, Tilford. Tell the president and try and stop me."

"Why would you bomb LA? You're an American!"

In a sinister voice, Hawthorne played up the role of terrorist. "The United States is like a lost sheep waiting to be slaughtered. Without the Global White Alliance, the US is driving itself into the grave. Our country is full of Communists disguising themselves as Liberals, and before long, we will all be speaking Chinese."

"You know damn well Liberals aren't Communists."

"That just makes you one of them."

Tilford said, "Calling the right wing a bunch of fascists, *that* I can believe."

"We *had* to become fascists," said Hawthorne. "America forced our hand."

"America forced you to declare war on your own kind?"

"My kind of people are white people, period. And white people have lost control of this country."

"You don't know your own country's history," said Tilford.

"Shut. Up," said Hawthorne. "I am sick and tired of this bullshit melting pot lie. America is failing because we let colored people in. The white race is becoming the weak minority and now is our time to fight back. We must kill America as we know it, so the GWA can rise!"

Tilford said, "You're one sick bastard with this White Power conspiracy talk. You can't just declare war like this!"

"I just did," said Hawthorne calmly.

"Christ on a crutch! I oversaw your Navy SEAL training. I made you into one of America's most elite fighters!"

"That's right, you made me a killing machine, and now it's time for me to kill. It's Armageddon. White people will dominate the world. It's God's will."

"Hawthorne, have you completely lost your mind?" asked Tilford.

"You're damn right! It's World War III, baby! Sayonara, Los Angeles! What doesn't kill 'em in the nuclear blast will get 'em in the meltdown! Let's get it on!" Hawthorne hung up and tossed the phone on the ground.

"Hello? Hello? God fucking dammit!" Tilford called his assistant. "Jonathan! Rex Hawthorne just declared nuclear war on the United States! Get the president on the line and get my jet ready. I want clearance to fly to LA within the hour!"

"Sir, LA is a war zone. Are you sure you want to—"

"Don't question me! Make it happen."

Back in the hideout, Hawthorne half smiled and gave a shrug. Katya and Wilder were both slack-jawed. Wilder asked, "Did you just declare World War III?"

"It was the best plan I could think of," said Hawthorne casually. "It seemed like the fastest way to get them to DEFCON 1."

Katya asked, "Are you crazy?"

"On the contrary," said Hawthorne. "I finally woke up. Maybe this time tomorrow we won't all be vaporized and we can talk it through."

"What kind of plan is this?" asked Wilder.

"Honestly, it's reckless as a motherfucker," said Hawthorne. "But it gives us our best chance at survival. We gotta stop that bomb."

"I'm with you. We stop the bomb," said Katya. "How?"

Hawthorne said, "We're going to do something they will never see coming."

47

INVISIBLE WARRIORS

Secretary of Defense Tilford landed on the naval air strip at Catalina Island, a few miles southwest of Los Angeles. Tilford was in command, greeted by Admiral Edward Jenkins, second lieutenant of Spec Ops. Ahead of Tilford's arrival, military forces rapidly transformed Catalina's decommissioned and ill-equipped base into the epicenter of the military's crisis response to LA's nuclear threat. Tilford and Admiral Jenkins headed directly to the war room on the base's top floor, which had a clear view of Long Beach. Every military base in California and the Southwest was on high alert and patched into the Catalina war room.

The scene in LA was a sustained panic. With the declaration of martial law, thousands of civilians fearing a military occupation flooded the streets in protest. Coupled with the race wars breaking out, chaos gripped the entire region. Hour after hour, the US Army and Marine Corps drove fleets of tanks, Humvees, buses and trucks from Camp Pendleton toward Los Angeles County. They surged north and fanned out from San Onofre throughout the LA city limits.

The Air Force dropped dummy bombs to suppress a violent civilian uprising. On the ground, soldiers fired tear gas and rubber bullets into crowds, but their show of force wasn't enough. Subduing so many guerrilla militias proved impossible.

Against orders and fearing for their lives, troops met crowds with machine-gun fire. Civilian militias fought back.

Soldiers executing citizens escalated horrifically, and military vehicles began running people over. Viral videos of explosions, shootings, beatings and deaths swept the internet. Entire blocks of buildings burned, billowing smoke across LA.

The Pentagon was losing control of large pockets of military forces. TV stations refused to stop covering the warfare and kept their helicopters in the sky. They claimed freedom of the press, insisting the world had the right to know what was happening. Online conspiracies spread like wildfire, including baseless theories about a Communist plot to take over California. Some said it was the precursor to the end of times and the wrath of God. Others claimed it was an alien invasion.

From the war room on Catalina Island, Tilford called Nowak at the Pentagon. Nowak sat quietly at his desk watching two monitors with live broadcasts of the LA mayhem. Tilford had no idea that Nowak was part of the Global White Alliance, much less that he could be the mysterious Karen, the so-called second head of the snake now running the US faction of GWA. Nowak's patience had paid off, and his moment to strike was fast approaching.

"Tell me what you know, Tilford," said Nowak.

"The nuke is somewhere in the Port of Long Beach," said Tilford.

"I don't believe there's any nuke close to detonation," lied Nowak.

"Assume it's happening. We act without hesitation here."

"Agreed," said Nowak. "You know, Hawthorne is to blame for everything. All this violence is because of him."

"Hawthorne? Come on, he can't be behind all the violence."

"He's a declared domestic terrorist."

"That is true," agreed Tilford.

"What if he's leading his own army? I have seen intel on that."

"That's over the top—but so is the uprising in LA. Anything is possible."

"I actually have contradictory intel—some says Hawthorne is working for China, while other people think he's commanding a group of white militias—not just in LA but nationwide."

"China? That's ludicrous. Where are you getting this from?"

"I'll send it along when I can. Who knows? Hawthorne could even be the head of the US faction of the GWA, now that Renfree is dead." Nowak relished in this particular lie since he was referring to himself.

Tilford clenched his jaw. "Dammit Nowak, these conspiracy theories make no sense. All I know is, the nuclear threat is a hundred percent real and we gotta stop the bomb. That's our number one priority. No more debating."

"Yes, sir," said Nowak. "Have you told President Garner?"

"Of course I fucking have," said Tilford. "Are you with him now?"

"No, I'm in my office," said Nowak.

"What are you waiting for? Get to the Situation Room. You're standing in for me and I need you to advise Garner. He may be able to declare war, but he sure as hell doesn't know how to fight one!"

"Right away, sir," said Nowak.

Tilford hung up and cursed under his breath. He got Admiral Jenkins on the line. "Jenkins, we're sending all our best men into LA city limits on this one."

Inside the airplane hangar in Catalina, the base was packed to the gills with military officers and Special Forces. Helicopters crowded the tarmac, lifting off nonstop to monitor the coastline and highways. Even the most battle-ready soldiers were on edge. If a WMD detonated in LA, it would vaporize them in the initial blast of radiation.

Awaiting orders, thirty teams of Navy SEALs and another fifty teams of Green Berets stood around angrily debating each other. Everyone had patchy intel. Some units believed the video of Hawthorne was real, which meant the head of Senate Intel betrayed the United States in the name of the GWA. Others believed the conspiracy theory that the video was a deepfake and Hawthorne was a Communist double agent working for China. Whatever the truth, the manhunt was in full swing. It was the largest terror threat on US soil since 9/11.

Admiral Jenkins grabbed a megaphone and called the SEALs and Green Berets into an auditorium. "Listen up, soldiers!" Jenkins commanded. "Secretary of Defense Tilford is sending you into the battle zone. Everyone head to the main building auditorium."

Tilford placed a phone call to President Garner, who put him on speaker surrounded by his advisors in the Situation Room. Nowak sat across from the president.

Nowak was plain faced in his deception. "President Garner, I just received top-secret intel confirming that Hawthorne has the WMD. He's going to war on behalf of China."

Tilford's baffled voice came over the speakerphone. "Who gave you that intel?"

"China, really?" asked the president. "Mother of God, what next? I don't know what to believe anymore. All I know is we have to stop the bomb. At all costs. We will figure out who the real threat is—I honestly don't believe that China crap—but first we stop that bomb."

"That's right, Mr. President," said Tilford. "That's exactly what we're going to do."

Tilford ended the call and looked toward the Port of Long Beach through a set of binoculars. Admiral Jenkins informed him, "The auditorium is full."

Tilford walked to the front stage, stepped up and grabbed the mic. He issued orders to find and neutralize the nuclear terror threat by any means necessary, and to kill Hawthorne on sight. Tilford commanded maximum fleets of aircraft in the skies and fortification of the Long Beach makeshift headquarters running ground operations. He left the mic and hurried back to the war room.

Among Spec Ops factions in the auditorium, arguments

broke into fistfights. A handful of men began hailing the Global White Alliance. They were secret loyalists chanting, "G-W-A!" proudly claiming Hawthorne as their own. They carried on about a legion of Communists threatening national security, and it was Hawthorne and GWA who were going to stop them. Others yelled back that Hawthorne was a real American hero defending the Republic by killing Renfree and exposing the WMD plot. The utmost confusion had reached the highest ranks, and men praising GWA were detained.

"I'm with Hawthorne!" yelled a white supremacist as he was carried off.

"No, I'm with Hawthorne!" yelled a man prepared to die before letting GWA factions overthrow his government.

Another round of fights broke out. Two more GWA loyalists cropped up, this time firing gun shots. They killed three men until a Green Beret shot them dead in return fire. The crowd stopped brawling. Everyone looked in shock at the dead bodies of their fellow soldiers.

Admiral Jenkins grabbed the microphone, flanked by the Navy SEAL unit he commanded. Jenkins was vehement. "Detain the traitors among us and stop fighting each other! None of this matters if a WMD blows up LA! We must defend the United States and stop the nuclear threat."

Soldiers held their firearms drawn, eyes darting around the room. Then they nodded in agreement with Jenkins and put their firearms away. For the moment, men fell in line, but the fight among the ranks was not over.

Back in the Situation Room, it was a scene of high anxiety. President Garner wrung his hands and broke into a cold sweat. He took a deep breath and leaned back in his chair. He stared at the ceiling and tried to clear his thoughts.

Nowak knew it was time to strike. The moment for GWA to rise had finally come. He stood up across the table from Garner and said, "Mr. President, I'm Karen."

"Huh?"

Nowak quickly drew his concealed Glock 26 from the front of his waistband and fired three shots at the president. Secret Service agents simultaneously pumped Nowak full of bullets. Garner fell over the back of his chair. Nowak's blood spattered everywhere and he collapsed.

Special Agent Peterson dove to President Garner, who lay on the floor. Garner blinked his eyes in a state of shock. "I'm hit."

Peterson asked, "Where, Mr. President?"

"My chest," said Garner. "It hurts!"

His physician rushed to help, pressing his palms on the wound to stop the flow of blood. "Paramedics, now!"

Agent Peterson looked up at the wall behind the president's chair and saw two bullet holes. "He only shot you once."

His physician confirmed, "The gunshot is up toward the shoulder. That's a good thing, sir. Stay with us."

"Nowak . . . betrayed me," said Garner. "I should be dead."

Garner's physician helped him sit up. "Not today, Mr. President."

Peterson looked down at Nowak's body. "The threat is eliminated."

"How did I not see it?" Garner asked.

"None of us did, sir," said an agent.

Peterson said, "You're lucky. Most men don't miss at close range."

"God, it hurts," said Garner.

Paramedics rushed in, treated and dressed the wound. They tried to get President Garner onto a gurney, but he insisted he stand up of his own accord. "Tell Tilford. Tell him GWA will fail. We will stop the WMD, and we will stop the Global White Alliance."

"Get on the gurney, Mr. President," said the head paramedic. "You lost a lot of blood."

"A gurney is too much," Garner said. "Get me a wheelchair instead."

"OK, Mr. President," confirmed the head paramedic. "We can do that."

"What about the intel on China?" asked Agent Peterson.

"It's a lie, all of it," said Garner. "This is GWA."

"It adds up with what we're seeing in LA," said Peterson.

"Declare them the top threat and a domestic terror cell," said Garner.

"What about Rex Hawthorne?" Peterson wondered aloud.

Garner said, "What about him? Give me a break, I just got shot."

"Yes," said his physician. "Try to stay calm. Here, drink this—it's a mild sedative."

Garner remarked, "In this situation, whether Hawthorne is a bad guy or not makes no difference. Just stop the bomb."

48

THE PAYLOAD

Inside the shipping container on the *Garganta*, Perez and Bailey assembled the rocket, a Chinese DF-11 short-range ballistic missile retrofitted to launch with the nuclear payload. They had given up on wearing handkerchiefs over their noses and mouths, because Stein's rotting corpse was indescribably pungent. His bloated body had popped and collapsed, with a few gallons of milky black fluid seeping like engine oil across the floor.

All boats in the bay were anchored and refused permission to dock at port. The *Garganta* floated a quarter mile off the coast of Long Beach.

Perez asked, "Are you hearing all that helicopter activity above us? The military must know about the nuke."

"They can't stop us now," said Bailey.

"You're damn right," said Perez. "They might be trying to find us, but they don't know where to look."

"What makes you so sure?"

"If they knew our location, they would be right on top of us. The sound of the choppers is coming and going, patrol style."

"Good point," said Bailey. "What about that guy, Hawthorne?"

"What about him?"

"You said he was the one big loose end on our mission. What if he knows where we are?"

"Hawthorne is a liability, that's for sure. But if that cocksucker knew our full plan, he would have come for us already."

"Is there any possibility that could still happen?"

"Extremely unlikely," said Perez. "This mission was highly protected."

"Yeah, but he's a Navy SEAL, right?"

"True," said Perez. "Look—Hawthorne doesn't matter now that we're in position."

Bailey said, "Yeah, I guess nothing really matters anymore."

Perez patted the hull of the missile. "It's beautiful, isn't it?"

"It really is," said Bailey.

"Did we assemble it right?" asked Perez.

"Yes, sir."

"I'm glad I didn't kill the engineer," said Perez. "Help me lift it onto the launchpad."

They muscled the rocket onto the cannon bay pointing at the ceiling of the shipping container. Bailey said, "Locked and loaded, sir."

Perez took a deep breath. "The nuke is ready to launch. Don't you dare touch the controls. I have earned the honor of starting this war."

"It's a historic moment, sir," said Bailey.

"Long live the Global White Alliance," said Perez.

"Long live the Global White Alliance."

Perez said, "Now that the bomb is ready, the only reason I'm not gonna kill you is I don't want to do this alone."

"Sir, I'm on your side. This is our moment of glory."

"I trust God and myself only—but you've proven your merit." Perez booted the system. "After I flip this switch, the roof opens, I hit the detonate button and there's no going back."

"LA will be flattened," said Bailey. "How many people do you think will die?"

"So damn many," said Perez coldly. "The radiation cloud will be massive. All of the dead will be martyrs for the movement."

Bailey assessed, "Hundreds of thousands dead."

Perez said, "It's necessary. It's the only way."

Bailey's heart sank. "Sir?"

"What is it?"

Bailey said, "Right now we still have a choice. We don't have to do this."

Perez asked, "Are you going soft on me?"

"Think about it, sir, we could still see our families again."

In the blink of an eye, Perez lunged at Bailey and got him in a choke hold, covering his mouth and nose. Bailey could not defend himself and suffocated to death.

"Damn coward," Perez muttered.

With two dead bodies beside him now, Perez sat awhile and then changed his clothing. He wore all-black baggy fatigues and military boots. He pulled a skeleton-faced balaclava over his head. Last he pulled a pair of ski goggles over his eyes and his face was completely covered. It was crucial to be unrecognizable by cameras before the nuclear blast.

Perez got shifty and hummed a song to himself, but it didn't calm his nerves. He unlocked a case and pulled out a cell phone. He stared at it for a long time and then dialed his wife.

"Hello, my love."

"Benny?" said Linda. "Oh my God, you're alive!"

"Sorry I haven't called," said Perez. "You know how these missions go." His eyes watered.

"Sweetheart, have you been following the news?"

"Not for a few weeks, actually."

"Your whole team is dead except for you and Hawthorne."

"Hawthorne's alive?"

"Yes."

"So you know then," said Perez. "Things went wrong in Africa. A lot of guys died."

"The news aired a video of Hawthorne shooting Senator Renfree from the Senate Intelligence Committee. After that everything went crazy. Sweetheart, LA is burning."

"Renfree from Senate Intel?"

"Yes, Benny. He was torturing civilians and talking about nuclear war and the Global White Alliance."

"Hawthorne shot Renfree?"

"That's right," said Linda. "And now LA is ground zero for a WMD threat and it's martial law."

"You can't be serious." Perez faked innocence.

She said, "I'm serious. Baby, where are you? I need you to come home."

"I can't come home right now," said Perez.

"At least try," she pleaded.

"Hawthorne must be with the Chinese."

"Chinese?" Linda was befuddled. "Baby, if you're somehow part of this, we will sort everything out."

"Honey, I can't come home. My mission's not over," he said with a lump in his throat. "How are the kids?"

"They miss you. None of us can sleep."

"Well, get some sleep. They need their mom. You know, the country gets nuclear threats all the time."

"Not like this," she said.

Perez said with certainty, "If there's really a WMD, it's China."

"Where are you getting this?" she asked.

"I can't tell you that," he said. "Did you say people are talking about the Global White Alliance?"

"Yes, it's all over the news," said Linda. "Somehow, Hawthorne is at the center of it."

"There's a lot of guys in that GWA movement."

"Benny, are you a part of that? Are you in the GWA?"

Perez didn't answer.

Linda said, "I know you always said you wish your father wasn't from Mexico."

"Yeah, but I'm not Mexican," said Perez defensively. "But they aren't the problem. China is the real enemy."

"Baby, what's gotten into you? Listen to me. I need you to come home. The kids miss you. I miss you. Everything is going to be OK."

"No, you listen to *me*, Linda," Perez said sternly.

"You never call me Linda."

"War with China is inevitable," Perez said. "This great nation is getting torn apart by our own weakness. And the Chinese have infected our brains."

"You do not sound like the man I know."

Perez's body trembled. He paced inside the shipping container, his shoes sticking to the floor with each step. "We either go to war with China or they bring the war to us. And even if China doesn't attack, we're gonna have a civil war anyway."

"Civil war? Benny, please come home. You need help. We can get that for you."

"I have trained all my life for this moment."

"What moment?"

"Things have to get very bad for our country before they get good again."

"Benny, what in God's name are you talking about?"

"I know they are listening," Perez said. "And they know I'm right."

"Who do you think is listening?"

"Linda, don't let the last thing you say to me be something stupid."

"Oh Benny," she cried.

"I love you forever," Perez said.

"You're my forever love," Linda said back.

Perez hung up the phone and sobbed uncontrollably.

49

FLIGHT OF THE *PYROIS*

Back at the hideout, Wilder and Katya lay slouching on a sofa—both were exhausted and emotionally frayed. Hawthorne unlocked a safe and pulled out another burner cell phone. He dialed a number.

"What's up, Ladybird?" he said. "Yep, it's Hawthorne. No time for that. I'll give you one guess where I'm calling from . . . I'm at Area Fifty-Never. Yeah, no shit. You still stationed in the desert?"

Ladybird was on base in the Mojave. "Yeah, our team is in Ridgecrest," she said. "Most of our units were called to LA. For fuck's sake, Hawthorne. What the hell have you gotten yourself into? Did you uncover a plot—or are you starting a war yourself?"

"Maybe both."

"LA is absolute madness," she said. "California is under martial law."

"I figured that might happen," Hawthorne said. "Listen. I found the location of the nuke. We're gonna lead Spec Ops right to it."

"You have the nuclear intel . . . ? Of course, you do."

"It's Wilder Kole who helped us find the nuke."

"Are you still with that Russian spy?" Ladybird asked.

"Yeah, she is here. She's with us."

"Are you sure?"

"One hundred percent."

"And you're with that kid, Wilder, too?"

"Yep."

Ladybird asked, "Hawthorne, what the hell are you doing at Area Fifty-Never?"

"I needed a guaranteed hideout, and we're getting ready to fly the *Pyrois*."

"The *Pyrois*?" she asked.

"It's our best shot."

"You idiot, the *Pyrois* is extremely dangerous, you know that."

Hawthorne said, "We can't risk being spotted until we're right on top of the WMD. We have to go all in."

Ladybird said, "I don't know what your plan is, but I fucking hate it."

"We're on the brink of nuclear war. Are you with me or not?"

"Do I have a choice?"

"It's an obvious one."

She sighed. "I'm with you, Hawthorne."

"Good," he said. "Write this down. Latitude 33.75, longitude minus 118.21. On a ship called the *Garganta*. Six thirty tomorrow morning."

"Is that the nuke's location?"

"It's as reliable as intel gets."

"Why don't you just tell the Pentagon?" asked Ladybird.

"Because they will fuck it up," said Hawthorne. "Believe me, I tried."

"What makes you think I won't tell the Pentagon?"

"And jeopardize the mission? This magnitude of failure would be too much to have on your conscience."

Ladybird sighed. "You've really lost your mind."

"Everybody keeps saying that," said Hawthorne.

"But I can see what you're saying," she said. "God, what a mess we are in."

"I need to know your team has my back. You got me?"

"I already said I'm with you," said Ladybird. "What are you, crazy *and* deaf?"

"And your team?"

"I'll do my best. They'll buy in."

Hawthorne said, "Good, OK. So here's the deal. Wilder is my pilot. I'm gonna need you to pick him up. Otherwise, he's a sitting duck."

"Dear Lord," said Ladybird.

Hawthorne continued, "Come get him. Our satellites and desert surveillance web will be able to spot the bunker after the launchpad comes into sight."

"It will be a miracle if you're not all dead by the time I get there."

Hawthorne said, "Pray for a miracle then."

"What's the plan after that?"

"We are sort of winging it."

Ladybird said, "You really piss me off, you know that? You want me in, but you won't tell me the full plan. And you don't trust the Pentagon with your intel, but you trust me?"

"Affirmative."

"Even though there's a goddamn nuclear threat in Los Angeles?"

"That pretty well sums it up," said Hawthorne. "Listen, I've gone over and over it. This is our best chance."

"Alright, Hawthorne, you already know. I'm all the way in," said Ladybird.

"We gotta stop that nuke."

"You sure you don't want to run your plan by me first?" she asked.

"Trust me."

"I hate that I have to ask. Are you on the right side here?"

"I'm on the side of peace," he said.

"But Hawthorne—this is war."

"Yes, it is. Just trust me and come get my pilot."

"And you trust that kid, Wilder, to be your pilot?"

"Yep."

"Dear God. Where will you be?"

"I'm gonna be riding the *Pyrois*," said Hawthorne.

"What does that even mean?" asked Ladybird.

"You'll see. Gotta run. Over and out." Hawthorne hung up and tossed the phone back in the safe. Wilder and Katya looked even more befuddled than before. Hawthorne asked, "Why are you looking at me like that? Come on, there's no time to waste."

Hawthorne walked into the launch room and powered on the *Pyrois*.

"You need me to fly *that*?" asked Wilder.

"Yeah, takeoff is the hardest part," said Hawthorne. "We have a very short runway and it might explode."

"Why don't *you* fly it?" Wilder asked.

"Because I'm getting inside of it," said Hawthorne.

"Inside?" Wilder was incredulous. "What about Katya?"

"She's gonna be inside of it too."

"I am?" Katya asked.

"Two commandos are better than one," said Hawthorne.

Katya protested, "Even if we survive takeoff, what will we do after that?"

"We fly over Long Beach port and basically base jump."

"Base jump?" asked Katya.

"Yeah, except at high speed," said Hawthorne. "Ever wear a flying suit?"

Katya said, "Only once. I flew into a cliff and almost died."

"Oh good," said Hawthorne. "So it's not your first time, then."

"I don't like this plan," said Katya. "Why are we doing this?"

"Never underestimate the power of surprising your enemy," said Hawthorne.

Katya locked eyes with Hawthorne and nodded. "OK, I'm in," she said.

"Let's go save LA," said Wilder.

Hawthorne spent an hour with Wilder on how to fly a drone, with particular flight instructions for the *Pyrois*. Wilder memorized as much as he could.

Hawthorne opened a trunk and pulled out a pair of sky-blue wing suits. Handing one to Katya, he said, "See if this fits. These are custom made with 4D tracking, a satellite mic hoodie and micro-infrared video."

Hawthorne and Katya stripped and put on the wing suits. "This one fits fine," said Katya. They strapped AR-15s on their backs.

Wilder said, "This is sexy in an end-of-the-world kind of way."

Hawthorne looked at the clock on the wall. "We need this thing in the air in less than five minutes." He knelt down under the *Pyrois*, opened the bomb-hatch door and motioned to Katya. "You first. Get in."

Katya crawled underneath the drone and climbed up into the hull. Hawthorne squeezed in after her, and she clung to his back.

Hawthorne said, "Wilder, shut the hatch."

"How?"

"Slam it—just like the trunk of a car."

"Yeah, right," said Wilder. He shut the hull with Hawthorne and Katya secure inside. He sat down at the flight console commands, talking into the mic for an audio/video check.

Hawthorne said, "Loud and clear, kid."

Wilder took a deep breath and said, "Katya. I love you. I mean I really love you. Don't you die on me."

"I have no plans to die," said Katya.

"Put us in the air," said Hawthorne.

Wilder said, "Roger that. Opening the roof now. Let's put the runway in place." A hundred-foot section of the steel roof descended at an angle, and sand rained into the hideout. The roof hit the ground with a loud clang.

"Runway is down," said Wilder.

Hawthorne said, "Wilder, activate invisibility."

Katya asked, "Is this the part where we might blow up?"

"No, that's liftoff," said Hawthorne.

Wilder watched through the thick glass window. He flipped a switch and the drone vanished right before his eyes.

"Sweet Jesus," said Wilder. "I can't see it! I can't see you either! It really works!"

"Incredible, right?" said Hawthorne. "Alright Wilder, get ready to hit full throttle."

"I love you," said Katya.

"You mean him or me?" asked Wilder.

Hawthorne said, "Never mind that. There's no time. Punch it!"

With a surge of blue flame, the drone shot into the sky. Wilder grimaced, waiting for an explosion but it never came. The drone arced upward into the clear sky.

"Wilder, you did it!" yelled Katya from inside the hull of the drone. "We're still alive! This is amazing!"

"Well done, brother!" shouted Hawthorne.

"Yahoo!" Wilder said, aiming the drone's ascent steeper from inside the bunker.

Hawthorne said, "Get us just high enough to clear the mountains. Don't go over five hundred miles an hour, or we won't be able to breathe."

"Roger," said Wilder.

At just over ten thousand feet, Wilder leveled the *Pyrois*.

Hawthorne said, "Dear God, this is absolutely glorious. If I die today, at least I saw this."

That pissed off Katya. "Nobody's dying today. This is no time for enjoying a view, and these damn AR-15s are stabbing me."

"I never said this would be comfortable," said Hawthorne.

"Good thing I'm not claustrophobic," she said.

Hawthorne said, "Wilder, enter the destination coordinates and put us on autopilot. My friend Ladybird will arrive at the bunker any minute."

Wilder hit autopilot and took off his headset. He turned and saw a silhouette walk down the runway. Ladybird stepped onto the hideout floor. She was a black woman with short dreadlocks and a tank top. "You must be Wilder," she said.

"You must be Ladybird," Wilder said.

"Is the *Pyrois* on autopilot?"

"Yes."

"Good." Ladybird commanded, "Give me the flight console and follow me." She shoved the laptop and VR headset into her backpack and slung it over her shoulder.

Ladybird motioned to Wilder. "Come on." They ran up the runway onto the desert floor, where a sprinter van sat idling. "Get in," she said. She took the wheel and they sped over the sand toward the road.

Ladybird sped toward Highway 15, linking the flight console to the sprinter's Spec Ops server. She handed him the laptop and VR headset and said, "Strap into that chair and log back on."

Wilder strapped in and put on the headset. He pulled up the *Pyrois*'s signal high above the Mojave Desert. He said, "Ladybird, I see Hawthorne and Katya inside the hull. How do we know if the *Pyrois* is still invisible?"

Ladybird said, "I'm sure the drone is still cloaking. If the military had eyes on it, they would have blown them out of the sky by now." She drove to the overpass at Barstow and headed south. "Wilder, link into the flight chair and set up the full station. You're gonna need the big monitor when we take the drone off autopilot."

Wilder patched his headset into a large motherboard and pulled the whole system online. "OK, the *Pyrois* is on the big screen. Holy crap, the resolution on this monitor is insane."

"Where are they?"

"They just cleared Mount San Antonio," he said.

Ladybird plugged in an earpiece, punched a button and a monitor folded down above the windshield. "I see them too," she said.

Wilder turned on the mic. "Hawthorne, Katya, can you hear me?"

"Yes, yes, we can hear you!" said Katya. "Great job, Wilder!"

"I'm with Ladybird. She picked me up."

"Good action," said Hawthorne. "It's just mountains below us now."

Wilder asked, "Ladybird, any chance you could put me through to President Garner?"

Ladybird said, "This vehicle can do that, yeah."

"Do it for me, would ya?"

"This is no time for nonsense," she said.

"Let him do it," said Hawthorne over the mic. "He's earned our trust."

Ladybird dialed a number on a phone and handed it to Wilder.

"Hello, may I please speak to President Garner? Yeah, this is Wilder Kole. That's correct." Wilder couldn't help but laugh. "I'm on hold."

"Don't be a smart-ass," said Ladybird. "How you ever got this deep is beyond me."

"Yes, hello? Mr. President? This is Wilder Kole."

The president was back in the Situation Room. "How did you get this number?"

"My Navy SEAL friends," said Wilder.

"Surrender now and I'll spare your life," said the president.

"No surrender," said Wilder.

"Where's Hawthorne?" Garner demanded to know.

"Hawthorne is deploying the element of surprise."

"What the hell is that supposed to mean?"

"Listen—those Long Beach coordinates are real."

"What coordinates?"

"I'm sure you've seen the intel I'm talking about," said Wilder.

"Long Beach, huh?"

"The WMD is in Long Beach. Me and Hawthorne's crew are gonna stop it."

"What about the Russian spy?" asked the president.

"Katya's on our side. She's helping us stop the bomb."

Garner said, "We will find Hawthorne and kill him. He has turned LA into a war zone."

"It already was a war zone," Wilder said. "You just didn't know it. Trust me."

"Alright, Wilder Kole, let's say I trust you. Where's the bomb?"

"Keep your eyes wide open for Hawthorne. He'll lead you right to it."

"Where the hell is Hawthorne?"

"Element of surprise, remember?"

"Don't fuck with me! I am the president of the United States!"

Wilder said, "I'm asking you to work with me—I'm trying to save my city!"

"Is Hawthorne in LA?"

"Mr. President, please. Clear the sky of your helicopters over Long Beach Bay."

"What for?"

"Please trust me," pleaded Wilder.

"I have no better option," said Garner grimly.

"You're gonna want a full view of what goes down in the bay."

"What's going down?"

"Just give us a pocket of sky and follow Hawthorne. This is how we stop the nuke."

"Don't fuck with me, Wilder Kole. You're not making any sense."

Ladybird shouted, "Wilder, time to hang up!"

"It will all make sense, Mr. President," Wilder assured him. "Just do it!" He hung up.

Ladybird said, "Track the flight path of the *Pyrois* closely."

"I'm flying great, admit it," said Wilder. "We're headed toward Anaheim, see? And calling the president was a good idea. He's gonna give us a pocket of sky, watch."

"Get ready, Wilder," she said. "It's go time."

The president trusted his instincts and issued orders for helicopters to clear the skies over Long Beach Bay. Pilots obeyed the president, but there was an insurrectionist cell of Navy SEALs flying Apaches over Redondo Beach. Navy SEAL Unit 30 was entirely GWA. They heard the orders and had plans of their own.

50

LA TRAFFIC

"*We're entering the valley now,*" said Hawthorne. "Wilder, fly low. They might hear us from the ground but they still can't see us."

Wilder marveled, "This cloaking feature is un-fucking real." He pointed the nose downward and the *Pyrois* sailed over the urban sprawl of LA's inland empire.

"Wilder," said Hawthorne, "get ready for a lot of traffic in the skies. You're gonna have to maneuver the hell out of it."

"Look at all that fire and smoke," said Wilder. "LA is a full-on war zone."

Hawthorne said, "Listen kid, when we get over Long Beach and I say *go*, turn off the cloaking."

"Turn off the cloaking?"

"Yeah, it's the only way to exit the hatch."

Wilder said, "I got you, Hawthorne. Oh, and—you didn't tell me Ladybird was so good looking."

Katya said, "Wilder, focus!"

"Are you jealous, Katya?" Wilder asked.

She fired back, "No! I'm thinking about not dying! Even if we make it to Long Beach Bay, I don't know if I can open my wings in this flight suit. Especially at this speed."

Hawthorne said, "Katya, there's one thing I didn't tell you. These suits don't have parachutes."

Katya asked, "Why the hell not?"

"They just don't," said Hawthorne. "Don't worry, we can decelerate by swooping up at the last minute."

"Are you kidding?"

"We will land on our feet."

"How can you be so confident?" Katya asked.

"Right now, there's no other way to be," Hawthorne said.

"This is suicide," Katya said.

He said, "Don't worry, we got this. Wilder, just get us above the *Garganta*."

"What's the plan after that?" Wilder asked.

"We land on the *Garganta* and stop the bomb," said Hawthorne.

"That's it?" asked Katya. "There's no more plan?"

"I told you," said Hawthorne. "We have to improvise."

Wilder said, "Holy shit, LA is straight-up on fire, and there are so many helicopters I can't even count them."

Hawthorne said, "If you can't fly around 'em, fly under 'em!"

"I got this!" said Wilder. He swerved around a fleet of Chinooks and flew into a huge cloud of smoke. "I can't see a thing!"

"Dive—or we will collide with a chopper for sure!" screamed Katya.

Wilder dove the *Pyrois* and they ducked just in time under another fleet of helicopters. "That was too close!"

Hawthorne said, "Lower Wilder! Lower! There are too many of them to avoid!"

The *Pyrois* flew one hundred feet above the ground. Now Wilder was weaving between tall buildings.

"Not that low!" said Hawthorne.

Ladybird said, "Nice flying, Wilder! Hawthorne, we got your back! Our team is the only one that knows you're coming."

Hawthorne said, "OK, team, let's do this."

Ladybird said, "Once the military sees us, we won't be able to tell who's on our side. All branches of the armed forces are on the brink of chaos."

Hawthorne said, "I knew that would happen."

Ladybird said, "There's fighting at the highest ranks. GWA is exploding."

"Soldiers are choosing sides," said Katya.

"What sides?" asked Wilder. "What sides are we talking about?"

"The GWA and the United States as we know it," said Hawthorne.

Ladybird said, "Just stop the fucking bomb. We worry about the rest later."

"Roger that," said Hawthorne.

"God will sort them out," said Katya.

Hawthorne said, "No more talk on the intercom. Everyone, focus!"

51

THE GREAT MOMENT

From the sprinter van a hundred miles away, Wilder steered the flight of the *Pyrois* soaring over the urban sprawl and toward city limits. Horrific scenes of violence continued on the ground, and helicopters filled the skies.

From inside of the *Pyrois*, Hawthorne and Katya looked down at the fire and smoke blanketing Los Angeles. "Visibility is next to nothing," said Hawthorne.

"Tell me about it," said Wilder. He zigzagged as low to the ground as he could fly because more and more helicopters clogged the higher altitude.

However, skies were still clear above Long Beach Bay. After President Garner's orders, the Air Force fell in line. But the Apaches from insurrectionist SEAL Unit 30 had joined the fleet encircling Long Beach waters. Their goal was to wreak havoc in the air the same as on land, and they were prepared to die.

Team 30 commanding officer yelled, "Fire on Dock 9's choppers! Take them out."

A Hellfire missile rocketed toward a Night Stalker. It erupted on impact into a fireball that plunged into the ocean. Over Huntington Beach, another insurrectionist helicopter fired a second Hellfire missile. Dock 9's second Night Stalker exploded.

In a flash, ten helicopters exchanged rocket fire and seven fell out of the sky. A Black Hawk crashed into Lincoln Boulevard in Santa Monica, engulfing a group of protestors in burning fuel. From the ground, disoriented Army platoons pointed their rifles skyward. Some soldiers held their fire and others emptied their rounds.

Across LA, GWA insurrectionist troops began turning on their fellow soldiers, shooting anyone they knew was against the alliance. Fleeing the violence, civilians stampeded the streets and hundreds were trampled to death.

The full-scale urban warfare couldn't have gotten any worse, but the Air Force appeared to regain control of the sky. The pocket of sky once again cleared over Long Beach and intel spread wide that the WMD was somewhere in the bay. The nuclear threat was incalculably bigger than the GWA insurrectionists trying to spark a civil war.

From inside the war room in Catalina, Tilford cut all lines of communication except the Spec Ops monitoring the Long Beach skies.

Wilder sat up at the flight controls. "We're almost over Long Beach! Now what?"

"Spot the *Garganta*!" said Hawthorne.

"I see it!" said Wilder. "We're approaching fast, almost on top of her."

"Deactivate the cloaking!" Hawthorne yelled.

"Roger that!" said Wilder.

Out of thin air, the *Pyrois* appeared in full view three hundred yards over Long Beach. The drone ripped across the sky.

"Now!" exclaimed Hawthorne.

"Drop us!" yelled Katya.

Wilder opened the bomb hatch, and Hawthorne and Katya leaped out of the bottom of the drone.

At breakneck speed, their bodies hurled toward the *Garganta* anchored in the bay. Hawthorne and Katya shot open their arms and legs, and their flight suits caught air. Careening toward the *Garganta*, their bodies plummeted.

Ladybird pulled over and prayed. She said, "Hitting the ship or even the water surface will kill them instantly at that velocity."

At the last moment Hawthorne swooped upward and his body skidded across the *Garganta*'s cargo deck. He slammed into a wall, knocking him unconscious. Katya followed his path darting in a sharp curve onto the boat. She hit the ship deck at a full sprint and landed on both feet.

The drone crashed into the ocean, and all across America people watched live in shock and terror.

Inside the shipping container, Perez heard them land and opened the roof. The DF-11 missile with the nuclear warhead came into full view from above. Perez hovered his hand over the launch button. He slammed his palm down and initiated the irreversible countdown to nuclear detonation. Perez grabbed his AK-47, opened the side door and headed toward the cargo deck.

Katya knelt over Hawthorne, slapping his face. He was out cold. Out of the corner of her eye, Katya saw Perez duck behind a crane.

I'll take him myself, thought Katya. She unstrapped the AR-15 from her back and beelined toward Perez. He saw her closing in, and Perez leaped into the open. He sprayed gunfire from his rifle. Bullets narrowly missed Katya and embedded into metal all around her. She took cover behind a shipping crate, inhaled deeply and then popped up firing. Perez exchanged fire again. Katya's shots ripped into Perez's chest and neck. Perez's head rocked back in a bloody shower and his body hit the deck.

Hawthorne regained consciousness and ran up to Katya. She said, "Perez is dead. I took him out."

She grabbed Hawthorne by the arm and hurried toward the shipping container with the WMD. Standing in the open doorway, Hawthorne and Katya stared at the nuclear missile bay. The countdown beeped ominously.

Hawthorne adjusted his head cam. "Wilder, are you seeing this?"

Wilder said, "I see it."

"It's going to blow."

"God help us," Wilder said.

Hawthorne and Katya stood over the controls. "What do we do?" asked Katya.

"Hit the off button!" said Wilder.

"There is no off button," said Hawthorne. "Detonation is irreversible."

"Then change the coordinates!" said Wilder.

Hawthorne asked, "Can I do that?"

Wilder said, "I don't know, you're the one looking at the controls!"

"There!" Katya exclaimed, pointing to the interface. "You can change it."

"Three minutes!" yelled Hawthorne. "Wilder, give me some coordinates."

"OK, um . . ." said Wilder. "Latitude 33.5, longitude minus 122."

"Got it," said Hawthorne.

Wilder said, "Change the altitude too!"

Hawthorne said, "OK, five thousand feet."

"It's gonna launch!" said Katya.

The countdown began at T-minus 10. Hawthorne and Katya ran back onto the ship deck to avoid the launch blast. They dove behind another shipping container. In a flash of white fire, the nuclear rocket shot skyward. The DF-11 arced west, climbing higher and over the sea away from Los Angeles. The nation watched with incomprehensible fear. From the ship deck, Katya and Hawthorne followed the thin line of the nuclear missile's jet stream.

The passing seconds felt like hours. Hawthorne and Katya held each other close in the fearful final moments. At five thousand feet altitude and ten miles offshore, the WMD exploded in a gigantic mushroom cloud.

The cloud expanded high off the coast of Southern California. The radiation waves would not reach land and offshore winds helped. Completely terrorized Americans felt a moment of collective relief. All across the LA area, the warfare stopped.

Katya and Hawthorne stood embracing in the middle of the *Garganta*'s ship deck. Their image aired live internationally. Hawthorne dropped to one knee, raising an outstretched arm with his hand in the peace sign. Katya knelt beside him, put her arm over his shoulder and raised the peace sign as well. They kept their peace fingers up, lowered their heads into each other and deeply sobbed.

"I love you," said Hawthorne.

"I love you too," said Katya.

52

ROAM OF THE CHINOOK

With the mushroom cloud hanging ominously in the sky, a single Chinook helicopter approached the *Garganta*. Tilford ordered all aircraft to hold fire. Hawthorne and Katya covered their ears and watched it land on the far side of the ship deck. Soldiers jumped out, waving, and motioned them over. Hawthorne recognized Ladybird's team of SEALs. He nodded to Katya and they climbed into the side of the helicopter. The Chinook hovered over the *Garganta* and banked skyward.

With world war on America's doorstep, President Garner got Tilford on the line and ordered, "All forces stand down. Total cease-fire."

"What about the helicopter lifting off the vessel?"

"Protect their lives. They saved Los Angeles. They saved us all."

Tilford asked, "Mr. President, they stopped the bomb, but how do we know what side they are on?"

"They're American heroes," Garner said. "Give them clearance to Camp Pendleton."

"We can't bring them to Camp Pendleton, Mr. President."

"Why not?" Garner asked. "They're no longer targets. I'll issue a declaration."

Tilford said, "If they're with the GWA, they could still start a civil war."

"I'm positive they aren't. You saw them. Do the math."

"In that case, they could be killed by GWA. Our ranks are divided, sir."

President Garner was in disbelief. "But they stopped the nuclear bomb."

"Yes, but we have a military insurgency. The situation is still volatile. We're better off killing them and making our own story about them."

"We will do no such thing," said Garner.

Tilford said, "I already issued the command." A moment later, a dozen Nighthawk helicopters surrounded the Chinook carrying Hawthorne and Katya. There was no escape. The helicopters hovered in midair formation ready to launch their missiles.

"Dammit, I'm the commander in chief," declared President Garner. "Stand down."

Tilford ordered them to stand down. One by one, the Nighthawks peeled away from the Chinook. Hawthorne said through a headset, "That was close."

Crawford was the pilot, and he said, "Yeah, that was way too close. OK, I'm cutting all radio signals. Then I'll see if I can get a line to Ladybird."

"Holy shit, we did it," said Hawthorne.

"Holy shit is right," said Katya.

"Ladybird, come through," said Crawford.

"I hear you, brother!" said Ladybird over the intercom. "We did it!"

"Yahoo!" said Crawford. "We got Hawthorne and Katya. You still with Wilder?"

"Affirmative," said Ladybird. "This kid pisses me off but he's one hell of a pilot. See you at the rendezvous point."

"Roger that," said Crawford.

*

Across LA, everyone stared up at the distant mushroom cloud. Smoke still billowed from burning buildings, and dead bodies were strewn in the streets. The city looked like hell.

Soldiers with GWA made another rallying cry. "We will not stop now! Now is the time for GWA!" Once again, they opened fire on their fellow Americans, both military and civilian. Squadrons fractured into greater chaos and another two thousand soldiers died.

New cease-fire orders came through from the Pentagon. Within an hour the fighting mostly stopped. Many GWA loyalists surrendered, and many more blended back into the ranks. All over the world, people watched the news unfold.

The president went live on television and gave the speech of his life. "We are a nation suddenly at war, but we cannot turn against ourselves. Today our country's best forces thwarted a nuclear attack. All of us—each one of us—needs to take this moment as an inflection point for our lives, our nation and who we are as a people. As president of the United States, it's my honor and my duty to do everything in my power to preserve this great nation. No terrorists, domestic or international, will destroy our way of life. Our spirit is unbreakable."

He continued, "In recent days, we've seen horrific tragedies, American civilians and troops at war with each other, traitors and cowards among us and countless innocent citizens killed. We will bring each and every traitor to justice. We owe a debt of gratitude to all those brave soldiers and people who fought back.

"But today we also saw something more important. We saw a small group of true heroes take Southern California in the palms of their hands and save hundreds of thousands of lives. An ordinary citizen piloted the aircraft that led our heroes to divert the WMD. Think about that. An ordinary citizen. What extraordinary acts of courage. And a Russian woman, from a country we call our enemy, working together to stop a world war. All humanity should use these shining examples of heroism as fuel and inspiration for our highest hopes. It's time for us all to dig deep and find that same courage within ourselves."

The president paused for dramatic effect. "Now, I can't lift the order of martial law in California until I am certain our citizens are safe. I call on all Americans, I call on all of you, because I am but one man. I am your president but you the people must act. Our only true choice is to unite, to stop fighting and to stand for the Republic. I can assure you, we will hunt down the terrorists responsible for the nuclear attack, and we will make them pay."

The president said, "Now let me address the Navy SEALs on the helicopter, those brave souls who saved us. Let the soldiers on the southbound Chinook be absolved, and all accusations leveled against Rex Hawthorne pardoned. The only thing Hawthorne is guilty of is being willing to sacrifice his life for humanity. I've issued the orders to let those brave men and women on board that helicopter fly where they may. Let our heroes roam free. They have earned this and more. I will say it again, let our heroes roam free, for they are the symbol of our great nation's highest values. May God bless America and God bless our troops."

With those final words, the president took a knee and raised his right hand with the peace sign.

All across LA, people went outside their homes. Citizens dropped to one knee, raising an outstretched arm and the peace sign, just like President Garner mirroring Hawthorne and Katya on the deck of the *Garganta*. The people of LA knelt in unity with peace signs high.

It aired live and within minutes the movement swept the nation. Taking a knee and raising fingers in peace signs became the symbol of that day. News coverage around the globe aired the lone Chinook helicopter carrying Hawthorne, Katya and the crew. With the helicopter in the foreground and the mushroom cloud behind it, they continued south, flying offshore of San Diego and into Mexican airspace.

53

SOUTHBOUND RENDEZVOUS

Back in the sprinter, Ladybird and Wilder headed southbound on the 79. Wilder felt an unbelievable mix of emotions and landed on what felt most true—intense pride, fulfillment and love for Katya and Hawthorne, the two other people besides himself who just changed the world.

Wilder wondered for a moment how Chuck and Kim were doing but then took stock in his newfound faith that somehow everything was going to be all right. At that very moment in Camp Pendleton, Chuck and Kim were brought together, debriefed and informed they were now regarded as American heroes and no longer prisoners. Until further notice, at President Garner's orders, they were to remain under protection of the Pentagon's best.

Northeast of San Diego, Ladybird switched freeways to the 8. It dawned on Wilder and he said, "I need to clear Hawthorne's name."

"That's not your responsibility," said Ladybird.

"He and I are the only ones who have seen the intel from Morocco."

"What intel?" she asked.

He said, "A video showing the sale of the nuke. Hawthorne tried to stop it from falling into the wrong hands."

"You have that video?"

Wilder said, "I uploaded it to YouTube."

"YouTube?"

"Don't worry, it's really well encrypted."

"You're shitting me," said Ladybird.

"Not shitting you," he said. "Can I have your phone? Let me download the decryption key and text it to the president."

"Of course you can have my phone." She tossed it to him. "You stopped the nuke."

"I couldn't have done it without you—not to mention Katya and Hawthorne."

Wilder opened the phone, texted President Garner the link to the YouTube video and attached the decoder key as an executable file. He powered down the phone. "Worth a shot anyway."

Ladybird said, "Nice of you to think of him, but Hawthorne can handle his own karma."

Wilder said, "Tell me again—why are we fleeing to Mexico?"

She said, "The military is crawling with white supremacists who are loyal to GWA. Most of them have gone back into hiding, but not for long, and they would kill you if they had the chance. The GWA uprising is here."

"Say no more," said Wilder. "Let's go to Mexico."

When they reached Pine Valley, Ladybird turned down a bumpy dirt road, drove into a driveway and up to a gate. A plainclothes guard entered numbers into a pin pad. The gate opened and she drove slowly into the sprawling ranch. It was mostly open land.

At the end of the driveway, several cars were parked in front of a humble one-story house. A half dozen men stood around in the lot, and one of them motioned for Ladybird to park inside the barn.

Ladybird stepped out, followed by Wilder. Inside the barn, they were greeted by a middle-aged Latino man wearing a large belt buckle and cowboy boots. "Wilder Kole. It's an honor to meet you in person . . . They call me Jefe." He extended his hand and Wilder shook it.

Wilder said, "Jefe? Aw shit, are you the guy I stole money from?"

Jefe smiled. "You don't owe Casta Cartel anymore. We owe you. You saved LA, man!"

Ladybird nodded. "He doesn't look like much, but he really came through for us."

Wilder high-fived Ladybird. "Now what?"

"The Casta cartel generously offered to be our escort. We can't report back to the US military—someone with GWA might kill you."

"Right," Wilder said, and nodded.

"We're not letting nobody kill you today," said Jefe. "You're heroes, man! I'm giving you first-class treatment. Whatever you need, anything at all, just name it."

"I'll take a double espresso," said Wilder.

"That's all?" Jefe laughed. "We're giving you an unlimited lifetime bank account—and you're asking for a five-dollar drink?"

"Hmm." Wilder was intrigued. "How about a waterfront mansion and a speedboat?"

"You got it. I'll get you the double espresso too. But first, come with me."

Inside the barn walls, Jefe led Wilder and Ladybird into the basement and down a long flight of stairs. He opened a door and they walked inside together. Jefe pointed to a futuristic-looking train car with a rail leading into a tunnel. "Check it out."

"What is it?" asked Wilder.

"It's a miniature bullet train," said Jefe.

"Bullet train?"

"Yeah, man. It goes two hundred miles an hour."

"Holy crap, that's fast," said Wilder.

Jefe bragged, "It runs on magnets. This thing will take us to Tecate in less than a minute."

Ladybird said, "You're going to have to stay south of the border for a while, somewhere no one can find you."

"Sounds good to me," said Wilder. "Does anybody know what happened to Chuck and Kim?"

"I'm sure they'll stay in military custody awhile," said Ladybird. "This whole thing will shake out. They'll be alright in the end." She climbed into the cab of the train and gave Wilder the front seat. Jefe took the last seat in the back.

"What's in Tecate?"

"Tecate is a nice town," said Jefe, "but we're gonna take Autopista Trés and go deeper into Baja. What's your favorite meal? You name it, I'll get it for you."

"Is it crazy that I can't remember?" asked Wilder.

"Not at all," said Ladybird. "You've been through a lot."

"Keep your chin down so you don't get whiplash," Jefe said.

"Punch it," said Wilder.

The train shot into the tunnel and moments later they were in Mexico.

54
THE CANTINA

After an hour flight, the Chinook touched down in a dusty parking lot in Ensenada. Twenty Casta cartel soldiers carrying M16s stood guard around the perimeter. The pilot cut the helicopter's engine, and four SEALs from Ladybird's team stepped out. Across the lot, Ladybird opened an SUV's door and let Wilder out first. Hawthorne and Katya jumped out of the Chinook and threw their arms around him. They all cried tears of joy.

"I have cried so much today," said Katya.

"What do we do now?" asked Wilder.

Katya said, "Whatever the hell we want."

"Damn right," said Hawthorne.

"Not exactly." Ladybird said, "I've asked our friends with the Casta cartel to put you in hiding for a while."

"You sure these guys are friends?" asked Wilder.

"We have some mutually beneficial arrangements," said Hawthorne. "The lines get blurry with the whole 'good guys' and 'bad guys' thing."

Ladybird handed large military backpacks to Hawthorne, Katya and Wilder. "Here are your go bags." She and her team of SEALs stood by the Chinook and prepared to lift off. Ladybird shook Katya's hand and said, "It's an honor to meet you."

"Same to you," Katya replied.

"Keep these two knuckleheads safe." Ladybird hugged Hawthorne and said, "Thank you for trusting me with this mission. Me and the crew gotta head back to San Diego. The Pentagon is gonna want a full report."

"You better do that," said Hawthorne. "You were perfect today."

"You too," Ladybird said.

"I wasn't totally perfect," said Hawthorne. "I didn't stick the landing in my flight suit."

"That's true." Katya laughed. "He hit that wall and passed out cold."

Ladybird said, "Well, friends, take a load off but watch your backs. This isn't over."

Hawthorne put one arm around Katya and another arm around Wilder. They stood back and watched the Chinook lift off.

Jefe said, "We better get you inside." He escorted them into a small concrete building with a faded sign that read, CANTINA LA NÚMERO DOS. Hawthorne said, "I have fond memories of this place."

Jefe motioned to the bartender. "Marta, give our guests of honor a bottle of our best tequila. I will be outside." She pulled a bottle off the top shelf as they set down their go bags and sidled up to the bar. Marta served them generous pours with chips, guacamole and pico de gallo.

They clinked their glasses. Wilder and Hawthorne knocked back their shots and Katya took a sip. She nodded to Marta. "This is the best drink I've ever had."

"Glad to hear it," said Marta.

"So, Katya . . ." Wilder smiled mischievously. "Between Hawthorne and me, who would you rather fuck?"

Katya replied, "I've been thinking about that, too."

"Same," said Hawthorne.

Katya loaded up a chip and took a big bite. "How about a plate of tacos?" she asked Marta.

"Of course," she said. "You want carnitas, chicken or lengua?"

"What's your favorite?"

"Carnitas."

"I'll have that."

"Carne asada burrito for me," said Hawthorne.

"Of course," said Marta.

Wilder said, "I'm gonna have the cheese enchiladas." Marta nodded and walked to the kitchen in back.

Hawthorne looked Katya in the eye. "Well . . . ?"

"Let's eat," said Katya. "We can talk about sex later."

"Works for me," said Wilder. "Also, what's our plan?"

"What do you mean?" asked Hawthorne.

"The whole world is watching," said Wilder. "The cartel got me here undercover, but you flew in by helicopter. How do we get out of here?"

Hawthorne assured him. "Our team of Navy SEALs is one step ahead."

"You better be," Katya said. "We stopped the nuke, but the GWA uprising has just begun."

"True," said Hawthorne.

"They will come for me first," said Katya. "I know too much."

"Ladybird gave us a rock-solid exit strategy," Hawthorne said. "I got this."

Wilder said, "That's my line."

"*I got this* is your tagline?" asked Hawthorne. "People say that all the time."

"Yeah but, I call dibs," said Wilder. "*You* don't got this, *I* got this."

Suddenly, machine-gun fire erupted outside. "Get down!" yelled Katya.

They dove to the floor and Hawthorne opened his go bag. He handed Katya and Wilder each an MP5 submachine gun and grabbed one of his own. He commanded, "Katya, take the left window. I'll take the right. Wilder, shoot anyone who comes through that door."

Marta hoisted an M240 from behind the bar. "I got the roof." She headed up a spiral staircase.

An entourage of masked men stormed toward the cantina. Dozens of bodies dropped in a fierce exchange of gunfire. From the windows, Katya and Hawthorne emptied their magazines and took down multiple assailants. The gunfire outside stopped. Katya and Hawthorne crouched down to reload.

After a long silence, Hawthorne said, "I think we held them off." Just then, a low thunder and a loud screeching sound pierced the air. "Oh shit," he said. "What the hell is an M1 Abrams doing in Mexico?"

"Tank!" yelled Marta from the roof. "Tank!"

"*¡Corre!*" shouted Jefe from the parking lot. "Run!"

The M1 Abrams rolled down the street and turned to face the cantina. Hawthorne ordered, "Follow me!" He bolted to the kitchen with Katya and Wilder on his heels. He ripped a fake light switch off the wall and punched in a code. A laser scanned his retina. With a loud click, steel pins disengaged the lock on a blast door inside the wall. Hawthorne threw aside a dishwasher and yanked on the door's vault wheel. "Get in the safe!"

Wilder, Katya and Hawthorne rushed inside. The M1 Abrams fired a sabot round into the cantina. A giant fireball billowed toward the vault door just as it shut.

AUTHOR'S NOTE

During the Iraq War and presidency of George W. Bush, as a proud American I was upset by international conflicts and the US government's wartime decisions. I was particularly upset with what I imagined soldiers were going through—traumas I viewed as unnecessary. I was experiencing addiction to alcohol and marijuana as well as prolonged, acute mania from untreated bipolar episodes. Years later in recovery, I learned to view my experiences with compassion, from both a psychological and medical perspective.

During that tumultuous time in my life, I harmed my closest relationships and experienced both voluntary and involuntary hospitalizations—with more mental health challenges to come in future years as well. After two years of sobriety, I made amends with loved ones, took a job in a detox clinic and began my master's program in mental health counseling at Antioch University in Seattle. I saw a therapist every week for a few years, and I healed significantly. I also witnessed many tragic stories of addiction and people struggling to overcome their own mental health issues. Not everyone is blessed with recovery, and though it is available to anyone, the playing field is not level. I reflected on my white privilege in particular, concluding that I was lucky to be unincarcerated and alive.

There are dimensions of healing and a lack thereof that have left scars within me. However, over the years I underwent a grand experiment that I would describe as a success. My memories of episodes of psychosis, paranoid delusion and bizarre interactions with people and myself—well, they were not going away. Just because I understood that these memories were not based in reality did not change the fact that they were imprinted on my mind. Trauma flowed like water in irrigation ditches where the neurons fired within my psyche—memories that occasionally disturbed me to the point of hypomania and worse. Medication and counseling helped only so much, especially when processing paranoia felt next to impossible in conversation with almost everyone.

I came to call my experiment "Alternate Narrative Therapy," which I began by writing down my memories in notebooks while visiting cafés and practicing gradual exposure response theory to PTSD treatment. To be clear, I do not have PTSD, nor do I appreciate the cavalier way in which this severe diagnosis has entered the modern lexicon of armchair psychiatry. However, I did have significant trauma that I began to process by separating the fictions of my memories from my experiences themselves. In recovery, I also found kernels of truth woven into these paranoid memories. I contemplated deeper philosophical topics and found a home for them in writing. Who are we, truly, compared to the characters we think we are and who we pretend to be? It's fascinating how our identities intersect with artifice—I imagine this is an ever-present truth in the life of a spy.

Over the years, I have healed in large part from my most difficult memories and removed their sting and triggering effects. I'm skipping over a lot here, including the friends who helped me along, especially my wife, rock and best friend, Kara. Eventually, I wrote a book—*this* book, *Rogue for Peace*—which ended up being quite a fun experience.

Warmly,
Ben

Made in USA - North Chelmsford, MA
85464_9798879744415
03.12.2024 2116